The Darcys & the Bingleys

PRIDE AND PREJUDICE
CONTINUES

A TALE OF TWO GENTLEMEN'S MARRIAGES TO TWO MOST DEVOTED SISTERS

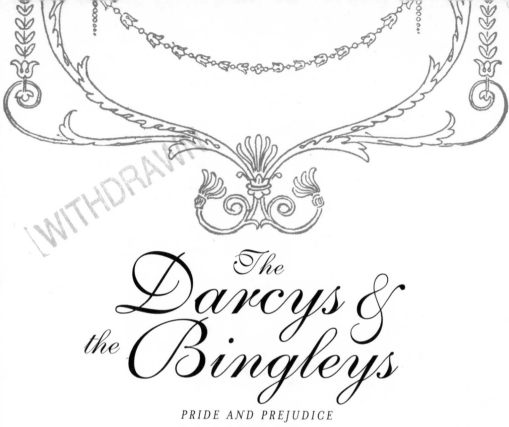

The Darcys & the Bingleys

PRIDE AND PREJUDICE
CONTINUES

A TALE OF TWO GENTLEMEN'S MARRIAGES TO TWO MOST DEVOTED SISTERS

MARSHA ALTMAN

SOURCEBOOKS LANDMARK™
AN IMPRINT OF SOURCEBOOKS, INC.®
NAPERVILLE, ILLINOIS

Copyright © 2008 by Marsha Altman
Cover and internal design © 2008 by Sourcebooks, Inc.
Cover photo © Bridgeman Art Library

Sourcebooks and the colophon are registered trademarks of Sourcebooks, Inc.

Published by Sourcebooks Landmark, an imprint of Sourcebooks, Inc.
P.O. Box 4410, Naperville, Illinois 60567-4410
(630) 961-3900
FAX: (630) 961-2168
www.sourcebooks.com

Library of Congress Cataloging-in-Publication Data

Altman, Marsha.
   The Darcys & the Bingleys : a tale of two gentlemen's marriages to two most devoted sis-
ters / Marsha Altman.
      p. cm.
   I. Austen, Jane, 1775-1817. Pride and prejudice. II. Title. III. Title: Darcys and the
Bingleys.
   PS3601.L853D37 2008
   813'.6--dc22
                              2008010395

            Printed and bound in the United States of America
               VP 10 9 8 7 6 5 4 3 2 1

Dedication

To the cheetah kid
You don't know who you are, and I don't remember your name,
but thanks for the eighteen years of inspiration.

Book One

A BIT OF ADVICE

THE DEAL

CHARLES BINGLEY, A MAN in possession of fortune and of good standing, had been for several years now in want of a wife. Now he stood at the culmination of his efforts and found it almost alarming.

For the first time in many years, the shooting season had passed, and Charles Bingley didn't give it a second thought. He had to look his best at all times for the numerous guests that were filling his hours. Normally, hosting was something he did gladly, but other forces were pulling him in directions away from his abominable guests and well-wishers.

This must be how Darcy feels all the time, he mused, and allowed himself a rare smile—rare in that it was at the expense of his friend. For he had no doubt that whatever sufferings he was enduring at Netherfield by having the flux of people and priorities keep him from his beloved Jane, Darcy was probably feeling them more, because Darcy went into the intense period of social events with a predisposition against them. As a guest in

Bingley's estate, he was normally entitled to all of the privacy he wished and could hide in his room with a pile of books for all Bingley cared. But that was not the case when one was engaged in what was looking to be a rather controversial wedding.

Perhaps controversial was not the right word, but Bingley chose it anyway, at least in his own mind. Certainly, there were those who opposed it, but none that he and Darcy were not willing to stand up to. He could never have imagined his unshakable best friend bending to the will of his aunt and marrying Anne de Bourgh, but then again, he also could never have imagined his friend falling in love with someone deemed below his station by the world at large. If anything, the master of Pemberley was more than aware of his station and the social standing that he was required to maintain, something Bingley would not wish on himself for the doubling of accounts that it would bring.

So, it seemed, life was full of surprises, because Darcy was quite possibly more in love with Elizabeth than Bingley was with Jane, even if he was being subtle about it and apparently had been since the moment they met. Only after much teasing and a persevering interrogation did Fitzwilliam Darcy admit to falling in love with her at first sight, of all places and times, and he only admitted it with a passion in his eyes that indicated that, if Charles Bingley were not his best friend and companion, he would be inclined to thrash him with his walking stick for asking such a question.

But even all of his purported and very real hauteur and intimidating posture and grace could not save poor Mr. Darcy from the necessities of prenuptial social business. There were the trips to Longbourn that were not frequent enough and the various well-wishers (and non-well-wishers) streaming into Netherfield that were all too frequent. He also had to travel to London no less than three times in a month for reasons of finance management and general legal wedding preparations. Bingley, a man of smaller fortune, only had to go once and entrusted to his steward that all the rest would be well.

In fact, it had reached such an extreme that standing in his room, waiting for the appearance of his waistcoat, Charles Bingley could not think of two or three words he had spoken to Darcy in the past day, despite living under the same roof. Not that he was totally unaccustomed to absences, and not that he was helpless without the person whom he would never bring himself to call—to his face, anyway—a sort of elder brother, but he could think of no better way to idle away the time which they were forced to be away from their respective fiancées by social circumstance than talking, even if it was idle chatter that would result in Bingley quite knowingly running his mouth off and Darcy impatiently rolling his eyes. That, at least, would be a bit relaxing in its own way.

No, there would be no return to normalcy. In three days, they would no longer be eligible bachelors who were the talk of every ball. Bingley's beloved sister would no longer be batting her eyelashes at his best friend (or, at least, Bingley *hoped* she wouldn't), and he would not be returning the favour with dismissive witticisms. All right, Bingley admitted he was a bit oblivious at times, but he was not dim-witted, even if he had missed Darcy's obsession with Elizabeth Bennet. But then again, *everyone* had missed that, probably including Darcy himself. Darcy was jubilant when writing to his sister of the arrangement, and he took great pains to make his face even more unreadable than usual when he gave the grave news to Caroline Bingley. It was a masterpiece of a performance and went well with Charles's considerable relief that he didn't have to do it himself.

All cousins, sisters, distant relatives, attendants, hired planners, paperwork officials, and local guests made two matters particularly vexing for the normally unvexible Charles Bingley. First, and most obviously, despite the many trips to Longbourn, he could not get nearly as much time with Jane as he would have liked, but he was assured that he had the rest of his life to make up for it. The second matter was more pressing, if less emotionally invested: he needed Darcy, alone.

It took him several weeks to admit even to himself that he had questions that were better answered before the wedding and that Darcy was the best person to answer them. He was lacking a father—though that would have been an awkward situation anyway—and Mr. Hurst was, he decided, with all of his good manners and intentions, the last person he wanted to ask.

That left his friend, confidant, and evermore-experienced-at-everything brother figure. If he could just get him alone long enough to properly work up the courage to ask the appropriate questions, then all would be well. Darcy wouldn't answer, of course. He would look indignant and find some reason to stomp off or find no reason at all and still stomp off. Or maybe, maybe, he would actually have some advice that could be pried out with excessive trying.

And Bingley was ready to try.

Now there was the apparently irremovable obstacle of getting some time alone with Darcy. The halls of Netherfield were out of the question. Even if he could shoo away the servants, he would have enough trouble with Caroline and Louisa walking in and out as if they owned the place. Maybe he should have put his foot down earlier, but they were his older sisters, and he felt a particular amount of respect for their wishes. "Retirement with the gentlemen" on premises would involve Mr. Hurst, and that was right out.

Longbourn was also not the answer. Aside from the obvious notion that their fiancées and future in-laws were around, even the after-dinner brandy and conversation could not happen without Mr. Bennet, a man with whom he was most eager to leave only the finest impression.

That Bingley was a varied outdoorsman and willing to admit it at the slightest temptation was about his only reasonable means of expediting the process. So was Darcy an outdoorsman; though, as with everything else, he kept silent about his own personal habits. The master of Pemberley wouldn't even admit to owning dogs or knowing their names or personally caring for them before Bingley caught him red-handed actually playing with one on the grounds when he was sure no one was around. When a man would not be seen even playing with his animals, that was the very measure of privacy—which was precisely why Bingley knew he needed to talk to Darcy about his concerns.

After much internal debate and fretting about timing, Bingley eventually decided that the best approach was a direct one and conspired to find Darcy when he was alone, even if it meant tromping into his dressing chamber. Fortunately, it did not come to that. Darcy had been breakfasting earlier than normal, either because he had business or because he had a great desire to avoid the leisurely feast with Bingley and Caroline, as a normally awkward situation was made even more awkward by Caroline's shock and disapproval, made obvious despite many layers of proposed civility. In fact, when Bingley inquired, Darcy barely sat down at all, merely pacing the room with a cup of coffee and glancing at the paper to see if it contained anything particularly scandalous about him *that* day.

"Darcy," Bingley said, announcing himself to his friend, who had discarded the local paper and was staring out the window with his morning liquid refreshment. "I hear it is to be a most pleasant day for the weather."

"Yes," was all Darcy answered, perhaps a bit surprised to see him so early and so eager, but offering none of that with his usual neutral expression.

"Perhaps we might go for a walk—not to Longbourn, necessarily. I just cannot let Netherfield's fine woods be neglected any longer."

Whether Darcy believed him or not, he gave no indication. "If it is your wish."

So it was that easy. Because of the hour, they managed to escape almost everyone who could not be shooed away with a gesture. The morning sun was not at full force yet, with the mists still shrouding the estate in an eclectic sort of charm.

"So," Darcy said when they were well out of sight of the grand halls of Netherfield. He did not continue.

"Is the quiet not very pleasant—?"

"Out with it," Darcy said, not entirely harshly—for *Darcy* anyway. He had a whole spectrum of impatience, one that could only be discerned with careful research, and Bingley judged himself rather low on the scale—so far. "I know full well we are not making a surprise visit to Longbourn, unless you are mistaken as to the proper direction, and I believe you are not. And as much as I appreciate the opportunity for peace that you have afforded me in your offer, that does not mean I intend to dally the day away while you decide whether to ask me whatever you intend to ask me."

"You know me too well. I fear I am quite readable."

Darcy gave an odd sort of smile. "I would not do you the dishonour of admitting it." That he just did went unspoken between the two of them.

Now they had come to it, the moment he dreaded. "We are to marry in nearly two days—"

"It has not escaped my notice, I assure you."

"—and I find myself in need of some . . . advice."

If Darcy were a tad less clever, Bingley supposed he would have asked him if he was worried about doing the right thing by marrying Jane Bennet—but Bingley knew that Darcy knew that he had no such concerns. He was madly in love with her and had been for a year now. It was not a question for an intelligent person to raise, and he considered Darcy to be quite possibly the most intelligent person he had the pleasure of knowing.

Instead, Darcy took a moment to ponder all of the meanings Bingley could be implying. Financial? Surely not, as that would not require such great fortifications of privacy. Merely nervousness? That was only to be expected.

Bingley was sure that Darcy had arrived upon the answer himself because a look of pure horror washed over his face.

"It is not what you think. I am quite aware—"

"One would hope," Darcy said. "No, no, I would never suppose you to be *that* naïve."

"Then you see it's not a matter of technical . . . knowledge. I just—," and he did not even begin to curse himself for stuttering like a fool, because if there were ever a time when this behaviour were excusable, it was now. "I—I just want to be . . . what I'm saying is—"

But Darcy didn't finish his sentence for him. *Damn it,* he was so good at that. Why couldn't he be so kind now? He merely replied with utmost calmness, "You are destroying your hat."

Because he was. Bingley was playing with his removed hat, shoving it around in his hands and wringing it out as if it were a rag. He had destroyed any number of hats this way, so it came as no great surprise. Fortunately, he had been wise enough to put the one purchased for the wedding away until the appropriate time. "I am perhaps my haberdasher's favourite client," Bingley said, mainly to relieve the tension that only he seemed to feel. Darcy was an impenetrable wall. It made him very patient but unhelpful. "Please don't torment me. You know what I mean."

"And you assume that I am somehow more experienced in this area."

"You are more experienced in most areas," Bingley freely admitted. "In fact, I cannot think of a single area where you have not bested me."

"Except in proposing marriage."

A rare admission for Darcy. Bingley was too busy to be stunned. "Only with your incessant prodding was I successful. But no matter, it is in the past. My point—"

"Yes, your point."

"My point is—," but he didn't want to say his point, and Darcy was going to torture him by making him say it out loud, even though he knew full well what they were talking about. *The bastard!* "I want—I want my wife to be very . . . happy."

"Satisfied."

"Yes!" he said, and then judged it to be too enthusiastic a response. He felt like smacking himself.

Darcy huffed a bit before answering, "Surely there are enough married men in England that you can find one to help illuminate the subject—"

"Darcy, please, don't make me beg you or suggest I resort to Mr. Hurst. Find some kindness in your heart. You may keep it hidden, but I know you have it." Bingley pleaded, "Do you want me to get on my knees? Because I will."

"I am merely affronted that you assume that I am some kind of expert on the subject," Darcy said, even though he didn't sound all *that* affronted. "Surely you do not categorise me with Wickham in this respect."

"No, no, of course not! You have always been very discreet—or I assume, I assume, you've been very discreet." Now he didn't want to hit himself; he wanted to kick his own teeth in. He wondered if that was possible. "I'm assuming."

Darcy raised an eyebrow. "You are assuming a lot."

"Don't torture me, man! I remember Juliana quite well."

"Juliana?" There was, as best as Bingley could tell, no look of recognition on Darcy's face.

"Juliana. Good God man, you don't even remember her name?" Now it was Bingley's turn to laugh. He was being daring now, treading the line of inciting Darcy's anger, but it was worth it if it helped him make any progress.

"Juliana," Darcy repeated, trying to dredge up old memories. "Cambridge?"

"The faculty soirée."

"Where we met. Not very formally, as I recall," Darcy said. "I'm afraid my impressions of the evening are—well, they're a bit lost over time. I may never have learned her name."

"Oh, you knew her name." Bingley would chastise himself for this later, but at the moment, it was good to gloat and ruffle Darcy's unruffable feathers. "You were moaning it the whole way back to your quarters."

Darcy's mouth was agape. It was such a sight; Bingley had never seen it. "How do you know?"

"Because I carried you back. You could hardly stand." Bingley revelled—this was an expected delight, plus it further put off his uncomfortable and very technical questions. "But apparently you don't remember much of that, either. Do you wish me to enlighten you?"

"No," Darcy said, returning to his cold voice. "No, what I have of my memories is quite all right, thank you very much. If I have need of your services in the future, I will let you know. But back to the matter at hand—"

"Yes, the matter at hand." He did not relish in returning to it, but it *was* why they were out here in the morning chill, with their clothes damp from the morning dew.

"Despite whatever you may have heard or seen, I will make no claims to be consummate at the arts of feminine wiles," Darcy said, as stoutly as he was capable of—which was not particularly stoutly at the moment.

"But you know *something*. You are . . . a man of the world."

"Yes." Darcy seemed annoyed at admitting it, but that was not unexpected. "Hmm. I now am curious as to how I unduly embarrassed myself at my alma mater."

"It was hardly the talk of the town, but it was amusing to some," Bingley said. "Having not drunk nearly as much as you, I think I may actually be a better judge of the events in this regard."

"Then I must make a deal with you. Actually, I am not required to do so, but in the interest of friendship and the success of your marriage, I will offer this to you," Darcy said. "We share our account of that certain . . . evening . . . and I will tell you the little that I could claim to know of the mysteries of the female disposition."

"I find those terms very agreeable," Bingley said, and he offered his hand. To his great relief, they shook on it.

THE PARTY

1795

FITZWILLIAM DARCY DECIDED TO approach the night with a heavy level of caution. Accustomed to doing this as he was, he still spent his afternoon overpreparing and driving his good manservant crazy. Darcy liked to think his voice was calm and betrayed nothing of his apprehension, but he looked at his pocket watch and realised he had spent more time on selecting a wardrobe for this evening than he had on any other day since the Christmas Ball at Pemberley.

There was something to be said for academic robes. Darcy was in the unfortunate station in life where what he normally wore was very important, yet he cared nothing for it, and had he anything to say on the matter, he would go around with the same frock coat every day. But the future master of Pemberley was expected not only to be presentable but fashionable, something that in his opinion was a waste of his good time. The saving grace of his position and wealth was that it provided him with practically a retinue of people who made it their business to have indispensable advice on the matter.

University was a retreat from that, and he supposed he would have enjoyed it more if it didn't come with its own share of difficulties. He did not find the work particularly challenging and rather enjoyed having a reason to immerse himself in literature for hours on end, but he was not headed for further academia. That would practically require him to take holy orders and to dispense with his responsibilities at Pemberley, something he had no wish to do.

Young Mr. Darcy went to Cambridge because it was what the landed gentry did. He found some pleasure in it and probably would have found more if he were not practically struck down by homesickness as one is with a fever. Wickham being sent down from the University during his second term was an ease to Darcy's senses, especially after his father's gift of two Irish wolfhounds to keep him company. Perhaps the elder Darcy sensed his somewhat retiring son was lacking in the area of friends. It was not to say that he was ill at ease among other men, but he was not the gregarious character that his father had apparently been.

Most of Darcy's studies came not from classes, where he was far more studious and serious than most of his fellow students out of a sense of duty, but from the fencing club. Even at the illustrious Cambridge, his social standing had some influence, and he was able to manoeuvre his way into the very exclusive fencing halls quite quickly for an underclassman. (He liked to think that some actual talent might have had something to do with it, but it was not something he would admit.) That he was sparring with the future heads of England was less of a concern to him;

he merely enjoyed the sport, which reminded him a great deal of home and even exceeded it in the availability of trainers.

It was then unavoidable that he would not go totally unnoticed and begin to be drawn into the social circles that surrounded the fencers. The best and brightest athletes of England were his companions, and they were not averse to the attention it brought them, even if he was. Eventually, the invitations began to stack up to the point of becoming unavoidable.

Such was the case with the "faculty soirée," as it was called. It was well known that it had little to do with the faculty beyond some supporting members, but the presence of authority made it appropriate for the intrusion of the fairer sex, whereas Darcy could very much spend his time on campus during the day without looking upon a woman.

Not that he didn't want to. It was more a matter of propriety. It would not be totally unknown to have a young mistress to dress his arm or even a marriage prospect, but he expected more from himself in this area. His indiscretions, then, were as discreet as was possible, and Cambridge the town was not without its willing populace of young women to service the one need even he could not totally control. He thought at first college would be a several-year experience in monasticism, but there were some things even the young Mr. Darcy could not stand. Fortunately, Cambridge was full of ways to be discreet.

But tonight it was the farthest thing from his mind. Well, not the farthest, but he was preoccupied with this social invitation that he could not avoid, thanks to the overwhelming generosity of his fencing master in personally handing it to him. There would be people there he didn't know, and he would have no idea what to say to them beyond the banal pleasantries required of conversation. He did not follow local politics; he was not one to engage in speculation about women; and he could only hope that, being at the illustrious Cambridge, he would at least not be the most eligible bachelor in the room.

To his relief upon entering the foyer, he was not. There were several titled gentlemen in the room, some who were his sparring partners and some with whom he was not formally acquainted. He was assaulted instead by his captain, who was surprised that Fitzwilliam Darcy would finally put in an appearance at such an event. "Darcy, Darcy, you must sample the punch!"

Indeed, he must. He decided that it was the best course of action, as being engaged in the act of drinking was the easiest way to avoid having to say something, and he very much wanted to avoid having to say something, as Wentworth took him by the arm and introduced him to every young lady in the room. From the way they looked at him, it seemed they could be distracted from the future lords of Britain long enough to evaluate some wealthy gentleman from the north. Darcy was well aware that his well-toned physique, tremendous height, and brash attitude would do nothing to dissuade them. After the eighth introduction, he was very willing to give half of Derbyshire to be the ugliest man in the room.

Perhaps noticing his nervousness, the duteous servants kept his glass full, and he found it convenient for two reasons. First, it prevented him from shaking hands if he held it in the right hand, and second, it gave him something to do with his mouth. Whatever it was—not always just punch—he swallowed it and found a third reason to like this situation very much. He was not entirely unfamiliar with intoxication, but he was certainly not on the level of his colleagues, as he considered public drunkenness ungentlemanly and below his station, even if he had occasion at college to witness men far above him in standing quite in the cups. So, he decided not to consider himself intoxicated. He just felt less uneasy after the fourth or fifth glass, and anything that made him less uneasy was a great comfort.

"And this is my second, Mr. Darcy." Wentworth put a hand on his shoulder, and the rocking motion made Darcy a little dizzy. He had no idea as to whom he was being introduced—he had missed that part of the conversation entirely—but it was a man at least. Just because he was not at his full senses did not mean Darcy was inclined to throw himself at every flirtatious female in the room. He was much more comfortable with this man, with sort of wild reddish hair and a pale composure but a very pleasing smile on his face.

"Of course," said the man—more of a boy, really. *Must be a first-year.* They shook hands. "Pleasure to meet you."

"You, as well," Darcy said, and hoped there would be no exam as to who this man was or what he was doing here. He was not a fencer, so Darcy did not recognise him at all.

"I will tell you a secret, Mr. Bingley," said Wentworth. "Our team this year would have suffered a most ignoble defeat to Oxford had it not been for Darcy here. As captain, of course, I'm not supposed to admit it was that close, but he literally saved the day by defeating their top man by a point—and the future Earl of Gloucester, too!"

Darcy smiled vaguely at the memory. He was not the type to bask in his victories, but he felt like smiling. Odd, because he almost never felt like smiling. "You are exaggerating my abilities to this man, good sir."

"Hardly a smudge on the old honour of Pemberley," said Wentworth. "If you'll excuse me, Darcy, I have a mission of utmost importance."

"Do you need a second?" Darcy said jokingly, knowing Wentworth did not, as he had his eye on a fine brunette who was a bit overdressed in a ball gown. Wait, had he just made a *joke*? What was *wrong* with him?

Wentworth left him alone with the underclassman— Bingley, right? He didn't want to gape and ask, so he took one of the available chairs beside him. Even through a considerable fuzz, he could see that this young man was nervous and out of sorts for entirely different reasons than he was. Darcy didn't like social soirées; Bingley just seemed to think he was out of place. There was the possibility that he actually was, but it was not a topic to broach. At the moment, in fact, Darcy was content just to be sitting down.

"So you are Mr. Darcy of Pemberley?"

"And Derbyshire and all that, yes," he said, before realising he had answered the question as if he was mocking the way he was normally announced to people beneath him. Bingley, for whatever reason, saw some humour in this. "And you?" *Oh please, say your name again.*

"Just Charles Bingley, I'm afraid. I suppose I'll have to wait until after my degree to purchase land and become 'of' something, unless you wish to include a townhouse in London."

"A named townhouse in London is of stature," he assured him, though he really had no idea why. He could not account for his actions at all this evening. His next question was completely inappropriate. "Trade?"

"Yes. Shipping, mainly wool. My father's business, obviously." But the point was that he was of wealth, even if its means were not as established as just inheriting centuries of wealth probably hoarded from wars with France. Darcy was vaguely aware of the D'Arcys of Normandy and suspected, upon perusal of the old histories of wars between the two countries for his classwork, that at least some of his wealth had nothing to do with Derbyshire and everything to do with some looting during a prolonged war—after all, was that not how great fortunes were made? In a few generations, the Bingleys might have a great landed estate and be socially beside the Darcys.

"Perhaps you're right," said Bingley, and to his horror, Darcy realised he must have said some, if not all, of his musing *out loud*.

"You will excuse me," he said quickly, and stood up just as quickly. This was clearly a mistake. He did not even notice Bingley steady him with his own arm before it happened, yet another indignity. The Darcy name would not survive this night if he weren't careful.

The room had stopped spinning long enough for him to get his bearings again, when he was practically assaulted by the brunette Wentworth had been talking to. They had been introduced earlier, though for the life of him he couldn't recall her name, but now that he had a moment (or *needed* a moment—to steady himself) he found her to be quite something for Wentworth to be chasing after. She nearly embraced him. "Mr. Darcy, Mr. Wentworth has told me all about your brave victory over those ruffians at Oxford. I must know more from the man himself."

"I assure you—he was exaggerating," he said, but he was smiling when he said it.

1803

"And that's really all you can remember?"

Fitzwilliam Darcy, now nine and twenty and standing on the dirt road that led away from the notable estate of Netherfield, home to his best friend and soon-to-be brother, could only shrug. "You have cornered me. It is so. Now tell me how I truly embarrassed myself."

"I would not say you did that," Bingley was quick to defend. "Certainly, not at the party, or there would have been some mention of it that would have gotten back to you. Am I correct?"

"I suppose you are," Darcy said, thinking it over. Bingley was right. Best he could recall, there was no gossip when he was back in the changing room the next day and no knowing winks from his captain. Surely if there was some assault on the Darcy honour, he would remember it distinctly. At the moment, all he remembered was a pounding headache. "That is some small comfort. Now, as your part of the bargain, you must finish the tale."

Bingley, who rarely had a one-up on anything with Darcy, was apparently much obliged.

1795

Charles Bingley came to Cambridge with a considerable amount of apprehension. His father was kind to him, but he knew he was expected to do well, being the first in what would hopefully be a line of sons with diplomas. While he was hardly the most impoverished student at the University, he was untitled and his soon-to-be inherited fortune was in the abominable area of trade. His father did not have a living but earned a living. He was so good at working, in fact, that his son would not have to, and neither would his daughters, provided they married well. Bingley's first sister was engaged, in fact, to some man named Mr. Hurst, but Bingley knew very little about him, consumed as he was with his studies. Academics were not a major difficulty for him, but they were not exactly his first love.

What he did have going for him was his personality. He decided quite early that he liked his classmates and his tutors and just about everyone else he met, as was his habit. There was no use (or time, with all of the work!) in seeing the bad in anyone in his opinion, unless he was in some kind of investigation, and Charles Bingley did not desire to be a barrister. He was content with where his life was taking him as it was and saw no reason to alter course.

Where he suffered in lack of atmosphere—used to being out of doors, as was his preference—he did not suffer in the area of social interaction. There were plenty of people to meet at Cambridge and women to be found when he hesitantly ventured beyond the vaulted doors of Cambridge. He was not at a loss for acquaintances—acquaintances that his father constantly reminded him would hopefully one day be helpful friends and contacts. To Charles Bingley Senior, Cambridge was to be the foundation of his son's social standing if he would only make friends with the higher ups of Britain, which he knew his son would not fail to do.

If making friends was his duty, Charles Bingley Junior did it exceedingly well. He was not half a term into his program before he was busy running from gathering to gathering. Even he was surprised somewhat when he was invited to the infamous faculty soirée, as it was mainly for people of high esteem in some fashionable extra curriculum, and that did not include Bingley. He did like hunting quite a lot, but sadly, that was not offered as a regular club and would have had no place to operate in a college town. That he was of some acquaintance with the fencing team captain was probably the explanation for the practically gilded invitation. His only nervousness about the event was his desire to make a good impression, but on this, he could at least feel some confidence.

He showed up, what he deemed was, fashionably on time—not too early—and Wentworth briefly showed him around then left him on his own. There were a number of ladies who piqued his interest, but he reminded himself that he was a college man, and he was actually alarmed by their forwardness. He was a socialite but admittedly inexperienced in certain . . . areas. Some insecurities would not be overcome in just one night.

After several hours of standing without dancing, he found himself retiring on one of the few chairs available for a brief respite when Wentworth reappeared with a fellow fencer on his arm, a dark-haired man with a look of discomfort on his face, marred only slightly by a mild drunkenness. Perhaps because of his own state, Wentworth was more than oblivious to this, but Bingley could read him quite well. "Charles Bingley, I'd like you to meet a good friend of mine, if you'd do me the honour."

"Yes, yes. I would—"

Wentworth patted Darcy on the shoulder, causing him to wobble. "And this is my second, Mr. Darcy."

"Of course," Bingley said, and shook Darcy's hand. "Pleasure to meet you."

"You, as well," said the man, his speech a little slurred, but not easily noticeable.

Wentworth went on to sing the praises of his fellow fencer, though this Darcy fellow seemed oblivious, even a little annoyed at his captain. Bingley was quite sure he saw a roll of the eyes, though he picked up a mention of Pemberley. *Was that not that great estate in Derbyshire?* Well, in this crowd, it was hardly unexpected that he would find many men far above his own station. Derbyshire—he had a great desire to see it, but he did not want to bother this new person who seemed ill at ease with himself in the room.

It was not long before the ever-busy Wentworth was chasing after some lady, and Bingley found the man known as Mr. Darcy sitting beside him, apparently enjoying the break far more than he was. He almost wanted to leave him alone entirely, but he was curious, and eventually he could not hold his tongue.

"So you are Mr. Darcy of Pemberley."

Darcy took another sip from his glass and answered, "And Derbyshire and all that, yes." The way he answered it, he had clearly answered the question to many admirers—and, undoubtedly, scouting women—and seemed truly annoyed with his own station. This gave Bingley cause for a very inappropriate chuckle, one that he was sure would quickly dissolve this acquaintance. A shame, really, because he looked like a lost puppy in this crowd.

Mr. Darcy made an enquiry as to who Bingley was associated with, as if he had missed it the first time, which he probably had, but Bingley was not about to slight him for it. In fact, he even let it slip that he was in trade, to which Darcy seemed not at all put off and had no fear in saying this in a very slurred mono-logue. When Bingley responded, he quickly excused himself, as if embarrassed by his own outburst. Here was a man of wealth and stature who was not as comfortable at parties as Bingley was and looked half-terrified when he ran into the brunette that Wentworth had been chasing. Not to come between a man and a woman, Bingley turned his attentions elsewhere. He did not even notice Darcy's disappearance until some time later, when it occurred to him in passing. Well, no matter; it was a party, and people were coming and going.

As the evening progressed, Bingley felt less inclined to stay because it seemed that the longer he did, the more cups of punch and wine he had to refuse, and he felt very guilty refusing any-thing. When he was quite sure he was thoroughly introduced to everyone in the room, he bowed and made his exit.

His dormitory was relatively close by, and he had only a brisk walk home. Not at all inebriated, he felt confident that he had weathered the evening with considerable success and was in the midst of congratulating himself when he stepped into the com-mon room and was greeted by the rush of a ball gown. It turned out to be a woman, a very familiar woman he did not quite recall the name of, having been introduced to her only briefly. She bumped into him, nearly knocking him from his feet before unapologetically disappearing out the door with all haste.

Bingley barely had time to recover when he had to face the angry dorm master, who merely looked at Bingley with surprise, perhaps at his sudden appearance. "I suppose I should just let the harlot go," he said with a sigh. "Do you know her, Mr. Bingley?"

He correctly answered, "No."

"Good. Now if you will excuse me, there's the matter of the student in Master Stuart's room—"

"What matter?" he asked out of curiosity.

For whatever reason, perhaps because they were on exceedingly good terms, as Bingley was as well-behaved a gown as anyone could imagine, he said in passing, "A previous occupant seems to have given the lady a key to the common room, and she took liberties to bring her . . . gentleman here. You will help me drag him out?"

"Of course," he said, because the dorm master was old and, frankly, he was interested in a way that was totally inappropriate. Of course this woman was not a loose person, and she did not abscond with keys and impressionable University students. This was clearly a minor misunderstanding.

Following the dorm master, Bingley was surprised to find Mr. Darcy in Mr. Stuart's room. He wasn't on the bed precisely—he was sitting on the floor next to the bed, his coat removed, his clothing very much askew, and muttering incoherently in a very drunken manner with a bottle in his hands.

"I will take him," Bingley immediately offered. "If he can stand."

"Do you know him?"

"No, but please, you must have other things to attend to," he said. Unaccustomed as he was to lying, it was certainly necessary. He helped Darcy to his feet. The man could walk, but not on his own. "Mr. Darcy—"

"Juliana—" Darcy said, and reached for his flask, which Bingley took from him and pocketed in his own waistcoat.

"Where do you live?"

"Where did she—"

"Gone, and you're the better for it. Let's go," he said, and without explaining himself further, he put one of Darcy's arms over his shoulders and helped him leave the dormitory just as quickly as the woman in question. Because of the lateness of the hour, they were able to make a relatively peaceful journey, but Bingley felt compelled to not leave Mr. Darcy with the doorman. "Your quarters. The number?"

"Juliana—ugh—Pemberley. I live in Pemberley."

"Yes, yes, I know. But in the dormitory."

"The dogs. Where are my dogs? Why can't they find me? They know my scent. They're hounds."

"Will you *please* point me in the right direction?"

Darcy gestured, and they made it back to his sizeable quarters, which were empty, his manservant apparently dismissed for the evening. Bingley was greeted by two massive wolfhounds that nearly toppled them both. Bingley barely succeeded in getting Darcy past them and to his bed—or what he assumed was Darcy's bed—as it seemed the most logical place to put a man who could barely stand. But Darcy would not lie down, despite his inebriation. He sat on the bed, his hair frazzled, and blinked several times. Bingley wasn't entirely sure if he comprehended where he was or who Bingley was, but he didn't toss him out.

"I think—I think I have made a fool of myself," Darcy mumbled. "No, no! The Darcy honour, man! The Darcy honour!"

"I imagine it will survive, as nothing untoward occurred at the party itself," Bingley said, meaning it to be a comfort, because he very much wished to take his leave and did not want to deal with a sobbing man.

"I am lost," Darcy mumbled, and keeled over. Bingley made a brief inspection to see if there were any more spirits about, and finding there were not, he thought it best to take his leave.

"Good night, Mr. Darcy." He bowed stiffly.

"By God, good night indeed!" said Darcy, and Bingley exited.

When he saw Darcy again, a week had passed, and it took him a moment to realise it was the same man. In full gown, with a glowering look of propriety and a stiff back, he was the very model of an ideal young man of wealth, and Bingley decided to treat him as such. He would not have engaged him at all had Darcy not done it himself when they saw each other walking across the quad.

"Mr. Bingley," Darcy said, and bowed briefly to him. Bingley merely tried to hide his surprise that he remembered his name. If he remembered anything else, he gave no indication, and Bingley wasn't about to enlighten him. "I believe we met at the faculty soirée."

"We did, Mr. Darcy," he said, and bowed.

"Mr. Wentworth has told me much about you."

"All good things, I hope."

"Of course. Would you care to join me for lunch?"

Bingley decided that he would.

1803

Not enough time had passed in eight years for Mr. Darcy to fully recover his demeanour—possibly because this was the first he had heard of the subject—because at various points in the narrative his face had gone bright red.

"It seems . . . I am in your debt," he finally stammered.

"It has been many times repaid. After all, you were the one who pushed me back to Netherfield—"

"Only after I had taken you from it—"

"Let us call it even. Except, of course, in the matter of which I first enquired."

"Yes, yes." Darcy was still visibly recovering, but he was recovering quickly, as he always did. "It is a very sensitive topic—" He paused, looking down the road. "And it seems I am saved."

"How—" but then Bingley saw no one coming down the road but the dreaded Mr. Collins. While he could usually not bear to think ill of anyone, at this moment, he was quite ready to pound Mr. Collins soundly with his walking stick merely for his sudden appearance.

"Mr. Darcy, Mr. Bingley," the cleric said, bowing to them both more deeply than was strictly necessary. "I was looking for you as I thought to inquire if I may give a wedding toast? I know it is rather late, but I was withheld by Lady Catherine for some time—"

Darcy explained very patiently and politely that they had already granted that honour to Mr Bennett, but thanked him very much for his time and gently suggested they return to Netherfield or Longbourn, for poor Mr. Collins looked positively exhausted.

"You *will* answer my inquiries," Bingley whispered to Darcy as they headed back.

"Yes, yes, of course," Darcy said with a smile, having avoided his duty for a further time.

THE WALK

ELIZABETH BENNET, SOON TO be Elizabeth Darcy—a notion she could hardly believe herself—was becoming just a bit frustrated at her apparent inability to see the man to whom she had promised herself for the rest of her life. She did see him almost every night at Longbourn or Netherfield for dinner, but she had realised long ago that Darcy loathed public displays of affection and she was resigned to it, as he seemed to make up for it quite readily in the little privacy they managed on long walks during their engagement. Still waters did run deep, so deep that both of his passionate proposals came to her as complete surprises and yet could not have been delivered with more honesty and emotion, even if he had bungled it the first time with his own pride. While Jane and Mr. Bingley—no offence meant to them—seemed quite content to gaze lovingly into each other's eyes, Elizabeth knew Darcy's true intentions would only be revealed when they were alone, and so she was all the more in want to have some time with him before they were married. Not that she at all doubted that he loved her or that she loved him perhaps equally in return, but a woman could not help but be curious about her obsessively secretive betrothed.

Georgiana's appearance did something to calm her fears. The lovely Miss Darcy arrived at Netherfield for the wedding a few days before and was more than happy to spend as much time as possible with her future sister and sister-in-law. She had much more access to the Bennet sisters and their end-of-the-wedding preparations than her brother did. Completely without bidding, she was her brother's best advocate, and her happiness at his happiness—and the obvious total innocence of her character— was a great testament to the private Mr. Darcy. She was not a sister singing praises to propose a match but an affectionate sibling who saw no reason not to express her feelings. Elizabeth felt she was more like Jane in personality—trusting and loving—and would make a terrific companion at Pemberley, for Elizabeth was already feeling the loss of no longer sharing a room with her beloved older sister, as she had all her life. If one knew nothing of Mr. Darcy but through Georgiana's mouth, he was a candidate for sainthood.

This diminished her worries but did not satisfy Elizabeth's longing for time with Darcy, something she expressed to her sister, and Jane quickly admitted the same for her own beau, but there was nothing to be done. They were busy with dresses and flowers and preparations, and the men were busy with finances and their own costumes and greeting the many people coming in for the double ceremony. In fact, Elizabeth wondered if they would spend the duration of the honeymoon sleeping to recover from the exhausting process.

But this was apparently not to be, or so they were about to be informed. The dresses had come in from London, and Elizabeth and the maid were checking the final fittings on Jane's lovely dress when Mrs. Bennet and Mrs. Gardiner burst in the room. More specifically, Mrs. Bennet burst in, and her sister followed her in a calming manner.

"Jane, Lizzy," her mother said with a certain gravity. "It is time."

Jane stared at her with a look of confused horror. Elizabeth decided just to be cautiously intrigued.

"Come, let us sit," Mrs. Bennet said, gesturing to the bed. "Be careful with your dress, Jane. You look so beautiful in it."

"Indeed," said Mrs. Gardiner, who sat down in the rocking chair.

They took their seats very properly, quite unclear of the situation. Surely if there were some bad news, it would have already been said at this point, and at a much louder volume.

"Oh my dear daughters," Mrs. Bennet said with her usual degree of melodrama, unintentional though it was, "you are so soon to be married."

"Yes, we are much aware," Elizabeth said, deciding not to hold herself back, even if it elicited a look from Jane.

"There is so much to tell you—about being married—and so little time. Oh, because of my nerves, I have put it off! I am quite an unsuitable mother!"

When they had no reaction to this, the mellower Mrs. Gardiner decided to pick up the slack. "What we mean to say is, dearest nieces, if you are to be adequately prepared to be wives, that from which your maiden ears have been guarded must no longer remain so."

"Yes, yes!" Mrs. Bennet said, "lest you be taken totally unawares! That would be most unsatisfying to your husbands indeed!"

Elizabeth realised her meaning first, but that didn't make her feel one bit better about it.

The carriage from Netherfield arrived earlier than dinner was ready, so a particularly frazzled couple decided to take a stroll. Darcy could account for his own countenance—it was becoming harder and harder to avoid Bingley entirely—but he could not understand what perturbed Elizabeth. At the very sight of their future husbands, Jane looked ready to bolt, her sister less so. The walk would do them all good. The walks always calmed her.

"My dearest Elizabeth . . . ," Darcy said finally when they were far out of view of the house and, he assumed, away from whatever was distressing her, because he couldn't imagine something he had done—today, anyway. "I must inquire—"

"I am perfectly fine, thank you very much."

She said it so quickly and insistently, it was obviously a lie. Darcy just looked away and muttered, "Of course."

"You are also not in the most pleasing of moods."

"Have you ever known me to be so?"

So, he had caught her. She had that look on her face, like she was developing a witticism with which to smite him but having a bit of trouble doing so. "If you tell me why you are distressed, I will tell you the same; for should we not exchange everything? Though honestly, we have only two days—"

"No, you are perturbed, and I will not stand for it," he said, thrusting his walking stick into the ground in an indignant manner that he knew she would find amusing. "You will tell me what

34

has made you so upset that you can hardly stand the sight of me, as I can think of no untoward behaviour on my part . . . at least, not in the last few months. But perhaps I am mistaken, and I could not stand to be mistaken."

Again, she was looking for something to say. "It is not what you did . . . or will do. It is a womanly matter."

"Oh," he said simply. It took him a moment to decide he did not entirely believe her. That wouldn't give her reason to be nervous around *him*.

"And you?"

"And me?"

"Yes, you. What has put you in such an ill mood?—though admittedly, not the most dour of moods I have ever seen you in."

"I perhaps shall take that as a compliment for the sake of argument." Then he realised he still had to answer the question. "It is a gentlemanly matter."

"How clever an answer."

"It is the truth."

"Hmm," Elizabeth said, looking off into the distance as they walked. "So we have learned nothing, because certainly I knew before this point that men and women kept things private from each other—though, I had hoped, not husbands and wives."

"When you are my wife, I will be happy to enlighten you. Before that, I do not think it would be proper, especially in the case of another man's privacy."

"So Bingley is involved?"

He stopped and shuddered. "I will admit that I sometimes wish I were betrothed to a less intelligent woman. Now, I cannot speak more on the subject!"

"If he is going to mistreat my sister—"

"He is not going to mistreat your sister. He has only the finest intentions. That is precisely the prob—" But he stopped himself, even if it was too late. "Perhaps we should turn before I further embarrass myself and Mr. Bingley's confidence."

"Hardly! After such an admission, I am now obligated to admit my own personal shame," she said, taking his hand for the first time that day, "though it is highly improper. I may burn your gentlemanly ears, and you may no longer wish such a wife."

"There is nothing I can think of that would make me wish you not to be my wife," he said, and looked at her. Elizabeth was too innocent to actually have done something . . . untoward. Of that, he was positively sure.

She seemed convinced enough to continue, "Today Jane and I had a most unpleasant conversation with our mother about . . . being wives."

Darcy's mouth simply made an "oh"—he didn't have to actually pronounce the word. It took him some time to get the courage up to ask, "And how was it unpleasant?"

"Surely this must wait until we are married."

"On the contrary. If you are uneasy now, let me put the matter to rest. I will not stand to have you upset for any length of time, be it only two days." He shrugged. "Besides, everyone else has made a hobby of asking me uncomfortable questions at every possible moment, so let at least one of them be my lovely betrothed."

"Mr. Bingley has—?"

"No more talk of Mr. Bingley, please, for the sake of my . . . just about everything that could need steadying," he said, trying to smile, but he knew he was mainly just blushing. "This is about you—and your mother."

"And my aunt, who fortunately provided some kind of balance, though her differing account was mainly . . . puzzling." She leaned on his arm. "You know of what I speak. Please don't make me say it."

"As you wish," he said. "Your mother has finally told you about relations, and now you are terrified because she has made it seem a horrible experience. No doubt she said something about wifely duties and made it seem like a necessary evil."

"You know my mother uncommonly well, sir."

"Hardly. She is just repeating the same nonsense that your cousin will drone on and on about in church. That it is a duty you must endure with great suffering." He sighed. "Elizabeth, the best thing I can think of to say is that if there was no fun to be had of it at all, the world would not be nearly so populated."

"And you are an expert on this—"

"Well, I wouldn't say 'expert'—" And he had to stop himself again. This time, he was ready to smack his own face just to keep his mouth shut. "Lizzy, you will forgive me—"

"No, no, of course," she said, though she had lost *some* composure. "I could not expect that you, who have been to University and travelled through Europe and are a man of great wealth and standing, have not—"

"You don't have to say it." He put his hand on her shoulder. "Elizabeth, I love you more than I have loved any woman I ever met, so much so that it seems I am incapable of keeping secrets from you, even when they would benefit both of us. You make a fool of a very proud man, so it must be love, for love makes fools of us all."

"How clever of you to quote poetry to placate my fears," she said, but not in spite. She seemed somewhat relieved, in fact, and they were able for the first time in several minutes to move on, though this time they did not separate their hands. Conversation ceased, and there remained only their physical selves, their touch, and the surrounding forest.

"How many?"

This brought Darcy back from his dreamlike state. "What?"

"Surely it was more than one."

"Oh God," he said, blaspheming quite openly now in his terror. "It is not about numbers."

"That many?"

"Perhaps you should just be grateful that I am not an inexperienced twit."

"Like Mr. Bingley?"

He glared at her. On everyone else, this worked perfectly. On Elizabeth, it was just a further enticement. *Blast!* If not for her perfect eyes . . . and wonderful personality . . . and loving soul . . . and so many things . . . damn her! "As I would do anything for you, it is only fair that you would do anything for me. So I beg of you, please, to stop mentioning my good friend in the course of this conversation. *Please.*"

She smiled one of her charming smiles that spoke volumes. "Of course, if that is your desire."

"Then the matter is cleared."

"Yes."

"And your fears are waylaid, at least to the extent that I can waylay them at this moment in time?"

"Perhaps," she said, now toying with him, indicating a vast improvement in her mood. So she was placated.

"And you will mention nothing of this to Jane?"

"She is my sister! Does she not deserve to be comforted? She is more terrified than I was."

"Then soothe her in some clever way that does not involve mentioning me or Bingley. You certainly have the wits to devise a strategy."

She appeared to hesitate, but it was probably just to torment him further. "All right."

"I have your promise?"

"You have my promise. I will speak to my sister in the most discreet way possible." She frowned. "Yes, this will require some strategy."

"Speaking of strategy," he said, patting her arm. "I am afraid I must be off to London tomorrow."

"That will leave us—"

"Time will pass just the same whether I am here or not," he said. "And it seems as though our time together is limited these days anyway. But I assure you, this is something that cannot wait. I will be back tomorrow evening, but perhaps not in time for dinner."

"And this mysterious errand will require you out at all hours?"

"I hope not. And don't give me a look, because I will not reveal its nature." He straightened his waistcoat in a mock fashion. "'Tis a gentlemanly matter."

Elizabeth smiled at him. "I see."

Surprisingly, the morning without Darcy passed with remarkable expediency. In fact, one could venture to say that it was passing *too* quickly, no offence meant to Elizabeth's beloved

Darcy. There was the final fitting for her dress, and the matter of the arrival of her sister Lydia in time for lunch.

Not that it should have been a "matter" at all for Lydia was not bringing her own husband along, claiming regimental duties he had and glossing over Mr. Bennet's refusal to ever see Wickham on the grounds of Longbourn again. But there was *another* matter to be settled, that of her comforting Jane, and she decided quickly that it had to happen before Lydia's arrival, or at least before Lydia found the time to talk to Jane—and knowing Lydia, it would be within moments of her arrival, as men were, in all likelihood, still her favourite topic of conversation. Despite her marital status, if her letters were any indicator, her interest in the latest man to behold did not wane with time.

Elizabeth had little time for pondering, so she did it expediently, staying up half the night with her own thoughts and those of her sister. Darcy had not truly removed all of her hesitations and fears about the . . . nature of conjugal union, but he had done an admirable job, and she could not imagine that the fastidious Mr. Darcy would ever do anything untoward, even in the privacy of his bedchambers. His standoffish nature did prevent him from outward displays of affection (and, in the beginning, any indication of affection entirely), but Elizabeth had come to realise that he was mildly uncomfortable in anyone's presence, much less someone he was keenly interested in. Well, he was forgiven. What he lacked in social abilities he obviously made up for in passion, or at least, in the ability to express it with his eyes. She found it very hard, despite her mild terror at what she was about to enter, to look at his deep brown eyes and imagine he would ever do anything but make her happy.

These were not words she found so easy to express to Jane. Though she was deeply in love, Jane was still shy to admit her own feelings about the particularities of Mr. Bingley, and Elizabeth did not want to say something that would make her future brother seem lacking by complete accident.

By morning she had decided on an ally in the elaborate scheme Darcy had urged her to concoct. Charlotte Collins was perhaps her only true confidante beyond Jane, and if she was not willing to be part of an elaborate but very proper charade, she was helpless.

"This will be quite hard to explain," Elizabeth said to Charlotte, after the seamstress had disappeared to acquire more ribbon. It did occur to her that, standing on a stool, wearing a virginal white wedding gown of considerable note and train, the conversation was even *more* inappropriate. "But I simply do not want my sister to . . . I don't want her to . . . be terrified."

"And you are not?"

She knew, without looking in the sizeable mirror before her, that she was blushing. "Perhaps a little. Mr. Darcy was very reassuring."

Without pausing, Charlotte said, "Lizzy, your forwardness does not in the least surprise me, so there is no reason to be embarrassed. Though I am assuming, he was a perfect gentleman about the whole matter."

"Yes, of course," she said. "It wouldn't even have come up if— if he hadn't asked why I was so perturbed, if I hadn't acted in such a manner as if I did loathe the sight of him. So it is my fault. But the point is, my concern is chiefly with my sister. I wish to reassure her without telling her the truth of my source of comfort."

"Why ever not? It is the most logical conclusion."

"Because Darcy made me promise."

"Oh yes." As usual, Charlotte understood everything. "He is the model of privacy."

"Precisely."

"So . . . you need an anonymous source—quickly."

Elizabeth smiled. "Yes."

"Well, I need hardly be anonymous, Lizzy. I have been married for nearly a year."

"I would not presume—"

"Presume all you wish," Charlotte said, much without regard. "I am but two months with child."

"Charlotte!" And then it occurred to her that she was in a very complicated dress. "Please come to me so that I might embrace you without turning myself into a pin cushion. How long have you known?"

"A few weeks. I have told no one but Mr. Collins."

They embraced, to the extent that they could, and Elizabeth could not help but notice that her friend looked truly ebullient. Perhaps she was not so ill married after all. "Though I must say in all honestly, I cannot imagine that you told Mr. Collins, and yet I have not heard of it from him, and at great length."

"Some things are just between husbands and wives until their wives say otherwise," Charlotte said with a twinkle in her eye. "The whole Rosings crowd will know in good time, but I have put my foot down on the matter and that is that."

"Charlotte, I must congratulate you first on the obvious and second on taming Mr. Collins."

"It was not so hard," Charlotte said with a smile. "My husband is not deficient in *all* things. I will be a very willing subject to this experiment."

It took Elizabeth a moment to grasp her meaning. "I have to confess, you have put a very nasty thought into my head."

"Lizzy, every married couple has done the same. Your parents at least five times—*at least.*"

She hadn't thought about it—or at least, she'd tried not to think about it, but one could logically conclude . . . she had to hold her head. "I think I am going to faint. Oh no, I am turning into my mother!"

"Should I get the smelling salts?"

"Do not mock me! I cannot stand it!" But at that moment, despite her agitated state, the seamstress reappeared, and she said quickly in a hushed tone, "So we will speak to Jane, before Lydia arrives."

"Yes."

She was relieved, but she decided she would be more relieved when she got the image of the awful Mr. Collins out of her head.

Charlotte did what Elizabeth recommended, despite her lack of experience on the matter, of reassuring Jane in the best and most complete manner without getting into the specifics of her own relationship, which she seemed very happy about but neither Bennet sister could accept as anything other than odious. The process took some time, and they were nearly late to lunch.

Lunch at Longbourn was an even more crowded and noisy affair than usual, as they were joined by the Gardiners, the Collinses, and Lydia Wickham, and there was certainly much to be discussed. Lydia embraced both of her sisters most enthusiastically, but the conversation kept going for all the preparations that still had to be made the next day. At the head of the table, Mr. Bennet attempted to create a fortification with the newspaper between him and the company, but Mrs. Bennet would have none of it. "Mr. Bennet, you cannot possibly be so relaxed when we are all so agitated!"

"You are correct in that assumption, Mrs. Bennet," he said mildly. "I admit that I am not as relaxed as I appear to be, but somehow over the years I have become quite accomplished at appearing so, if I may say so myself. I owe it to much opportunity for practice."

Elizabeth giggled and was not sure if her mother knew she was being insulted or even had time to acknowledge it. Lunch was a quick affair between appointments, and Elizabeth thought maybe they would escape Lydia altogether, but she managed to corner Jane and Elizabeth upstairs in the early afternoon.

"Dear God," Jane said bluntly as Lydia began her monologue about the delights of matrimony. "Am I to be assaulted with advice and reassurance from every person in Hertfordshire? Is not any mystery to be left of it at all?"

That silenced them all completely for several moments.

"We are just concerned—"

"And I am overwhelmed by the kindness of my sisters, my mother, my friends, and my more distant relatives, but surely there is more to marriage than relations! Would someone like to give me advice about when to expect visitors or how to receive relatives?" She went on, to everyone's stunned expressions, "Is Miss Bingley going to burst in and give me suggestions of the most untoward kind? Because please, let me at least put on a better gown for it."

The strange silence of several gabby women, quieted entirely by the outburst of their beloved porcelain sister, was only broken when Elizabeth began to laugh. "Just when I thought I knew everything of my sister's character, you have surprised me. Brava!"

They were only interrupted by Mr. Bennet's voice at the bottom of the stairs. "Jane, are you all right?" Whether he had heard the particulars of the outburst was doubtable, but the very fact that his eldest daughter was shouting was probably of some concern to him.

"Yes, Papa! Everything is fine!" she called back, opening the door to her father. "We were just having a discussion."

"I am very accustomed to discussions in this family; it seems I cannot avoid them no matter how hard I try. This, instead, sounded like an argument of some kind."

"No, no, Papa," Jane rushed to reassure her father, taking his hand. "We were just discussing . . . matrimony."

"I can't imagine why not. It is the topic of the day."

"And the specifics of matrimony," Lydia cut in. "I will not stand to have my sisters go into their marriage beds without any idea as to what they are to expect."

The elder Mr. Bennet blinked and then said slowly and carefully, "Oh." After a pause, he added, "Well, I will be in my study until it is time to leave for dinner. If you have any great need of me, I wish you the best of luck at finding an axe, because the door shall be soundly locked."

Dinner at Netherfield was not officially the pre-wedding dinner, which would come the following night, but it was in all likelihood an unintentional rehearsal. The room was so crowded with guests that tables had to be brought together. At one end was the man of honour and the host, Mr. Bingley, and to his immediate left, Mr. Hurst in Darcy's usual place, for his friend had yet to return from London. (He broke the news to Elizabeth politely and quickly as they arrived.) On his right were his sisters Caroline and Louisa, the former constantly requesting the wine to be passed. Then there were the Bennets, all seven of them; the Gardiners; the Collinses; and the Lucas parents. All pretences for coherent conversation were quickly abandoned, as one could hardly shout across the table without being rude to the person next to them, and the atmosphere was undeniably cheery. Elizabeth contented herself seated between Jane and Georgiana, her sister and sister-to-be, though she did keep an unintentional eye on the door. Only when it began to rain rather badly—so noticeably that it could be heard in the background of the clamorous dinner—did Elizabeth begin to worry.

"Do not worry," Georgiana said quietly. "This is not the first time my brother has been caught in the rain, and I can barely believe that he would allow it to alter his plans."

"I wish he would, for his own safety, be caught in Town rather than in a downpour."

"He is Fitzwilliam Darcy, and he has quite a resilience. He once rode all the way from Pemberley to Liverpool in the middle of the night, stayed only a few hours, and then returned the next evening. I believe his clothing had to be disposed of."

"Oh yes," Colonel Fitzwilliam said, at Georgiana's other side. "I remember that well. I'm surprised you remember it at all. He was but seventeen, so you must have been—"

"Pray, I never did learn the reason," Georgiana said, and winked to Elizabeth, knowing full well she was just as curious.

Fitzwilliam grunted, "Humph. Well, um, it is not for me to say. It was connected to some boyhood prank, I believe. That and he was at the age where he was quite sure he was the best rider in all of England—you know, the time in a man's life where he feels he is invincible. When he was needed in Liverpool for some reason, he jumped at the chance to be as brash and daring as possible."

"Mr. Darcy! Really!" Elizabeth exclaimed, having to restrain her voice so they were not overheard, even though everyone around them was engaged in their own conversation. "It does not seem like something he would do."

"If you imagine that your betrothed has never done anything rash in his life, then you have no idea what he did to his aunt the evening before he proposed," Georgiana said.

"Really? You must tell me!"

"Well . . . I suppose I shouldn't, because I only heard it from Anne de Bourgh in later correspondence, but, apparently, when he heard from Lady Catherine that you had refused to swear you would never marry him, he made her repeat it several times, as if he had a hearing deficiency, before thanking her for aiding him in his quest to win your hand. She wouldn't stand for it, of course, so he left her alone in his London apartment while he rode off to Longbourn! In the middle of the night!" Georgiana giggled. "Somehow I imagine you can believe it."

"I can. Though before that day, I would have not," Elizabeth admitted.

Dinner seemed to pass too slowly, perhaps out of her growing concern for Darcy. When it ended there was hardly a change in situation, because they were all stuck there but for the weather. Card games and the pianoforte diverted them, and the men removed to the study for cigars. Eventually, though everyone was enjoying himself, Mr. Bingley had to make arrangements with his servants about who was to sleep where because there were those who were inclined to retire. Only a few were left at the card table when a rapping on the door shook them out of their conversation. The servants who stood by the door had retired, so Bingley did not wait for another to appear and opened the massive door himself.

It was, of course, Mr. Darcy, a completely soaked Mr. Darcy. When he removed his hat, a splash of collected water hit the floor, creating a considerable puddle in Netherfield's hallway.

"Mr. Darcy!" Mrs. Bennet shrieked, as various servants rushed to attend him.

"I apologise," he said, bowing very tiredly at the crowd assembling quickly before him. "There was a problem with the carriage, and I was forced to take the rest of the way on horseback."

"On horseback!" Mrs. Bennet was livid. "Poor Mr. Darcy, off to bed with you, for the sake of your health! Please!"

Darcy paused, probably deciding if he wanted to be treated by his future mother-in-law as if she were his *actual* mother, but just quietly answered, "I regret my absence at dinner. Please excuse me." He bowed again and allowed the servants to practically carry him off to his quarters.

"Mr. Bingley, we must have some food sent up to Mr. Darcy! A starving man is very easily taken ill!" said Mrs. Bennet.

"Of course," Bingley said, still stupefied enough by Darcy's sudden appearance to defend the competence of Netherfield's well-paid staff to tend to Darcy properly. He *did* have the sense to turn to Elizabeth and say, "Perhaps, Miss Bennet, you shall oversee the preparing of food, if you are not too tired yourself from the late hour?"

She gave him a smile that obviously meant she was grateful that he read her mind on wanting to have an excuse to attend to Darcy. "Of course." She curtseyed and quickly scurried off to the kitchen. As she left, she heard her mother further discuss Mr. Darcy's health, apparently in fear that he would drop dead before the wedding.

"I believe a great philosopher once said, 'One does not die of a cold,'" Mr. Bennet reminded her, and Elizabeth smiled.

The food business was just an excuse, of course. Not that Elizabeth was wont to engage an exhausted Darcy in a long conversation that would not be to his liking, but she did want dearly to at least poke her head in. With the servant bearing the tray behind her, she knocked on the door and was allowed entrance by the servant after he announced her and she heard Darcy mutter something in approval.

He was still mostly dressed, but he did not rise to greet her for obvious reasons. He was seated on the chaise lounge, and a servant was pulling off his boots. She curtseyed to him.

"Elizabeth," he said softly, "there is no reason to be alarmed. I am in quite good health, though I will be very happy if I do not see the back of a horse for a few days at least."

"I see you have not lost your sense of humour. That is the best sign. Well, I will bother you no longer—"

"It is good to see you," he interrupted. "I apologise again for my lateness. It was an important errand."

"Was it?"

"Yes, but I am not inclined to divulge it yet," he said, somehow managing a twinkle in his eye despite sheer exhaustion.

"Very well then," she said with a smirk. "I will wait until morn."

He held out his hand as some kind of invitation, and she took it briefly and leaned over, kissing him on the top of his still-wet head. "Good night, Mr. Darcy."

"Good night, Miss Bennet." He said the name strangely, as if he was tired of it.

Yes, they were both ready for a change of names.

THE BOOK

IN THE MORNING, THE weather had cleared, and the various unintended guests were off in a hurry, far too much for Elizabeth's comfort. Darcy was still sleeping soundly, even through a noisy breakfast, which was not like him at all, and Elizabeth was eager to invent an excuse to remain at Netherfield at least until he woke, even though she had plenty to do at home on her last day as Elizabeth Bennet.

Fortunately, Mr. Bennet in his wisdom said kindly, "Lizzy, I have some business with Mr. Darcy, and I must stay until he is up and about. Perhaps you would take time from your busy schedule to spend a morning with your father before he gives you away?"

She gladly obliged. Fortunately, she had done most of her packing already, for Mr. Darcy had insisted that most of his wife's possessions be sent on ahead to Pemberley so that she would not be waiting for their arrival when they got there, after a brief stay in Town to break up the travelling. She saw her sisters off and then retreated with her father to the library of Netherfield.

"And what business do you have with Mr. Darcy?—if it is something you can divulge," she said, as he wandered the impressive library, glancing at the titles.

"Just some matters involving your inheritance, of course—purely legal nonsense that forces men to vex themselves on behalf of their wives and daughters."

"Papa, I have no desire to vex my husband!"

"Certainly not, but he is a proud man, and if anyone is to give him an occasional ribbing about it, I think it ought to be you, for he is so in much love with you that he would forgive you if you called him a donkey," Mr. Bennet said.

"Oh, Papa," she said, embracing him. "Sometimes I cannot bear the thought of the distance to be between us because of this marriage. If I were to be an old maid, you would at least have my company until the end of your days."

"But I would not be nearly as happy as I am to see you happy with a husband such as yours," he said. "I will miss you dearly, but it does not come as a complete surprise to me that my daughters would eventually leave me for other men. It is just a pain fathers must bear—mothers, too."

"You will visit me at Pemberley, as often as you like."

"In time. When I was a newlywed, I was not much inclined to visitors for the first few months."

Before she could comprehend his meaning, there was a knock on the door, and a servant entered and bowed to them both. "Mr. Bennet, Miss Bennet, I am to inform you that Mr. Darcy is recovering quite well. The master has gone to see to him now, and he will report back to you."

"He is not sick?"

"No, marm, just very tired."

"Then let him rest all he wants," said Mr. Bennet. "He has enough to do tomorrow, I should say."

Mr. Bingley was a bundle of nerves for too many reasons to count without throwing himself into a fit, but the top thing on his mind was the health of his good friend. In the years they had known each other, Darcy had never failed to rise before Bingley, and yet today he slept well until noon. A local doctor was called, and he made his assessment as soon as Darcy showed signs of rousing.

"He is not ill," said the doctor, and Bingley was quite prepared to wring his arm in thanks. "He is suffering from minor exhaustion. With some rest and plenty of food he should be fine for the celebrations tomorrow."

"Thank goodness. Thank you, Doctor," he said, and gave orders to his servants to inform the waiting Bennets before hurrying up the stairs.

Finally, Bingley knocked on the door to Darcy's bedchamber. He felt a bit guilty about cornering him by means of Darcy's ill health, but the situation was rather desperate in his opinion. The servant answered, carrying an empty platter.

"Is Mr. Darcy well?" asked Bingley.

"He is recovering, Mr. Bingley."

"Good, very good. Is he awake? Would he stand a visitor?"

"He is indeed at awares, sir." He bowed and quickly left, leaving the door open in his wake.

Bingley peered in and knocked again. "Darcy?"

A moan issued from inside the room. "Come in."

Bingley entered and found Darcy alone, quite dishevelled in his undershirt and propped up on a copious amount of pillows. "I came to see how you are doing."

"Yes, how delightfully obvious," Darcy said, his mood excusably lowered by the fact that he looked exhausted despite sleeping most of the morning. "I am not sick. I am just very, very tired."

"And it was raining."

"Only for the last hour or so," Darcy said, the memory dragging his voice down into a lower and angrier octave. "Very tired and sore. I will be fine for tomorrow."

"Of course." Bingley seated himself on the chair beside the bed. "Did you ride—"

"The entire way from Town, yes," Darcy said. "The carriage wheel broke but two miles on the road. I would do to point out, in my defence, at the time I took to the horse, it was not raining." He put his head back and shut his eyes. "This is, of course, your fault."

"My fault? Are you serious?"

Darcy merely pointed to the dressing table, where there was a small package wrapped in paper and string. "A wedding present— though it would be better for you to see it now, as opposed to after the wedding. So perhaps we shall call it a betrothal present."

"For me?"

"Bingley, just because I am not dying of a cold does not mean I am willing to listen to you stating the obvious all morning." He corrected himself, "Afternoon. Is it afternoon? I have an appointment in Meryton."

"We called for the tailor and he is coming to Netherfield. It is being handled."

"And I am grateful for it. Now, do me the honour and make my miserable trip worthwhile."

Bingley cautiously approached the package, square, but not a box. He lifted it, and it was obviously a book from the weight and shape. He cut the string with his pocket knife and removed the wrapper, and what he saw vexed him greatly. It was an old book, not ancient but certainly dusty and well-travelled, and its title was in a script he had never seen. There was no picture on the cover, but on the bottom he found in English, "Translation by M. L. Watts." He opened the cover and found the first page in English, to his great relief. "Well, I'm sure Netherfield's library will certainly be enhanced by this rare—" And then his voice stopped. His brain just stopped when he flipped the page and saw the first illustration. He was educated enough to recognise the style of artwork, but this was not the type of subject matter he had studied in Cambridge. Terrified, he flipped quickly through the thick book and found page after page of foreign script titles, English explanations, and illustrations that . . . well, he was fairly sure his ears were so hot that they were at any moment to burn off.

Darcy—in whatever state of self-amusement, Bingley had no time for, so . . . taken unawares as he was—finally broke the silence. "It is from India, I am told. Or, it says so in the translator's notes. I do not know the man. I imagine such a man, who is obviously well-educated from the breadth of his research, would use a pseudonym. I believe it was published in Bombay."

When Bingley had recovered enough to speak—which was quite a while—he merely stuttered, "You went to London to look for such a book?"

"Not such a book, Bingley—*the* book. And believe me, I had to go to a number of shops before I located a copy. If bookshop owners are inclined to gossip, the Pemberley honour will never recover from my attempts to aid your marriage."

"*The* book." Bingley's mind was not totally centred on the conversation, being immensely distracted by the fascinating . . . content. "So you knew of it?"

"Yes, my father owned a copy, and like everything else at Pemberley, it passed to my guardianship after his death. Sadly, I could not have it sent for in time because I am the only one who knows where to look for it."

"You—you keep this—this *work*—in the hallowed libraries of Pemberley?"

"Certainly *not*! I keep it where my father left it, in a false bottom to a locked drawer in the desk in his study. You may wish to exercise the same discretion."

"Of . . . of course," he said, feeling like his hand was going to burn from just holding it. But on the other hand, he was per-versely fascinated by its contents.

And perversely was *definitely* the right word.

"So—you are familiar with it?" Bingley said.

"I cannot say I have mastered it," Darcy answered. "I cannot even pronounce the title. But let us say that the copy at Pemberley has been . . . much perused."

"In privacy, I'm assuming."

"I have gone through great lengths to keep it from Georgiana and the servants, and I will go through even greater lengths to render you crippled in some fashion if you ever reveal a word of this to any of them."

Bingley didn't doubt it. Darcy made no further comment, apparently falling back into a more resting state, and Bingley found himself ignoring his ailing friend entirely, utterly fascinated as he was. There was no way . . . there was no way he could ever . . . that Jane would ever . . . were these just flights of savage Indian fantasy? He could not think, despite his athleticism, of a way to even get in most of those positions. And surely the church would frown on this. Surely he was damned to hell for just reading this book right now in Darcy's room. He imagined John Calvin descending from heaven, with his black robes and long beard like the picture in his father's study, to point at him and scream about the unholy hellfire that awaited him.

"Darcy—"

Apparently brought out of a mild sleep, Darcy did not hide his annoyance. "*What?*"

"Please forgive my intrusion on your ill health, but . . . um, is this even *possible?*"

"Is *what* even possible?"

Bingley was obligated to bring the book forward, sitting down on the edge of the bed and holding up the very graphic and bizarre picture. Darcy squinted. "Oh, yes. Very difficult, though. Takes some practice."

And now, Bingley was quite sure, they were *both* going to hell. Well, if that notion entered Darcy's mind, it didn't seem to perturb him, and there was a mind inside that tired head so full of knowledge Bingley was desperate to mine.

"How about this?"

"Give it here." Darcy took the book into his hands. "I confess I do not believe every method proposed in this book is physically possible, unless the Indian locals are somehow differently built than us."

"I did suspect such a thing."

"Perhaps if I were double-jointed," Darcy mumbled, flipping casually through the tome as if it were a local newspaper. There was something almost . . . studious about his posture, as if he were looking at a very uncomfortable subject very academically, weighing options and opinions. "Here we go. This one." He passed the book back.

There were so many; Bingley had not seen them all. He was flummoxed by the illustration and read the description several times before finally saying, "This cannot be very gentlemanly."

"But it does work—*quite well*." Darcy was so at ease. Was he basking in the glory of watching Bingley squirm and blush so hard he might pop out of his skin at any moment? Or was he recalling fond memories of the past? "There is even a Latin name for it, I believe."

"I cannot possibly—"

"You asked for my advice, Bingley, on the very delicate matter of pleasing your wife. I have gone to great lengths to make sure that you at least have some source of reference to do so beyond the wisdom you received from tavern chatter. It is your turn to use it wisely—and, of course, to never speak of it with me again."

"Of course," Bingley said, trying to recover. "Of course. You are truly a wonderful friend, and I am grateful for it. Now, I cannot inconvenience you further by having you ill for the wedding." He stood and bowed.

"You sound like our mother-in-law," Darcy merely said, and rolled over, presumably to go back to sleep.

"I am afraid to remind you that you have some business with Mr. Bennet this afternoon, and Miss Elizabeth is eager to see you."

At "Elizabeth," Darcy sat up and said, "Please have a servant bring me some decent clothes at once." Bingley nodded in complete understanding.

As Bingley left, he took a great effort to hide the book within the inner folds of his jacket until he could dash into his room, where he dismissed the servant and then was free to fret about the best hiding place for his wedding present. When he felt that it was thoroughly hidden under the mattress, he heard the bell for lunch and quickly collected himself, splashing water on his still-hot face. Only when his normal natural paleness (due to a partial Irish ancestry no one would admit to) had returned was he willing to make an appearance. At the top of the stairs, he looked down and saw at the bottom Miss Elizabeth Bennet, clearly waiting for some news of Darcy's health.

This of course caused him to blush entirely anew. By the time he got down the steps, he must have been beet red, because he could not help but think that if Mr. Darcy was as scholarly on a certain Indian subject as he seemed to be, the future Mrs. Darcy was perhaps the luckiest woman in England.

And she had no idea as to why.

After some waiting, Elizabeth was permitted entry into Darcy's bedchambers. For reasons of propriety, the servant would not be dismissed, at least not until Darcy insisted. He was dressed properly, but he came unsteadily to his feet to greet her.

"Do not," she insisted, and pushed him down on the bed. It occurred to her that this was the first time they were ever on a bed together. "You need your rest."

"I am sorry to keep your father waiting."

"Do not worry for a moment. He is entranced with the library and will be happy for some time. It is I who must return quickly to Longbourn—but I could not, before seeing you."

"I am not ill," he said, sounding like he was tired of saying it.

"You did ride to Hertfordshire from Town on horseback. Though, I heard, it was not your wildest ride, even if it was raining."

Darcy blinked, clearly having no idea as to the reference, so she went ahead and filled him in. "Your cousin told me last night of an adventure to Liverpool, but very strangely, he would not give me the particulars."

A look confirmed that he would have to tell this story, so he sighed and went ahead with it. "It was a foolish thing to do. I suffered a great deal from it for weeks, I suppose, as punishment for the reason. I assure you it was not scandalous, but it was rather stupid."

"Then you will tell me?"

"I would tell you anything," he said. "The reason Colonel Fitzwilliam perhaps did not engage the specifics is because it involved Wickham, if in a rather harmless way for Wickham to be involved in anything."

"Of course," she concluded. "Georgiana was present."

"Yes. Well, it does not reflect well on my character, or at least on my intelligence. I was stupid, and Wickham was . . . being himself. At the time, I was seventeen, and he was sixteen, I believe, and we were in competition over everything, not always the friendliest kind, as when we were boys. At that particular time, it was in the area of riding. So it was that my father had a document waiting for him in Liverpool and mentioned it in some conversation, and Wickham, ever looking to get in father's good graces, told me he would ride to Liverpool overnight to fetch this document instead of making a servant do it because he was such an accomplished rider that his method would be most expedient. Being the headstrong beast that I was—"

"And still may, on occasion, be—"

He did not get angry. Instead, he sort of smiled at her. So her father's theory was correct. "I immediately challenged him that I could make it to Liverpool and back with greater urgency. And so it became a private challenge, for we told my father nothing of it, intending it to be a surprise. We took slightly different routes, I suppose to not be on edge at constantly seeing each other, and I arrived in Liverpool with little idea of where Wickham was. I was grateful that he had not overtaken me, but I had to wait until sunrise for the clerk's office to open and for me to obtain the document, and I dared not to sleep. When I did obtain it, I thought nothing better than to return home as quickly as possible, I suppose to drive the point home, so to speak. I was there and back in nearly the cycle of a day.

"Wickham did not reappear for several days. It seems he got lost and sheltered at an inn, where he found some woman to his liking, and realising that he had already lost, he decided to weather there for some time before returning home to my gloating. So as to not be unseemly, I did not mention his involvement in the affair at all when I presented the document to my very surprised and confused father. I may have told Colonel

Fitzwilliam at some point, but I do not remember. All I remember is spending nearly a month in bed with a terrible fever and
terrible muscle pain. I did not mount a horse for another month
beyond that."

"I can imagine," she said, giggling. "Or, I am creative
enough to do so."

"Yes, I imagine," he said. "So last night's exploits were really
nothing in comparison. I am quite well."

"So you have explained. But you still not have explained the
reason for taking off and returning so hastily."

He raised an eyebrow. "Do I need a reason? I have had much
business in Town since our engagement was announced."

"I will venture a guess and say this was not a business dealing."

Darcy sighed and lay back on the pillow. "Clearly, I should
not be marrying someone of such great intuition. I will never
have a secret again."

"Clearly."

"But allow me a day's respite. This was a matter of . . . research."

"And then you will tell me?"

"No, Elizabeth," he said. "Then I will *show* you."

THE DINNER PARTY

DESPITE THE INTRICACIES OF the planning, the pre-wedding dinner was somewhat delayed in starting, as the muddy roads prevented the best choice of meats from arriving on time. Despite Bingley's mild worry over the inconvenience, his many, many guests seemed content to feast on hors d'oeuvres and a good amount of wine, and he could put himself at some ease. In fact, he had enough time to glance at poor Darcy, who despite his robust appearance was entrenched in endless inquiries about his health. Bingley smiled sympathetically at him, and Darcy only returned a pained grimace before turning his attentions back to a very insistent guest. It was that very decidedly stealthy Darcy glance that said, "I would give considerable thought to the notion of killing everyone in this room to escape." Maybe Elizabeth would be the exception, but they were not yet married, and so, at least in such a social atmosphere, some distance was kept—consciously or unconsciously—between them. Perhaps when Elizabeth would properly dress his arm, the introverted Mr. Darcy would at least be able to manage company a bit more easily.

But Mr. Bingley's concerns were not entirely focused on Darcy and Elizabeth. In fact, they were only peripheral. The same reason that kept Darcy and Elizabeth at opposite ends of the room also kept him from his beloved Jane. Perhaps he should have ridden miles in the rain, been stuck in bed, and skilfully forced Jane to attend to him. Alas, if it had all been a plot, he lamented that he were not as clever as Darcy by half. He barely got a glimpse of Jane, surrounded as she was by guests, and he had hosting duties that could not be ignored, especially with the minor disaster in the kitchen. Someone had to retrieve extra salad plates from the storeroom downstairs, and in a great desire to expel some nervous energy, Bingley decided to insist on doing it himself. Not that he had ever been to the storeroom, but it was his manor, and he figured he had best be acquainted with every nook and cranny, so he took directions from the flummoxed cook and headed down the stairs. Hopefully he would return quickly and not find too many dead bodies and Darcy arrested for manslaughter.

The dark humour of his grim thought was enough to keep him smiling and distracted, so much so that he almost dropped the box of plates right there on the stairway upon the sight of Jane at the top.

"Mr. Bingley!" she said, obviously surprised by his appearance. "I did not mean to—"

"You are not intruding. Just . . . allow me to put down this box or we will have no proper plates for the third course," he stuttered, and put the box down, knowing there was no way he could concentrate on a container of porcelain with proper attention with his country beauty standing right there. He joined her on the landing, and it occurred to him that for the first time in many days they were quite, if briefly, alone—and very close. "How . . . how are you, Miss Bennet?"

"Very well," she said, but her voice was full of mixed emotions, and he had enough sense in him to guess that she had the same feelings he did: love mixed with anticipation, nervousness, anxiety, and quite possibly absolute terror. "I should not keep you from your duties—"

"No, no," he sputtered. "It can wait, of course. Anything can wait for . . . I mean, anything can wait . . . for you." God, he would give anything for Darcy's golden power of speech at this moment. "How are you?"

"You already asked that," she said with an amused smile.

"I did? Yes, I suppose I did." He allowed himself to laugh. "I am ridiculous, am I not?"

Jane merely answered, "In a very endearing sort of way, Mr. Bingley."

He suddenly didn't know what to do with his hands. He needed a hat to strangle the life out of. Instead, he was stuck rubbing the sides of his waistcoat. "This will not do. You must call me Charles. I cannot take being 'Mr. Bingley' to you any longer."

"Then I will have to be Jane," she said, "though I have not heard Lizzy call Darcy anything but his formal name. And, come to think of it, neither have I of you."

"That's because Darcy is Darcy, you know," and he said in a very stentorian voice, like a servant announcing him, "'Darcy of Pemberley and Derbyshire,' and all that." They shared a giggle at his friend's expense.

"So you have never called him anything else?"

"Never!"

"And what does his sister call him?"

"'Brother.' I believe he is not much endeared to his baptismal name—besides, I suppose, the inconvenience of Colonel Fitzwilliam being his cousin, though . . . they do look quite different."

"So you've never heard anyone call him Fitzwilliam?"

"I have heard someone call him 'Fitzers,' but that is not a story I can repeat, as it does not end well." But when Bingley's future wife looked at him, he felt even more compelled than usual to be obliging. "Oh please, do not look at me like that. I cannot betray his confidence."

Her smile was so kind; it completely ruined the intended effect of her answer. "I would never ask you to betray Mr. *Darcy's* confidence."

She wasn't really asking, and he knew it. He could easily sideswipe the issue entirely, but standing there next to her, quite alone and quite giddy, he felt in the mood to be light about it. "On the other hand, I have never had a chance to tell it, and I can think of no better person to ask for the strictest confidentiality than a wife."

"Minus fifteen hours."

"So we are *both* counting!" he said. "All right, I must oblige you on this, but privately." He skipped up the steps and closed the door, then returned to the landing. "And you cannot tell your sister. No, I cannot ask that of you. That is too cruel. I suppose I will just have to suffer the indignity of being a gossip."

"You do not have to, Charles."

"But I will—for you," he said, again keenly aware that they were alone—now in a closed, very small space. "You must understand that Cambridge is a place of much . . . well, to be blunt about the subject . . . drinking—and other behaviour that does not enter this conversation. But this is not to say Darcy was an alehouse regular, nor I. Quite the opposite, in fact. He was most studious because he is Darcy of Pemberley, and I was most honoured with being the first of my family to attend University, so I had better things to do than fail. But there was one night—," he bit his lip. Thank heavens he wasn't telling *that* story! "On this night, I was invited to a particular . . . tavern and hadn't the faintest idea of where it was. At this point I had known Darcy for a few months and he was, I admit, being somewhat protective of me. I did not realise it at the time, but it is something in his nature that he does with the people he cares about, so I suppose I should have been honoured but—I am prattling on." He tried not to look at Jane—not because he didn't want to, but because he couldn't imagine what would happen if he did. "So . . . he knew the place and decided to accompany me. I must confess that I was terrible and became so involved in my conversation with a man in my logic lectures that I did not notice how uneasy Darcy was. Truly I am an awful friend."

"Truly you are too hard on yourself."

He did not want to contradict her. He never wanted to contradict her on anything, ever. "At some point, I do not recall exactly when, someone approached Darcy at the table, presumably someone he knew from fencing. Not to say there was discord between them, but this man thought himself a better friend to Darcy than Darcy thought of him. He proceeded to immediately engage him in a long conversation about local sport, to which Darcy said hardly anything. I did not even take much note of it until the man, when congratulating him on a recent match, quite liberally slapped him on the shoulder and called him 'Fitzers,' or some such nickname. In fact, he slapped him so hard and unexpectedly that Darcy sort of swooned and knocked over his wineglass—or, all three of them . . . and a mug of ale."

"And Mr. Darcy's reaction?" she asked, because now she was obviously too invested in the story not to know its conclusion, however unbecoming.

"He slammed a fist on the table and challenged the man to a duel. To first blood or what I do not know—I am not a fencer, and I have never been in a duel. Darcy did not explain himself at all, but he was incensed, and it took a minute for the man to even react to this. Now you must understand, Darcy was at this time second only to the captain of Cambridge's fencing club."

"So the man would have lost."

"And he could not have been unknowing in that. But it was that intensity in Darcy's eyes—everyone in the room was staring at him as he awaited the man's reaction. His colleague merely said, 'Are you serious?' And all Darcy had to do was stand up, one hand still on the table, and stare him down."

"And?"

"And he ran—the man, I mean—right out of the tavern. I never saw his face again."

"Quite an accomplishment for Mr. Darcy!"

"More than that man knew, because Darcy was in no condition to duel, however talented he might have been," Bingley said. "It turned out that only his hand on the table was keeping him upright. As soon as the man was soundly gone, he collapsed on the floor. It took me and the bartender to get him upright again." He added quickly, "There is something to be said for not regularly partaking in vast quantities of spirits, but it does nothing to build up your resistance."

"Are you saying Darcy is a lush?"

"Perhaps." He giggled again. "Please, please, I beg of you, never tell him I told you this."

"I would never do anything to insult the considerable Darcy pride," she said semi-jokingly.

"Because it *is* considerable," he said. "Oh dear, we are up here laughing at Darcy, and we have left him to the wolves downstairs."

"Charles! Some of those wolves are my relatives! And some of my relatives are not even wolves!" They were roaring with laughter again, preventing any further conversation for some time. The dishes were now thoroughly forgotten.

"I am being a terrible host."

"I forgive you of this great sin."

He chuckled. "But I will gladly endure the same of being a notoriously bad master of Netherfield if it means I must instead spend my time alone with you."

To this, Jane was silent. She was shy; he was shy; and they were both aware of it and of the irregularity of his outburst. Most of their moments of privacy—well, almost all of them—had been on walks outside, and more mundane topics were discussed. This moment was not so much the case, and there was much averting of the eyes.

"Jane," he said, after gathering some courage. *Imagine you're Darcy*, he thought. *You can say whatever you please and somehow not only get away with it but secure the second-loveliest girl in England for your bride.* "I am overwhelmingly grateful that we can laugh together now . . . when there has been so much between us."

"Not so much."

"Well, two days ago, you looked like I was going to eat you alive."

Instead of shrinking back in horror, she actually giggled again, covering her mouth. "Oh, that was nothing to do with you—just some apprehension thanks to being assaulted with marital advice by my mother."

Mrs. Bennet giving Jane marital advice of any kind—*there* was a most unpleasant image. He did not want to bring up his own travails, at least, not in detail. He had already shamed himself and Darcy enough in the last few minutes. "I admit to being somewhat nervous myself—not for any reason related to you, just . . . fear of the unknown, I suppose." *And you have completely bewitched me. Can I mention that? Would it be unbecoming? Would I terrify you?* "But I suppose it is natural and ultimately irrelevant."

"Yes, of course."

It was not anything she said or the way she said it. It was that their gazes met for the first time in several minutes, and there was a meeting of not only the eyes but the minds. She was up against the wall and he was kissing her, trying to decide that if the act itself was as good as the simple sensation of having her arms around his neck.

Fear of the unknown was definitely a most illogical human emotion. The unknown was wonderful, especially when it was her fingers moving through his hair.

"Bingley!"

Damn that knocking, and damn that Darcy! Well, at least it was Darcy and not a servant—or, heaven forbid, one of his sisters. He loved his sisters dearly, but this was not the moment for brotherly affection. It was the moment for removing himself from Jane and taking a deep, well-needed breath. They looked at each other, as if expecting the other to invent a solution.

"Bingley, do you wish half the servants in this house looking for their master or not? And make no pretence of being elsewhere, because I've looked in half the rooms in this estate on your behalf already!"

"Coming, Darcy!" he said, as he straightened his waistcoat. "It seems I must return."

"I think we must *both* return," she whispered.

"Fifteen, then."

"I believe it is more like fourteen, but yes."

He smiled at her a very private smile before straightening himself one last time and opening the door to, fortunately, only Darcy. Seeing both of them, Darcy's face registered no particular emotion and he bowed politely. "Miss Bennet."

"Mr. Darcy," she curtseyed and quickly slid past him and back upstairs.

Bingley stood there watching his best friend give him a once-over—with his head of mussed hair and reddened face. Darcy merely said in the most even voice possible, "It seems you are besting me at everything these days."

"I did not know you were inclined to consider this a competition," Bingley said, and could not account for his own shrewdness. Maybe it was something in Jane's influence that brought it out of him. "But seriously, you have not—"

"We are not having this discussion."

"So I can assume—"

"The longer you stay down here, the longer your guests will have to avail themselves of the liquor cabinet on empty stomachs, and if I must endure another impromptu drunken sermon by Mr. Collins, I will permanently hold it against your character. Now *go*." He handed him the discarded box of plates and nearly dragged him up the stairs. "And if you can invent a proper reason, send Elizabeth down."

To this, Bingley decided he did not have the wits to craft a response.

Darcy did not have to endure another impromptu drunken sermon by Mr. Collins, at least not at the dinner table. There were simply so many guests and so much chatter that one could be easily ignored, and since he was not able to mention Lady Catherine without provoking Darcy's considerable anger, his conversational abilities were cut in half.

But Darcy was not inclined to be angry, at least from what Bingley could tell. If Darcy was not turned directly to his left, he could not tell anything because he could hardly hear anything or make out any conversation a few seats beyond them. Though he was not wont to say, it was fortunate that Lady Catherine had not attended, for she would have insisted on the traditional formalities that a twelve-course meal demanded, while Bingley was more inclined to let his guests revel in the pre-wedding festivities. For matters such as this, he usually referred to Darcy for his expertise, as it was only under Darcy's subtle hand that he had been schooled in being master of Netherfield, but both men were busy with other things and content to let matters fall where they may.

Despite the variety of food, unusual even by his considerable standards, Bingley found himself eating little, his stomach not the least bit settled, he assumed out of nerves. He instead contented himself with partaking in the socialisation or merely observing it. There was a certain triangle among his adjacencies, as Miss Bingley put up a considerable show to appear to like her new sister a great deal, and Bingley was sure he could see Darcy occasionally smirking at the flagrancy of the act. It was some relief to Bingley that Darcy would no longer have to fend off Caroline, though he was unsure if the matter had ever truly vexed him. Certainly if it had, Darcy would have said something or made his feelings known by less readily spending time with the Bingleys, and yet he was Bingley's closest companion.

There were toasts to the host and to the two couples, and the glasses were raised quite a few times before the dinner was over. Mr. Collins was about to stand up when his wife found herself overwhelmed by either the food or the atmosphere—that could not be determined properly—and insisted that he escort her outside for fresh air. Elizabeth whispered something in Darcy's ear, and he waited until there was a moment when chatter had resumed before saying quietly to Bingley, "You owe a great favour to Mrs. Collins."

Bingley held himself back from proposing a toast.

Time was pressing, and the dinner was brought to a conclusion so that the various guests could retire, and the Bennets and Gardiners could return to Longbourn. As it would be the last time he would see his fiancée before she stood in church, Bingley was a bit emotional and looked to Darcy who undoubtedly was doing well at hiding any emotions *he* felt—but Darcy could not be found. Darcy and Elizabeth were missing as the crowd gathered around the carriages and reappeared only moments before the carriages set off, with no proper explanation. Everyone was too busy to notice this, but the carriages could not leave without Elizabeth Bennet, so their timing was impeccable. "Till tomorrow," Bingley said with no lack of enthusiasm as he waved good-bye.

That left them with their Netherfield guests. The women mainly retired or took to the drawing room, and the men to the parlour. "Bingley," Darcy said from behind him, ever the mysterious man. "I fear Mr. Bennet was left behind. He is in the library."

"Oh no. He said he wanted some more time to think and wouldn't get a moment of it at home. He will take a carriage later this evening," Bingley explained. "Shall we share a glass of port?"

"Yes, I desperately need something to settle my stomach," Darcy admitted.

"Goodness, Darcy, are you all right?" Darcy gave him the cold glare of a man tired of being asked that question. Bingley decided to continue as if it had not occurred. "So then, the port."

"Indeed."

Bingley opened the double doors that lead to the parlour and was greeted by a rousing cheer from his male company at their appearance. Bingley looked to Darcy, who merely covered his forehead with disgust.

THE LONGEST NIGHT

ELIZABETH'S SHARED ROOM WITH her sister was practically empty but for the furniture. Her things were packed and on their way to Pemberley or in trunks downstairs. She barely had her nightgown and a brush. Jane, with less of a distance to be travelling, had nonetheless prepared herself for no longer being a resident of Longbourn, and the sisters were quite alone but for the beds and each other—and soon, they would be without both.

Nonetheless, a generally giddy atmosphere pervaded even when they were finally left alone, with their mother telling them to get a good rest. Clearly, there would be none of that. They were far too excited—anxious, too, but it was better not to think of it.

"I am quite sure of it now," Elizabeth said. "You *can* die of happiness. They will have to prop my corpse up for the wedding."

"Lizzy, don't be so morbid!"

"I fear the only thing keeping me alive at this very moment is that tomorrow night I will be far away from you," she said, lowering her tone somewhat as she squeezed her sister's hand. "But you shall visit."

"There is much convenience in the fact that our husbands are practically inseparable. We must make a pact that we will conspire to never allow them to fight."

"And we must make another pact that we must never allow them to find out about *our* pact, for they could never stand to know that we were meddling in their private affairs," Elizabeth said. "Or perhaps Mr. Bingley could, but Darcy would be affronted."

"Why I am the one to make this revelation, I know not, but dear sister, Mr. Darcy is affronted by *everything*."

Elizabeth lay back on the pillow, propping her head up with her elbow. "Oh yes. But how fortunate that he is insufferably adorable when he looks disgusted."

"So I am to be invited to Pemberley?"

"What? Why ever would you think not?"

"Because of Charles's train of sisters, of whom your beloved is so overly fond."

Elizabeth giggled. "Who is this vicious woman, and what has she done with my sister, who can only see the good in everyone?"

"I did not say *I* do not like them. They have been perfectly civil to *me*."

"Perhaps because one of them is not trying to marry your intended."

"Poor Miss Bingley," Jane said, sounding somewhat sympathetic. "She had such a similar method to you, and now she is a spinster. If only she had your heart behind her."

"You are not *seriously* comparing me to Caroline Bingley!"

"No! Not in all manners. But . . . will you say honestly that you never did anything intentionally to vex Mr. Darcy? Did you not engage him in a manner that would provoke his ire?"

"Only when he was begging for it! How could I not? And that was before . . . before I was even considering not hating the man!"

"Oh yes, Lizzy, I'm sure."

Elizabeth hit her sister with a pillow—not hard, just enough to make the point that Jane was right and Elizabeth didn't care for the truth at that moment one bit.

"We are supposed to be getting our rest!"

"Yes, our 'rest,'" Elizabeth said, "while our husbands are up at all hours enjoying their last bit of bachelorhood to no end. We must be perfect ladies while they have the time of their lives!"

At that exact moment, Mr. Darcy was swallowing a third glass of brandy and trying to decide honestly whether it would be better to simply hit Mr. Collins in the face or to expel the contents of his stomach all over him. Surely, the latter would be improper, but it was likely to happen in a few minutes anyway for unrelated reasons, and the grovelling vicar would surely forgive a very rich man of standing and potential future patron. But a solid hit would be so very satisfying. The gut certainly would shut him up without putting a bruise all over his face for the wedding or knocking one of his teeth out. Darcy, to his best recollection, had only done that once, and Wickham had whined about it for weeks afterwards. How bad could the loss of a simple back tooth be? Perhaps it explained Wickham's lack of wisdom.

Regardless, Darcy remained in his chair opposite the prat-tling parson, mainly because he did not feel inclined to stand up. Instead he gave the best impression that he was listening to every word the man was saying, something he considered him-self very talented at.

"—has to say about the sanctity of marriage, but I won't bore you further with the words of the great—"

Darcy could not help but roll his eyes. Fortunately, Mr. Collins was interrupted by a tap on the shoulder from Mr. Hurst, a very imposing figure when he was standing up straight. "If you would, Mr. Collins, I would like a word with my future brother-in-law."

"Of course, of course," he said, because Mr. Collins was agreeable to everything said out loud, even if he was oblivious to every subtly. He relinquished his treasured throne in front of the prone Darcy, who was doing his best to hide that he was either ill or drunk, as Mr. Hurst sat down. Darcy said a silent half-serious prayer that the chair wouldn't collapse.

"Mr. Darcy," Mr. Hurst said, with a sort of formality that put Darcy off, "I know you are a man of great standing and a man of education. You have travelled to the continent and shown yourself to be a true master of a great estate. I am much hon-oured to be closer in association to your family." Darcy nodded politely. "I cannot help but then offer my humble advice, from one man to another, in the one area in which I may have some more . . . er . . . *expertise*." Darcy sunk further into his chair. "Now I'm sure you've had your jaunts, what with the sort of man you are, tall and proud, fending 'em off—like Caroline. Good job on that one." He gave Darcy a gentle nudge on the arm, something Darcy absolutely despised, but he hoped his groan wasn't audible. "No offence to my sister, but—well, you know. To put up with her—all those years. But to the subject at hand—yes! The bloody subject!" He raised his glass. Darcy made some effort to raise his, and Mr. Hurst continued in a lowered voice, "There is some difference, I must tell you, in having a wife and a mistress."

"*Really*," Darcy finally managed to say, raising one eyebrow to press the point. "I had no idea."

"You will make a jest of it if you please, but I am trying to help you, good man! There are particulars to each woman—though surely you have discovered that. But I mean long term—"

Darcy motioned to the servant and requested a pen and scrap of paper. "Please continue, Mr. Hurst," he said as he scribbled his note and gave the servant instructions to deliver it to Bingley posthaste. "And bring more brandy, please."

On the other side of the room, Bingley was just as entrenched, fending off the attentions of Sir William Lucas and Mr. Collins, both very respectable men who seemed to be eager to remind him that he was getting married tomorrow, as if he could forget.

"Sir," said his servant, and handed him a paper. He apologised to his guests, unfolded it, and read in Darcy's precise (if a little wobbly) script, "I will give you my half of Derbyshire to get me out of this room right now. D."

When he looked up, Sir William Lucas had gone for more refreshment, and he was left with Mr. Collins, who had literally cornered him against the wall. "Mr. Bingley, if I could have your ear but for a moment—"

"Yes, yes, of course," he said, holding the note behind his back.

"You will excuse me, Mr. Bingley, if I do not sound like a proper churchman for what I am about to say, but I believe that marriage should be held in the highest regard and therefore is worthy of some low speech to make this particular sacrament more palatable. And I might say, with all humility, that I have some experience in this area."

"Oh yes, of course—of course, Reverend Collins. You have my full attention—as soon as I handle this missive," he said, and quickly motioned to the servant for a pen. Once procured, he put the note against the bookcase and scribbled on the back, "And I will give you Netherfield to get me out. CB." "Please, if you would, deliver this to Mr. Darcy. Now, you were saying, Mr. Collins?"

"Lizzy?"

"Mmm?"

"Who do you think our sisters will marry?"

Elizabeth sat up. "Surely you do not expect me to have names and fortunes ready."

"Throwing aside circumstance, who do you think they would be likely to fall in love with, if they are so lucky to marry for love?"

"They can take the veil for all concerned, but I do not see Kitty doing so."

"Pray, whatever do you mean?"

"She will doubtless fall in love with some colonel, but this time, we will do a thorough check of his social standing and background before agreeing to allow her a moment alone with him. So all will be well, when she finds one satisfactory to all of us. Oh, and gambling debts—we must look into gambling debts. I should write this down so I do not forget."

Jane covered her mouth. "But you cannot tell Mr. Darcy, or he will be all over Town saving the family again." Hesitating, Jane asked, "Are you intending to keep secrets from your husband?"

"Nothing so horrible! It is merely a matter of leaving things out. If you were to, say, tell me something in confidence about Mr. Bingley—"

"Which I would not—"

"Of course not, but *hypothetically*, if you were to tell me something in confidence—about anything—I would not immediately run and tell Darcy. Some things shall remain between sisters."

"Of course," Jane said, and their hands tugged in a sort of unintentional handshake.

"And she can find it to be very pleasing—"

Mr. Darcy did not want to know what was potentially pleasing to Elizabeth Bennet. He did not want to know what Louisa Hurst found pleasing. He did not want to know another single thought that might be contained in Mr. Hurst's mind. He would have gotten up a long time ago, but he was not sure he could do it without losing his dinner. It turned out that alcohol was *not* medicinal, and this night was the night to learn it.

He had Bingley's reply in his hand, but there was nothing he could do about it. He was meant to suffer. Perhaps this was some divine punishment for the torture he had once inflicted upon his bride, as if he had not been punished enough by her and circumstance. Her and circumstance combined left him in a stupor for half a year. He was ready to get on with his happy life with the greatest beauty in England, if only this man would *shut up*.

But it was not to be, and he had not the strength to fight it for some reason. It was only when the double doors opened that he lifted his head, assuming it was some servant to refill their glasses. God, that was all he needed. But he looked, and it was not. It was Mr. Bennet.

"Good sirs," he announced properly. "If I may pull my two new sons away from you for a bit before I must return home, I would be a very grateful man."

As he was the father of the brides, everyone was obliging. Darcy was surprised at his own ability to stand up, though it did give his stomach an ominous turn, which he swallowed back down. He accompanied Bingley and Mr. Bennet to the library. Once they were safely inside, he closed the lock and sat down with his book and own brandy. Darcy collapsed in a chair, but Bingley just stood there, expecting something.

"Well?" Bingley finally dared.

"Well what?" Mr. Bennet said, not glancing up from the text. "I just supposed you might want some respite from your wonderful guests. If you're not inclined to retire just yet, I could recommend a few books from your own library that do not look as if they have been read in ages."

"So . . . no advice?"

"Of course not. Takes all the fun out of things." Mr. Bennet finally looked up long enough to see Darcy. "Mr. Darcy, I dare say, you look rather ill."

"I fear I am," Darcy decided to admit, realising now it was not the drink—though that certainly hadn't helped. "Bingley, could you—" But before he could finish his sentence, servants appeared to help him into the next room, where he lingered for some time before being well enough to return. If he looked any less green twenty minutes later upon his return, no one said anything.

"Perhaps some tea," Bingley offered, and Darcy nodded weakly in agreement.

"Yes, very good for the stomach," Mr. Bennet said, turning his chair around to face them better as Bingley took a seat on the couch next to Darcy. "Well, since we're all in this room together, I might as well entertain you with a story that I have never told anyone, and all of the Longbourn staff who knew of it are long since expired, so I feel safe." He stood up, his back to the roaring fire, towering over the men he was willingly giving his daughters to—one a little dizzy with nerves and one obviously ill. "It's not a terribly long story, so don't worry. The night before my wedding, I was a nervous wreck. In fact, I was for weeks ahead of time, so that night I took great care not to eat or drink anything exceptional. It did not help one bit, and I spent the entire evening being ill. I showed up to the altar with barely three hours of sleep and absolutely nothing in my entire digestive system, I am quite sure. And yet we married all the same and had many happy years together and will continue to do so, provided I do not keel over any day now as has been so repeatedly predicted."

Neither of them had any response to this. This, too, Mr. Bennet seemed to expect, and he continued just the same. "I suppose this does come as some surprise, but as Mrs. Bennet can be a particularly nervous and vexing personality, I cannot blame her, shouldering the responsibility of five daughters to marry off and an estate to manage while I sit in my study and read books that tell me that it is *my* fault we have no sons. She occupies her entire life seeing to the care of the people she loves, no matter how little care they actually desire. I would not have anyone else. Though, if you're searching for a proper Christmas gift for your father-in-law, please make it a nice pair of earmuffs. You know, those new-fashioned ones that reduce noise."

"Gladly," Bingley immediately answered, and Darcy's main reply was to rush off again. Bingley glanced in concern, but Mr. Bennet put a hand on his shoulder.

"He'll be fine. He has swallowed all of his nerves like any stoic gentleman, and now they are having their revenge."

"Mr. Bennet," Bingley said, "how did you get so wise?"

"Years of living with Jane and Lizzy," he replied.

GUESTS, UNEXPECTED
AND OTHERWISE

CHARLES BINGLEY DID NOT take his morning constitutional. Almost instantaneously upon his waking, his servants were all ready for him, for his grooming needed exceptional attention, and it was everyone's opinion that it was best to get it out of the way. He breakfasted quickly on a tray in his room before having to stand in front of several mirrors and be exquisitely dressed. Not that he minded at all—he picked the outfit out himself—but he was just overwhelmed by the whole experience.

"Mr. Bingley," said his manservant, and took from him the third handkerchief he had torn by wringing it obsessively. He had the notion that they were intentionally handing him bad ones at this point.

"My apologies," he said with a stutter.

"Please hold still, sir."

But he could not. His hands were shaking. Oh, how was he ever to survive the day? Surely Darcy was doing better than he. Wait, Darcy! He immediately sent a servant to privately inquire after his friend's health, as he himself had not made it past the door of his dressing chamber yet. He had only retired the night before after many reassurances from Darcy that he was quite well, thank you very much, and wanted only to sleep.

"Sir," said another servant, entering the room, "Miss Bingley, if you are available."

He was fully dressed, and they were only making the final adjustments on the most complicated cravat he had ever worn, so he said, "Yes, of course. Tell her she is most welcome." Actually he was surprised at the announcement—what could she possibly have to say to him now? He wasn't entirely sure how to feel about it, but the rest of his emotions were busy overwhelming him anyway, and he barely had time to properly sort out her possible reasons to appear when she strode in, not in her usual unnecessary ball gown, but in an elegant but modest dress. "Caroline, you look—very nice."

"I am glad you went with blue," she said, taking a turn around him. He was unable to read her intentions, but then again, he was never able to read them, at least when Darcy wasn't in the room and she wasn't making them obvious. In fact, her behaviour since the announcement of Darcy's engagement had been in general downright bizarre, but he had hardly rushed to quiz her on it. His attentions were admittedly elsewhere. Perhaps that made him a bad brother. "You are quite fetching." She gave a playful tug to his coat to straighten it. This turn of affection was odd.

"You will be honest with me," he said, because, after all, if there was one person in the world—well, one woman in the world—that he could trust to be brutally honest, she was his sister. "Do I look proper? I mean, for a wedding?"

"There is not a girl in England who would not marry you now, Charles," she said, and for once, there wasn't a hint of sarcasm in her voice. "And I have seen Miss Bennet's dress—stunning."

"Please allow me to be surprised."

"Of course, brother." She ran a line down his sleeve, and he took her hand. "My little brother, getting married."

They were not an affectionate family. At least, they had not been in years, since Bingley's sisters had entered society. He had vague recollections of being depressed at the prospect because suddenly Louisa and then Caroline were all grown up, and he was left to be the only child in the family for a few more years, perhaps the loneliest in his life. And then he went to Cambridge, and when he came home for his father's funeral, he was the man of the house, not the little brother, and one of his sisters was married and the other quite expecting to marry as soon as she found someone suitable. They still had their moments of treating him as their baby brother—three years Caroline's junior and five to Louisa—but he, Charles Bingley, master of Netherfield and their London townhouse, controlled their fortunes however graciously and unwittingly. The entire Bingley line rested on him, and he had to act like the senior member of the Bingleys, while he often felt some trepidation at the idea of the role. Only because Darcy had prodded him had he purchased a country estate, and only at his sister's prodding had he abandoned it, because he knew he could truly deny them nothing. And then Darcy's prodding again—about the only thing he did totally on his own was propose to Jane, standing alone in the room before the proposal because Darcy had out-right refused to accompany him on the return trip. She was right—he was the little brother, and he was getting married. Caroline was right.

Caroline was also crying. Her eyes were a little watery, the sort of thing she would deny, but she was crying. He tugged at her hand. What was he supposed to say? *Yes, I'm getting married? To the family you despise? And sorry, Darcy's unavailable?* What was this about? No, he was being cruel. "I know," he said, being utterly without other words.

"Papa would be so proud," she said. She hadn't mentioned him in years. It was not a topic of conversation between them, and he was taken aback. What would he be proud of? That he was marrying a country girl? That he was setting up a household and was finally going to continue the Bingley line? Not that he had put it off exceptionally long—he was just . . . it was hard to think of his father now, when there was so much else to deal with. Maybe he was a bad son that he hadn't thought of his parents, looking down on him from heaven (and hopefully not seeing his reading material). "We are all proud of you, Charles."

On any other day, he would have doubted it because it was Jane Bennet he was marrying, not Georgiana Darcy or some other person of relative station. Yes, his sisters were civil to her, but first only in a joking manner, then in an awkward manner when the matter became very real, and he could not comprehend their true emotions. "Thank you, Caroline." But she had gone into full sob mode, something he had not seen even at their father's funeral, and he could only think to embrace her, as his manservant rushed to stuff a towel between the well-dressed Bingley and his sister's tears. "There's no need to be sad."

"I am not sad," she said, looking at up him. Another rare occurrence—she was taller than he, but he was very high up on a stand at the moment for the dressing. "Forgive me."

"There is nothing to forgive."

"You are too kind. It is only fitting that you would find the kindest girl in the kingdom to be your bride," she said. "For all of our vexations, we only wanted to see you happy, Charles."

He could say with all truthfulness, even if his voice cracked when he said it, "I am *very* happy, I assure you."

"I know." She pulled away, but only reluctantly. "Forgive me; I am ruining your wedding coat."

"Hardly." And because he could think of nothing better to do, and because he had the rare opportunity of being taller than his sister, he kissed her on her forehead. "I am grateful for all of your support."

She was still crying, but not as badly, as she curtseyed and smiled a weak good-bye smile before leaving the room, which was suddenly very empty. The servants had disappeared at the displays of sibling affection, and he felt alone.

But it was not to be for long. The door was left half-open, and Darcy did not even bother to knock. "What was that?"

"What?" Bingley said, being brought back to awareness. He realised that Darcy must have seen Caroline upset, though there was hardly enough time to have a conversation with her. "It was family, Darcy." He hoped that would be enough.

It seemed to be. Darcy, refusing to wear the blue and wearing a more modest dark green, but still very formally attired, switched gears entirely. "I decided to relieve your staff of the liberty of reporting my condition to you, as they are quite busy. I am perfectly fine now, thank you very much."

"Did you eat?"

"I had some tea. Must I tell you every detail?" Darcy didn't look truly annoyed; Bingley could tell he was just nervous. He paced the room, looking out the window. "I am sorry for keeping you up. I hope you are at least partially rested."

"I confess I was up some time after you retired." He swallowed. "Reading."

"Oh?" It seemed to take a minute to register with Darcy, which was a minute slower than it usually took. He was definitely preoccupied. "Yes . . . well—" He stopped short. "Can I borrow it for a moment?"

"What? Oh, yes, I suppose."

"Where—"

"Under the mattress," Bingley said, pointing to his bedchamber.

Darcy bowed to him. "Thank you." And he quickly disappeared into Bingley's bedchamber. Bingley himself was busy, as his manservant returned, removed the towel, and straightened his clothing once again. As long as no one else cried on his chest this morning, he would be all right, he decided. It was not a few moments before Darcy reappeared, flipping quickly through the book in question. "Just a moment."

"Looking something up?"

"We are not having this conversation." That was Darcy's way of telling him to shut up. "Oh yes, okay. Here we go." He did not enlighten Bingley as to what chapter he was reading, and when Bingley tried to peer over without getting off the stand, Darcy grunted and repositioned the book so its contents were out of sight. Eventually he finished and slammed it shut. "I am in your debt." He then disappeared back into the adjoining room, presumably to return it to its hiding place.

Bingley let out the giggle he had been withholding at Darcy's actions as soon as he was gone. He did not have long to revel in his solitude, however, for another servant appeared at the door. "A guest, sir. He asked to be unannounced."

"Unannounced?" Bingley said, but before he could inquire further, the guest in question sideswiped the servant on his way into the room.

It was George Wickham.

Bingley swallowed. "Mr. Wickham, I don't believe we've ever had the pleasure of being formally introduced—"

"Of course." Mr. Wickham was all charm, and perhaps if Bingley had no idea as to who this man was, he would suppose to like him immediately, as he offered his hand. "George Wickham."

"Charles Bingley." Yes, truly, there was nothing that appeared displeasing about this man at all, but he did not doubt Darcy's account for one second. "Darcy! Perhaps this is not the best time—"

"I cannot think of a better one. I very much desire to meet my future brother and of course to congratulate Darcy on his considerable 'catch.'"

"We are not fishing," Darcy said harshly, announcing his presence in the room as he entered from the bedchamber and leaned impatiently against the wall. "Or participating in any other sport, for that matter."

"And this is how you greet your future brother?" Wickham was all smiles. "At last, I suppose."

"You will remain my brother until Mrs. Wickham comes to her senses and kicks you out of Newcastle," Darcy answered coldly, to Bingley's surprise. Even though there was no anger in his voice, that he was holding it back was visible enough. "Excuse me, but this wedding costume is making me a bit heated." And with that, he opened the windows and looked out. "There, much better. Now, I assume you are here on some matter of business."

"Matter of business? On your wedding day? You can't be serious."

"And you are not going to make jest with me? Do you have some reason for being here?"

"I was invited."

"*Lydia* Wickham was invited, because it could not be prevented."

"And it would only be proper to invite both husband and wife to a wedding of relations," Wickham countered. "And of course, Darcy, you are a master of propriety, so surely you know that, and the lack of my name on the invitation was merely an error."

Truly, Wickham was a master at the art of conversation, at least in the area of inciting Mr. Darcy to levels of barely controlled rage. His posture said nothing, but his eyes said everything. Bingley wanted very much to duck behind the dressing screen and let them have it out, even if this was his manor and they were both his guests.

"Now that we have dispensed with pleasantries," Darcy said, "I must inquire again as to your appearance. While I'm sure you are here to wish us well, the thing has been said, and so we must press on. Is there anything else on your mind, Wickham?"

"You are quite keen on reading me, Darcy. But I have only the noblest of intentions. My wife would like very much to visit Pemberley this spring, but for some reason, I am prevented from entering the grounds."

"How odd," Darcy said. "Well, *Mrs.* Wickham is welcome to visit Pemberley whenever our schedules are agreeable—but that is entirely Elizabeth's decision. I am sure you can find some other amusement for yourself in her absence."

"Come now, Fitzers, we are finally brothers—"

Bingley raised his hand to shield himself from Darcy's rage, but Darcy's voice, after a pause in which undoubtedly numerous emotions were suppressed, was surprisingly light-hearted. "And I suppose as your brother, I must be the mischievous pest. And as the youngest of the three, Bingley must be my partner-in-crime, the impressionable young lad that he is. Right, Mr. Bingley?"

"Um . . . yes." Bingley had no idea as to where this was going, but he was hardly going to contradict Darcy.

Darcy began to pace the room, circling Wickham. "For example, I could be an annoying older brother and for no reason whatsoever, hit you with this walking stick." And then, suddenly, he took Wickham's walking stick and smacked him on the back of the head, causing Wickham to double over. "Then, because the youngest brother inevitably follows his senior, Bingley could help me toss you out the window. Bingley?"

Bingley opened his mouth to put up a protest, but Darcy gave him a look that told him that resistance would be indefensible. And so, oddly enough, he helped Darcy heave Wickham out the window. They did not hear the cracking of bones, or even an audible thud, but it was not a long drop from the second story.

"Will he be all right?"

"Oh, yes," Darcy said as he closed the window. "The manure pile there surely broke his fall."

Before they made haste for the church, there was one more guest to greet. "She's arrived!" Georgiana practically screamed, running into her brother's arms as he came down the steps. "She made it after all!"

"Who?" Bingley asked, following Darcy down. "I can't seem to keep track of my own guests."

"Something else must be on your mind," Darcy said. "I assume we are speaking of Miss de Bourgh."

"Yes! I just saw her carriage over the bend. Oh, Mr. Bingley, you look wonderful!" Georgiana, as usual, was all smiles. "She should be arriving now. Thank you for agreeing to host her if she is not well enough to travel home tonight."

"Of course, but I must see her in!" Bingley ran to the door, leaving Darcy with his sister.

"Oh, and of course, you are very handsome," Georgiana said. "But you already knew that."

"As you selected the costume, I cannot fault you by saying anything else," Darcy said as the doors opened and Charles welcomed Darcy's cousin Anne de Bourgh. She was not dressed in nearly as dark shades as she normally was, and Darcy had to admit to himself that she looked the best he had seen in years, even if her health was in obvious decline. "Miss de Bourgh," he said, bowing to her.

"Mr. Darcy," she said. "Thank you so much for the invitation."

"Thank my sister and her abilities of subterfuge." For they had sent a formal invitation to the de Bourghs, knowing it would be refused. Another one was sent, quite inappropriately, to Anne alone, hidden in a letter from Georgiana. "You are looking well."

"We are so happy to have you here," Georgiana said. "I do hope you do not get in much trouble with our aunt."

"I am visiting you, and that is not a lie. That it happens to be on Darcy's wedding day is of no consequence to me," Anne said. "Georgiana, if I may have a moment with your brother before the festivities begin?"

"Of course." Georgiana curtseyed, and Darcy took Anne's hand and led her into the drawing room. This was the closest he had been to Anne since his last visit to Rosings, the disaster that he did not wish to recall even when wrongs had been righted. "Please, sit. Shall I call for some tea?"

"I do not intend to hold you up for so long," Anne said. "But I would appreciate some, yes."

He called for some tea and then shut the door behind the servant, taking a seat at the desk away from her. Despite the bizarre situation of the day—or what his aunt considered a bizarre situation—they were quite comfortable with each other. While she was hardly his confidant, they had a friendship over the years, and he was grateful for her kindness to Georgiana, who was often too shy to make friends easily. Well, he admitted to himself, neither of them made friends easily, but for entirely different reasons. "I *am* honoured that you chose to come against Aunt Catherine's wishes."

"She is not so harsh with me as she is with everyone else. Perhaps because she believes I will break."

But he knew that wasn't true. Anne was sickly, but inside she was strong. She was, after all, a de Bourgh. She would make someone a fine wife, even if they had decided together long ago that it was not to be him. "How is Aunt Catherine? She did not see fit to respond to my invitation, even to refuse."

"As can only be expected."

"Of course, I am sorry for breaking her heart—or at least, her well-laid plans."

"If it was her heart or yours, let it be hers," she said. "Your heart has belonged to Miss Elizabeth Bennet for some time."

"Was I really that obvious?"

"You were practically stalking her at Rosings," she said with a sly smile. "Colonel Fitzwilliam said something to me about it. He asked me if there was a reason why you were so distant to me and everyone else during that trip."

"And what did you tell him?"

"I told him you have always been a mystery to me."

"But you had me figured out the whole time."

"Of course. You were being perfectly readable. But Fitzwilliam is a man; Mr. Collins is a bit of a fool; and my mother . . . has her blind spots. She was so busy disapproving of Miss Bennet that she did not notice you staring at her during every meal."

"I hardly think I was *staring.*"

"Darcy," she said gently, "*you were staring.*"

He decided to point out, "You mentioned nothing of this to me when we talked."

"Of course not. Falling horribly in love is hardly something a man will easily admit to." She smiled. "I do hope she is kind to you, because I know you will do whatever she says for the rest of your natural life."

"Now you are just insulting me," he said playfully.

"But am I not wrong."

"No. I will admit that much."

"Darcy," she said, "I do wish you the best of luck. Elizabeth is a wonderful woman."

"Truly." He rose because he knew he had to be getting on, and when she offered her hand, he kissed it. This was the secret Anne, away from her mother, that he knew and loved—kind and clever.

But it was not Anne who appeared in his dreams at night.

Chapter 8

THE CEREMONY

LONGBOURN WAS IN THE appropriate uproar.

"I must enquire," Elizabeth said from her dressing stand, "that if it takes me no less than two hours and a seamstress to get this dress on, how I am supposed to ever get it off?"

"Lizzy! You will have servants enough as Mrs. Darcy to do whatever you please!" Mrs. Bennet assured her from her couch. She was in such a state of nerves, she could hardly stand up without aid. "Ten thousand a year! And half of Derbyshire! I would like very much to see it someday."

"And you shall—perhaps at Christmas?" She had not proposed the idea to Darcy, but she could not imagine that if there were to be a family gathering for the holidays, it would not be at Pemberley—though perhaps minus the Wickhams. At least Lydia had had the decency to show up for the wedding without her husband. He was not invited, but Elizabeth knew that would hardly stop Lydia from bringing him if she saw fit.

No, Elizabeth decided she was being unfair to Lydia. She was sixteen, had every right to be silly (though no right to be scandalous), and had actually been in repose since Jane's outburst. Lydia had not endeavoured to tell them any more secrets of intimacy, perhaps because they had both done their best to avoid being cornered by her. With all of the festivities, it was not overly difficult to do so. Then there was Mr. Darcy's health, which had kept Elizabeth away at Netherfield for half of a very crucial day, even though he was obviously much recovered by the dinner.

"I cannot think," Mrs. Bennet fretted as she looked her daughter over, and Elizabeth decided not to make the obvious joke. "There must be something I have not told you—some advice I have not imparted—"

"Mama, please—I have quite enough advice to last me a lifetime. Oh, Jane!"

For Jane had entered, very carefully with the train that was following her. Elizabeth had no notion or care as to how she herself appeared to the world—her only concern was for Darcy, who seemed to love her even in the most misshapen of walking gowns—but Jane looked like an absolute angel, bathed in white, even without her veil on.

"Oh, Jane, my dear Jane." Apparently afraid to touch her gown, Mrs. Bennet ran to her oldest daughter and cupped her hands around her cheeks. "You are so beautiful. It is too much to part with you."

"Mama!" Jane said, worry on her face, mainly because it was obvious that Mrs. Bennet was beginning to cry. Though she had her fits, to see real tears of happiness was such a rare occasion that it was unsettling.

"But I know it must be so," Mrs. Bennet said, holding Jane's hand and turning to Elizabeth. "We are giving you both away to the best men in England and that should at least comfort me, yes?"

Elizabeth embraced her mother, but only after checking that there was nothing left in her dress to puncture them both.

The silence was broken by the appearance of Mr. Bennet, poking his head up from the stairs. "I hate to interrupt all of this mysterious mourning on what is to be the happiest day of my favourite daughters' lives, but there is some matter of business at the church, and I believe the vicar will look at me most unfavourably if we are late."

And with that, he disappeared back down the stairs, putting on his hat as he went. Mrs. Bennet removed herself from her daughters, wiping the tears from her eyes. "Of course, we must make haste. Your sisters are already downstairs, and the others have gone on ahead. Do you have all of your things? Wait, no matter. They can be sent for. We must not make your husbands wait!"

Somehow, seeing her return to her normal state of worried impatience was relieving to them both. Mrs. Bennet followed her husband down the stairs, leaving the two sisters alone for what occurred to them would be the last time in months.

"So."

"So."

And they both giggled at the gravity at which they had said it.

"They are waiting for us, Lizzy."

"I know."

"Are you nervous?"

Elizabeth swallowed. "Perhaps I will concede to some natural trepidation."

"Well, then I will make the full concession. I did not eat anything this morning in fear that I would be ill. I will not deny that I am timid, but pray, this must be natural."

"I'm sure. Mr. Bingley has probably worn out the carpet at the church with his pacing."

Jane added, "And Mr. Darcy has focused so hard on suppressing all tension that he may well explode."

"Come then, let us get there before we get a stone husband and a bill from the church for a destroyed rug."

Their laughter seemed to carry them all the way down the stairs.

"I say, my daughters seem to be in some sort of a competition," Mr. Bennet said. "The first husband I must pay; the second I have no obligations to; and the third pays *me*. Mary, if this pattern is to continue, I will consent to you marrying a man of no less than twenty thousand pounds a year. And Kitty, nothing less than royalty will do. I perhaps will settle for Scottish royalty, but only if he truly loves you."

"Mr. Bennet!" was Mrs. Bennet's natural reaction because she had an uncanny ability to fail to recognise when he was joking. In this area, everyone else was not lacking, and there was a good deal of giggling among the three sisters while the carriages were prepared. "You will never cease in your attempts to incite my nerves!"

"At this point, it would be reprehensible of me to do so," he said. "But here come the brides."

After much hemming and hawing on the part of the tearful servants, Jane and Elizabeth had finally made it out of Longbourn, at least as far as the carriages.

"Oh, Mr. Bennet!" Mrs. Bennet cried again and this time literally fell sideways into his arms. He did not impede this at all, putting an arm around her as she wept.

"There, there, dear," he said. "I fear you must keep your promise to me and allow me to ride with Jane and Lizzy in their carriage, because if you accompany them instead, they will arrive thoroughly soaked, and their husbands will toss them out on the doorstop." But before she could put up some response to this, he kissed her on her forehead and beckoned his relatively shocked daughters into the carriage.

In the first carriage went Jane, Elizabeth, and their father. Their mother and sisters followed in the remaining ones. "You must forgive your mother," Mr. Bennet said without reservation. "Despite all of this talk of marriage, there was a time when it was very hard for either of us to imagine that we would have to give you up. I believe the period began with Jane's birth and lasted until a few years before you all entered society."

So removed from it they were, neither sister could imagine being infants to a young Mrs. Bennet. "I imagine she was just as nervous for a whole different set of reasons," Elizabeth ventured.

"No, she was quite the composed mother. It was I who acted abominably." Since he was facing them, it was impossible not to catch their shocked looks. "Very well, I was hoping to escape this, but it seems I must now tell a story from my own past which brings me much embarrassment, especially because it may well happen to your husbands. Jane, when you were born,

I remember vividly sitting in my study with Mr. Gardiner, awaiting the announcement of a child. You may find me a reserved man now, but on that particular day, I was terrified of so many things that I was out of sorts. While Mr. Gardiner did his best to comfort me during your mother's travails, you know that shouting carries very well through Longbourn's walls.

"Anyway, when I heard a baby crying, I decided I could wait no longer and left my refuge and raced up the stairs. The nurse, unprepared for this improper rampage, greeted me with you, Jane, in a bundle in her arms. I then did what any man completely ill prepared for the position of fatherhood would do: I fainted away completely—head right on the floor."

The light-hearted way he said it made it seem like a cheerful story, and they both giggled, which seemed to aid his telling. "But that, sadly, is not the end of the matter," Mr. Bennet said. "While I was not injured, it took some time to rouse me, and Mrs. Bennet heard of it immediately and would not let me hold you for several weeks unless I was sitting down. So upon her second confinement, I had Mr. Gardiner standing right beside me when I was presented with you, Lizzy, even though I insisted that I would be all right. I was, of course, not all right, and this time around, he caught me. It was not until Mary was born that I finally took your mother's good advice and received her sitting down."

"Papa, I cannot imagine it," Elizabeth said at last.

"Then find some time when your mother is cross at me, and I have no doubt that she will tell you the whole story in great detail—or Mr. Gardiner, if he is in a particularly gossipy mood. But it is the honest truth that women are far more prepared than men for parenthood, if I am any judge." He sighed happily. "There, that is all the wisdom I have to impart: If you are to have children, do make sure the servants have your husbands sitting down."

While last minute arrangements were made in the church, the two grooms were sent for a moment of reflection with the vicar in his study. After instructing them on their marital duties in a very formal and churchly (and boring) way, he excused himself, leaving them to fret until they were called to take their places. Darcy immediately took a seat and poured himself some tea. "Do not inquire as to my health. I am tired of it. I merely want some tea, as I think it would be better than eating at this juncture."

"Yes," Bingley said, and, after looking briefly at the small religious paintings on the walls of the study, began to pace.

Darcy merely opened his hand, as if asking for a coin. "Your hat."

"What?"

"I will not see you destroy it. Now give it over."

Bingley frowned indignantly, but he did hand Darcy his hat. "I am just nervous. My stomach feels like it is full of butterflies."

"If you wish to expel the contents of your stomach," Darcy offered, "I can tell you what Mr. Hurst told me about your sister last night. That should do the trick."

"Louisa? What did—" And it struck him like a lightening bolt. "No! Do not even start! I do not wish to know!" He put his hands over his ears. "See? I am not listening to you any longer."

"You are so nervous you cannot take a joke. How odd," Darcy said. "I would never repeat the contents of that vile conversation."

"And you are not nervous. How do you do it, Darcy? Tell me your secret."

"It is very simple. I am too terrified to be nervous. One emotion overrides the other."

"Well, I don't see how—you, terrified?" Bingley stopped pacing for a moment. "Darcy of Pemberley, who pushed his new brother out of a window this morning?"

"Not without an admirable second. And that's the least of what I've done to him over the years. Or what he's done to me." Darcy took a sip of the tea that had been set out for him. "We are true siblings then, I suppose."

"You will not ignore my question."

Darcy hesitated before answering, as if he needed to chew on his words a bit first. "Bingley, I assume you are aware that I am marrying perhaps one of the cleverest, most headstrong, and most independent girls in England. That, coupled with the fact that I am completely surrendered to her means that I know very well I will be doing her bidding for the rest of my life with no complaints—is it not a daunting prospect?"

"Don't be ridiculous. You are a perfect match because you are as stubborn as she is."

Darcy merely grunted subtly in reply; he was either too uncomfortable with making his feelings so obvious or he was unwilling to admit conversational defeat. Bingley was not a fool; the inscrutable Darcy was deeply in love, and Elizabeth unwittingly had him wrapped around her finger. And Bingley doubted she would be so unwitting for long. Not that he did not feel the same way about Jane himself, but their countenances were different, if similarly matching. He could not imagine ever even raising an objection with Jane in the room, and yet Darcy and Elizabeth had been trading quiet insults since the first ball. That true affection had been born of this strife had surprised everyone.

"Miss Elizabeth is one of the most agreeable ladies I have ever met," Bingley said at last. "And I have no doubt that all of your worries are just nerves. Perhaps she has the same."

"And would you venture to suppose that Miss Bennet is thinking the same right now?"

"No, I—," but he couldn't finish the sentence. What if Jane were having second thoughts? Oh, cruel Darcy! Bingley usually knew better than to get in a battle of wits with him. "Are you trying to make me nervous? Or, I suppose, *more* nervous?"

"I must admit it did distract me from my own nerves for a moment," Darcy said with a grin. "You will forgive me. If we must talk, let us talk of something more pleasant. Why don't you pick a topic?"

"Fine," Bingley said, regaining his ground. Now he wanted the edge on Darcy. "So, by some happenstance, I had the pleasure of finally telling *someone* the 'Fitzers' story that you have had me keep secret for so long."

"Now you mean to terrify me! Who was it? Oh, of course, it must have been Jane." He took a sip of his tea as if it were some kind of consoling spirit. "And she probably immediately told her sister. My reputation is ruined, depending on which one you told."

"There is more than one?"

This gave Darcy pause. "There are a number of them, all involving me and Wickham, except for the one you were present for. So I assume it must have been the Cambridge incident, wholly unrelated to my new relation." His eyes widened. "Good heavens, you didn't tell her the part about my passing out?"

"She found it quite amusing. Though perhaps this would be averted if you were not so secretive as to why you will allow no one to call you anything but Darcy."

"Perhaps. Well, Elizabeth can call me whatever she pleases," Darcy admitted rather suddenly.

"Provided it is not 'Mr. Wickham!'"

The smouldering rage on Darcy's face was apparent. "Now you are just *trying* to torment me."

"Only because you were doing the same a few moments ago! And made me throw a guest out a window!" Bingley had more to say but was interrupted by Colonel Fitzwilliam entering the vicar's study. He did not get a word out before Bingley pointed directly and rudely at Darcy and said, "He is trying to irritate me! On my wedding day!"

The colonel did a double take, looking at the quivering, accusatory Bingley and the smug Darcy in his chair. "Perhaps leaving you two alone was not the best idea on this day."

"Perhaps," Darcy said, attempting to return to his usual demeanour.

"Well, the carriages have been spotted, so it is perhaps time for you to take your places, assuming there will be no wild escapes."

"Oh no," Darcy said. "Enough people have gone out the window today. Lead on, Fitzwilliam."

Thankfully, his cousin did not ask for an explanation of that particular comment.

By the time they arrived at the church, preparations were in their final stages, and the girls were ushered into a waiting room with their immediate family before they took their places.

Mary, to their great surprise, provided her sisters with two silver crosses on chains. Where she must have picked them up and at what expense was a mystery. "You don't have to wear them. Just keep them along with you."

"Of course," Jane said, and kissed her sister.

Kitty gave them both beautiful purple ribbons. "All the fashion in Paris, I heard," she said, her usual giggling manner somewhat subdued.

It was Lydia, though, who appeared before them and shamelessly said, "It was my gift to you both that I didn't bring Wickham."

The humour in her voice was obvious; perhaps she was not the dunderhead they assumed her to be, and they both lovingly embraced her before she left the small room.

"My dears, my dears," their mother said nervously. "Oh, there is so much to say now and so little time to say it. Always be good to your husbands, and be careful never to irritate them with your fits."

"Wise advice," said Mr. Bennet.

"And if they ever do make some quiet comments at your expense, it will suit your marriage to pretend that you do not hear," she replied. She gave Mr. Bennet no time for a response before kissing both her daughters on the cheek and leaving them alone with Mr. Bennet.

"Having been outdone," he said, "I fear I have nothing more to say."

Fortunately for him, the music started.

"Three daughters married!" Mrs. Bennet said, but her exclamation was in a hushed tone as Mr. Darcy and Mr. Bingley took their places.

"I fear we must find another match as quickly as possible because my sister will need something new to say," Mr. Gardiner whispered to his wife in Mr. Bennet's absence.

In response, she swatted him playfully with her decorative fan. "I am so *very* glad we visited the grounds of Pemberley."

"Yes, the fishing was exquisite."

She smacked him again with a giggle. "You know what I mean."

"If only we could claim we were witting in our plans to bring Lizzy to Derbyshire, and then we would have even more right to drop in unannounced when the weather is particularly good and they have just stocked the lake."

"I think our niece will be a very gracious hostess."

"Maybe she will even have us," Charlotte said to her husband, patting him on his forearm.

"If Lady Catherine discovers we attended—"

Anne, who was in the row behind him, stood up and coughed, "What is this about my mother?"

"Miss de Bourgh!" A very flummoxed Mr. Collins found the church pews did not give him proper room to turn around and bow. "I . . . I had no idea—"

"Shhh, darling," Charlotte shushed him. "The music is starting."

Up at the altar, Darcy and Bingley turned to the aisle where their brides would be appearing momentarily. "Any last words?" Bingley whispered.

"Chapter 15."

"What—Darcy! We're in a church!"

"I was of course discussing the book of Leviticus. I don't know why *your* mind is so filthy these days, Bingley."

"That's *your* fault!"

"You asked for my advice, and you have it. Chapter 15."

Bingley swallowed, but then the doors to the church opened and all conversation ceased.

The day Mr. Bennet gave away his two eldest and most beloved daughters was a beautiful December day. The sun was bright and shining when they left the church and returned to Netherfield for the wedding feast, which was more for the guests than the new couples, who were very eager to be off to Town. Darcy and Elizabeth were taking an evening before going north to Pemberley, and Bingley and Jane had decided that Netherfield was a bit too crowded for their tastes at this juncture and the Bingley townhouse in London would do just fine. The Darcys made their escape quicker than the Bingleys, as they were not the hosts, and the Bennets saw them off.

"Oh, Mr. Bennet," his wife said, not in a shriek but in a melancholy tone. "Our house will seem so empty."

"Indeed, Mrs. Bennet, I've given this matter much thought and decided that if Kitty and Mary do not do their fair share, we will have to have some more daughters to liven up the place."

"How can you talk such rubbish?" she said, but she was not at all mean. In fact, she was sort of smiling, in a sad way. "At your age, you could hardly take another fall, and we cannot always rely on Mr. Gardiner to catch you when you swoon!"

UNION

"Dearest Elizabeth," Darcy said as he took hold of her arms, "you are the love of my life, and I never wish to be parted from you again. I have been looking forward to this day since I first laid eyes upon you. And yet, I must tear myself away from those lovely eyes for a brief moment because I fear that I will die very shortly if I do not *eat something*."

Elizabeth decided that this was a perfectly logical explanation. In fact, the passion with which he said it was outright amusing. He had had every opportunity to consume something at the festivities, but they both had their minds on the solitary idea of getting out of there as soon as possible, with no love lost to their relatives. In Darcy's London house, which was vacant except for the servants absolutely necessary for their night's stay, they now had what they only had a few minutes of in Bingley's closet yesterday—privacy. And without speaking, they both knew what the other was thinking: that it was worth its weight in gold.

The few servants available were asked to cook up—to quote the noble and upstanding Mr. Darcy of Pemberley—"whatever is around." He gave Elizabeth a kiss and let her be led to her dressing chamber to finally escape the very complex dress and its hazard of a long train. She was unaware of what the protocol was now—was she just supposed to lie and wait for him? But her stomach made its own decision, for she had eaten little since the night before, and she shooed away the attendants and dressed herself in a pretty but simple frock—she supposed he would like it all the same, now that he had no choice in the matter—and returned to the dining room to find a dish of mutton waiting for her across from him. She did not need any further enticement to devour it whole and anything else that was quickly put in front of her.

By the time they were both finished and tea was served, their impromptu feast had cost them most of their energy, and they were left languishing in their respective chairs, quite unwilling to be anything but upright at the moment, basking in an easy and satiated silence.

It was only then that she noticed Darcy had stripped himself of most of his wedding costume and was down to his shirt and breeches. He did look very fetching, but she felt odd saying it. "I must confess, Mr. Darcy . . ."

He looked up when he heard "Mr. Darcy." "You thought I was going to pounce on top of you like a feral cat when we entered the apartment?"

There was the significant temptation to wrinkle her nose because Darcy's laid-back composure was positively unnerving compared to the pillar of respectability he had been throughout the wedding—minus some very loving and almost sultry glances during the ceremony. But she decided instead to treat it in jest, because he seemed so inclined. Perhaps this was his true nature, hid behind the curtain of propriety that he so readily displayed in open society. "Yes . . . I suppose."

"Then I have disappointed you, and I should never be forgiven. Or I have greatly relieved you and should be forever looked on with great respect." The table was set for two and not very long, and he sat straight up enough to reach over and put his hand over hers. His touch had a tingling sensation, perking her up just a bit. "Some things deserve just the right . . . planning."

"Which involves a full stomach?"

"Apparently. I confess that you have driven me to such distraction over the last few days that I have lost whatever I attempted to ingest."

"That and your wild stag party last night."

"If you would call being cornered by Mr. Collins and Mr. Hurst a wild stag party, then you are much mistaken about the affairs of men," he said, and kissed her knuckles, "my dear Lizzy."

"So there was no drunken debauchery?"

"There was some drunkenness and tales of debauchery that came from men from whom I have never desired to know their intimate secrets, however keen they were on telling them. Then your father called us out of the room and saved both of us; I lost my stomach many times and went to sleep. There, you now have the full account of my wild stag night, minus the spoken details that I never want to think of again in my life."

Elizabeth laughed. "How ridiculous! All I had was a pillow fight with my sister."

"Then in some respect, this 'woman's lot' that I hear so much of is not so terrible."

"You are omitting a few things from a woman's lot, Darcy."

"Oh yes. There is also having to endure the total devotion of your husband, to be the mistress of a great estate, and to drive me insane trying to satisfy your every unconscious want and need."

"And to produce an heir," she could not help but mentioning.

"Lizzy," he said, and his eyes were quite honest, "if it was just you and me until the day we died, I would be the most satisfied and complete man in England."

"Truly?"

"Truly."

She did not know the protocol. She tended to her own toilette and put on her nightgown, but the servants had mysteriously disappeared from sight, perhaps partially because she had shooed them away earlier, unaccustomed as she was to being so attended. Being unlaced by someone else was helpful, but beyond that, she was uncomfortable in such luxury.

In actuality, she was uncomfortable about a lot of things, but she was not terrified. He had not, as he so eloquently put it, pounced on her like a feral cat. In the washroom she had to smirk at the phrase. He certainly had a way with words, whether he meant to insult or to reassure. Still, he hadn't said he wasn't *about* to jump her.

Not that it was so daunting a prospect. However brief they had been, their closeted kisses the night before had incited her to the idea that perhaps the more amorous accounts of marital rites were not so far gone. So now whatever fears she had were mixed with a perceptible anticipation—but not of the bad sort.

When she emerged into what was to be their bedchamber, at least in the London estate, he was still dressed, perhaps not to terrify her. "Elizabeth . . ." was all he said as he kissed her. She tasted brandy.

"You drank?"

"It was that or the mutton taste. Which would you prefer? It was merely a mouthwash," he said. "And I will now tell you a dark secret if you wish."

"Yes, I wish to know all of your dark secrets, Mr. Darcy." She said the last bit mainly because she knew it made him turn his head. They sat down on the bed, casually, like old friends, even if they were anything but.

"Very well," he said. "I am, it seems, a cheap drunk."

"A man of your countenance?"

"Yes. Being formal and daunting has nothing to do with susceptibility to intoxication. And it has caused me no end of troubles."

"So you are saying," she said, as she took his hands in hers, "that if I ever wish to take you down off your high horse—which you may, I will venture to say, dear husband, occasionally be on—I merely need to spike your usual wine with something stronger?"

"Precisely. You now know my weakness. Let us leave it at that."

"We certainly shall not! I must hear at least one story of your drunken escapades, if you can find one becoming enough."

"Or if I can *remember* one becoming enough," Darcy said, frowning in the candlelight. "I suppose your sister told you the one about the duel in the tavern."

"She did, just this morning."

"Am I to have no secrets, then?"

"Of course you are. But we were not married just *then*," she said with a smile. "Now you may tell me all you want in confidence, and I will not tell my sister, and she may tell me all she wants in confidence, and I will not tell you. That seems only fair. And you may have your own confidences with Mr. Bingley."

"I am not a gossip with Bingley," he said. "You surely realise that. Everything untoward he knows of me is something he was present for."

"So you have no confidant."

"I have you, Lizzy."

"Then tell me something confidential."

He laughed. This was not the Darcy she met at the Meryton Assembly, so haughty and of ill demeanour. It had taken her months—nearly a year—to learn that this was his public face, one that was required of him, like a mask that he retreated behind because of his insecurities. Yes, it was cruel to think of her husband as having insecurities, but he had openly admitted it to her at Rosings, even if she did not understand it with proper gravity at the time. And yet here they were, and he was completely at ease and not hidden behind a social mask, and the real person that was Fitzwilliam Darcy was quite happy and charming. "Hmm. I suppose I should tell the story of my sister's pianoforte."

"The one you bought for her?"

"Yes, precisely that one. How it came about that I felt she needed a new, nicer pianoforte when Pemberley had a number of perfectly good ones has everything to do with my making a fool of myself and attempting to cover it up."

She found herself stroking his arms as she begged him, "Then you must tell me."

"I must, though there is some sadness in the tale, as it happened right after the incident at Kent in which you told me some things that I needed to hear."

"You mean, when I soundly and cruelly rejected you?"

"Yes, precisely. So, as you know, I left Rosings and went home to Pemberley almost immediately, where I stayed for several months despite pressing business in Town. On the first morning home, I did what any man would do after being rejected by the loveliest woman in the entire world. That is to say, I drank a fine single malt straight from the bottle to the point where the room was spinning. My plan was to remain locked in my study all day, wallowing in self-pity, but it was about then that Georgiana heard of my sudden arrival and burst into the room, wanting to know all of the particulars of my visit to Rosings. As you may know, she is a great friend of Anne, if from a distance and mainly by letter. I barely had time to hide the bottle under my desk, but there was no way I could have a coherent conversation with her at that moment and disguise my inebriation. Eventually, I devised a plan, which was to beg her to play the pianoforte for me, as I was tired from the journey and much desired to hear it. She was of course very willing and went straight ahead to play what I assume was a very beautiful piece of music."

"You assume?"

Darcy nodded. "I did what any drunken fool would do when in a very comfortable chair and with wonderful music playing— I fell asleep during the fourth or fifth bar. She did not notice this for some time, apparently, and her attendant later told me she played the whole piece before turning to ask what I thought and finding me out cold. Being the dear sister that she is, she did not disturb me at all, and when I awoke several hours later with a blinding headache, I found a blanket draped over me. She never demanded an explanation, but over dinner I did my best to reassure her that I was just very, very tired and that her playing was very lovely indeed. Though she seemed to accept this as an answer, I felt so guilty that I immediately began my research to find her the best pianoforte I could acquire to assure her of her musical talent." He added, "And that must be a secret between husband and wife."

"Surely," she said, and kissed him. "But that cannot be your only secret."

"I do not have the sordid past you may be imagining," he said. "All I have to my credit are a few cases of inebriation that led to untoward behaviour and some duels with Wickham that were hardly verbal."

"But you are a far more disreputable character than a simple country girl. I have nothing to compare. But you still haven't told me of your trip to Town."

He rolled his eyes playfully. "And I did promise, didn't I? I needed to procure a certain book."

"That's it? A book?"

"Well, not the kind of book you would find in your father's library, Lizzy. It was more of a . . . reference book."

"On?"

"No, no." He put a finger to her lips. "I promised to *show* you, not tell you."

She was about to put up some kind of objection to this, because what he said made very little sense on a logical level, but he kissed her in the sort of way that was not a quick peck that could be easily interrupted, nor did she desire for it to be interrupted.

Fortunately, for all of her worries, the wedding gown was long discarded and the nightgown was easily removed. Was this the way it was all supposed to work?

Elizabeth decided she was quite eager to find out.

The sun was rising in London, and the servants at the Bingley townhouse were beginning to rise for their morning chores, unawares that they were the only ones in the house who had any significant amount of sleep. The morning light was creeping in through the curtains, leaving little lines on the bed as Bingley finally fell into an exhausted doze. Jane was beside him, her head nestled on his shoulder, trying to remember what she was going to say and if it was worth disturbing him, but she was finding herself a bit muddled in the head herself. Something about the servants? Breakfast? Opening the curtains? Was there some formality of wealth that was going to interrupt them to announce a new morning? Yes, something like that, but she couldn't bring herself to say it. Instead she stroked his auburn hair, considerably more mussed than it usually was—which for Charles Bingley, was saying quite a lot. He had that dashing young "I am so exciting, my hair is trying to escape from my head, and it is a hopeless cause" unintentional style that was so adorable. Maybe it was his wild but hidden Irish heritage that no good English family would admit to. His hair was very soft, and she was very content to ruffle it further as she drifted into her own half-sleep, still very aware of her position but not willing to move from it.

"Are they going to wake us for breakfast?" she finally asked, breaking a considerable silence.

Bingley, facing away from her, didn't seem to mind, his voice blissfully relaxed. "Only if they can pick the lock on the door."

Somehow, she still had the energy to giggle, and he had the energy to join her in this new endeavour. He flipped over to face her, at least partially awake, or unwilling to drift off entirely at this moment. This consensus was reached without words, even though they were both exhausted and barely capable of doing anything other than holding hands.

"I do not believe I have ever been so happy," Jane said. "The day of your proposal will now have to be relegated to second place."

"I the same," Bingley said. "Third would be the Meryton Assembly."

"Really?"

"Really, my love."

"It was not marred by your sister's and Darcy's glowering looks all night?"

"I do not remember a single other thing about that night," he said, "except that Darcy refused to dance, insolent man that he was. And remember, she is your sister now."

"So now I have *seven* sisters. Oh dear, this will be confusing."

"And when the rest of *them* marry—"

She covered her mouth, but she was giggling. "Charles, don't!"

"Very well, I will torment you no longer. I am sure Pemberley at Christmas will hold us all." He kissed her, which was meant to be an affectionate peck but quickly turned into something more.

"Charles," Jane said when they finally broke apart, at least for the necessities of breathing, "I have to confess a very naughty thought to you."

"Then I must confess that I am in great anticipation to hear it," he said, but his cheeks started to match his hair.

"I assume, of course—or I *did* assume—that you came into this marriage with only the purest, loveliest innocence. However, considering—"

"Yes, that third thing was a little odd. I don't even know if it has a name."

"Considering," she said, also blushing now and trying to stay composed, "that I have heard such differing tales of marital rites, but none of them have quite been on the level of—"

"Jane, I assure you, at this time yesterday, I was as pure as snow. With that said, I am a very well-read man when I care to be."

She raised an eyebrow as if not completely convinced.

"What I mean to say is—" But he didn't want to say what he wanted to say. Instead, he laughed. "It is too embarrassing."

"Charles, we are husband and wife in basically every possible way at this exact moment. There is nothing that is too embarrassing that I can imagine."

"I will not fault your imagination, because I could never bring myself to fault anything in you," he said, "but um . . . well, there is this book—"

"Surely not!"

"I was as surprised as you were when it was given to me as a gift, but apparently it is available by import."

"A gift? Pray, by whom?"

He considered his answer before giving it in an answer. "Must you ask?"

Jane erupted in a fit of giggles, which he was content to let pass, as it prevented him from having to answer any more awkward questions. Finally she asked, "Does Lizzy know?"

"This is something that I will never inquire of her."

"An excellent idea."

They fell into another silence, punctuated only by the early morning sounds of London coming to life. Jane, again, broke it with her announcement. "I must see this book."

"Oh no!" It was not a refusal as much as a cry of unfairness. "'Tis ungentlemanly for me even to own it."

"Conveniently, I am not a gentleman. And I will insist."

"If—," but he turned and looked at his wife's beautiful face. "You have me at your mercy. Surely you realise that. Now you are taking advantage of it."

"The book, Charles."

Bingley grunted nervously and turned back over, swinging his legs over the side of the bed. Jane stroked his bare back as he reached under the bed and retrieved the book stashed beneath his blue top hat and several other books, one of them a Bible. He passed it over his shoulder before climbing back into the bed and under the considerable covers.

"My heavens," Jane said as she opened the innocent-looking cover. "Where did you get such a book?"

"I have already told you."

"I mean, where would such a book originate?" She added, "Are these people human or monster?"

"It is from India, and that is their style of drawing. This

much I do know from my illustrious Cambridge education, though the nature of the drawings in the books there were more concerning local religious figures."

"It is very unrealistic."

"Yes, but nonetheless very instructive."

Jane leaned over and kissed him. "I have no complaints."

But she did not return the book. Instead, she put it on the table on her side of the bed.

Chapter 10

THE NICKNAME

THE CARRIAGE DRIVER FOR Mr. Darcy of Pemberley and Derbyshire was not accustomed to waiting. It was not that the coachman was a particularly impatient man, but years of conditioning had taught him that Mr. Darcy valued promptness and never once made his servants wait when an appearance time was set. Therefore, he could hardly believe it when Mr. Darcy's manservant came down and said that they would be delayed a day. In fact, he didn't believe it until Mr. Darcy appeared himself, all prim and proper, to explain himself. "Well, you know . . ." then he trailed off very uncharacteristically and went back into the townhouse. He was told by the servants to report back the next day at the same time, and when it was quietly explained to him that there was a Mrs. Darcy also in residence, he nodded with complete comprehension.

Back in the confines of his bedchamber, Darcy hastily shed all of the complex layers of wool that he had put on just to step outside. The whole process was ridiculously long even with his manservant's help on one end and Elizabeth's help on the other, a notion she found very amusing. "Just to speak to the driver?"

"I will not appear in public as a rogue."

"Yes, because you would look quite villainous without the proper knot on your cravat."

"What would Town think of me then?" he said with a smile, finally willing to laugh at his own ridiculousness. "I will not stand for it. The Darcy honour is too great."

"Not great enough to regulate your behaviour to your wife."

"And how else am I supposed to behave in front of a wife?" he said, and then frowned.

"Darcy, what is it?"

"Now I have the terrible image in my head of my mother and father rolling around on the bed, to be blunt about it."

Elizabeth lay across their wide bed as he knelt on it in front of her. "Well, considering the evidence of the existence of both you and Georgiana . . ."

"And considering the existence of your *four* siblings, your parents must have been very adventurous indeed."

She covered her mouth. "Darcy, now you've done it to me!"

He gave her that innocent look, which of course meant it was anything but innocent. "I was merely stating the obvious."

"Sometimes the obvious does not need to be stated! Now it will not leave my mind."

"Hmm." Darcy smiled, and leaned over her. "I will have to distract you, then." As he kissed her, she tugged his shirt off and was indeed very distracted. There would be no trip to Pemberley today, they had decided. A very long ride was a very daunting prospect when things were perfectly lovely here in Town. Not that she would be without entertainment on the road, as she had a whole number of things to wring from her husband's mind, but some things just couldn't be done in a carriage.

She was right about one premarital notion—that the events would leave her quite exhausted. *Which* events would leave her most exhausted she was mistaken about, but they did spend much of the next day, when not otherwise engaged, sleeping soundly in each other's arms. Trays of food were left at the door, and eventually they decided to make a ragged appearance at the dinner table, which required leaving the bedchamber for the first time in nearly a day. Even on short notice, the servants had a sizeable (and this time, more presentable) meal prepared, but there was no formality to the dinner whatsoever beyond what the servants were wearing—wigs and all.

"Darcy, we look more like two ruffians who have broken in and taken our leisure of this wealthy man's apartment," she stated, when the servants had stepped out. As amused as she was, it was still downright bizarre.

"If it would suit you, my dear, I would put on all four layers of waistcoat and dress myself up for a royal ball," he offered, "but then I would have to spend quite some time taking it all off again."

"Quite right."

They retired as early as they could manage on full stomachs. She had never seen Darcy like this, though she had hints of it during his second proposal and that night at Netherfield. She decided that if this was what the illustrious Darcy of Pemberley was like in private, she soundly approved. No wonder his sister was so ready in her expressions of sibling affection. She wondered if anyone else had ever seen this side of him—perhaps his servants, but she doubted it. Bingley was an unlikely candidate, but honestly, he was the furthest thing from her mind at the moment.

"What are you giggling at?"

"That you are so different in the ways you present yourself, Darcy," she said. "So, I should call you Darcy like everyone else?"

"You may call me whatever you please," he said. "Though I would prefer whatever nickname you invent to display some affection and not be a formality like Mr. Darcy."

"'Of Pemberley and Derbyshire.' Yes, suppose I were to call you that every single time, as if I were constantly announcing you."

"You would tire of it quickly, I am sure," he said as he tickled her on the bed. "What bothers you so about 'Darcy'?"

"Nothing. I am merely curious as to the range I am to be allowed. I hear many stories about how you are a great lover of your baptismal name."

"*Many* stories? I know you know but one."

"Unless Bingley has spread that one around considerably, there must be another, because I have never heard anyone call you by your name."

"I think it is that more people are following in other's footsteps on the matter."

"I confess I do not entirely believe you."

He was trying to hold out, she could tell. But she tapped him on his chest with her feet, and between that and her smile, it seemed to be enough to drag him out of whatever closed stance he was trying to enter into. "Fine. I will tell you the whole story, though it does not reflect well on either person chiefly involved."

"I will forgive you in advance and assume the other person is Wickham."

"You know me too well." He kissed her foot, the closest available body part. "Once upon a time, I was a very small boy who could not pronounce his own name."

"Really?"

"I was three, Elizabeth! I do not even remember it, but you can confirm it with Mrs. Reynolds if you wish. Apparently I found the 'z' particularly perplexing and went about calling myself 'Fissers' until my tongue was old enough to do otherwise."

"And what did you call Colonel Fitzwilliam?"

"What, do you think they dressed him in a uniform and bought him a commission when he was six? I called him Richard. But that is not the point. To my father and mother I was Fitzwilliam; to everyone else I was 'Master Fitzwilliam'; and to Wickham I was Fitz. I did not care for it very much, and I think Richard may have picked up on it, because he started calling me Darcy, and I decided at some point that I liked it much better. Eventually Wickham gave in, and the matter was dropped—or so I thought."

The Darcy she knew was brief, honest, and to the point. This Darcy was laid back on his own pillow and paused for some drama, amused at his own telling even if he did not care for the contents. Only her curling up to his side would convince him to resume his narrative. "Now we come to the part when I was in Cambridge, and Wickham's true colours began to show. There were hints beforehand, and we were always rivals on some level, but in the area of women, I usually allowed him to soundly beat me. But there was a girl—I do not remember her name or even if I ever knew her name, but we met in a tavern Wickham insisted on dragging me to after he decided I had been 'studying too much.' I will fully admit now, I suppose, that I had some mild attraction to this woman. There was something in her eyes . . . Well, I am much endeared to attractive eyes." He looked into hers, just in case she didn't get the message. "This was, I believe, the first time I was seriously pursuing someone in front of Wickham, at least in terms of seeking her conversation and goodwill. And so he decided to usurp me by approaching me while I was sitting alone with her. Sarah was her name; that was it—and he called me 'Fitzers.' This brought great amusement to her and no amusement to me, so he decided to tell the whole story about my infant tongue. He even went as far as to say that I secretly loved when women addressed me as such, knowing full well that I hadn't heard the name in years and it was likely that nothing was further from the truth. In other words, he completely ruined my chances, because I immediately lost my temper, which was his intention all the time by proceeding to flirt with her while discussing *me*."

"If I may interject," Elizabeth said, "I have to say that I am very glad that he was successful in tearing you away from her."

He did smile at that. "This was not so romantic. Remember, I was but nineteen at this time. I cannot even recall properly now what she looked like. Anyway, I did what I suppose any uncouth, jealous, romantically driven boy would do, which was to punch him soundly in the jaw."

"In front of her?"

"In front of her—thoroughly destroying my chances, but Wickham did suffer only a pyrrhic victory, because he lost a tooth in the process—one of the back ones. When he recovered, he proceeded to engage me in an all-out brawl. Now I will say, as humbly as possible, that I pride myself on having *some* fencing abilities, but I am not one to wrestle or engage in uncouth sports such as boxing. The first time, I merely managed what I did by surprise. Fortunately for me, we were both kicked out of the tavern posthaste, and with our dorm supervisor strolling outside, we had to separate before he could beat me into a bloody pulp, which is probably what he would have done. I was taller than him, but he was not unfamiliar with barroom and alleyway tactics. Though, I have to admit, aside from my pride, I emerged largely unscathed."

She had her head on his stomach, and she rolled over. "So you are saying that if I call you 'Fitzers,' you will strike your wife?"

"No, of course not. I will politely say in a very respectful and quiet voice, 'Dearest Lizzy, love of my life, if you call me that again, I will have no recourse but to annul our marriage and send you to a nunnery in Ireland.' That should be warning enough to clear the room."

The shocked silence was broken by shared laughter almost instantaneously.

After some time, when no actual comprehensible words were spoken but a lot of noises were made, Elizabeth turned to a half-sleeping Darcy and said, "I suppose we should depart tomorrow for Pemberley."

"Yes."

"And then I shall be mistress of Pemberley."

"Dearest Elizabeth, I am sure that it was last night that you officially became 'mistress of Pemberley.'"

With pseudo-indignation she said, "I am quite sure that I am a wife and not a mistress."

He propped his head up on the pillow. "And would you prefer to be treated as a proper wife of good standing even in private? Should I call you only 'Mrs. Darcy' and seek you only for impregnation, locking myself soundly in another room on all other occasions? Because I shall do anything you prefer!"

"Now you are mocking me!"

"I shall do my best to be an upstanding gentleman, ignoring your presence almost entirely in company, and never endeavour to gaze upon you or whisper private jokes in your ear at parties—"

Her response was to kiss him. Well, to kiss him and to climb on top of him, the ultimate assertion of authority. "That is *not* what I prefer, *Mr.* Darcy."

"Then we are in agreement. I will treat you with great love and compassion in front of guests and as a wanton wench in the bedchamber."

To this, she could not find a reason to raise dispute.

Mr. and Mrs. Bingley arrived in time for dinner at Netherfield. Many guests were still in attendance. Georgiana would return to the Darcy townhouse in London once her brother vacated it, and Colonel Fitzwilliam would see her there and then ride north. Bingley's sisters would eventually also make their way to London, but their comings and goings had always been a mystery to him, and even with a new wife at his arm, he was reluctant to toss them out. They were, after all, his sisters—two of *seven* as Jane reminded him jokingly on the carriage ride back.

Jane showed a little apprehension about the way the servants of Netherfield greeted her. Not that they had ever been anything but of the utmost standing in their positions as servants, but she was now Mrs. Charles Bingley, mistress of Netherfield, and thus she was received in a ceremony more elaborate than she wished. Charles merely put his hand on her arm for comfort as he led her in, and that seemed to be enough.

Seating at dinner was of course rearranged. Jane took the proper place at the table as Bingley's wife, and her new sisters showed all respect, though there was an occasional—though accidental—"Miss Bennet" over the course of conversation, but these lapses were entirely overlooked by everyone. Georgiana was all smiles and her usual eager conversation alike with her new relative, even though she did not bother to inquire after her brother. Mr. and Mrs. Darcy had not been heard from, but this was a surprise to no one.

Jane made a quiet comment to Charles about this in passing when they were moving between rooms to the after-dinner entertainment.

"Maybe they are too exhausted to send a correspondence," was all he said, and she knew very well what he meant and had to duck into a corner to keep herself from being seen with a flushed face. The implied type of activity was quite improper and odd for both of them, or perhaps would have been not two days before.

Bingley regretted his own social obligations, but he performed them, taking a glass of port with Colonel Fitzwilliam and Mr. Hurst as his sisters played cards. Fitzwilliam had some news of troop movements in France, and of course an impending war would be of great interest to the trade-engaged Bingley estate, so Bingley made every attempt to be interested, however noncrucial the information was at the time or however distracted he was at the moment, while Mr. Hurst snorted indignantly at the French and made occasional comments on the weather there.

At some point when he ventured into the parlour, he noticed Jane was no longer at the card table and inquired as to her whereabouts.

"She is retired for the night, I believe," Louisa said. "She had some business upstairs and then announced that the last few weeks have been exhausting and very politely excused herself. I must compliment her, Charles. She is a quick learner at cards."

"She bested me twice," Georgiana said. "I am not half as skilled, and I have been at this since Miss Bingley began instructing me last Christmas. I fear I am a poor pupil. Jane is so much better, is she not, Miss Bingley?"

She had, of course, trapped Miss Bingley into complimenting Jane. "Yes, I dare say she is." And it was hard even for Charles to tell if she was not being sincere.

"Well, I am glad to hear that she is under your tutelage, Caroline," he said, most happily. Yes, he had many things to be happy for this day. The only thing on his shoulders was that as host he must endeavour to stay downstairs until his guests retired. Normally sociable and content in this duty, he did find it a bit trying but decided to take a page from the wisdom of Darcy and hide it as best he could. He was grateful when his sisters took to their rooms, Louisa practically carrying her soused husband up the stairs. Georgiana also retired, and with a slap on the back to Bingley, Colonel Fitzwilliam disappeared.

He did give the servants instructions for the morning breakfast he doubted he would be attending. In that way, he was a very
bad host, but his reputation would have to endure that attack.
As soon as the room was cleared, he raced up the stairs with
enough speed to nearly trip the maid on her way down with the
day's laundry.

Officially, they had separate rooms, but he could hardly stop
himself from knocking on her bedchamber door. If she was truly
asleep, so be it, but to his tremendous relief she immediately
answered, and he entered without reservation.

She was not asleep, or even half asleep, as one would think
of someone who had retired a few hours earlier. Multiple lamps
were lit, and she was sitting up in bed, a book in her hands,
pleasantly satisfied with her situation.

"I—I did not mean to disturb you," he quickly explained,
even though the situation required no explanation on his part.
"I mean, if you were tired. They said you were."

"I lied."

"Oh."

Surely an explanation would follow, but other things busied him
for the moment, such as removing his considerable layers of clothing down to his underclothes and climbing into bed next to her.

She, of course, beat him to it. "I am not afraid of socialising
with your sisters. In fact, they have been charming to me, and
Georgiana is always a pleasure. However, I had more pressing
matters that did not involve them."

He rearranged himself more comfortably on the many pillows, and only then did he glance over at her reading material.
It did look astonishingly familiar.

"You know," Jane said nonchalantly, no doubt as she watched the horror wash over her husband's face, "there is a whole bit in here about other people's wives . . . and courtesans."

"I did not read that part."

"I am not saying you did," and she said it with a smile, which meant she was teasing him. "I am merely pointing it out."

"So you are telling me you lied to my guests and deserted me so you could sit up reading the most illustriously wicked book ever written?"

"I don't know about that. Have you ever actually read the Bible, Charles? There are some early passages I find rather disturbing. Something about Noah and his daughters," she said with mock hauteur. "But yes, I did what you have accused me of. I am a terrible hostess indeed."

"I think we merely have wicked guests for keeping us away from each other."

At this, they both shared a laugh, and he kissed her on the cheek. This was pleasant enough, but not satisfying to either of them. Their sleeping schedule quite out of sorts, they were both awake and, at long last after many trying hours, alone. Once their guests vacated Netherfield, they could do as they pleased, but until then . . . well, it did not matter. Bingley decided that many little things in this world—like family, duty, and being the master of an estate—did not matter as much as getting his shirt off at this exact moment.

"Charles," she said, as soon as she could find a time for interruption.

"Pray, what?" he said, his breathing heavy with anticipation.

She merely handed him the book, open to a certain chapter, one of the ones Darcy had pointed out to him as being exceedingly productive—hence the reason he recognised it. That did not make it an undaunting prospect. "Clearly, I should never have let you see this book."

"Is that a no?"

"Jane, dearest, I could never say no to you." He added, "And I have a feeling that you know it."

Chapter 11

LETTERS TO PEMBERLEY

As FALL APPROACHED, NETHERFIELD Park had fallen into an easy rhythm, uninterrupted by the London summer season, which the Bingleys did not attend. As the weather began to chill, Charles Bingley decided to take pleasure in every remaining burst of warm air and slipped out for his morning constitution with exceptional diligence. Sometimes his wife accompanied him, but she usually preferred the bed at that hour, and he was not wont to push her into something she had no wish to do.

Sometimes he walked toward Meryton, sometimes in the direction of Longbourn, but never reaching a particular destination. It was nature he admired, and he was content to occasionally wander rather aimlessly, getting lost and showing up hours later with a coat torn by thorns. And Jane would say, "Oh *Charles*," in such an adorable way that it would make any following admonishments worth it. But he was very determined to inspect every inch of his property now that he was considering relinquishing it.

Sisterly affection had not waned with marriage, and Jane and Elizabeth corresponded to such an extent that the post bin was always full. Jane missed her sister even more since the Darcys' visit and recent departure. Mr. Darcy, who was like a bird in his nest at Pemberley, content never to leave if he did not have to, could not be coaxed from his roost for a full six months, and then only to visit the Bingleys. As much as he liked Netherfield, Bingley was not ready to rule out the rest of England as being bereft of suitable places to live. In fact, with the renovations done for his purchase, Netherfield's worth had increased considerably, and there were buyers at the ready to his advantage. He had a list of places closer to Pemberley, but this was not something to be done in haste, not when he was uneager to rock the calm waters at home. Jane was open and even eager to the idea, but it was something to be done with great care, and they both knew that, so it was not a topic that was discussed with any immediacy.

His only immediate concern at the moment was getting back to his manor, now with an overcoat thoroughly soaked by morning dew. Despite the fact that breakfast was on the table, Jane was not downstairs, and when he inquired as to why this was, the maid merely bowed.

Always one to take the initiative no matter how ridiculous it made him look, he leapt up the stairs and knocked on her door. "Jane?"

To his surprise, Jane's attendant answered the door, looking proper but out of sorts. "I'm sorry, Mr. Bingley, but the mistress is not available."

"Not available?" He blinked and tried to imagine why. "Is she ill?"

"Only in a very minor way, sir," she said, apparently knowing the words "Jane" and "ill" would immediately send him into full panic mode. "I will ask her if she wants a visitor."

"Has someone sent for a doctor?"

"It may not be necessary."

"Necessary! A doctor must be sent for right away! And not some Meryton quack. Town!"

The maid rolled her eyes and disappeared back into the bedchamber, shutting the door behind her. Bingley turned to his manservant who had the good sense to appear immediately and listen to his careful instructions. By the time Bingley was finished, the door reopened, and to his surprise, it was in fact the housekeeper, Mrs. Eddings, who curtseyed to Bingley and shuffled out.

"Jane?" he called as he entered, and found her on the chaise, sitting straight up and looking very pale. There was an empty bucket beside her. "Jane!" he practically shouted, and rushed to her side. "Are you all right?"

"I am better," she said. "It is nothing serious. I was ill, and now I feel better." She leaned on his shoulder as he sat down next to her, wrapping an arm across her shoulders.

"Was it something you ate?"

"That was my inclination—about a week ago."

"This has been going on for a week?" *How did I not notice it?* was the greater question. He was a terrible husband, filled with guilt not to notice an ongoing illness.

"It is only in the morning, and you are often out."

"Then I will not be out anymore. I have sent for a doctor from Town."

She smiled, but it was an odd sort of smile, and took his hand. "Mrs. Eddings has informed me that it will not be necessary."

"So you are fully recovered? To be plain, you do not look it. You are obviously in much distress, and I will not have it."

"Charles," she said very slowly and carefully, as if he were a child. "I am not ill. I am pregnant."

To this, he had nothing immediate to say. All of his mental energy was taken up by gaping. Jane very politely closed his hanging mouth and kissed him on the cheek. "I would prefer a doctor to confirm it, though, but evidently this illness is the first sign—that and the lack of a certain feminine affliction when it was due." She looked at him oddly, "Charles, say something."

Apparently he had to, but first he had to break himself from his shocked stupor. "P-pregnant?"

"Yes."

Pregnant, with child—it meant a confinement, and with heaven's help, a baby in . . . the early spring, maybe late winter. A child, a Bingley heir, to welcome into their lives. His life complete, as if he were not happy enough with Jane. He laughed with joy. "It's wonderful. Jane, it's so wonderful." He was not sure whether he was referring to this new prospect or to life in general.

"Should I ring the bell?" he asked, wiping his tears, realising now he was uncertain what propriety called for in the case of announcing a pregnancy. Confinement, yes, he was familiar enough with, but should they wait?

"Perhaps not until the doctor has come, if he is coming anyway. And I would prefer to not have everyone treating me like fine china just yet," Jane admitted. "But I must write to Lizzy."

"Perhaps you will give her leave to tell Darcy herself, as I have just posted to him earlier this morning, when I did not have this wonderful news."

"Of course, dearest," she said, and kissed him on the cheek. Yes, she would be the one to tell Darcy, and Bingley would be content to quietly bask in his accomplishment until he saw Darcy next—something he was definitely looking forward to.

When the postman finally arrived at Pemberley, he was nervous. Mr. Darcy was rather benevolent for a landlord, but even he was not necessarily about to excuse a considerable delay, no matter how bad the rains. Fortunately for him, the master of Pemberley was rather distracted by other business and merely took the considerable stack of mail and disappeared with it.

Mr. Darcy headed into his study and was not the least bit surprised to see Elizabeth at his desk, no doubt composing a letter to her sister or to Georgiana. One day Elizabeth had apparently decided that, when it was vacant, his writing station was the most preferable one in the house. The only way to solve this was of course to get her one of comparable size and expense, as— even though she had said nothing—she would not be satisfied by a simple feminine writing desk. If the servants had anything to say about the usurpation of his sacred male temple of business, they did a good job of keeping it beyond his ears.

"The post has finally arrived," he announced, and set it down across from her on the desk. The stack was considerable. Elizabeth looked up and stopped writing as he began to sort it. "Mostly business letters . . . business . . . business . . .

Netherfield." He passed it to her, and she immediately opened it and went to reading the several-page letter from her sister. "Oh, and Longbourn."

"Mother's handwriting or Father's?"

"Mrs. Bennet."

"Oh," she said without looking up from her letter. "It must be her monthly enquiry to see if I am yet pregnant. Will you do me the favour of writing her a quick response that I am and that she should stop asking?"

"Anything you—*what?*"

"Yes," she said with a nonchalance he thought only *he* was capable of. "I am with child. This will please her to no end, especially if it is a boy."

He was stuck in place, holding the letter from Mrs. Bennet, his mouth frozen for some time before he could say, "How long have you known?"

"It was confirmed a few days ago—the nurse who visited briefly?"

He puffed himself up with considerable partially mocking disgust. "And *this* is how you chose to tell me?"

"I did deliberate over it for some time about the best way and then decided that if I am to suffer nearly a year of sore muscles, stomach pains, and ballooning to a bovine, then I should at least have the pleasure of seeing that adorably miffed look upon your face just once more."

Her voice was perfectly serious and dismissive, the exact way she obviously wanted it, and when he realised the joke was on him, the tension fell away from him, and he ran around the desk and picked up his wife, twirling her around. "You will drive me to Bedlam!"

"And then I will have Pemberley and Derbyshire all to myself! My plan all along! Oh no, you have discovered it!" She kissed him. "But please, as much as I do love you holding me, another twirl and I will be ill—which is *your* fault."

"I thought it was those bad clams I insisted on you trying."

"For two weeks?"

"Perhaps I am not the most observant husband."

She kissed him again. "You will do."

She giddily returned to her letter, and he went back to the pile of mail, opening the letter from Mrs. Bennet and composing a hasty reply. He was only interrupted from his assignment when Elizabeth said, "Oh!"

"What?"

"It seems I am in good company, as Jane is also expecting."

"Wonderful news!" he said, and then thought on the matter. "Did she give a date for her confinement?"

"She estimates it should begin sometime after New Year's. Why?"

"And the date for your confinement would be—"

"Sometime after New Year's."

He bit his lip. "So, we don't actually know who—"

"Darcy! It is not a competition!"

"No!" he said appropriately quickly. "No, of course it is not." And he returned hastily to the letter to give the appearance of his mind being on other things.

"Darcy," Elizabeth said as he stamped the wax on the letter to his mother-in-law, "there is a package beneath the other letters."

"Really? I did not notice it." He returned to the desk and tossed the other post aside. The reason the pile was so high was that at the bottom lay a small package sealed with string, small in size and weight but bigger than an envelope. "It is from Bingley." It said Netherfield, but he recognised the script. "The knife in the drawer on your left, if you would." She handed it to him, and he cut loose the strings and removed the wrapping paper to reveal a dusty brown book.

"What is it?"

"I don't know." He frowned and read the title, "*The Ananga Ranga*." At the bottom was printed in tiny letters, "Translation by M. L. Watts."

"Bless you."

"That is the title." He opened it and found a note from Bingley.

Dear Darcy,

I apologise for the delay in returning your considerable favour, but it took me some great time to locate a book that would be even remotely comparable to the one you have provided me with. I do not know much about it, but I did peruse it when it arrived with the East Indian shipment, and suffice to say, you may be the only man in England who owns it. I apologise for a lack of illustrations, but this was the only English edition I could find.

CB

He did not need to open past the table of contents to know precisely the nature of the book.

"Pray, what is it?"

Very calmly and with the best monotone he could muster, he told his wife as he put the book behind his back, "Merely a book on shipping I have been inquiring about. The title is a bunch of nautical terms, I believe."

"Oh," Elizabeth said. Yes, he was in the clear! With his letter to Longbourn finished, he took his leave to post it. He was halfway out the door when she said, "You are lying to me. This may make me very annoyed, which would be bad for the baby. Surely you know that."

In the doorway, Darcy silently cursed then turned around and put on his best smile. "You know me too well."

Elizabeth merely crossed her arms in expectation.

"It is really noth—"

"The book, Darcy."

"I could not betray Mr. Bingley's confidence."

"So he told you in the letter not to mention a word about this to me on pain of death? What does it contain, an entire sordid history of his own family? Surely they would not bind that and give it such an obscure name. Anyway, if you are just to put it in the library, then I will eventually find it."

"I will not put it in the library," he responded.

"Then you will put it in the false bottom of this locked drawer." She motioned to her right. "The one with the lock that matches the key you keep in the dresser by the bed stand?"

Very few people could render Darcy speechless. Elizabeth was one of them. No, in fact, she was the only one. Unfortunately, he had married her. "You have me at your mercy," he said at last.

"Then give me the book."

"Allow me at least to read it first."

"Fine. I will wait in the drawing room while you peruse it."

He sighed and decided it was time to give up this game. "Very well." He placed it on the desk before her, and she scooped it up with entirely too much interest.

Elizabeth Darcy put her hand over her mouth to hide her expression. She had, it seemed, some propriety left. "My goodness."

"I cannot account for—"

She slammed the book shut. "You do not need to account for it." With that, she stood up, taking the book and the letter from Jane with her. "If you need me, I will be in the library." And with a quick kiss on his cheek she added, "Reading."

To this, he could form no proper response before she was gone.

THE VISITOR

As December approached, the Pemberley staff was at the appropriate frantic level of anticipation. Only their master seemed particularly calm, probably because he had the natural ability to seem calm in any situation whatsoever, except perhaps a military invasion or someone tying his cravat wrong. There was no amount of guessing (or betting) on the part of the servants as to how he would act toward the end of his wife's first confinement, as the only time he showed his true emotions was around his wife or his sister, and the former was burdened with producing the heir to Pemberley.

At the moment, that was not Elizabeth's chief concern (though it hardly truly left her mind for a moment). She had to assemble a guest list, and as mistress of Pemberley, it had to be done with a ridiculous amount of care. She was surprised then when Darcy, avoiding eye contact by staring out the window as he said it, casually asked that she invite the Wickham family—husband, wife, and relatively newborn son.

When queried on this, he replied, "It's the proper thing to do, and I know he won't come." To this, he left no explanation and quickly exited the room.

In his infinite wisdom, Mr. Darcy was not wrong. The Wickhams returned post with the message that they were embedded at Newcastle and would decline the invitation. Elizabeth was sure she saw her husband give one of his quiet smirks at the news.

The list needed careful consideration this year, as it involved two wives very near entering confinement, and so was restricted to their very extensive families. Lady Catherine immediately sent her refusal, and it was regrettable only that they could see no way to invite cousin Anne de Bourgh away from her home on Christmas under any pretence. Though Darcy did not mourn the loss of Mr. Collins as a guest, he was aware that Elizabeth did feel the loss of any acquaintance with Mrs. Collins, now that all relations with Rosings were for the most part hopelessly severed. "It will not do to lose your relationship with your aunt," Elizabeth said. "I mean, you may do as you choose, but I will not suffer the loss of Charlotte as a friend."

"And I will not suffer the loss of Anne as a friend."

She looked at him incredulously. "Anne de Bourgh? Your former betrothed? Whom you refused? We speak of the same person, correct?"

"Correct. That does not mean she is nothing to me. In fact, our refusal of my aunt's intentions was mutual, and she has been a great friend to Georgiana. I would be honoured if you would take some time to write to her. We could send it with my sister's letter, as we did for the wedding."

She looked at him as if she could not believe it, but his face was perfectly amiable, and he was never known to lie. "Very well, I shall happily write to her, and perhaps she can find an excuse to be in Derbyshire in the spring."

"The weather here is known to be quite relieving to the body," he said. And the matter was settled.

Their first guest arrived a week early, to their great surprise but also to their great delight.

Mr. Bennet had weathered over a year without visiting his favourite daughter. He did delight in her company when they came to see the Bingleys at Netherfield, but with all of the commotion and the brevity of the visit, Mr. Bennet felt that he rarely had a proper moment with Elizabeth. He resolved that he must visit Pemberley but put it off.

At first it was merely to give the newlyweds their proper privacy, though the rumours were that the estate was so vast that they would have no problem avoiding anything if they so chose, while he had at Longbourn only his study as a sanctuary. Then the weather chilled, and his wife protested for his health. At first he found this odd, as with their financial situation secure, his death would no longer be the disastrous event that had so long been her worry. At the fourth or fifth protest at his suggestion of visiting Derbyshire, he looked more carefully at his wife of nearly five and twenty years and, after much consideration, decided that there was a slim chance that she was *actually* concerned for his person— as a *person*. He did not mention this to her, for as much as she talked about herself, she did not care much to be talked *of*.

He did, however, smile.

This bizarre state held him in Longbourn until he at last gave in and gave his wife and daughters permission to go to Brighton, with the explicit understanding that Mrs. Bennet would be the most diligent chaperone. "I have learned *that* lesson, Mr. Bennet," she said. He even convinced Mary to go, taking great pains to tell her of the spectacular scenery that might be observed in the area, so that he might be at his leave to appear at Pemberley before the official arrival date. He had a great desire to see the place in some privacy first, but this involved getting his remaining daughters out of the house so that he might secretly vacate it, and the task took him nearly a month to arrange.

It was late in the first week of December that he finally got in a carriage and took the long trip to Derbyshire, farther north than he had travelled in a great number of years. He was very sick of trees and fields—that was, until he reached Derbyshire. "Quite a lovely place," he admitted to himself when they stopped for lunch.

That was until he saw Pemberley.

"My goodness," he said as it came into view, with its reflecting pool and great columns. Even far away from the entrance, he took off his hat as if he were entering church. He had yet to see the new Bingley estate at Chatton Hall, but he had a notion that nothing would compare to this. "Well, well, Lizzy, you have done well for yourself."

If Mr. Bennet were a man to be cowed, the great halls of Pemberley would have rendered him speechless. He was not, however, that sort of man, though there was a significant hesitation to his step as he entered and had his walking stick and hat taken by the servants. He was approached by a servant. "May I help you, sir?"

"I am here to see Mrs. Darcy, though I prefer to be unannounced, if she is in the mood to be interrupted from whatever business she has as mistress of Pemberley"—as it was midafternoon as he'd planned it, and she was well with child. "That is, if she would see her father."

The servant blanched and then said he would make haste to find her, and would he mind sitting in the drawing room until she was located? Of course he wouldn't, because the "drawing room" was probably, by his rough estimation, larger than half of Longbourn and its shelves filled with so many books that he could hardly imagine the actual library's collection. "I definitely should have intruded earlier," he muttered, glancing at the titles.

He did not have to wait very long. The doors opened, and before she could be announced, Mrs. Darcy scampered into the room like a little girl—even though she was certainly no longer dressed like one—and immediately embraced her father. "Oh, Papa!"

"Lizzy," he said, though having some difficulty, partially because of his emotions at seeing her and partially because there was much more of her to hold. She was, to everyone's estimate, in her sixth month, and while not yet overburdened, she was undeniably pregnant when she removed her shawl. He kissed her and then withdrew from the embrace, but not from holding her hands. "You look splendid." In fact, she looked positively astounding, considering her particular burden. All of his fears—however irrational—about her interest in her marriage to the aloof Mr. Darcy were quickly dissolved entirely in his mind. He could have chalked up her visit to Netherfield as just excitement about seeing her family, but here at Pemberley she was still more radiant than on her wedding day, the look of a woman most happy in her present situation. "I am very sorry to intrude—"

"You do not look very sorry," she chided. "I see you came alone."

"Your mother and sisters are in Brighton, admiring all the officers from a very respectable distance. At least a foot, I told them, though I have no idea if they will abide by it. I would have said at least thirty feet and bought your mother a pair of looking glasses, but she would not have it. They will arrive closer to the holiday, though I challenge even Mrs. Bennet and Kitty to fill these immense hallways with their squalling."

"You are being ungenerous," she said, her voice thoroughly mocking. "Oh, but I did not think to have someone call for my husband because I rushed to you."

"I imagine there is someone around here who has thought of it, what with the massive retinue of Mr. Darcy. If His Majesty has any desire to invade the Continent and has need of stout men, he has only to call on Pemberley." He tugged her hand. "But seriously, Lizzy, unless you are better at trickery than I know you to be, I assume Darcy has made you quite a happy woman."

"Indeed, he has," was all she could say before the subject of discussion entered the room. "I'm so glad someone found you."

"Mr. Bennet," Darcy said, bowing to his father-in-law.

"Mr. Darcy." Mr. Bennet returned the gesture but could not help but recall, without an inward chuckle, about the night before his wedding when he had been in such an intimate setting with Mr. Darcy; the poor man was drunkenly ill. Now his son-in-law was all smiles—and not just the quiet, subtle smiles he would sneak across the table at Elizabeth when he was sure no one else was watching during their engagement. Marriage had obviously been very good to him. "I apologise for my intrusion into your privacy."

"Not at all. In fact, we were wondering when you might be venturing north for several months now. I hope you find Pemberley to your liking."

"I find nothing that anyone could ever dislike."

"I am relieved to hear it." Where was the proud Darcy who cared nothing for the approval of those decidedly below his station? Perhaps Elizabeth had merely married a different man with the same name. "If you will excuse me, I have a most pressing matter with my steward, and I assume that you wish more time with your daughter. I will see you at dinner, Mr. Bennet." He turned to his wife. "Remember about the gardens, if you would."

"If my father wishes to see the gardens of Pemberley on this mild afternoon, I would be a most discourteous daughter not to guide him."

"Lizzy, I would rather have you a discourteous daughter than a discourteous mother, and *you know it*," Darcy said in a whisper, perhaps imagining Mr. Bennet was hard of hearing.

"Mr. Darcy," Mr. Bennet said, having no intention of being left out of the fun, "I must confess to you right now that the only time a Bennet ever intentionally sabotaged another Bennet's health was in not providing Jane with a carriage when it was raining and she was invited to some great estate in Hertfordshire, and the outcome was most advantageous to us all. Still, I will not try the master of Pemberley's patience."

"That is my job, Papa," Elizabeth chimed in, but she did lean in and kiss her husband on the cheek before he bowed and took his leave.

They were alone again, and Mr. Bennet did not hesitate to venture, "You were absolutely correct, Lizzy. You are both so ridiculously stubborn that somehow you are a perfect match. I assume this garden business was he being overprotective of your condition."

"To his credit, it *is* winter, but we have had many mild days." She tightened her grip on his hand. "But I think you have had enough scenery for a while and would prefer to remain indoors. And there is so much to discuss. Come, let us repair to the parlour."

"I'm not sure how far away this parlour is and if I am well enough to make it to it," he said. "Please tell me it is under two miles."

"Papa!"

"You know I am only poking fun at how well a sworn spinster who considered herself too stubborn ever to attract a man has done so well for herself. Quite the reverse of conventional wisdom, but then again, when have you ever been conventional?"

"I will take that as a compliment."

They did make it to the parlour, despite Mr. Bennet's jokes, where they were practically assaulted by servants ready with tea for the esteemed father of Mrs. Darcy. Mr. Bennet found himself in a state of perpetual self-amusement at the whole proceeding.

"How is the family? I have not written enough, I know."

"I must confess, I am somewhat surprised by the changes at Longbourn," he said. "Though I do miss you and Jane every day, your mother's countenance has . . . almost returned to normal."

She looked legitimately confused. "Whatever do you mean?"

"You do not mean to imply that I married a fluttering imbecile with a chronic nerve condition? No, I confess I had almost forgotten it myself that she underwent a particular transformation when Jane came out, and suddenly she had the daunting prospect of five marriageable daughters who were in desperate need of prospects. And seeing as how I was only a very reluctant aid in the matter, so attached to you all as I was, it is amazing that she accomplished so much in so little time." He did not give her time to comment before continuing. "Kitty is doing well, though still quite silly, but in that endearing way that some officer will no doubt find amusing. And having learned that lesson, we will make sure to check his gambling debts before agreeing to see her have a moment alone with him."

"And Mary?"

"Yes, Mary, who is usually complacent with her books, has asked of me that she be sent to study on the Continent. I feel almost compelled to oblige her in the fall. Surely then she will fall for some scholar who is as good at giving unrequested sermons as she is, and they will spend a happy life amusing themselves at the dinner table by talking about proper manners and the severity of life." He sipped his tea. "I find myself oddly at ease with my existence now, minus the absence of my favourite daughter. Fortunately, I believe she is with child, and that will give me a tremendous excuse to dally by her side for her confinement, if her stubborn husband would permit it."

She smiled slyly at him, "But Bingley is not stubborn at all!"

"Now you intend to mock me, though I say I do enjoy it more than when any other relation does it. So I will let it pass.

I have no idea how you will settle the matter of the confine-ment. Mr. Bingley could have hardly moved all the way up here just to separate his wife from her sister for three months."

"My husband and Mr. Bingley are in an argument about it."

"An argument, you say?"

Lizzy smiled again. "Not an *argument*, proper—more of a gentlemanly game of theirs. We have yet to inform them that they have no say in the matter, and Jane and I will decide at New Year's, and that will be that."

"So you have completely and utterly conquered your hus-bands. I see your mother has trained you well."

"Are you joking? Every correspondence I have had with her since the wedding has told me of my wifely duties and that I must be entirely obliging to my husband's every whim and desire. Does she expect me to be only a combination of a maidservant and breeder?"

He set his teacup down with some ceremony. "I have given some thought to the matter, and considering that Darcy has five times my income, you are required to produce no less than five and twenty children—all daughters, of course."

"Now you are deliberately trying to tease me!"

"I have always said," he laughed, "that of all my daughters, you had the quickest wit and perception, and you have never proven me wrong."

Dinner was a peaceful but splendid affair, and though in front of the servants Darcy was more reserved, he was still the welcoming gentleman that he had been in the parlour earlier. To

Elizabeth he was expressive enough, and that was Mr. Bennet's chief concern, which was much abated now. It was only when he briefly disappeared to attend to something that Mr. Bennet remarked, "I must say that my son is a rather puzzling sort of man in the way he presents himself. It is not at all consistent."

"It is not a matter of pride at all," she said. "I have come to the conclusion that he is extremely shy."

"A man is never shy, Lizzy—certainly not one of his standing."

She giggled but tried to stifle it. "I was trying to be polite. I think he is merely . . . I do not know the term. I will have to stand on *shy*." She lowered her voice further. "He does not find company easy to bear if he does not have a keen interest in them. I do think this is a failing on his part as much as it is something instinctive."

"Well, that he has a *keen interest* in you is, I suppose, all that matters," he said with a smile.

To this, she could only blush in reply.

CHRISTMAS AT PEMBERLEY

As CHRISTMAS ARRIVED, so did the Darcys' guests. Georgiana returned from Town first, followed quickly by the three Bennets from Brighton. "Oh! Oh my dear Mr. Bennet!" his wife said, and Mr. Darcy instantly insisted that the very qualified Mrs. Reynolds give his mother-in-law a grand tour of all nine and fifty rooms of Pemberley, and that Mrs. Bennet be given ample time in each room to say whatever she pleased and inquire after the expense of every single piece of furniture to her heart's content. Fortunately, he had already given Mrs. Reynolds a sizeable Christmas bonus, so all was well, and Mrs. Bennet was gone into the deep lairs of Pemberley for almost an entire day.

Colonel Fitzwilliam returned from his business in the north and was happily greeted by both his cousins and Elizabeth. The Gardiners were delayed in Lambton by the weather only for a day before making their appearance. It was, in fact, the Bingleys who appeared last, having the least distance to travel and so weather and delays were no concern, but as usual, Mr. Bingley was all concerns for his wife's health to such an extent in his various posts that it came as a surprise to everyone when she appeared at the door looking well and full of colour. With him came his sisters and brother, happy as always to be at Pemberley no matter who was on the guest list—or if they had any objection, they hid it well.

Diversions were many in the vast halls of Pemberley, and it was actually a while after the first dinner that Colonel Fitzwilliam finally caught Bingley and Darcy in the billiards room, temporarily escaping their guests. They were happy to let him join their game. "So," he said casually, "I have heard some speculation concerning the delicate matter—if I may be so bold—of the location of confinement."

"The matter remains . . . unsettled," Bingley said.

"Don't be ridiculous, Bingley," Darcy said. "Fitzwilliam, we've already decided to settle the matter in the most gentlemanly way possible."

"So, you mean, some sort of contest," he surmised.

"Precisely," said Darcy. "By duelling. Rapiers, shall it be?"

Bingley gave his friend and brother a horrified look. "I agreed to no such thing! You know I would lose horribly. You are not making the slightest attempt to be fair." Straightening his waistcoat, he added, "It shall be shooting."

Colonel Fitzwilliam raised his eyebrows. "Red eight in the side pocket. You know, Darcy is very good at shooting. It would be a close match."

"I have been practising," Darcy said confidently.

"Very well then—dancing!"

"Surely not!" Darcy replied. "Chess."

"Sewing."

"Riding."

"First proposal."

"First *attempted* proposal."

"Drinking contest," Bingley said keenly.

Darcy raised an eyebrow. "Height."

"I do believe Jane is taller than Elizabeth."

"Only if she stands on her toes!"

"Good God," Fitzwilliam said. "You're like children! Why don't you just flip a coin like decent men? Or better yet, let your wives decide?"

"Don't be ridiculous," Darcy replied. "We will decide as men and then return to our wives, who will promptly ignore us and announce their own decision, which was probably made months ago—but still, propriety must be maintained."

"You mean your *egos* must be maintained," his cousin replied. "Despite your obvious respective marital bliss, I fear I must endeavour to find a more complying wife."

"My sister is out of the question, then," Bingley said, to everyone's surprise. "What? I was merely stating the obvious."

"It seems marriage has given you a spine," Darcy said.

"And destroyed yours."

Fitzwilliam sighed and put his pool cue down. "Darcy, I spent most of my childhood keeping you and Wickham from each other's throats. However good natured your relationship with Bingley may be, I will not spend my adulthood doing the same thing with another person."

"Fine, fine, a coin it shall be. Does anyone have a sovereign?"

Fitzwilliam produced a coin, and Bingley took it from him. "Heads, Pemberley. Tails, Chatton."

"Agreed."

He flipped it and covered it with his hand. Before the outcome could be revealed, however, there was a rough banging at the door. "Darcy!" It was undoubtedly Mrs. Darcy. "What have you done now?"

Darcy shushed him with a look and opened the door. "Darling—"

Elizabeth crossed him and entered the gentlemen's sanctuary, her hands on her hips, and stood before Darcy and Bingley. "Did you or did you not make a bet on who would deliver first?"

"No."

"No," Bingley backed him up.

"Of course not."

"Never."

Elizabeth gave her husband a look of smouldering rage.

"A small bet."

"Very small," said Bingley.

"A few pence."

"Very few."

"Nothing significant."

"Ten pence."

"Maybe a pound . . . at most . . . absolute most."

Elizabeth focused her intense eyes on Bingley.

Finally he croaked out, "Maybe four . . . f-five pounds?"

She turned back to Darcy.

"It really was five pounds," he said in a voice that could not be denied as truthful. "That is all."

"Four."

"Stop lying to her, Bingley. It's not worth it." He approached his wife and cupped her cheek. "Dearest—"

"There will be no such bet," she said, but her voice was softening.

"Of course not," he said, and kissed her on the forehead in an unusual display of affection for Darcy in front of other gentlemen, even his relatives.

"All right, I will leave you to your game," she said, apparently much relieved. "Oh, and the confinements will take place at Pemberley. Sorry, Mr. Bingley."

"Quite all right," he assured her, waving as she closed the door behind her.

As soon as she was gone, Darcy said, "I do adore the Gardiners, but it is perfectly clear that I cannot trust them with a secret."

"Indeed," said Bingley.

Jane had long retired when Bingley made his way into her bedchamber. In theory, he had his own adjoining one, but it was not in his habit to use it when unnecessary. In fact, she was soundly asleep. Jane liked to sleep on her stomach, but in recent months, that had become increasingly difficult and against the midwife's advice. He took great care at sliding into bed next to her, keeping a respectful distance so as not to wake her. Falling asleep after a long night and a few glasses of port was not exceptionally difficult.

He did wake several hours later, as would happen occasionally in the night, especially after some alcohol. He woke to find

Jane partially on her side, leaning her head on his shoulder. Her movement indicated that she was not entirely asleep, and he kissed her gently to see if this would elicit some response. She did smile but squirmed uncomfortably.

"Is everything all right?"

"'Tis nothing." When she realised that wouldn't satisfy him, she added, "My feet are a bit sore."

Without hesitation or request, he wandered down to the foot of the bed and began to rub them. Her ankles were swollen, which he supposed was not to be unexpected.

"Mmm . . . how do you always know exactly what to do, husband?"

"I am a good guesser."

Jane gave a contented sigh. "You're not upset that we chose Pemberley, are you?"

"It is the most logical choice," he said. "And with our absence, they can do the renovations."

"Chatton is suitable as it stands. We have had this conversation."

"It could be better. It should be perfect."

She didn't seem in the mood to argue with him, but then again, she never did.

When Darcy, with all of his hosting duties, finally slid into bed, he was a bit drunker than he wanted to be but certainly not tumbling over. He crawled in next to Elizabeth and kissed her softly on the cheek before turning on his own pillow. So far, minus abstentions for periods of indisposition and his being out of Derbyshire on business, they had not missed a night of marital pleasure. She was asleep and probably exhausted, and he was very eager to be the same (the former at least). He was nearly there when he felt the tremors of Elizabeth wiggling her toes and turning over to face him—a considerable feat on her part at this point in her condition.

"Yes, darling?" he mumbled.

"Five pounds."

He put the pillow over his head.

"Is that really all I'm worth to you? Five pounds?"

Darcy blinked and removed the pillow. "I am confused. Are you unhappy with the betting itself or do you want me to bet more? Because they are contradictory notions."

"I was just wondering how you came to the decision of five pounds—how the number value was reached."

"We felt compelled not to exceed it," he said, "lest our wives discover us." He looked over his shoulder, and Elizabeth's look in the light from the fire was not total disapproval. In fact, she looked amused. "What?"

"I find it rather silly," she said. "Men and your need for cockfights."

It took Darcy a considerable moment to decide whether he wanted to interpret her usage of the noun with its obvious intention or with the proper definition. "Now I think you're just insulting me."

"Well, someone has to knock you off your high horse."

"No more animal allusions! Please!" He buried himself in his pillow, but Elizabeth was giggling. "One man can only take so much."

"And my father has taken a great deal more than you. You should consider yourself lucky."

"I will not for long if you continue to torment me as such!"

"Really? Have I been so terrible a wife to you?" She ran her finger along his backside. "I must say these past months must have been positively dreadful for you."

He turned over to face her. "*Absolutely* dreadful." And he kissed her. Perhaps the conventional midwife would have some objection to their continued dalliances, but if they were to have this conversation with her, they had not one but *two* sources to back up their assertions that everything would be quite all right.

The celebrations on Christmas Eve could not have been more perfectly planned according to Pemberley's guests, and many congratulations went to Elizabeth, who took them with gratitude but felt that they were undeserved. There were many toasts to everyone's health and happiness (and a certain two people's health and happiness *especially*). Mary Bennet thought spirits made one loose of tongue (and no one was willing to contradict her), and Mr. Darcy, as was his custom, stopped at the first glass. The Gardiner children ran to and fro along the long table, and no one felt compelled to stop them for the sake of decorum, as it was Christmas Eve and everyone seemed to be in a particularly delightful mood.

There was much after-dinner entertainment in the parlour, and fortunately, Mary's pianoforte abilities had much improved in a calmer Longbourn setting. She was happy to play a duet with Georgiana. Mr. Darcy was briefly seen, by those who were inclined to be eavesdroppers, arguing with his wife in the hallway, not about whether she was to play, but whether she should retire immediately out of concern for her health.

"Is this to be my last social engagement? Then surely you will *allow me* Christmas." And she said *allow me* with every indication that she was not inclined to let him have his proper husbandly say in the matter, however inclined he was to give it.

"Elizabeth—"

"I am perfectly well, Mr. Darcy."

He scowled but said nothing when she rejoined her guests.

Someone else was scowling on the other side of the door. "She should not aggravate her husband so!" Mrs. Bennet said.

"I don't know how you have not observed this," Mr. Bennet said in a hushed voice, "but I do believe it is the entire foundation for their very stable and loving marriage, so I am not inclined to give any advice that might dissuade it."

"Oh, Mr. Bennet!" and she swatted him, but very playfully, and he smiled and took her by the arm.

Though celebrations continued into the night, Mrs. Darcy and Mrs. Bingley did respectfully retire, not so much at their husband's inclinations as their own. Mrs. Gardiner put her overexcited children to bed, and eventually the company whittled down to the Bingley sisters playing cards and the various gentlemen of strong countenances. Darcy, as host, was obligated to remain with his guests, though he did make no less than two trips upstairs to check on his wife. Eventually the gentlemen retired to the smoking room where Mr. Hurst partook of a large cigar and not his first brandy of the night.

"And how is Mrs. Darcy?" Mr. Bennet asked, because he was not afraid of the intimidating figure of a very private Mr. Darcy, now considerably less at ease without his wife by his side.

"Resting," he said, hoping that would suit his father-in-law.

"Delightful evening," Mr. Hurst said from his position slumped in the lounge chair—for him, a rare compliment.

"Indeed," said Bingley, raising his glass and looking at the grandfather clock. "I believe it is the hour at last. Happy Christmas!"

"Happy Christmas," they said, raising their glasses, except for Darcy who looked out the window and was very content to do so until approached by Mr. Gardiner.

"No white Christmas for us this year, hmm? I suppose it does not matter."

"It rarely snows this early in the season," Darcy said, a long sentence for him, even in good company.

"Well, it has certainly been a delightful evening, I must say. Thank you for your hospitality, Mr. Darcy. Especially considering—"

"Yes," he interrupted. He liked his new uncle well enough, but that did not mean he wanted the matter to go any further. Something of a suspicious tremor was crawling up his back, making him less sociable than he wanted to be with his relatives, some of whom he was actually quite fond of. Maybe this would be a good time to check on Lizzy again.

"If I may be so bold, Mr. Darcy," Mr. Gardiner continued in that very pleasing way of his, which was no great comfort to Darcy, "as this may be one of the last times we could corner you—"

And Darcy suddenly realised in that room he *was cornered.*

"I know you are inclined to be to the point about things, so I will indulge you and do the same. You are about to enter, God willing, into fatherhood, something that requires much care."

Oh God. Where was his ability to curse this man with the legendary Darcy stare of indifference? Why was it failing him now? "And?"

"Having some experience on the matter, if I could, perhaps, offer some advice—"

Darcy looked at Mr. Bennet, who actually stood up and seemed to be joining Mr. Gardiner in this well-meaning but horrible endeavour. Mr. Hurst, as usual, was half conscious and would be of no use. Now desperate, Darcy turned to Bingley who was holding up two glass bottles. "Whiskey or brandy?"

Without hesitation, Darcy answered, "Both."

HEIR TO A GREAT HOUSEHOLD

NOT ONLY DID JANE and Elizabeth spend their confinements at Pemberley, but Mr. Bennet was a welcomed guest as well, even when the Bingley sisters and Mr. Hurst retired to Chatton Hall. He seemed to know when best to make himself scarce, which was easy enough in the halls of Pemberley, especially in the tremendously intimidating library. He occasionally got a letter from his wife, who had returned to Brighton and was wintering with the officers. Kitty had apparently made friends with one of the officers, this one of considerable standing and reputation, and would he be so kind as to inquire into his credentials? Of course he would. When not distracted by the marriage possibilities of one of his two remaining unmarried daughters, Mr. Bennet busied himself with a glass of brandy and a book in one of the many reading rooms, or observing his two sons fret endlessly. Bingley paced until there was some actual concern on the housekeeper's part for the carpets, which the master of the estate dismissed with an unusually reserved word. Mr. Darcy, when not with his wife, spent much time staring out the window. He was not unpleasant but unusually quiet, a bastion of reserve—so much so that Mr. Bennet commented to his daughter, "I fear if you do not deliver soon, your husband may well explode."

"Or spontaneously combust," she laughed. "And then poor Mr. Bingley will catch on fire as well, run around the house, and all Pemberley will be ablaze."

"To lose such a large house!" Jane said. "All because of the natural order of things."

"It is no surprise then that wives often outlive their husbands," Mr. Bennet said. "We have solved that great mystery at least."

It was at that point that Mr. Darcy had the misfortune to poke his head into his wife's sitting room. "What is it?" He seemed concerned at the noise.

"Nothing," Elizabeth said, making no effort to control herself. "We are merely laughing at your expense."

"Oh," he said with no particular surprise. "Well, I should hardly interrupt you, then."

"What was it?" came Bingley's voice, from somewhere down the hall.

Darcy turned back and shouted, "They were laughing at your expense, Bingley!"

"What?"

"I did not say that!" Elizabeth said in her defence.

"Yes, but if it distracts him for at least five minutes, it will be worth the deception," Darcy said with a smile as Bingley crashed his way into the room.

"What did I do?" he demanded breathlessly, and his wife merely bade him to come over and kissed him on the cheek, which required quite a bit of bending over and manoeuvring on his part around her considerable girth.

"Nothing, Charles," she said, "except given me a child that is kicking rather relentlessly."

"Much like its father," Darcy said, and then ran straight out of the room to escape Bingley's exasperated ire as he followed him.

"I must admit that I have never seen two unrelated men take to being squabbling brothers so easily," Mr. Bennet observed, and his daughters could not do anything but agree.

The thaw came early in March, but Georgiana did not retire to London as usual, not only for the obvious reasons that another female influence was desperately needed around the place, but because she had to plan for her coming out. Assuming that all went well with Elizabeth's condition, the Darcys would be unable to make the London season, and so she would have to come out at a ball held at Pemberley sometime in the summer season. To this idea, Darcy was most disagreeable but not in front of his sister.

"She is seventeen," Elizabeth gently pointed out.

"She'll be seventeen when I damn well say she is!" her husband said, facing out the window in indignation. There were so many obvious reasons for his unusual outburst—stress concerning his upcoming fatherhood, his usual overprotectiveness of his sister, the fact that there had been no marital relations in two months—at which Elizabeth could only laugh in reply. Darcy was in a perpetual foul mood, and having to hide it from everyone merely made it worse.

Unfortunately, on that very day Colonel Fitzwilliam arrived.

"If he asks for a friendly duel, refuse," Elizabeth said to the colonel in private. "He nearly ran his coach through last week."

"And the reason for his discord?"

Not having any inclination to enlighten him on her husband's source of frustration—at least the one usually relieved by ferocious duelling—she merely feigned innocence in response and gave the usual reason of nerves concerning the confinement.

It was at dinner that night that Fitzwilliam broke the dual news: first, that he was affianced to Miss Anne de Bourgh, second, that she would be joining him—if permitted by the master of Pemberley—shortly in Derbyshire, for she had much desire to see her relatives. Coming with her, he pointed out, would be Mrs. Collins and her eight-month-old daughter, carrying special instructions on Anne's every care, lest the Pemberley staff be ill equipped to handle her delicate condition. (Mr. Darcy did not point out that this was hardly Anne's first trip to Pemberley.) Lady Catherine would, of course, not be journeying anywhere near Derbyshire, and Mr. Collins had his own responsibilities in his vicarage and would have to weather his wife's brief absence.

Despite his disinclination to visitors with the current state of affairs, Darcy heartily agreed and politely excused himself to tell his wife, who was no longer joining them for dinner and rarely left her chambers. (On this matter, she had relented to his considerable will and concern for her health.)

With several great carriages arrived Miss Anne de Bourgh, looking well by her own set of standards, and she was eagerly embraced by Colonel Fitzwilliam before being formally greeted by Darcy, who quickly ushered her in from the cold. Whether

Darcy had occasion yet to quiz Fitzwilliam on the nature of how this came about was anybody's guess, for he gave no indication, only a mildly approving eye. The affection between them, everyone else admitted, was obvious.

Charlotte Collins came behind her, carrying her eight-month-old daughter, Amelia Collins, whose presence was no end of delight to both confined ladies, as she was a pleasant and energetic baby, who thankfully seemed to take mainly after her mother in looks. She liked very much to have her mother hold her up and attempt to stand on her knees, as sort of play walking that as was amusing to everyone as it was fun to her. That Charlotte was beaming with motherhood brought great relief to Elizabeth, who shared this separately but privately with her sister and her husband.

"It seems I did Charlotte a great favour in rejecting Mr. Collins," she said, and to Darcy's look added, "I am surprised as you are."

"You—he—" Mr. Darcy was at a loss for words. "He made you an offer of marriage?"

"Yes. Did I not tell you? Oh no, it was before even your first proposal—shortly after the ball at Netherfield. Less heated but with considerably less regret on my part."

He merely repeated in total shock. "*He made you an offer of marriage?*"

She raised an eyebrow. "Yes, darling."

"I should run him through!"

She took hold of his balled fists. "I think you are in such a state that you would gladly run anyone through. Do not take it out on poor Mr. Collins."

"To think that—"

"I *rejected him*," she said clearly. "Without a second thought. The matter is long settled. You are just upset because you are so . . . stymied."

"What?" It took him a second to grasp her meaning. "I am *not!*"

"Yes, you *are*."

In frustration, he flung himself on the bed next to her. "Fine. Maybe. A small amount, I will grant you."

"Whatever did you do before me, husband?"

"I believe I was a proud, inconsiderate man lacking in social manners who would obsess about a woman because she had lovely eyes to the point of getting drunk and having to buy my sister the most expensive musical instrument in England to make up for it."

She raised her eyebrows. "That I cannot dispute."

He sighed and rested his head on her shoulder, facing away from her, and she stroked his hair.

"So you are expectant when? Three weeks?"

"It is not an exact science! And besides, there will be a period of indisposition afterwards!"

He put the pillow over his head and moaned.

Thinking on the matter, she said, "Surely there must be something in the book for this."

He immediately removed the pillow. "Yes! I am sure there is. I must check." And he ran out of their bedchamber with a speed she had never seen before, which brought her no end of laughter for some time.

Darcy had his head buried beneath his desk when his servant entered. "Miss Anne de Bourgh to see you, sir."

He slammed the drawer shut and picked his head up. "Oh, of course. Send her in." He immediately stood and bowed. "Miss de Bourgh."

"Mr. Darcy." She curtsied and quickly took the seat offered to her facing the desk. "Thank you for inviting me to Pemberley on such short notice."

"Think nothing of it. You are always welcome at Pemberley, especially since we are to be—" he frowned. "Double cousins?"

"I'm sure there is a proper word for it."

"I'm sure I don't know it. Nonetheless, my most firm congratulations, for I see you are very happy with this arrangement. Though I have to ask—"

"It was done not without my mother's consent. I am not to be banished from Rosings," she said. "But it was not her *idea* if that is what you are inclined to think."

"Still, it does come as some surprise. Though my cousin is a pleasant and affectionate man—"

"Who is often at Rosings—"

"And is not without social stature." He blinked. "I cannot see why it comes as much surprise to me, then. Clearly, men are somewhat blind on these matters."

"Clearly, marriage has done wonders for your insight."

He did not take it as an insult, as it was not meant as one. "And engagement has done wonders for your health." For—though it was improper to say it—this was the first time he could rightfully recall that she had some colour on her face.

"I am feeling much better these days," she said, and almost looked like she was beaming as she rose. "I will not keep you from your work." She offered her hand, and he kissed it. "I am glad we have both found happiness, even at the expense of my mother's wishes. Though, do not be surprised if we produce children of opposite gender and she proposes another infancy engagement."

"For that," he said, "she would have to get my wife to agree. And I do believe she will not find Elizabeth as agreeable as my mother on the subject."

Darcy went to great lengths to make sure his wife did not have to play hostess to so many guests, however welcome they were or happy she was to see them. He took great pains to keep the men outdoors when the weather improved, and Mr. Bennet was quite happy in the library. It was only when Mrs. Bennet and her remaining daughters arrived that he was persuaded by his wife and Mrs. Reynolds—who teamed up on him in his chambers—to give up on the matter entirely and let nature take its course. He was only willing to stray within a certain distance of the house, but that was far enough for some casual shooting, which Mr. Bingley was eager to do.

"So," said Colonel Fitzwilliam as they were reloading, "I hear that there are some plans for a ball for Georgiana."

"What, is she finally coming out?" Bingley said in his usual oblivious voice.

"She'll come out when I'm cold in my grave," Darcy said without looking at either of them, which Bingley took most severely and Fitzwilliam only took with a laugh.

"I am her guardian, too, and I consent to it. She is seventeen, Darcy."

"But you are not her brother; therefore, I overrule you."

"Hmm, that is true. Perhaps I will ask Mrs. Darcy her opinion on the matter."

"If you are thinking of having her enter a conspiracy against me on this subject, I will have to run you through at our next fencing match," Darcy casually replied.

"Surely you would not do that and make Anne suffer so."

Darcy growled. "You have caught me."

Fitzwilliam jovially turned to Bingley. "We should have a celebration for this, for the master of Pemberley is so rarely caught."

"He's like a wild bird."

"When did I become a source of amusement for everyone?" Darcy asked.

"Since you've been managing your wife's confinement worse than she does," Fitzwilliam answered.

Bingley added, "That's because he hasn't found chapter three and twenty yet."

"What?"

But before Bingley could enlighten Fitzwilliam, Darcy was charging at him like a wild boar, various curses coming out his mouth as he chased him all the way around the stately home of Pemberley.

Whether Jane was merely early and Elizabeth late was never determined, but Mrs. Bingley delivered a healthy baby girl a full two weeks before her sister, ending her confinement—and making Mr. Darcy five pounds poorer. There were no great theatrics on Bingley's part when presented with his daughter, as his father-in-law held him firmly in his chair by both shoulders. Elizabeth later remarked in privacy to her sister that it was Darcy who looked the palest of them all. As to naming the child "Elizabeth," Mr. Bennet objected soundly, saying his old brain would be much befuddled by the confusion despite their considerable age and height differences. And if the two great families weren't united enough, Bingley mildly said, "I've always liked the name Georgiana." His wife agreed, and so she was christened, and everyone immediately took to calling her Georgie.

Bingley did not benefit much from the bet and the result of the financial transaction, for despite their intense secrecy, Elizabeth immediately demanded that the funds be donated to a local poorhouse, and both husbands decided to be obliging. In fact, when Geoffrey Darcy—named after his paternal grandfather—was born two weeks later, Darcy and Bingley got into a sort of competition of piety about local donations to the point where the house manager was exasperated at the repeated appearances of both of them. Some of the orphans were eating out of silver spoons, and Elizabeth told her husband to swallow his pride lest Pemberley become the home of every orphan and destitute child in Derbyshire.

"I did not know you to be so ungenerous," Darcy said as he held their son, now a week old.

"I did not know you to be so competitive," a still-tired Elizabeth replied from her bed. "But I suppose you must have something to amuse yourselves with while your wives do all the work?"

"*All* the work?" he said. "There was at least . . . an hour of my time spent on . . . this," he said, cradling his son.

"My dear husband, you are being *very* generous with yourself in your estimation."

He decided that with a physically weak wife, it was better not to be affronted. "Well, I suppose, since I am considered the most generous man in Derbyshire at the moment, I am allowed that." Geoffrey giggled in his arms or made some kind of sound that sounded like a giggle and hopefully was not a precursor to a crying fit. His father looked at him hopelessly, only to be greeted by a face full of drool, and he quickly coloured and relinquished the infant to the nurse, all the while having to endure his wife's laughter.

With the stress of his wife's confinement (for giving birth was a dangerous prospect for any woman) and the weight of producing an heir off his shoulders, Mr. Darcy was free to enjoy all of the many pleasures life had to offer him. Despite the constant wailing of an infant, Geoffrey Darcy was a lively child and had his mother's eyes, and basking in the glow of parenthood, neither parent could find fault in him—no matter how many cravats and waistcoats he ruined with various unexpected discharges. Normally, a man of Darcy's stature was expected to maintain a distance from his infant son, having him only brought to his father in his study, but Darcy felt no sense of obligation to this particular tradition; between him and Elizabeth, the child was hardly out of someone's arms, and how fast they went through clothing became a comedy to them and an exasperation to their servants.

The Bingleys returned to Chatton after the second birth, but there were many correspondences between them and the Darcys, and every small instance of amusement was described in detail. The babies did not see each other again until the Pemberley Ball some months later, when little Georgie appeared sporting a wild twist of red hair that could not be combed down no matter how hard anyone tried. Her own mother, in fact, merely shrugged and said she had long since given up, giving a wry glance to her husband.

Colonel Fitzwilliam was still in attendance, and Anne would make her last appearance as a maid before retiring to Rosings for preparations for her fall wedding. With a hesitant grace, Georgiana Darcy emerged in society officially as an eligible maiden, though every man she danced with who was not a relation got a cold glare from Mr. Darcy.

When the festivities were finally over and the guests more or less departed in every direction, Jane made one final announcement over the relatively quiet breakfast of the two couples in attendance—she was pregnant again. So there were more congratulations and smiles as the Darcys saw Bingley and Jane off, with their now five-month-old Georgiana Bingley in Jane's arms.

"I suppose this is my fault," Darcy said to his wife as they watched the carriage pull away.

"And how would that possibly be so?"

"Well," he said, "I gave him that damned book."

END OF BOOK 1

Book Two

THE QUESTION OF CONSENT

A Most Unexpected Visitor

For once, Mr. Fitzwilliam Darcy had his massive study to himself, but he did not revel in the privacy as he thought he would. Since her first days at Pemberley, Elizabeth had been fascinated by this male sanctuary and had thoroughly invaded it, even when he offered her many alternate locations for her own writing and reading and what little financial business she had to contract with her minor personal income. He had not the will to shoo her away, and she seemed to realise it. Her goings in and out became more of a silly war of personal space, one both sides were content to occasionally win and occasionally lose (though Darcy had to admit, he most often lost but was compensated thoroughly later at night).

As it was, on this beautiful fall morning, he had the room truly to himself because Elizabeth was three miles away tending to her confined sister at Chatton Hall. His only reason for being at Pemberley was for business, which he hurried to finish. Only his highest scruples would not allow him to sign contracts before reading them, even if it meant another few hours without Lizzy and Geoffrey.

His son was yet another loss in the study. Since he had learned to crawl, he spent far too long (according to Nurse) rolling around on the carpet in front of the desk. Usually when infants were brought to see their father it was largely for show, but Darcy was content to let the toddler have his way about the room, ruining whatever clothing he was bundled in. In fact, the servants had become adept at stepping around the young Master Geoffrey.

The servant this morning had no such worries as he entered. "Mr. Bingley, sir."

Bingley was in Town. Darcy knew that as a fact. Bingley had received a letter and had business of great import in London that could not be avoided. He was finally convinced by his wife to answer the call and hightail it to Town. That was only six days ago by Darcy's estimation, but he didn't question Bingley's reappearance and gave him an approving nod.

The man who entered immediately after the servant was indeed Charles Bingley, still carrying his hat and looking rather weatherworn. He had clearly been riding, perhaps from Chatton. "Please forgive—"

"What is wrong?" Darcy did not hide his concern. "Who is ill?"

"No one. I have not, in fact, been to Chatton, but I did hear that everyone is well."

Darcy frowned and bid him to be seated, but Bingley would not. He paced by the fireplace instead as Darcy observed, "You came here directly from Town?"

"Yes. Yes, I did." He practically spit it out. "I need your advice."

"On business I assume?"

"No. Yes. Sort of. Not the business you are thinking of." As usual, Bingley was a sputtering mess, but the truth would be out soon enough. The important thing was Jane and Elizabeth and the children were well. Everything else was irrelevant. "You recall I was told of pressing affairs in Town. The letter made it seem as if they were related to the business." Though he rarely spoke of it, the Bingley family was still very connected to the wool trade, as it was the source of their original fortune and had potential for future fortune, but Mr. Bingley Senior had raised his son a gentleman of leisure, so Bingley had little to do with his own business and relied on overseers and stewards to manage it almost entirely. "This was not entirely true."

Darcy simply gave him the same impatient look that said, "Do go on, silly man who is wasting my time" that he gave to practically everybody.

"As it turns out, my sister is engaged and was seeking my consent for her marriage to a certain minor earl. His name is Lord James Kincaid, and they are very eager to be married, but I suppose they must have imagined that I would not leave Chatton for another two months."

"And they could not come to you?"

Bingley shrugged. "I suppose Caroline wanted me to meet him in the proper setting."

"So I am to understand that Miss Bingley is affianced to Scottish nobility, and you are here to ask me . . . what, exactly? If you should give your consent?"

"No, not precisely." Bingley twirled around in frustration. "I dislike saying it."

"Saying what? I was not under the impression that you dis-like anything in this world."

Bingley frowned and leaned on the fireplace. "I do not favour this man."

To this, Darcy had to give pause—considerable pause. "In our entire history, I cannot think of a single acquaintance that you did not like immensely, even when there was ample reason for the contrary. You have spoken highly even of women who have slighted you and servants who have cheated you. So I must come to the conclusion that this man is either secretly George Wickham, or he is the most disgusting, disagreeable man in Britain."

"Precisely. Only he isn't. He's quite pleasant, and he seems . . . well, Caroline is pleased with the arrangement."

"So he is wealthy."

"Not by heritage. His particular region is not very prosperous, somewhere in the lowlands. But he went to Australia and made a fortune there and has just recently returned to settle down."

"The lowlands, you say?"

"Yes. Not so terribly far from here, so it is not a question of my not wanting the distance between us . . ." Because despite the general disposition of his siblings, Charles Bingley was a model brother and loved them dearly. "To be blunt about it, I don't know what it is that bothers me about him. I can find no proper reason not to like this man and eagerly consent to a marriage that would make Caroline happy." He paused. "And yet, here I am."

"And I am still waiting for your answer to my question. On what subject do you need advice? Surely you cannot ask me to judge the man from afar? Or for that matter, to have any real say in the matter of whom Miss Bingley marries."

"I know, but . . ." he hesitated again. "I would wish a favour from you, Darcy."

"You know you don't even have to ask."

"I would ask you to go to Town—secretly or to accompany, I care not. But—to put it correctly—you know something of discovering people's . . . connections."

"You suspect something of this man? Lord Kincaid?"

"I cannot even say that. But there is something I cannot describe that has caused me to withhold my consent. Not that Caroline could not be in the process of marrying him at this moment, as she is only my sister and has her own will, but I do not believe she would do so, or she wouldn't have called for me with Jane in confinement. Am I correct in my estimation?"

"She is your sister, Bingley!" Darcy said. "I am merely her brother by marriage whom she spent many years fawning over. I have no great insight on her present disposition toward this suitor. Normally, I would say let her be married at last and be even perhaps happy! But . . ." He stood up and looked out the window, his hands clasped behind his back, his own posture of deep concentration. "Tell me—what is her inheritance?"

"Twenty thousand pounds. But . . . he has made a fortune in Australia!"

"If you really believed that, I do not think you would have travelled to Pemberley to chat about your sister's romantic travails."

"You are so judgmental. You always see the worst in everyone."

"This is precisely why you called on me."

Bingley could not deny it. "Then do me this favour, please."

"Do you wish me to meet him or merely investigate him?"

"As you see fit. Though he does relish himself an accom-plished fencer if that makes any difference."

Darcy did not acknowledge that it did. "You realise we will have to stop at Chatton and tell our wives of this scheme."

"I didn't want to trouble Jane," Bingley said. "But I suppose it would look suspicious if we both suddenly return to Town."

"Precisely."

Jane Bingley's second confinement was considerably different from her first for a host of reasons. While reclined at home in Chatton, her "isolation" seemed anything but—with two toddlers, a host of nervous servants, and the prospect of her parents and sis-ters arriving in a few days. When Bingley was finally convinced to travel to London, because Jane felt he needed a breather more than she did, she was very content to be alone with Elizabeth, who often held Miss Georgiana in her arms while they watched young Geoffrey attempt to pull up on the furniture of the sitting room.

"He will not be still," Elizabeth said. "I think we've given up on the matter."

"From your side, surely," Jane observed, as they watched him try to stand again. He could get to his feet, but only with aid, and was not quite ready to walk. "He will be disappearing for long morning walks in no time. Oh, Lizzy, you will have to bundle him up so he doesn't catch cold!"

"Now you sound like Mama."

"But you will do it all the same."

Elizabeth found she could not contradict her. As willing as she was to let Geoffrey explore the ground, she kept a very careful eye on his available territory, and many of the sharper edges of their furniture had been wrapped in blankets. She was smiling at this memory when she noticed Georgie was trying to escape her grasp and climb onto her mother's sizeable belly. Every time Elizabeth experienced any anxiety that she herself was not again expectant, she merely looked at the fact that Jane had ballooned to a whale and felt a small, very selfish pang of comfort. Had they both been this large before, and she was merely imagining things? Or was her sister even bigger this time around?

The question was not asked. Instead, Jane's lady-maid entered and interrupted them. "Mr. Bingley and Mr. Darcy."

Elizabeth made a quick dive for her son, lest he be stepped on by either gentleman as they strode into the room. As she took him into her arms, she nearly crashed into her husband, who as usual strode so confidently into the room that he needed his athletic agility to prevent himself from colliding with whatever was in his path. He made a brief bow to Jane as he took Geoffrey from Elizabeth's arms. "Mrs. Bingley."

"Mr. Darcy, Charles! How was Town?" Jane said as her own husband quickly joined her and gave her a sitting hug, certainly not requiring her to rise in his presence. "You settled your business I assume?"

"Actually, no," he said. "It seems I must return, if you would permit it."

"If I would permit it?"

"I mean, considering—"

"Charles," she said patiently, "I am two months away. Are you planning to go to the Continent or something?"

"No. No, of course not. The matter is . . ." he hesitated. "Darcy, do you want to explain it?"

Darcy looked positively infuriated that all eyes were suddenly on him, which made him uncomfortable, even in the most comfortable of social situations. "Why should I explain it? She's *your* sister!"

"Explain what?" Elizabeth said.

"She's your sister, too!"

"Only by marriage!"

"Are we talking about Miss Bingley?" Jane interrupted.

"Bingley, this is your problem and you must explain it!"

"You should not phrase it like that!"

"Then tell me precisely how I am to phrase it!" Darcy said with as much stature as he could muster with a babbling infant tugging at his cravat.

"Someone had better phrase whatever it is you mean to say correctly and *soon*," Elizabeth said with her hands on her hips, "Mr. Darcy."

Darcy looked in terror at his wife and then at Bingley who finally spit it out. "It seems Caroline is to be affianced to a Scottish earl. She . . . requested my return to Town to give my consent. She failed to mention that that was the pressing 'matter of business' in the letter."

Caroline Bingley did not, actually, need his consent, but no one felt compelled to mention that. Charles Bingley Junior was now the master of the Bingley family and estate upon his father's death and had further elevated his status by getting married and settling in a sizeable manor in the country. Just being a man, despite a younger brother, gave him social status over his sisters, and that Miss Bingley had seen fit to ask for his opinion on the matter was a quiet nod to this.

"And?" Jane finally saw fit to ask.

"And what?"

"Did you give your consent?"

Bingley frowned and looked at Darcy. "No. Not yet."

"And on what grounds did you find him so objectionable?"

"Yes," Elizabeth said, backing her sister up. "If I may be so bold, if Miss Bingley has found nothing wanting in him as a potential husband, then I am having trouble imagining your objection."

"Does he have excessive warts or something?" Jane asked.

"Is he a fortune hunter?

"A gambler?"

"Is he Mr. Wickham in disguise?"

Bingley sighed and slumped onto the couch by his wife's side. "He is none of those things. He is the most eligible bachelor, in fact, and a man of some fortune as well as minor aristocracy. And my sister has given every indication of finding him as dashing and handsome as anyone who lives in Derbyshire and owns Pemberley."

"I heard that," Darcy said.

"So your objection was?" Jane pressed, now thoroughly confused as she balanced Georgie on her stomach.

"I have no idea."

This was met with considerable silence, broken first by the young Mr. Darcy suddenly and incoherently babbling, something that had increased considerably as of late. Real words were sure to follow.

"Exactly," Darcy said, as if his son made perfect sense. "Well, we must be off to Town. Good-bye, darling."

"*We?*"

"Yes, um, I've, uh, asked Darcy to come and . . ." Bingley played with his hands. "Well . . . perhaps Darcy should explain."

"As I have little idea as to why I am to accompany you and am going along because you asked so politely, please, Bingley, do explain—for *everyone*," Darcy replied.

Jane laughed. "Yes, I can safely say we are all thoroughly confused."

"Well, um." Charles managed to buy himself some time by taking Georgie into his arms and balancing her on his knee. "I do hate to think ill of anyone, but there is something about this man—his name is James Kincaid—that, well, bothers me. But I can't rightly put my finger on it. Perhaps I am just being overprotective of my last sister, but . . . I have asked Darcy to help . . . check his credentials and judge his character." He added, "Besides, he is uncommonly good at talking Bingleys out of marr—"

"Bingley, I see we must prepare for our journey, before your foot is more firmly inserted into your mouth," Darcy said, before anyone could even start to be mad at him. "Elizabeth, I will be only a few days—" But when he turned to her, she was giving him eyes of fury anyway. "*What?* He said it!"

"So you are just going to hightail it to London, then," Elizabeth said, taking Geoffrey from him, "leaving the women and children behind?"

"I *assumed* that you would not wish to leave Chatton at the present time. Did I assume incorrectly?"

"Lizzy," Jane said kindly, "do not assume that just because I am temporarily rendered an invalid—"

"Darling, you are not an invalid," Bingley said.

"Did something happen to your eyesight in Town?" she said, and turned back to her sister. "I am serious, Lizzy. You are not bound my side. You know our family will be here within the week, and between them and the servants I will hardly get enough rest as it is. You need not worry for me. You need only worry for Charles, who will find himself suffering a horrible accident if he ever renders me this way again." She rolled her head over to him but gave no indication if she meant it or not.

"Perhaps we should give them a moment," Darcy said quietly; his wife agreed, and they took to the hallway and closed the door behind them. "Lizzy, do be serious, you may accompany me to Town if you wish, but it is hardly necessary, and I would think you more inclined to remain with your sister."

After a moment, she answered, "You are correct in your assumptions. I am simply taken by surprise by the whole matter."

"I do not properly understand it either," he readily admitted. "Perhaps he thinks I will see some flaw he does not. Perhaps he does not have confidence in his perceptions."

"So? Surely this 'Lord Kincaid' may have some flaw, but if Miss Bingley is willing enough to marry him, it must be of no consequence. I am inclined to let a woman trust her instincts."

"As am I. But Elizabeth, this is the first time I have ever heard Bingley object to anyone—ever. Surely there is something here that he cannot express, or if not, then he shall see it out, and they will be happily married. But I cannot so easily dismiss his fears without seeing to the matter myself, and he has asked—practically begged—me to do so. Should I not be obliging?"

She patted his arm affectionately. "My darling husband, always the sentinel for all people good and just—even, apparently, Miss Bingley."

He said with a smirk, "Yes, apparently. Obviously, this matter must be concluded quickly if she is so intent to marry him, so I will be gone but a few days, perhaps a week. And I will write."

"And you will miss my mother's visit, or part of it."

"That loss I will have to suffer," he said, and kissed her then his son on the cheek. "You are not to speak until I return, for I promised myself to hear your first words."

"Baa!" said Geoffrey, and flailed his arms at his father.

"Someone is overdue for a nap," Elizabeth said, and fortunately for timing, Bingley emerged from the parlour.

"Should we be off, then?" he said, donning his hat. "I must try to be in Town by nightfall, two days hence."

"Nightfall? Two days hence?"

"I . . . may have not told my sisters I was going all the way to Derbyshire," he admitted, and bowed. "Mrs. Darcy, we will return with great haste, I assure you."

"I am assured," she said, and received another good-bye kiss from her husband before they both disappeared out the front doors. She returned quickly to Jane, who was handing little Georgiana off to a nurse. "It seems we are to be barefoot and pregnant wives indeed."

"I will not be barefoot," Jane said. Her feet were on a foot stand, clothed in slippers. "My feet are cold enough as they are." This sent them both giggling, as Elizabeth rejoined her sister in her usual position beside her. "So, was Mr. Darcy particularly revelatory about their trip?"

"I think he is as flummoxed as we are and Mr. Bingley is. No one can account for this conspiracy to save Miss Bingley from the horrible state of marriage, though I do take comfort in the amusing irony."

"I will take any comfort that is offered me," Jane said. "And when my husband returns, if I have grown any larger, I will take great comfort in wringing his neck."

THE MAN FROM THE NORTH

It was a long trip to Town, and Darcy was no fan of small talk so he got right to the inquisition. Six days prior, Bingley had returned to his townhouse, apparently to immediately be received not by his steward but by Miss Bingley, who explained that she had recently met the earl in question at the opera during intermission, and he had offered to take her up to his private box. The Bingleys held their own regular box; that she would have been a fool not to accept did not have to be mentioned by either party, including the pair in the carriage on an uncomfortable ride in the late season weather. The earl had just returned from Australia and was still settling his new accounts, but he was most eager to see the opera performed in England again, as he was a regular during his time in Town. He was no great lover of his homeland, considering himself more of an Englishman than a Scotsman (like many lowlanders), and had missed all things properly English in Australia. Miss Bingley then went on to give the earl's academic credentials, which didn't surprise Darcy in the least, though he made no vocal note of it as Bingley went on. Lord Kincaid, the earl of a small estate and lands near the border of England and Scotland, was well versed in the modern languages, quite good at cards, and even a match for Mr. Hurst at chess. (Darcy was surprised to learn that Mr. Hurst excelled at anything, but this he also kept to himself.) His lodgings, though elegant, seemed dreadfully empty, and so he often dined at the Bingley townhouse, at least in the few short weeks before he proposed. Caroline said she found him most pleasing, and he would make an excellent husband, but she wanted her brother's consent, of course.

"I, of course, said it was his business to ask me for her hand, if that is to be the procedure," Bingley explained. "And before he could do this—for this was just an hour after my arrival, and he was not due again for some time—I enquired of Louisa, and she spoke of nothing but praises for this Scottish gentleman. Even Mr. Hurst, who may rival you in xenophobia—"

"I never said I disliked the Scots," Darcy interrupted.

"Darcy, I know you have travelled the Continent, admired the ruins of ancient Greece, and seen the Arch of Titus and St. Peter's Cathedral. Tell me, have you, with a great estate in the north of England, ever been to Scotland?"

"No," Darcy said.

The point made, Bingley wisely moved on. "Even Mr. Hurst could find no fault in him and praised his accent, which he found 'very English.' Anyway, the earl in question quickly arrived for dinner, and we were introduced and made some conversation. I asked about his trip to Australia, and he gave me a mild travelogue and said if I was ever in want of a greater fortune, I should travel there myself. Then after dinner, he came with me into my study and asked for her hand."

"How did he do it?"

"The usual way, I suppose. I'm sorry not to be of help here, but my only experience was my own, and the only thing I really remember about facing Mr. Bennet was I could barely hear him with the pounding in my ears. How I acted I cannot properly recall. Anyway, it was a perfectly pleasant but formal affair."

"And your response?"

"You know my response. Do not tease me."

"I mean, what was the precise reason you gave for refusing your consent? If you gave a reason at all. You were not obligated to."

Bingley squirmed in his seat. "I said though I wished Caroline happy, I simply wanted to know him better, as she was my beloved sister. I may have blundered into some speech about that. I can't recall the precise words, but I begged of him a week's time to know him better, and he conceded and said his love for her would not diminish in a week's time."

"Noble indeed."

"Yes."

"Did you speak to Miss Bingley," Darcy asked, "after Lord Kincaid's proposal?"

"Yes." Bingley turned away uncomfortably and looked instead at the passing landscape. "Yes."

"Bingley, if I'm going to have to worm every last detail from you, then this will be a long trip."

Bingley sighed and gave in. "She inquired as to the reason for my refusal. I said I merely needed to know the man who was to be my brother better."

"Did she know you were stalling?"

"Undoubtedly."

There was a pause.

"I also asked—if she loved him."

"And her reply?"

He did not attempt to imitate his sister's haughty accent. Perhaps at that moment in time, she had not had one. "She asked if it made any difference."

Darcy settled back in the coach seat. "So she does not."

"I confess I have always found Caroline very hard to read . . . when she wishes to be, at least. She knows it is an advantageous or at least equal match, and she has been . . . well, since your marriage, I would venture to guess that she has probably felt some desperation."

It was probably true. Miss Bingley was thirty, had a younger brother married, and had spent most of her time on a futile endeavour during her prime years, so her prospects were dwindling. But was Lord Kincaid not a good prospect? He was nobility, and he was rich and, by Bingley's accounts at least, good-looking. (Bingley was known for being overboard in his estimations of people's good qualities, and so Darcy decided he would judge this Kincaid for himself, but if Caroline Bingley was happy, it would be hard to find fault in this man, truly.)

Darcy confessed the last bit of his musings out loud to Bingley, who merely shrugged as they approached London and the road became busier. It was a great relief to finally arrive at Darcy's townhouse. "So then, dinner?"

"At seven, yes. I will tell them you are here on business, of course." He added with more seriousness, "Thank you, Darcy."

Darcy had no comment. He merely exited the coach and opened his front door. No message had been sent forth to prepare for his arrival, so the butler was surprised to see him. "Mr. Darcy!"

He nodded, and apparently the outburst was enough to make it to wherever Georgiana was present because she quickly burst into the hallway and ran to embrace her brother in the doorway. "Brother!" She kissed him on the cheek. "I was not expecting you."

"I was not expecting myself," he said, and did not explain. "Everything is well. I will be in Town only a few days on some business with the Bingleys."

"With the Bingleys? Business?"

He sighed. "It is not for me to understand or explain. Suffice to say, we are invited to dine at seven at Bingley's townhouse, if you are inclined to join me, and we will meet Miss Bingley's fiancé."

"Oh, Lord Kincaid!" she said with no surprise, just her usual general enthusiasm. She reminded him of Bingley in many ways, this being one of them, though she had not his natural gregariousness with people she did not know intimately. As he could only think first of the trouble it had gotten Charles Bingley into over the years and the pains Darcy had taken to extricate his dear friend from it, he found this difference most pleasant. "I met him when I was walking in the park. He was with Caroline. A very pleasant man."

"And Miss Bingley?" He realised he had to clarify. She did not know of his real reason for being here, and he did not yet want to enlighten her. "I mean to say, was she . . . happy to be walking with him?"

"Yes, quite. This is the first I've heard of an official engage-ment, but it does only seem natural, the way they walked together, that they would be now affianced."

"They are not," he clarified. "Or, not officially. Bingley has not given his consent."

Georgiana frowned in confusion. "Why ever not?"

"It is as great a mystery to me as it is to you," he could say in all honestly. "Now if you do not mind, though it is a great pleas-ure to see you, I must ready myself for the evening. Elizabeth, of course, sends her regards."

"Oh, and Jane?"

"Jane is well." He had a sudden image of his sister swollen like Jane Bingley and felt a tremor down his back. "Will you be joining us for dinner?"

"Of course! And I will not bother you further now, but you must tell me all about Geoffrey and Georgie on the way to the Bingleys. Promise me, Brother!"

At this request, he was most ready and willing. "I promise."

Mr. Darcy was indeed a good brother and spent the carriage ride telling Georgiana all about Geoffrey and his various tenden-cies. "Once he learns to climb, we're done for," he commented, and Georgiana found this most amusing. She would join him at Chatton for the birth if it would not be imposing; she asked, and he answered that it would certainly not be.

They arrived a bit on the early side because he was Darcy, and he could do that without any social impropriety. Bingley was eager to have him there, looking very much the eager guest in his own home, as he was there so rarely now. "I'm so glad you've come. And Miss Georgiana, of course, you look lovelier every day."

"Thank you, Mr. Bingley. I hope we are not too early."

"No, no, of course not! In fact, you will be here for the earl's entrance; however grand it shall be, I can't presume. Please, come in."

The Darcys were familiar enough with the Bingley town-house, smaller than theirs but better used, as it was the rather permanent home of Mr. and Mrs. Hurst as well as Miss Bingley, so even Darcy had to admit that it was kept up a bit more.

Bingley, in his usual oblivious exuberance at greeting his guests, nearly slammed into a man coming down the steps whom Darcy did not recognise. He was not as well dressed, but a long coat covered respectable attire. Shaggy ringlets of wild, black hair and a pair of thick-rimmed glasses covered most of his face, and he nimbly stepped out of the way and bowed very seriously to Bingley as if it had been entirely his fault. "Mr. Bingley."

"Shall you be back tomorrow?"

"I am afraid so," he said in a wavering, nervous sort of voice. Darcy noticed he carried a black bag with him. "Daily treatments will continue for some time," he said in a more hushed tone to Mr. Bingley, though not hushed enough to escape Darcy's ears.

"Very well. Tomorrow, then," Bingley said, all smiles as usual as his guest scurried out. He turned immediately to Darcy. "Dr. Maddox. He treats Mr. Hurst's gout, which as of late, I understand, has become rather insufferable. I know shamefully little about it for a brother, but this one is apparently a good doctor with excellent credentials. Went to Cambridge," he added in a quieter tone to Darcy. "He's the fourth doctor they've gone through and the only one they've liked, so I'm inclined to keep him on for as long as they like."

"I see," Darcy said, and inquired no more on the matter as their coats were taken from them and they retired to the parlour, where Bingley was greeted with more fervour by his sister than Darcy could ever remember Caroline greeting him with.

"Charles! How is Jane? Is everything all right?"

Darcy realised, of course, that a string of lies had been involved in Bingley's escape to the north, no doubt involving something about Jane's health. He did not interrupt, and as Georgiana at his side made no indication of being aware of anything conspiratorial, he did not impede her from doing anything at the moment.

"Jane is fine. It was merely a fright over nothing," Bingley explained. "I apologise for my sudden absence at such a crucial time in our family."

"Of course. Anything for my sister's health," Miss Bingley said, and turned to Darcy. "Mr. Darcy. Miss Darcy."

"Miss Bingley," he said. "It is a pleasure to see you again."

"I hear you are here on some business. How detestable to be dragged to and fro across the country for things that could perhaps be settled on paper. But at least we can offer you a pleasant meal and some entertainment."

"I have no doubt."

"And surely you have heard the news from Charles? I cannot imagine my brother containing anything." Clearly, love—if that was the case—had done nothing to decrease her dry wit. "Or perhaps your sister enlightened you. She came upon us in the park."

"Yes, I've heard now two accounts and am eager to meet the man in person who is so highly regarded by everyone he meets," Darcy replied.

"Oh, I think you will like him, even with your very discerning tastes, Darcy," she said. "He is quite a fencer, I hear."

"Is he?" he said.

Further conversation was interrupted by the entrance of Louisa Hurst, followed by her husband who hobbled with a cane. "Do not be alarmed," he said, shaking Darcy's hand. "'Tis the best I've done in months—all thanks to that doctor, a miracle worker, I tell you."

"We were lucky to find him," his wife added. "So, Mr. Darcy, what brings you so suddenly to Town?"

Before he could answer, the door opened, and Mr. Bingley rushed to warmly invite the apparent lord into his house. "Lord Kincaid," he said, bowing. "Welcome."

It was only when James Kincaid stepped fully in, having the servants remove his decorous coat, did the Darcys get a full view of the man. He was not particularly tall but of good stature for a man and pleasingly stout. He was dressed, not in the ornamentals of his rank (or the pleated skirt of his ancestry), but in a waistcoat of exceedingly fashionable London, and his reddish-brown hair was combed down carefully. His face was full of smiles as he greeted his host and then, of course, Miss Bingley, who curtseyed to him as propriety only allowed.

"And please, let me introduce Mr. Darcy," Bingley said turning toward them a bit.

"Yes, of course," said Lord Kincaid, and bowed to both Darcys. His accent was undeniably Scottish but hardly the thick burr of the Highlands. Instead, it sounded more of a strange English drawl, like someone from very far north or most of Darcy's servants, though more respectably intoned. "Mr. Darcy, Miss Darcy, I understand you are both connected to Mr. Bingley by marriage."

"Yes, for almost two years," Darcy answered.

"Married two sisters, I believe. Forgive me; I am merely trying to recall what I was told. And Miss Georgiana, it is very nice to see you again."

"And you as well," she said, curtseying. Darcy said nothing.

"Well," Bingley said, "seeing as we're all here, shall we begin the meal?"

And a meal it was. The Bingleys were never stingy on food for their guests, and in his bachelorhood, Darcy had shamefully found one excuse or another to stay with the Bingleys when he was feeling particularly peckish but not interested in having to figure out a complicated meal plan for himself at Pemberley. That he was quiet and observant at dinner was no surprise to anyone, as was his normal habit— or so he assumed that it came as no surprise, and there was no clandestine reason for this surprise dinner party. Lord Kincaid directed most of his attention to Mr. Bingley, whom he was obviously most wont to impress (and for the most obvious reasons that they were hardly worth even thinking about), but there were passing glances across the table to Miss Bingley, and Darcy took great pains not to miss one of them.

"I have heard you are quite accomplished in the areas of literature," Darcy said after a long period of silence. "Where did you study, if I might ask?"

"Certainly. St. Andrews. I know it's nothing to Cambridge or Oxford, but my family has a long history there, one that could not be avoided. And parts of the area, I will admit, are very lovely."

"Yes, it can be quite a tourist attraction in the summer," said Miss Bingley, and the fact that it was neither a witty or cynical comment made Darcy take note of it, but he continued his inquiries as if nothing were out of the ordinary.

"And I hear you are an accomplished fencer."

"Well, nothing compared to the great fencing club of Cambridge, Mr. Darcy. Do not think your legacy there has escaped my ears."

"That was a great number of years ago," Darcy said. "I would be wont to think that my skills, whatever they might have been, have deteriorated somewhat with time. So you may wish to consider yourself less impressed."

"We shall have to settle it then—if you can find time, of course, if your busy schedule permits."

"I'm sure some time between appointments can be found."

The conversation turned to other topics, as everyone was quick to fawn over this earl, except for Bingley, who kept his usual exuberance to a minimum, and Darcy, who was too much lost in his own thoughts. As the evening ended, the gentlemen retired to the study where the time was set for Darcy's "duel" with Lord Kincaid, who insisted upon being called James. (Darcy insisted on being called "Darcy" and rolled his eyes at Bingley's stifled giggle.) They shook on it, and the prospective suitor rose to say his goodbyes to his beloved.

"So?" Bingley said when the door was barely shut.

"What an agreeable man," Darcy said. "Well educated, pleasing in appearance, a good conversationalist—and Miss Bingley seems pleased."

"But not in love."

He did not respond for a time. He saw the looks passing between Miss Bingley and Lord Kincaid, and they were the proper looks between two people who took note at their respective situations and personalities and saw the force in uniting them, as most proper people did. Perhaps his experience was too much coloured by the passionate looks he had given Elizabeth when she had been unknowing, or the outward admiration Bingley expressed for Jane within hours of meeting her. Maybe he fancied now that all people should be so horribly in love that they make asses of themselves in company, ignoring everyone else, but he had to remind himself that that was not the way of the world, and this courtship had all of the appearances of being normal. "Well, I don't know if you can expect that, Bingley," he answered at last.

"So?"

"So?"

"So?" Bingley, ever full of energy, spun the globe on his desk as if it was a toy. "What do *you* think of him?"

"You value my opinion over your own sister's?"

"Well, *obviously*."

Darcy did not think it was particularly appropriate to crack a smile, so he held himself back from doing so and said most seriously, "He is a most pleasing person. That said, I don't think he is to be trusted with a walking stick, much less your sister."

"And you have a reason for your suspicions?"

"No," he said, turning, ready to leave the room for the night. "But I am going to find out."

MR. BENNET'S GRAND PLAN

ALL THINGS CONSIDERED, THE Bennet party that arrived at Chatton was rather small. It included only Mr. Bennet, Mrs. Bennet, and Kitty, whose theoretical engagement to a Brighton officer had been negated by his being assigned to France, at which point Mrs. Bennet proclaimed a frustration with this complicated business of marrying officers who were always going to and fro, and perhaps it was better to marry a stable, civilian Englishman.

"I have suspicions of my wife," Mr. Bennet wrote to Elizabeth afterwards, "that with Mary gone to study on the Continent, she is feeling a bit lonely and is not in such a rush to marry off the only other person in the house capable of raising the ruckus to make Longbourn seem normal." His own sentiments he did not include in the letter.

Their arrival date had been continually put off by the bad weather as winter approached, but they did eventually arrive carrying many letters from Mary meant for her sisters. Mailing from the Continent was particularly expensive, and she had done it in large packages, all to Longbourn. Mrs. Bennet brought what seemed to be another trunk of baby clothes, most of these meant for her two Derbyshire grandchildren.

Any reservations Mrs. Bennet had for her eldest daughter moving so far away from home, when Netherfield was a decent place, were put out of her mind when she saw the newly renovated Chatton. "Is it not lovely, Mr. Bennet?" she said as they came inside. He assumed the question was rhetorical and did not answer.

Elizabeth greeted them in the hallway and was rushed by Kitty, then properly hugged by her father and mother. "Jane is in the sitting room."

"Oh dear! Why is she not in her chambers?" Mrs. Bennet said.

"Mama, where she chooses to spend her time in her own house is surely her business!"

"Besides," said Mr. Bennet, "I have sat in many cushioned chairs in my lifetime and have found them all to do relatively the same job."

"Mr. Bingley should insist on it!" Mrs. Bennet said.

"Mr. Bingley is in Town," Elizabeth informed her mother, trying to keep her voice polite. "Miss Bingley is to be engaged and has asked for his consent."

"And she could not come here? With my poor Jane in confinement! The nerve of that woman . . . but Jane! I must see her at once!"

Maybe it was age or experience or the fact that she was married now and in a different social position, but Elizabeth found her mother not quite so trying and was more than willing to show her to the sitting room. Or maybe it was her mother who did not seem so shrill, who was not actually so shrill now that the time of extreme desperation of the Bennet family was over.

But there was enough to deal with. Jane was in her armchair wrapped in a shawl (she had insisted on it, somewhat embarrassed of her girth), busying herself with some embroidery when her family entered. This situation had been carefully constructed by both sisters. Normally, she would be on the couch and have Georgie by her side, and Geoffrey would be crawling around, but the proper place for two toddlers was in their nursery under the watchful eye of Nurse, and it was decided that, for the sake of their mother's nerves, some pretence of propriety must be preserved. Jane did not rise to greet them, again a planned event, because she and Elizabeth joked earlier that surely Mrs. Bennet would faint if she saw Jane's size. "Mama!"

"Oh, Jane!"

They embraced what they could, and Jane put aside her needles to receive a kiss from an overexcited Kitty and then her father, who looked a bit horrified at his daughter's size but did his best to hide it as he seated himself in a proper chair some distance away so the women could chatter. "Please bring the children," Jane told her lady-maid, who curtseyed and disappeared as if this was a completely normal occurrence.

"I must know everything of Mary," Jane insisted, "and, of course, all the doings in Hertfordshire."

"And we must know of this business of Miss Bingley, if there is going to be another wedding!"

"Perhaps not," Elizabeth said too quietly for her mother to hear, but she was sitting close enough to her father for him to raise his eyebrows, and she returned this gesture with a very obvious "I will tell you later" glance.

"And where is Mr. Darcy?" Mr. Bennet said. "This is the first time I can recall in a long time he is not hovering about you. Miss Darcy must have some suitor that he is chasing down with a blade for him to be absent from your side."

"He is *also* in Town," she said between giggles, "on business. But it will bore poor Mama to death, so perhaps we should speak of it later."

"I see," he said simply, and was quickly distracted by the arrival of his grandchildren. Georgiana Bingley was handed to her grandmother at Jane's insistence, and her new handler quickly made every attempt at combing back that Bingley hair that stood up like a flame, with no success. Geoffrey Darcy was brought to his grandfather, and Mr. Bennet was shyly beaming as he took the child into his arms.

"Baa!" said Geoffrey, and being the lively child he was, it was not clear whether he was trying to escape the grasp or merely find a preferred position.

"No, no, Grandpapa. Can you say 'Grandfather'?"

Geoffrey mumbled incoherently.

"Grandfather." This seemed to bring Mr. Bennet amusement to no end. "Okay, how about her? Surely you recognise your mother. Can you say 'Mother'?"

"Don't tease him," Elizabeth said.

But Geoffrey would not be quiet or still. He flailed at his mother, who offered her hand, and he grasped her pinkie with his small hand and held it tightly. "Yeff!"

Elizabeth covered her mouth in horror. "Oh no!"

"Oh no?" Mr. Bennet said. "I do believe the child has said his name—or tried."

"But Darcy is not here. Oh, Papa, we cannot tell him his son said his first word while he was out preventing another marriage!"

"Well, then we shall have to—*What?*"

"Yeff!" Geoffrey repeated, apparently delighted at his mother's look of shock. "Yeff. Bah. Yeff!"

"Geoffrey," Elizabeth said, half serious, "you will cry and crawl all you like, but you will hold that in until your father gets home. Do you understand?"

"I daresay he doesn't," Mr. Bennet said. "Now, perhaps we should take my grandson somewhere else before he further incriminates himself in front of witnesses, and you will tell me all about Darcy's current marriage-related schemes."

They were actually able to make an easy escape into the parlour, what with the women fawning over the forcibly idle Jane and her daughter. Elizabeth called for tea as she took Geoffrey into her own arms and faced her father's inquiries. When the servants had left, she spilled all of the details, which was basically a summary of the entire visit of Bingley and Darcy, brief as it had been. "I've not heard from them since, but as it's only been a few days, there may not be news. Odd, is it not?"

"Odd, indeed." Mr. Bennet frowned his thinking frown. "Drawing from my own experience in talking people out of marriages—"

"*Papa*—"

"I still am inclined to say, with no informed perspective whatsoever on this matter, that surely if Miss Bingley has found someone suitable, then he must be suitable. But then again, if Charles Bingley has found some reason to disapprove—"

"Which he hasn't—"

"Yes. Stranger and stranger. I would say either he has some brotherly instinct or he is simply unwilling to let her go. Though the latter does not seem likely, knowing what I do of his general disposition. Thinking of it, it was insightful of him to go to Mr. Darcy on the matter. To be frank, Elizabeth, if any man is good at finding fault in people, it is your husband."

"I am not insulted," she said with a smile.

"And you say this suitor—he is Scottish nobility?"

"An earl. But with a new fortune made in Australia. His own estate is apparently in disrepair."

"Well, I am also somewhat an expert in old estates being in disrepair," Mr. Bennet said in all humour, "and I cannot fault him on that. It is a curious matter, though. So your husband headed off to Town—"

"He was more than willing to take me," she quickly defended, "but he was correct in his assumption that I would not leave Jane alone."

"But now that she is not alone—"

"I cannot think of a reason to join him. I barely know Town; I do not know what help I would be," she said honestly.

Mr. Bennet took his tea and went into his thinking posture. There he was for some time, and Elizabeth was busied watching Geoffrey, whom she had set down on the floor and who was making his way about the expensive carpet.

Out of nowhere, Mr. Bennet announced, "I have never been to the north."

"Never?" This came as no surprise. Her father was not a great traveller and spoke almost nothing of his trip to the Continent when he was a young man, except to say it included only the major parts of France. Despite his love of appearing at Pemberley, she was sure he did not enjoy the journey there one bit.

"Yes, I suppose I should see it once before my death, and if your mother is correct, I will surely drop any day now. We must go at once then—at least to the lowlands." He continued before Elizabeth could object. "It is not terribly far from here, I understand—three days or so to the border, perhaps less if we did not stop at the major sites to admire the grand beauty of the English countryside. Though of course your mother would have no interest, nor would Kitty, and they would be of great comfort to Jane in her time of need, or, at least, keep her utterly distracted. She might not even notice we are gone."

"The two of us?"

"Well, if we take my grandson, he might come home with not only his first words but a Scottish accent. And then the master of Pemberley would be most displeased on both accounts," he said.

"Papa, be serious. We have no reason to go to whatever barony this earl controls, nor do we know its location, only that it is in the lowlands."

"You said he is Lord James Kincaid? Then surely, there can only be so many earls named Kincaid living in the lowlands, and if my geography is right, the lowlands are not very large at all. I'm sure the information we need would be easy to acquire." He stood up. "Though, if you would prefer to stay back with the women—"

"Now you are just making fun," she said. "And what explanation should we give for this?"

"Give whatever explanation you like; Mr. Bingley is so accommodating that we could take six carriages with us, and he would not be the least perturbed. And if *this* is to be a thing to make Mr. Darcy fall so horribly out of love with you, I would be quite surprised."

"But Jane—"

He took her hands. "Jane still has plenty of time. And I would place my remaining fortune on a bet that she will not put up any objection to you getting some fresh air. But I think if we are to do this, then time is of the essence."

She could not imagine it. Actually, she could imagine it, but it still seemed like such a wild endeavour.

"Mr. Bennet!" came Mrs. Bennet's usual shrill cry.

"Also of the essence is a way to explain this to your mother," Mr. Bennet said. "You'd best think of something while I handle whatever crisis she has imagined now. You were always the quick thinker, Lizzy. I have no doubt you'll have the whole plan by the time I return."

He was right in his estimation, and as soon as the carriage was ready and Geoffrey put down for his nap, Mr. Bennet and his second eldest daughter were on the muddy roads of Derbyshire headed north.

There were many reasons why Mr. Darcy liked to fence. It was one of the few athletic endeavours he truly enjoyed beyond walking, not because he was a lazy man, but because he had no great love of killing birds or other animals, archery seemed entirely medieval, and there were few other sports which a man of leisure could be expected to take part in and not be considered an uncouth ruffian. He also liked it because he was quite good at it, or so he fancied himself. Perhaps this love had blossomed the first time he bested George Wickham at twelve years old. It was a time when a year was a marked difference between boys, and Wickham had already had a growth spurt despite his age, while Darcy was still a "boy" in appearance, and so he took great relish in his first successful duel against him. It was at that point that Wickham gave up the sport entirely, or at least gave it up in Darcy's presence.

And then there was Cambridge, where fencing was a way to arguably be "social" without actually having to chat much. Darcy considered talking during a match unprofessional, as did most of his peers, and by his second term he had invented multiple excuses to escape from the postmatch drinking bouts. He kept his athletic figure (which at times was more of a flaw than a boon, especially when being at balls), and he even wrote home that he had made "friends"—which delighted his father to no end, he imagined.

Though Darcy was never captain and probably would never reach that skill level, he kept it up over the years at fencing clubs and with his private trainer at Pemberley. During the period between his proposal at Rosings and his return to Hertfordshire, he had nearly worn his trainer out.

Darcy's wife, of course, had her own explanation for all of this—one he did not care to think of. He made every attempt to change the subject when she brought it up, but she had the wit to make such comments in bed, where he was entirely at her conversational mercy and merely waited it out, usually with a pillow over his head.

The final reason (if he counted Elizabeth's reasons) for his love of the sport was that it was, in his estimation, the best way for him to get the measure of a man. There was something about the intimacy of swordplay—an expression he did not use around his wife, lest it give her further ideas—that brought out the nature of a man. He knew he was exposing himself, in fact, as a man of great strength and determination but also of honour. He never cheated, or not intentionally and to his knowledge, and he never resorted to the dirtier tricks of swordplay that were somehow within club rules. Even as a fighter, he was Mr. Darcy of Pemberley and Derbyshire, and showing anything more or less would be an assault on his general character. He did not know if other fencers shared his beliefs, but he did not doubt that a few philosophers among them did.

There were numerous reasons why he had never fenced Bingley. The first and most obvious was that Bingley had only minimal instruction, and there was no way Darcy could properly lower his skill level to make the match even without making it obvious. The second was that Bingley absolutely refused and looked terrified at the prospect the one time it was brought up over a meal in Cambridge. The third and most complex was that Darcy had no desire to fence Bingley because he knew Bingley. Charles Bingley was a man whose character was generally obvious to everyone, even the last bit of it, the bit that was so much innermost to Bingley that he was hardly aware of it, even though Darcy knew just by being his acquaintance. In other words, Darcy could get the measure of the man, full and complete, from a few conversations. Bingley was kind, generous, outgoing, and good on every level. He was so determined to see the good in everyone and so agreeable that he willingly suffered the social consequences of occasionally looking like a dunderhead, but

Darcy was convinced that he was on some level *aware* of what he was doing.

Bingley was not stupid; in that unspoken estimation, Caroline Bingley and Mrs. Hurst were wrong, and it was one of the reasons that Darcy disliked them both so. Bingley was actually very intelligent. What little aspect of the Bingley family trade he did take part in, he was good at in terms of numbers. And in Darcy's estimation, he relied a little too much on his stewards and servants, but social propriety kept him from taking a real interest in the origins of his fortunes, and he knew it. It was, in fact, in academics that Darcy had truly come to know him. Though Darcy was in his final year and Bingley in his first at Cambridge, they both were in the same Latin lectures, Darcy having put them off for as long as possible, which was most advantageous to Darcy, for it seemed that Bingley was quite skilled in languages and, by the end of the semester, was practically Darcy's tutor.

So the one proposal for a match between them was quickly and eagerly denied by Bingley, and Darcy pressed no further.

But Bingley was not the matter at hand. Instead it was this Lord Kincaid, Earl of ____shire, who was enough of a fencer to have a visitor's pass at the exclusive London Fencing Club, to which Darcy paid membership dues whether he was there more than once a year or not.

The contest was to be in the early afternoon, after Darcy had finished his supposed business meeting. Of course he had nothing of the sort, with his steward at Pemberley, but he was reluctant to be seen strolling the streets of London when he was supposed to be here on most urgent matters, so he stayed inside his considerable townhouse. Unfortunately for him, Georgiana did not depart quickly enough, and she immediately noticed his hanging about. She found him in the parlour reading a book Elizabeth had recommended from his own library.

"Brother—"

As she went into her inquiries, he realised he could hide it no longer without a string of lies that he had no desire to burden his sister with. Clearly, if they were to be in the same house during this conspiracy, she was at least to know of it. "I must confess, I am not here on the type of business that would require a meeting with a steward."

"Oh," she frowned. "Darcy, you're keeping something from me."

"Am I that easy to read?"

"To most people, you are an enigma. But to me, yes, you are easy to read. And to my sister, you are an open book, I think."

He smiled at the memory of Elizabeth. "You have taken on some of her wit, I see."

"So you are saying I have no wits of my own?"

"All right," he said, and motioned to the servant for tea. "She is *definitely* a bad influence on you." When the servant was gone, he motioned for his sister to join him and explained the whole matter to her to the best of his abilities.

"How strange," Georgiana replied to all of this. "Everyone likes him—except you and Mr. Bingley, it seems. But you have no reason for it."

"Call it a brotherly instinct."

"I can speak for your brotherly instincts," she said, without having to elaborate further, and it was nice to see that even a passing, obscure reference to the Wickham incident did not only

THE DARCYS & THE BINGLEYS

not bring her to tears but could be instigated *by* her. "So how do you think you will go about this investigation? Though, I do not know much on the matters of business."

"I do, but not business abroad, beyond our holdings in the East India Company. I confess to knowing next to nothing about Australia. Bingley knows more than I, and his guess is as good as mine."

She bit her lip then said, "I should remind you, Brother, that you now have relatives in *trade*."

The Gardiners! Of course! And they were right here in Town! "Georgiana, I am in your debt. Would you care to join me on a call to the Gardiners?"

"I would love to." She put a finger to her lips. "And yes, I know—not a word of this to anyone. You do not have to say it."

"Clearly your intelligence surpasses my own," he said, and kissed her gratefully on the cheek after rising. "Now I must prepare for my *actual* business in Town. Thank you, Georgiana."

"Only promise me to keep me a part of all of your exciting conspiracies, as this is the most exciting thing to happen to me in months." She added with dramatic gravity, "I mean, *terrible* as it is."

He could not help but chuckle a bit. "Yes, terrible indeed."

Darcy arrived on time, but Lord Kincaid was already there. They shook hands before donning their protective gear. "I am still honoured to fight the master of Pemberley."

"Being master of Pemberley has nothing to do with fencing," Darcy said good-naturedly (something he had to put a good deal of effort into). "If it did, I would enjoy it a great deal more than I do."

They separated to warm up and faced each other in full armour, their face masks completely obscuring their expressions as the master watched on to make the calls. This lack of expression would be no trouble to Darcy, not as a fencer or a reader of other fencers. He was accustomed to the necessities of safety and had learned long ago that reading a person's body language during a fight was far more important than their facial expression anyway. By his own estimation, stance was nearly everything, the selection of movements a close second. He was not here to win, however much he would prefer it, but to make out this man's character, and he also knew all of the dangers of fighting an unknown opponent who had the advantage over him of knowing Darcy's reputation while Darcy had no such knowledge.

The contest was silent. Kincaid took an aggressive stance, Darcy cautiously neutral as he was with all unfamiliar opponents. He had stamina enough and would be as aggressive as he chose when the time was right, but at the moment, his interests were not in victory but in study. He parried and counterattacked where it was appropriate, which was easy enough. They were well matched by his early estimation, which made for an interesting match but only if he kept his side of it. Switching into an aggressive stance, he moved forward and awaited Kincaid's response. It was of course defensive, the intelligent move of an experienced fighter for more than the logical reasons. Kincaid could remain aggressive himself, but he had not yet seen Darcy aggressive, and he did not know the ferocity with which he would be attacked. Darcy considered himself to be, at the moment, quite mild, in fact, his mind admittedly on other things.

So successful was his advance, despite all of Kincaid's parries that prevented a match point, that Kincaid had nearly pushed out of bounds and the fencing master told him to take a step back. It was then that Kincaid's strategy changed, suddenly aggressive, and it was only Darcy's intuition and agility that caught it in time. Had Kincaid been drawing him out? He would have time to worry about that later. He did not have to see the hidden expression to know it. Undoubtedly, from the way the muscles in his collar and neck were tensed, Kincaid was seething that his initial attack had been parried, and he would stab until it succeeded.

Well, that could be dispatched. Darcy had not been second on Cambridge's fencing team for nothing. Having learned what he wanted, he parried the next strike and countered to the breast, hitting the layers of cotton and leather with his tipped foil. With a real sword, it would have struck him near the shoulder and possibly killed him, but that was not that situation.

"Match point!" announced the fencing master. "To Mr. Darcy."

They saluted each other, removed their masks, and shook hands with very tired arms. Kincaid's face was a mask of congeniality—but it was a mask. "It seems you are not a good enough advocate of your abilities, Darcy."

"You are quite skilled yourself, Lord Kincaid," he said evenly. "Excellent match."

"Indeed. Would you care to join me in the lounge afterwards?"

Darcy leaned against the pillar and considered. There were

reasons on both sides, and an excuse could easily be made for rejecting the offer to drink with this man. But this was not an opportunity to pass up, he decided. "I would be delighted. Half an hour, shall we say?"

"Delighted." Kincaid shook his hand again and disappeared to wherever he was going to change. Darcy, as a senior member, had his own changing room and a bath ready for him. He barely paid attention to the servant helping him change out of his sweat-soaked clothes. He had much to think about.

Fortunately it was midafternoon now, and even in the fencer's lounge, Darcy had an excuse not to get drunk with his new fencing partner, as was the habit of many of the regulars. In fact, he was inclined to have no alcohol at all, but that could not be avoided. When he appeared properly recovered and dressed, Kincaid was there to greet him again. "Darcy."

"Lord Kincaid."

"You have bested me. I insist you call me James."

"Very well then," Darcy said, but still didn't. They took seats at a small table, and Darcy ordered what he knew to be the weakest beer in their stocks.

"I confess, I'm a whiskey man myself," Kincaid said. "It's my only nationalist indulgence. We will remain in confidence of this, of course."

"Of course," Darcy said, "though you will not find Mr. Bingley the Anglophile you may believe him to be."

"My concern is of course with Caroline, primarily. You must know her habits," he said. "Not to be beat around the bush, but you were once her suitor."

"That would imply that I was pursuing her. But I had not your courage," he answered.

"You are being humble. There is no need, Darcy, if we are to be brothers, if Charles would come around. I cannot account for it."

"Nor I," Darcy said, which was actually reasonably honest.

"The point is, I am aware that it was considered a suitable match by . . . her family—and Caroline herself."

"Oh, yes." Fine, if Kincaid was going to be flippant, so would he. "And Bingley would marry my sister, and our families would be so ridiculously connected that no one would be sure who could marry whom after several generations. But life often turns out differently. And besides, had I not . . . to be blunt about it . . . not further engaged Miss Bingley in pursuit, then we would not be sitting here, and you would have to find another beauty."

"Then I am a lucky man indeed."

Darcy took a long drink. "Indeed." He was trying to imagine what this man's scheme was, because there had to be one. What would he possibly see in *Caroline Bingley*? All he could think of in her defence was that she had a nice brother. Perhaps he was being a bit cruel, but what was warranting this rather thorough investigation of this man, anyway?

"I will confess something to you, Darcy, if you would have it."

Darcy raised an eyebrow. "If you are so inclined."

"I know very well that my sudden appearance and pursuit of Caroline must all seem a bit hasty and alarming. Perhaps that is why her brother is so reluctant to grant his consent. I know I have not proven my worth yet, have no reputation, et cetera . . .

but three long years in Australia in the desert searching for gold with the natives can really put a man in want of good company." He stuttered, "I don't mean female company, to be crude about it—sophisticated female company. And you must admit, Caroline is a sophisticated woman."

"The very model of it," Darcy found himself saying. "I believe she knows . . . four languages. Is that correct?"

"Yes."

"She surpassed me in this endeavour. My French is barely tolerable, and my Latin has disappeared entirely over the years. If those are her requirements for a husband, I have no idea what she saw in me."

"I am not such a scholar either," Kincaid admitted, "but I do know French, which is all the rage in Scotland of course, practically a second language among the nobility . . . and some Italian. And I confess to having picked up quite a bit of the 'Aboriginal' language—lot of good it will do me here, though."

Darcy had to assume he meant the Australian native tongue. "Perhaps you could write a book of your observations of the culture and language."

"Perhaps. It would be a pursuit. I am so accustomed to being overworked that I haven't the faintest idea of what to do with my time now. But I suppose Caroline will keep me busy for long enough," he said with a sly smile that made Darcy's stomach churn. Caroline was a beautiful woman, but she looked too much like her brother. He had always tried to ignore the occasional creeping thought that relations with her would be too much like engaging with a female Bingley. "But I am too crude for a gentlemen's club." Kincaid slapped Darcy on the shoulder.

"Too long in the wilds of the Outback."

"Well, if you want proper English society, you've found it," Darcy said, raising his mug. "Cheers."

Their glasses clinked. "Cheers."

Darcy was changed and back at Bingley's on his usual early schedule for dinner. There was nothing complicated about his dinner dress, but he had spent some time in his room pacing and pondering while the manservant gave him a queer look. James Kincaid did not appear to be an overly complicated man and, in fact, gave every indication that he should be worth liking. Darcy could not account for his uneasiness at all, but he was fairly confident in his own instincts and certainly if he shared them with the usually unobservant Bingley. Whether Kincaid was deeply in love with Miss Bingley was still a question on the table, but he certainly presented himself as someone who cared about her enough to marry her.

He could only point a finger in one direction, vague as it was. As much as he wanted to know Kincaid, Kincaid wanted to know him. Fencing and drinking with him had told him that. He was as suspicious of Darcy's sudden presence as Darcy was of him, and he wanted desperately to be liked by this mysterious relative who had even once been Miss Bingley's ideal match (and might very well still be). Everything in his fencing moves said, *I can match you. I can play this game.*

It unnerved Darcy that it was a game at all.

On his way to the Bingley townhouse, Darcy made a mental inventory of the things that still needed investigating: Kincaid's finances, his plans for the future, what Bingley was thinking, what Miss Bingley was thinking. Was he actually going to have to talk to her? About *this*? Surely Bingley could handle *that*.

Georgiana had another engagement and had not joined him. Only Mrs. Hurst was in the parlour, and he had no desire to make any discussion with her, so he went looking for Bingley instead. He was a regular-enough fixture to make his own way about the place without anyone hassling him. He was about halfway up the stairs when he saw a flash of orange hair from the person on the second-story landing, but it was not *Charles* Bingley. Partially to avoid her and partially because he found himself rather enjoying his sudden career in sleuthing, he ducked behind the stairwell as she descended.

"Mr. Hurst is—?"

"Doing well, actually."

"So you—"

"—will be finished with the treatments soon. Not that I can cure him, but I can certainly get him out of this flare. And then I'll be out of your way."

He could see the two of them, now at the bottom of the stairs, as she curtseyed. "Daniel."

"Caroline."

He walked off and out the door in a nervous shuffle, leaving Miss Bingley to stand in place for some time before disappearing back up the stairs. It was only in relative safety that Darcy emerged from his hiding space only to find yet another Bingley coming down the stairs; this was the one he wanted. "May I speak with you?"

"Darcy, you're here! Of course." They quickly retired to his study. "I see you survived your match with the earl. I hope you weren't too harsh on him. In other words, I hope he's still alive."

"Please!" Darcy said, shutting the door behind him. "The only man I've stabbed—that was completely by accident. The tip broke. And it was just a flesh wound."

"So you kept insisting," Bingley said. "I do, however, seem to recall him calling you by a very particular nickname shortly before the match—"

"*Bingley.*"

"Fine." Bingley took up his seat at the grand desk, leaning back into it. "My father used to sit at this desk and lecture me."

"On what?"

"Oh, everything a man who is to inherit a fortune ought to know. Surely your father did the same?"

"He did," Darcy admitted, leaning on the fireplace. "It was very odd to take his place, even with the ample warning I had. The very first thing I did in his seat was pay off Wickham—using his check."

"I'm sorry," Bingley said. He was playing with the globe again, just an idle spin of it. "I often wonder if my father sat in here and worried about his daughters' marriage prospects."

"I have no doubt. I worry about Georgiana incessantly."

"Not about her prospects—just if she'll ever find one you'll approve of. When she turns thirty, you may have to lower your standards." He didn't give Darcy time for his cheeky reply. "You have some news."

"First, a question, a rather simple one—almost unrelated. How long has Dr. Maddox been in your employ?"

"I suppose we could pretend he is in Mr. Hurst's employ, but somehow I imagine his bill will turn up on my books when I inspect them more carefully. I don't know—can't be more than a month. Why do you ask?"

"And he is here every day?"

"Yes, he insists that Mr. Hurst have some soak, and of course my brother insists that the poor doctor stand there the whole time, as if something would go wrong while soaking one's foot in some salt water. But I suppose if you don't want to be working in the cholera wards, you will put up with whatever your wealthy patients want." Bingley frowned. "Are you looking for a doctor for your employ?"

"Perhaps." For some reason, he felt compelled to lie or at least disguise the truth of his concerns. There would be time for that. Kincaid was more pressing. "No matter. I am going to make some inquiries tomorrow into Lord Kincaid's fortune."

"So you doubt it exists?"

"I'm glad I'm not the first one who has thought of that!"

"Of course not, but it would be rather impolite of me to request records. That would make his marriage to my sister look like some kind of business transaction."

"Unless both families are penniless, *all* marriages are on some level a business transaction. Money was exchanged, no matter how reluctant we were to receive it and how insignificant it was. Lord Kincaid, Earl of _____shire, is to receive a small fortune upon marrying Miss Bingley, and that should not be forgotten until note is paid."

"I doubt my sister could live very long on twenty thousand pounds," Bingley said. "This of course means that if he is a fortune hunter, he is the worst kind. But we have no proof of this. Why are we so eager to suspect?"

Darcy shrugged with indignation. "You dragged me down here, Bingley! You tell me!"

"We are both going on brotherly instincts, then."

"Until the truth is made plain, yes. There is also the matter that neither of them is particularly in love."

"Caroline seems suited with the match. And she never seemed to me the type to be 'in love' with any man. She would have readily become your mistress, and yet she still made all kinds of snobby comments at your expense."

"This is true," though, he added privately, quite incendiary from the usually tolerant Bingley. Maybe his role as head of his family was wearing on him, especially with the enigma that was the unconfirmably rich Lord Kincaid.

"Well, I will go to the Gardiners tomorrow and learn what I can of Australia, begin looking into his actual prospects," Darcy assured him. "And then we will have our answer."

"Darcy, I don't know what I would do without you."

"They were your instincts that brought me here. I am merely doing the legwork so you can remain above suspicion." He mock-bowed to Bingley. "At your service."

"And I am grateful, so grateful." Something had put Bingley in a sad mood, and if Darcy had to guess, it was worry, for Bingley did care a great deal for his sister and would not see her ill married, no matter how well she sabotaged a marriage with her own personality. But that was not something Darcy could intrude upon anymore than Bingley could give him advice about dealing with Georgiana, so he bowed again more politely and left the room.

Back in the hallway, Darcy was greeted by the newly arrived Lord Kincaid, who was more formal with Miss Bingley by his side. They were a reasonable couple—not glowing as he remembered Bingley and Jane, but Bingley and Jane were the exception to the norm. He vaguely recalled being described as somewhat inscrutable and inexpressive at his own place at the altar, so he was not wont to point fingers, and they were happy with each other. Why should he not, with no great sin uncovered, bless this couple? Even if they relied on her wealth, they could ride on Bingley's coattails as easily as the Hursts did. Darcy and Kincaid would be sparring partners and maybe get drunk together occasionally. Was it such a terrible concept? Caroline's prospects were almost gone, and here was a suitable match, to minor aristocracy, even if it was Scottish. Darcy did not even have to be involved, and instead he was to play the private investigator into this man's affairs apparently. So Caroline was not deep in the bonds of love; most couples weren't, and he could not imagine her acting like a lovesick girl anyway.

In fact, the only time he had ever heard any feeling in her voice that was not sarcasm or false modesty but genuine emotion was the half hour before, as Dr. Maddox took his leave.

NORTH AND SOUTH

DARCY WAS UP EARLY as usual, and his coffee was hot and ready for him. He was already dressed for his excursion when Georgiana, usually a later sleeper, appeared in travelling winter clothes. "If you would permit me, I wish to accompany you."

"I have other business first—before the Gardiners—banks and the like. I am to call on them for lunch, if you wish to meet up there."

"Brother," she said, taking his arm in the way she did when she really wanted something. "Balls and shopping are only so exciting, and you know it. If there is to be an exciting mystery to be solved, I demand to be part of it."

"It may not be so exciting. It may involve bank records and talking to stewards."

"All the same." She twisted tighter around his arm and smiled at him. She must have known he could not resist that smile. Lizzy, it was her eyes; Georgiana, her smile.

"Very well. We will be the constables," he said.

"Elizabeth will never forgive us for excluding her."

"I will write and tell her to join us if we discover anything *truly* exciting," he said. "But I do doubt it."

It was a cold, clear day, and the London streets were, of course, disastrously muddy, but for their first mission, he had them descend from the carriage several blocks away before approaching the small offices on the corner. So small were they that the proprietor emerged to greet them even in the November cold. "What d'ya want?"

"I am seeking to inquire about a property in this district," Darcy said, tapping his cane into the mud with some authority. "I believe I have found a house most suitable to my needs, and I rarely see life in it, so I assume it is available. Would you be interested in showing it to me?"

"Which one?"

Darcy gestured. "The third on the left."

"Oh, I'm sorry, good sir, but it is most recently taken by a gentleman from the north, a Scotsman."

"I see. And he intends to stay?" Residences were transitory at the beginning, before they became established, furnished, and passed down from generation and generation.

"I don' know, sir, but he paid out the year. More I can't tell you. Wouldn't be proper intrudin' on a gent's business."

"Of course not," Darcy said, and slipped a sovereign into the man's palm. "I merely seek to understand the best way one should pay for such a townhouse."

"Cash," said the renter. "He paid in cash. Or so I was told by the owner of the block; if you want to talk to 'em—"

"No, thank you. I believe I will be making my further inquiries through the proper channels." He tipped his hat. "Good day to you, sir."

The man had no hat to tip, but he bowed rather grandly to the obviously wealthy gentleman before him, and the Darcys made their way back to the carriage.

"What does that mean?" Georgiana asked as soon as they were back in the safety of their carriage. "Do you think it a large sum?"

"Possibly. It could mean any number of things. The Gardiners, I'm sure, will be able to shed some light on the subject."

Before their luncheon appointment, they made three stops, all at different banks, inquiring to see if a certain Scottish earl had recently opened an account there. Banks were a bit more on the official side, and outright bribery and his own personal connections could only get Darcy far enough to tell that no, the earl had not opened accounts with these banks, but there were many banks in Town, and he could have gone to any one of them. With this tiny knowledge gained, a frustrated Darcy returned to his sister in the carriage, and they made for Cheapside.

He had sent a message ahead, so the Gardiners were expecting them, and their children delightfully rushed to them at the door. Georgiana was more than obliging, kneeling to their level after her muddy coat was removed. Normally, the formidable Mr. Darcy would be more put off with young children climbing all over him, but the last year had endeared him more to the idea. "Mr. Gardiner. Mrs. Gardiner."

"So lovely to see you," their hostess said.

"Odd circumstances, though," Mr. Gardiner said in that smirking way of his. Darcy had explained a bit in his letter, but only that he was looking into the credits of a suitor for someone in the family. Since they would have heard extensively from their sister had it been Mary or Kitty, and Georgiana was coming with him, it could really only be one person, and he guessed they had the ability to surmise that. "Shall we dine?"

There was some talk of recent events, and they asked fervently how Jane was doing, and he replied that she was weathering things well, especially with Elizabeth by her side, and Geoffrey would be walking any day now.

"Then you won't know what to do with him," said Mrs. Gardiner, clearly delightfully exasperated by her own children running to and fro.

"I hardly know now."

Once Mrs. Gardiner bid Nurse to retire her children, they got down to business.

"Australia, from what I've heard," Mr. Gardiner explained, "is a risky venture. They say there is gold to be found there, but I've yet to see a man return with a fortune in it or any at all. It's mainly thieves, ruffians, and natives—not a proper colony at all. But that, of course, says nothing of this earl's success."

"What about his lodgings?"

"You say he paid in cash? For a year on that street? It must have been a good sum."

Darcy nodded.

"I don't see," Georgiana said, refusing to be removed from the affairs. "Is it not the most efficient means to pay for something? Any landlord would take cash, and if he was meaning to be expedient, it would be the best way."

"Yes, but that amount . . . it would be unwieldy."

"But he had it—he made it in Australia!"

"Georgiana," Darcy said, "it is not as if he came on a ship with a bag of gold stuffed under his mattress. The only way to insure the safe return of the wealth would be a check of some sort written up in the capitol—"

"Sydney, isn't it?" said Mr. Gardiner.

"And then the funds would be ready for him here. But surely, to pay for the lodging he would pay by check for convenience's sake. One does not walk up and down the streets of Town with a bag of coins looking for a place such as that to live."

"Unless—unless he didn't want the money to be traced," Mr. Gardiner said, taking a sip of his tea. "Then he would want to pay in cash."

"You mean if the money was ill gotten?"

"Or nonexistent," his uncle explained for Georgiana's sake. "Suppose for a moment he had no money, only a reputation for having money, if we must assume the worst. He could go to a bank, perhaps a less reputable one, and say that the funds were in transfer and he needed some spending money, and he could take out a considerable loan. But a landlord on a square such as that would not take a note on an obvious loan, so he would go to another bank, redeem the note, and then have all the money to present himself as a wealthy man—for a time."

"Until he found someone suitable to pay off his debts," Darcy suggested.

"Precisely. Of course, this is all just conjecture, but I could make considerable inquiries into the banks I do regular business with . . . and the ones I do not. For the family's sake, of course."

"If you would, we would be most grateful. I have not had much luck. And it may all be for nothing, of course, and Lord Kincaid may be a most eligible bachelor."

"Indeed, he may be. But you don't believe it, do you, Darcy?"

Darcy could not reply with anything but that he didn't.

When they were back in the carriage, Darcy turned to his sister. "Georgiana—"

"What is it you want me to do?"

"You realise you should not be involved in these—"

"Most indelicate matters?"

He shook his head. "Definitely from Elizabeth."

"Why is she not here? Because of Jane?"

"Perhaps she will join us if the need arises. But until then, yes. So you will have to be my Elizabeth and have the very daunting task of distracting Miss Bingley and Mrs. Hurst for a while."

"Brother! It is not so very daunting," she said confidently. "I have been doing it for years."

He never should have doubted her, but he was wont to say it. They were relatively silent until they reached the Bingley house. It was now early afternoon, almost time for high tea. Darcy was fairly sure Bingley was out on some business with his steward, but he was not his objective. They were greeted by the servants and then by the Bingley sisters doing needlepoint in the drawing room, where Georgiana eagerly joined them and Darcy bowed, then disappeared up the steps.

If his timing was correct, Mr. Hurst was in the middle of one of his treatments. A knock on the door confirmed it. There was some muffled discussion and then a loud Mr. Hurst calling, "Come in!"

Darcy entered to perceive Mr. Hurst at a chair, his left foot soaking in a basin filled with coloured water. Beside him was

Dr. Maddox, who bowed stiffly and then continued fiddling with his various tinctures and equipment. "Doctor, if I may have a moment—"

"Of course," Dr. Maddox said, and scampered out. "Of course."

It was only when the door was closed and he was gone that Mr. Darcy turned to Mr. Hurst who for once did not look so soundly drunk or in pain. In fact, he looked quite comfortable and coherent. "Brilliant man. Done wonders for this blasted foot."

Darcy did not gaze at the exposed ankle in the water. "So I hear. Tell me, how long has Dr. Maddox been in your employ?"

"Oh, I would say . . . just over a month now."

"And his credentials?"

"Looking for a suitable doctor for Pemberley? You'll have to steal him from me."

"Perhaps I shall," Darcy said with a false but necessary smile. "How did you come to know him?"

"Recommendation. I went through several city doctors. Their treatments were all rubbish, of course, so I applied to a friend of mine, one with tumours, and he gave me a private recommendation. Dr. Maddox, as you may have heard, was trained at Cambridge; your alma mater, is it not?"

"Precisely the one."

"He's quite a scholar, you know. Speaks five languages. Caroline even gets to practice her Italian around him. She gets such little opportunity—perhaps what she sees in this Kincaid fellow."

"So Miss Bingley has had a chance to talk with your doctor?"

"Well, he's here so often, and of course, I'm not about to let him run off to another patient while my foot is soaking in . . . this." He temporarily lifted his foot out of the murky water, and

Darcy got to see the full extent of the poor man's gout. Only years of training in maintaining composure in all circumstances prevented him from turning away in disgust. "So he talks to Caroline. Or he used to."

"Used to?" He added quickly, "If I'm not intruding. It is just that I am not accustomed to hear of Miss Bingley making conversation with servants."

"I think they had a bit of a falling out around the time Kincaid showed up," Mr. Hurst said. "You can probably guess why."

"You are mistaken. I have no idea."

"Come now, Darcy. You're much smarter than I am; you've been here but three days and you're already in my room talking to me about Caroline and Dr. Maddox. When have we ever had a conversation such as this?"

When had they ever had a conversation *at all?* Mr. Hurst was usually in a drunken stupor by the dinner bell. But Darcy kept his cool composure. "What are you implying?"

"You know and I know that Dr. Maddox, despite being of rather distinguished birth, is no match for Caroline. His elder brother inherited everything and lost it on a venture in East India or something, leaving him nothing. And perhaps Caroline will not stand to live on Bingley's pounds any longer. I don't know. The woman's a mystery to everyone."

"I had no idea of his circumstances."

"You wouldn't. But I do. And Caroline does." He took a sip of his tea, which had been resting on the bed stand. "So now I think we have a perfect understanding of the situation."

"I wouldn't say perfect, but yes." It was taking a lot of energy to maintain his cool composure, so taken aback by Mr. Hurst's bizarre behaviour. "I confess it seems I have not given you proper credit in the past, Mr. Hurst."

"We are very different; I am a fat old fool, and you are a wealthy young man of stature. So we will continue these roles because it puts everyone at ease. I will be drunk and oblivious— which, I admit, after a couple of shots I might well be—and you will maintain your position as an impartial observer on this whole matter—which can hardly be why Mr. Bingley called you into Town so suddenly."

To this, Darcy could only say, "Quite right." He bowed and eagerly left the room.

This was all more complicated than he thought.

When Mr. Bingley did return home, it was with a glorious expression that could only mean he had just been designated Prince Regent or he had good news from Jane. "She says she is well, Darcy," he said, not reading the long letter in its entirety. "Her mother and sister have arrived and are keeping her company while Elizabeth is in the north."

"*What?*" It was not said in anger but in surprise. "She's in the north?"

"So it says, with Mr. Bennet. I've no idea why. I haven't gotten that far. Why don't—" But before Bingley could finish, Darcy grabbed the letter out of his hands and began to scan it himself, even though a letter from wife to husband was the most private kind. This was *Elizabeth* they were talking about.

She had gone north with Mr. Bennet; they were to visit the lowlands and see the Kincaid lands themselves. There were many assurances from Jane that she had tried to dissuade them and that they would be returning shortly, but Darcy had to hold back his instincts to crumble the letter—which was not his property—in disgust. "It seems Lizzy will not be idle. She's gone to the Kincaid estate in _____shire with our father-in-law." He handed the letter back to Bingley.

"Well," Bingley said, "you can't be *all* that surprised."

When Darcy was done imagining all of the horrible things that could happen to her on those terrible Scottish roads, he had to admit Bingley was correct. This was exactly something Elizabeth would do; he had to expect it, even be amused by it. "I could go after her."

"I would not stop you. However, by the time you catch up, she'll probably be on her way back. We must post to Jane to keep us updated. Or perhaps you will get a letter from Mrs. Darcy herself." He was trying to be assuring. "Darcy, you cannot be angry at her for this."

"I am not *angry*," he said. "I am just . . ." He couldn't bring himself to say, *worried*. "We should never have told them."

"Are you joking? When they found out they were left in the dark, we'd never have heard the end of it. And I'm sure Elizabeth will handle herself. Besides, she is under her father's care."

Yes, as if an aged Mr. Bennet as her knight protector was any comfort to Darcy. "Fine," he grumbled, seeing as how nothing useful could be done. "You will excuse me. I must dispatch a courier or two . . . or three . . . or ten thousand."

"Of course." Bingley put a hand on his shoulder. "She will be fine, Darcy. I'm sure of it." How he was able to go from the obliviously revealing idiot to the great comforter was truly impressive.

Unfortunately, Darcy did not have time to be impressed. He had business of the most urgent kind that, for the first time in several days, did not involve Miss Bingley.

Darcy was barely in the door of his own apartments when Georgiana greeted him bearing a letter. "From Elizabeth." It was still sealed. Without explanation, he frantically tore it open.

Dearest Husband,

By now Jane has probably told Mr. Bingley that we've gone north, and Mr. Bingley has unwittingly told the last person he should have told, which of course is you. Not meaning any deception on my part, but I will not have you riding all the way to Scotland from Town on my behalf when you have perfectly good business there (or perfectly bad business there—you have been rather lax about writing how matters are progressing).

Papa and I are well and have located the estate of Lord Kincaid, Earl of _____shire, which is currently occupied by his younger brother. It is not terribly far from the border, and our appearance there will be brief. Papa insisted that if you are to be involved in clandestine affairs in Town, then it is only fair that I should have my own secret investigations elsewhere, if this is to be a true and equal partnership, and is it not a sin not to honour one's parents?

Be assured that we have taken several men with us, and we shall be perfectly fine, though I am sure you will hole yourself up in your home now so you can secretly fret about

*where no one can see you. I am sorry to miss it because it is
rather amusing.*

*I will write as soon as we have more news. Please do
the same.*

*Know that I love you most dearly and do mean only to
aid you in your investigations in the best avenue available.
Geoffrey is well within the walls of Chatton, and he has definitely not said his first word, and it was definitely not a hilar-
ious pronunciation of his name—just so you know.*

Your Loving and Always Very Obedient Wife,

Elizabeth

"Well?" Georgiana said somewhat impatiently. "What does
it say?"

It always amazed him that Elizabeth had the ability to annoy
the daylights out of him and yet make him love her all the more
because of it.

When Mr. Bennet and his daughter finally arrived at the
castle of the Earl of Kincaid, the scheme had been cooked up
and properly spiced and was ready on a serving platter. It relied
on Mr. Bennet getting past the butler, but he could be exceptionally charming when he wished to be, and very soon they had
an invitation to see the grounds and the home and even meet its
master, Lord William Kincaid, a charming young man with a
thick lowlands accent that was not quite the Highlands burr of
most of his servants, who were in kilts while he was in pan-
taloons, but different in speech tones from their own. He was so

overwhelmed by the idea that anyone would want to visit his estate (which was a drafty castle with the insides converted into something more modern and suitable for living) that he decided to provide the tour himself.

Mr. Bennet was addressed as he had introduced himself to the servant, which was as Mr. Darcy's steward. "We only regret that Mr. Darcy himself cannot be present, but he is busy with business in Town—London. That and he trusts his wife's opinions implicitly." Mr. Bennet bowed to his daughter who had trouble keeping a straight face.

"Of course. Though to be perfectly honest, I cannot recommend this area as the ideal place for the construction of a summer home, but I will not be too harsh on my ancestral lands," said their host.

He went on for a bit, which was proper for a tour, and they saw most of the public rooms, which did not take very long, as the castle was no Pemberley and was full of mainly old furniture and knickknacks and even some weaponry that did not look as if it had been used in some time. Their gracious host took some delight in showing them a drinking horn, which he said his family was no longer in the practice of using. "And thank goodness."

"Why is that?"

"In the wild Highlands, they have a custom—I think they got it from the Vikings. When a man is to become chief of the clan—I, by the way, am not chief of mine—he must fill in a drinking horn with whiskey and consume it all in one chug. Whether he then succumbs to unconsciousness I think is irrelevant, but I would surely not be up to the task." Now intimidated by his own artifact, Lord Kincaid put it down.

They eventually arrived at the room that served as a portrait gallery where the Earls of Kincaid were pictured in the English style of portraiture. "And here is my father, the former earl, Lord James Kincaid. He gave his name to my older brother, of course."

"Who is to inherit, is that correct?" Elizabeth asked.

"No. We may be lowlanders, but my father insisted on the old clan custom that the next 'chief' be chosen among his sons, instead of the honour being granted to the eldest, to my brother's great dismay and to my delight. Of course, James—I mean, my brother James—could not have been all that surprised."

"Why ever not?" Mr. Bennet said.

Lord Kincaid sighed and turned to another portrait. "This is my brother, James Kincaid." The man pictured there, very handsome, did resemble him greatly. "He is in Australia now, or somewhere."

"Or something?" Elizabeth said. "I'm sorry, but are you in search of your brother?"

"I am not in search. I merely mean to say he went to Australia, and his correspondences have been more irregular than we have cared for."

Seeing the time was right and that this Lord Kincaid was not inclined to gossip and would be eager to move on if Mr. Bennet did not say something to continue the topic, he announced, "I believe your brother is in Town."

"You mean London?" the gentleman asked, spinning around to face them proper instead of turning to the next portrait. "What? How do you know this?"

"There is some talk," Elizabeth said quickly. "He is even affianced."

William Kincaid was obviously dumbfounded. "That is impossible, Mrs. Darcy."

"I believe it is true."

"No, it is certainly impossible. Of that, I am sure."

"But you just said—and I do not mean to intrude on a family matter—that you did not even know his location."

"Yes, that is true, but I do know that even if he is returned to Britain, he cannot be affianced to any woman, English or otherwise. My brother is married."

In unison the Bennets shouted, "*Married?*"

THE EARL KINCAID

IF THERE WAS ONE thing Darcy detested—and he did admittedly detest a great many things—it was being caught unawares. He attributed it to fuming over Elizabeth's departure and his overwhelming concern for her safety (and his inability apparently to do anything about it) that he was almost entirely distracted when he made his next visit to the Bingleys and was easily trapped in the billiards room alone with Caroline Bingley. "Miss Bingley," he bowed quickly when he finally noticed her entrance.

"Mr. Darcy," she curtseyed. "I'm sorry, but I refuse to carry on this charade anymore. If I know anything about you, I doubt you can stand it as well."

"What charade?" he answered honestly, because he could think of a dozen that were simultaneously occurring.

"Your presence here, Charles's refusal to grant his consent despite my repeated pleas—I can only assume there is some conspiracy here, and since I also know you detest disguise, you will not deny it now."

She *did* know him. And since she was in the perhaps unknowing position of victim in this whole situation, he felt compelled to be kind. "Very well. You are correct that my business in Town is directly related to surmising Lord Kincaid's character, but that does not mean you must assume the worst in me or your brother. As you are well aware, a proper suitor must present his credentials, and they must prove to be more than just smoke."

"Why does it upset you so that I may have found happiness, Darcy?"

If it were anyone other than Miss Bingley, it would have been a rather low blow with its implications. It was, however, Miss Bingley. "Because I have yet to judge that you have found happiness—not with Lord Kincaid, anyway. I will admit he is a pleasant fellow and a good fencer and that you think he is suitable, but a marriage should preferably be something that is more than just suitable."

She scoffed at him. "When did you become such a romantic? Oh yes, when you fell in love with Eliza Bennet's eyes."

"I will not deny it, though she *is* my wife, Miss Bingley," he said, not matching her tone but nearing it. This was the game they always played, even now when he didn't feel compelled to play it. "If we are to be so honest, then let us be honest. Even though marriage between us was never truly in question no matter how much you may have desired it, I am now Bingley's brother, and you are my sister, so I have some affection for you, of the kind where I am concerned about your future happiness. Maybe I will not chase down suitors with a sword as everyone seems to be implying I will do with Georgiana, but that does not mean I am completely without an opinion on the issue."

"But you would not have been had Charles not come to you."

"It is irrelevant. I simply wouldn't have known until some-one had told me as I live in Derbyshire and you in Town. And so Bingley came to tell me, and I knew and decided of my own wit to observe the matter myself. After all, if you are so intent on the match, this man is to be my brother-in-law and so I must have an interest in at least *meeting* him."

"But you will not deny that you have been looking at him with a most critical eye," she said.

"Miss Bingley, if you are so observant of my character, surely you know that I look at *everyone* with a most critical eye." He added, "Even Dr. Maddox."

She apparently decided to give this no proper response no mat-ter how many emotions registered on her face, so he decided to let it pass without further comment. She looked exhausted, as if this was as much a strain on her as it was on everyone else. He recalled the many sleepless nights during his own courtship, both the unhappy and the happy bits. Why should it not be the same for her? Finally, in a soft, strange voice unlike anything he had previously heard from her, she said, "We would not have made a good couple."

"No," he said, his own voice gentle. "We are too good for this sort of verbal sparring. But it does keep one's wits about one. We are better as brother and sister."

"Then do me a brotherly favour," she said, "and tell Bingley to grant his consent."

"If you ask him properly," he said, "in a way that conveys that you are in love with James Kincaid, he will surely grant it."

Again she did not respond. She huffed instead, like an angered peacock puffing up her feathers, and stormed out. She nearly slammed into Bingley, finally on his way to his appointment with Darcy. Smiling and oblivious, Bingley said, "What did I miss?"

Darcy slapped himself on the forehead and groaned.

"Yes, married," said a now thoroughly confused Lord William Kincaid. "His wife lives in a house in the north. She is a Highlander after all. But I refuse to be a gossip about my family's matters if you are merely here to discuss the country."

"And as you probably have already surmised," Mr. Bennet began, "we are not, though we did give our true names. Mrs. Darcy is my daughter, and I am not Mr. Darcy's steward, though he does know we are here."

Elizabeth curtseyed deeply, "My lord, we apologise for the situation, but the matter is apparently more grave than we thought. Your brother—if we are correct in assuming it is the same man, or you have other older brothers who went to Australia to seek a fortune—"

"Of which I do not—"

"Is newly returned to London and claims to have made a great fortune there and is to be affianced to my sister by marriage, whose name I will not mention for her reputation. My husband and her brother were suspicious of the arrangement and are now investigating his connections, but since my husband's estate is further north than they are right now, I decided to make some investigations here myself as to who this man was."

"And I, being an old man with little chance for amusement and not willing to see my daughter off to the north unaccompanied, joined her," Mr. Bennet said, bowing to the earl.

The earl sputtered for a few moments before speaking as he took it in. "Well . . . well, I don't know what to say, except that you should cancel the engagement as quickly as possible. I doubt very highly of his supposed fortune. In his limited correspondences with Fiona and me, he not only refused to come home but continued to draw on Fiona's inheritance, which is considerable. She even attempted to request a divorce, but he refused—repeatedly." He shrugged. "If he is so in love with your sister, now I suppose . . ."

"We do not know if he is in love," Elizabeth interrupted, "but the entire matter is extremely distasteful. I am sorry, but we know nothing of your brother's character and must judge him only on what you have told us, and if what you have told us is true, then he is intending to be a bigamist."

Lord Kincaid straightened and said with authority, "I would not doubt it, if he thought he could get away with it. And with the complex differences between Scottish and English marriage laws, perhaps he could. But I *do* know my brother's character, and I will stop myself and say only there is a reason our father chose me to inherit over James, and that you must do everything to stop this engagement to your sister." He rubbed his chin in thought. "I suppose the best way to confront him is for me to go down there myself, but would it be too late?"

"Frankly, I have no idea," Elizabeth said. "But I would not bother you with the task, as my husband is a most loyal protector of even his extended family and would be happy to sort the matter out. Perhaps you have some proof that the marriage to Lady Kincaid still stands?"

"Yes, in fact, I do," he said. "After all, she's been trying to obtain a divorce, so all of these documents were made ready and even duplicated. I have copies here myself that I would be more than happy to loan to you. He has already put Fiona through so much trouble; I will not see it happen to another woman. It is outright dishonourable, and we Scots do not stand for dishonour to the family or the clan." He called out to a servant and gave the necessary instructions for the documents to be located. "I can give you Fiona's address, but she is some distance north, and if you wish to speak with her, I feel you will just lose time. You may wish a correspondence, but that is at your discretion. Now, to put it quickly, is there anything I can do for you, Mrs. Darcy?"

She had already considered it. "Can you perhaps loan me a horse?"

"Lizzy!" Mr. Bennet interrupted, dropping all formal pretences. "You cannot seriously be proposing—"

"My own husband taught me to ride, and it will be quicker even than the post," she said. "And I would not trust such important documents to a courier, especially over borders. I will not push myself excessively, Papa, but someone must get to Town with the documents."

"It should not be you."

"And it will not be *you*," she said.

"I would ride myself," Lord Kincaid said, "but I do not know the way. I confess I have never been to England. But I could ride with you for your safety."

"You put yourself out, my lord."

"This is my brother and my responsibility."

He reminded Elizabeth quite a bit of a Scottish Darcy. The very memory brought her warm thoughts when otherwise all she could think of was disaster. "No, I will not allow it. You may follow in a proper carriage if you wish and see that the matter is carried out, but I will go, and I will go at the speed at which I choose."

"I can see there is no arguing with you, Mrs. Darcy."

"There never is," said Mr. Bennet.

"I will prepare the horse and the necessary supplies. Mr. Bennet, you will accompany me in the carriage?"

"Only if you promise to drop him off along the way," Elizabeth said, "at an estate called Chatton." She turned to her immediately questioning father. "Papa, you cannot go all the way to Town right now, and Jane must be told by someone with the calmness to do it properly. Besides, you despise travelling."

Mr. Bennet shook his head. "I cannot—well, I cannot convince you that your plan is madness and a danger to your health. All for the sake of Miss Bingley?"

"She is my sister-in-law."

"At this moment I wish she were not. But I see there is no convincing you otherwise. There never is." Mr. Bennet shook his head. "Lord Kincaid, thank you for your hospitality and all of your aid."

"Most gladly given, however unhappy the circumstances. *Sealbh math dhuit.*" He added, "It means good luck, Mrs. Darcy. You will need it."

Before entering, Bingley steeled himself with a shot of whiskey. It was not his custom, but it was not enough to make him

drunk (after all, he was not Darcy), and he needed the reinforce-
ment. Not only was Caroline smarter, older, and taller than he,
but she was as intimidating a woman as there ever could be, and
all past attempts to verbally spar with her had ended in disaster.

Still, he had no other recourse. He knocked on her door.
"Caroline?"

"Come in," she said, her voice entirely composed. When he
entered, her posture made it very clear that, though she was perfectly dressed and this was merely her dressing chamber, he was
invading her personal space. "I suppose Darcy told you everything."

"Very little, in fact. The rest was left to my imagination," he
said. "If you feel slighted by him for his actions these past days,
you must excuse Darcy. He is only acting on my behalf since I
requested his help in this matter."

"In this matter," Caroline scoffed. "You can marry a country
girl of no fortune, but when I find a suitable match, it becomes
a matter that involves even the master of Pemberley."

"That is not the point—"

"It *is* the point," she said, stepping toward him. "You rely on
him for every basic decision, Charles. It is pathetic."

No, he would not be cowed. He was Charles Bingley Junior
and the master of the Bingley fortunes. He was a member of the
landed class, even if he was untitled. He was a man of stature,
and he had every right to do as his conscience required. "That
is not the case at all. I did not like Lord Kincaid from the start,
and so I did what any good businessman would do—what our
father was so good at to the point of raising us to a high position such as our own—to find an expert and delegate authority.
Darcy is better at looking into the sordid pasts of people than I

am, and so I called on him. I practically had to drag him here, if you must know, but he did it as a favour to me and to you despite his own instincts."

"Because of what? What do you find so lacking in James?"

That was, of course, the question he could not answer properly, so he had to invent something. "He appears out of nowhere with no established property and no connections in Town and pays in cash for his lodging. If he made a fortune in Australia that is wonderful for him, but no one has seen a pence of it. I cannot help but, with your inheritance, to be suspicious. More importantly, I know very well you do not love him, and that is my greatest concern."

"You make many assumptions about my feelings, Charles."

He fumed. "I am not the idiot you plainly believe me to be. Your affection for him derives from his own charms and perhaps his fluency in Italian but has no solid foundation."

"This is what you believe?"

"You have yet to deny it."

At least Caroline seemed to recognise his determination. She took an unthinking step back. "What do you expect from me? Am I to continue to be the unmarried spinster, the laugh of all of Town?"

"You are being dramatic."

"In a few years I will not be!" she said, her voice unintentionally betraying emotion, something it rarely did. "I am thirty years old. I live off your fortune. Lord Kincaid is likely to be my last serious prospect for a good match."

He considered before answering. "Caroline, surely you have noticed that both Darcy and I would argue with you for what constitutes a 'good match.'"

"And you are both men with fortunes. The situation is entirely different."

He sighed. "To see you happy, I would gladly pay for your marriage to the Town's poorest pauper and buy him a great estate in Derbyshire."

To this, she had no proper response.

It seemed Bingley's responsibility, after some moments of awkward silence, to continue the conversation. "Caroline," he said formally, his hands behind his back, "I can't imagine . . . well, yes, I can imagine . . . where it was drilled into you that you must marry a man of at least equal, preferably greater, fortune to be a woman of any worth. You are a Bingley and must stand up to the name that father created. But he created that name out of smoke and hard work and clever business manoeuvres. And now our beloved father is gone and no longer makes the family policy on marriage. And since it falls to my shoulders, I will reiterate my stance: you may marry whomever you like, provided he is not a fortune hunter and you are truly in love with him—be he pauper, parish priest, or dare I say doctor."

Miss Bingley had turned away to the window. At this, she spun back around. "How dare you—"

"I am not blind, even if my stay here has been of short duration. But on this matter, I will remain silent. It is for you and he to decide. I will withhold my blessing on this Lord Kincaid until you fall in love with him or he proves to be a fortune hunter—whichever comes first. However long that may take, I shall gladly wait it out to see you happy in your marriage. And it cannot be more than a few days."

"That or it will have to be much longer. Am I mistaken, or is Jane not in confinement?"

This threw him off; it was her intention. "Yes, and I must be out within the week. But if Lord Kincaid is exactly who he says he is, he is most welcome to join us at Chatton for as long as he wishes. Until then, we shall wait."

"Because that is what you are good at," she said, "waiting."

He could take no more of this. It was either that or he had said everything he desired to say, and so the conversation was allowed to end. He signalled this by placing his hand on the door handle. "I hope you will consider what I said, because there is only one thing I will not stand for, and it is to see you unhappy in marriage."

She did not respond as he left.

Darcy had one comfort in the days that passed and one anticipated comfort. The actual comfort was his sister, who with Elizabeth's good influence had begun to emerge as the confident young woman he had always hoped she would be, and she almost delighted in their little trips to bankers and the Gardiners, trying to account for Kincaid's mysterious wealth. Her light treatment of it put him at ease. This was also his first long trip to Town since her coming out, and he was glad to see that she was not being assaulted by suitors on a daily basis, though she did have her social calls, mainly among female friends. She was not the homebody he was, and it suited her greatly, he decided.

The second thing was the correspondences from Jane Bingley, meant to comfort him. They, of course, had the opposite effect. Elizabeth and Mr. Bennet were somewhere in Scotland; even though Jane was quick to assure him, in writing him directly, that they were expected home at any moment, this was the first time since their marriage that Elizabeth was out of his reach, and it made him moody and anxious. He was also taking measure to avoid the Bingley house after his confrontation with Miss Bingley, as he felt he had not the energy for it with all of the things he was busy doing on her behalf, and that gave him only more time to fret.

Several days passed before a formal meeting with Mr. Gardiner settled at least one matter. With the accounts—or what they could muster of them—spread out before them in his uncle's study, they took in the measure of the matter. This time, Bingley was present.

"So there we have it," Mr. Gardiner said. "Not only do we have no proof of any fortune currently here or in transfer from Australia, but we have several loans made on unknown credit at banks of questionable standing, which presumably he has used to pay for his lodgings and other expenses. All I could find with all of my contacts and some very improper questioning on my part—"

"Thank you, Mr. Gardiner," Bingley bowed to him.

"—was that over the last few years he had money come from somewhere in Scotland, somewhere in the Highlands, where he must have some account because it is not from his estate in the lowlands."

"So," Darcy said, "no damning evidence but a lack of the fortune he claims to have."

"It is very troubling," said Bingley, staring at the materials. "If he could produce any evidence of his own fortune, I would happily disregard all of this information."

"And yet, he will not," reminded Darcy.

"But I cannot toss him out based on this. You know that," Bingley said. When it came to money matters, they were all very calm men. "I could talk to Caroline—"

"She will dismiss it," Darcy said. "Or she may not. I don't know. The thing to do is confront the earl."

"I cannot in all good conscience condemn a man who on paper has done nothing wrong!" Bingley said.

"But you cannot give him what he wants either," said Mr. Gardiner.

Bingley frowned and played with a handkerchief for some time. The only thing to break him from his deep concentration was the handkerchief that he tore in half. Fortunately, the air was too serious, and no one laughed. "There is one other thing—Elizabeth."

"Thank you for reminding me," Darcy deadpanned.

"I mean to say she has gone to investigate his reputation in his home. Either she is returning now with news or—though I am wont to say it—something has happened to her—which is *also* news that may help decide the matter."

"I am glad you view my wife's safety in regards to Miss Bingley's situation!"

"Am I going to have to call someone to keep you from throttling each other?" Mr. Gardiner asked in all seriousness. "Because you're both stout young men, and I don't think I could do it."

"Darcy," Bingley said calmly and in the most soothing tone he could manage, "I did not mean to imply that. I was merely stating the fact. Any moment now a letter could arrive—"

"I am sick of 'any moment now'! It is all your wife writes to me!" Darcy shouted, bringing immediate silence to the room. He used an occasional stern voice, but Mr. Darcy *never* shouted. "I am sorry," he said quickly. "I feel I must retire, and do . . . something." He did not want to explain himself. He wanted to find somewhere else to fret about Elizabeth. He stormed out of the Gardiners with barely a cursory bow and apology.

"Brother!" Georgiana, who had been playing with the Gardiner children, followed him in concern.

He did not speak for the whole carriage ride to their townhouse, and she did not ask him to. He was too focused, too upset, and too desperate not to show it. When he stepped out of the carriage at last, the cold late November air did him good, and only then was he shaken from his trance and noticed the unfamiliar horse being handled by one of his servants. He practically kicked in the door to find Elizabeth having her extensive winter garments removed by the servants. "Elizabeth!"

She turned to him, her face without colour, and she promptly swooned into his arms.

Chapter 6

MRS. DARCY RIDES AGAIN

HER FACE WAS FREEZING. Darcy called for everyone available to assist him in getting her to bed, even though he carried her himself right up the stairs without any aid. Georgiana fetched the warm water and brought a cloth to her forehead as quickly as she could.

"Darcy," Elizabeth whispered.

"Elizabeth," he said, his voice almost cracking as he stroked her cheek, "are you hurt in any way?"

"I am very sore," she said, "but that will pass. I am . . . sorry for the spectacle."

He gave her a supportive smile. "I would expect nothing less from you than some sort of memorable entrance. Next time, try not to let it involve your health."

She smiled and kissed his hand as it passed. Her lips at least were warm, even if they were still a bit blue.

"I take it—you rode here? Some long distance?"

She nodded.

"How long?"

"All of it."

"From *Scotland?*"

Again, a nod. "There are documents . . . from Lord Kincaid, the brother of this man Miss Bingley wants to marry." She coughed and then straightened herself on the pillow. "He is married. I have a copy of the contract."

"*What?*" Georgiana, the first to respond, nearly dropped the bowl where she was standing.

"Lizzy, this is true?" he said, taking her hand. "He is currently married to a woman in Scotland?"

"And he refuses a divorce."

"Damning evidence indeed," he said. "Our suspicions were correct, then. I confess, we achieved here in Town not half of what you did, and we even had Mr. Gardiner aiding us. But surely, could you not have sent a courier?"

"Are you implying . . . you would rather see a courier . . . than your own wife?"

"Lizzy," he said. "You will send me to Bedlam yet."

"Always my intention."

Georgiana interrupted, "Should I send for someone? Mr. Bingley maybe?"

But he could not think of Bingley at the moment. "In time. Unless Miss Bingley and Kincaid are somehow by magic at Gretna Green right now against his wishes, there is no rush. And if they were, then nothing can be done anyway. Please, we should let Elizabeth rest, and then she can tell us the whole story, and *then* we can go to Bingley."

Georgiana knew enough not to argue with him and excused herself. A nurse was called in and, after a quick inspection, decided Elizabeth merely needed rest. Darcy shooed her and the other servants away, closed the door, and lay down on the bed beside Elizabeth, above the covers, without even removing his boots. It was now midday, but he was in no mood for luncheon. In fact, he found he was exhausted himself, and now that his wife was beside him, he drifted off to sleep and did not realise it until he woke some hours later to find Elizabeth staring at him with some amusement.

"I rush here from Scotland," she said, her voice having regained much of its strength, "and the first thing you do is take a nap."

He smiled and kissed her. Her body heat had returned. "Worrying about one's wife can be quite exhausting."

"So can be preventing a marriage. You should have warned me in your vast experience."

"Vast experience? It was one . . . two times!" he laughed. "Now I suppose it will be three. Perhaps I should declare it my profession. But, my darling, whatever propelled you, who just recently learned to ride, to cross the country in November on a horse?"

"I made a bet with Wickham. If he hasn't appeared, I've won." Darcy laughed into his pillow.

"So am I to wait here all day for you to tell me what you've been doing in Town while I've been accomplishing everything?"

"I love you."

"That is not an answer, Darcy—or at least not a full one."

Thus, very happily, he recalled all of the events since his arrival in Town, leaving out what he judged irrelevant or not important at the moment. Even though it had been a stress on him at times, in her comforting presence it gave him no angst to retell any of the events. It all seemed now something of the distant past. "And if it would not tire you further, I would very much like to hear about Scotland."

So she told him, and he immediately excused his father-in-law for impersonating his steward. He even laughed at parts of the story, at least until they began to seriously discuss the marriage of the would-be bigamist Lord Kincaid. "Well, the marriage is off," he said. "I suppose she will have to finally come to her senses about the doctor."

"What doctor?"

"Oh, did I leave that part out? I suppose I was trying to be prudent. It seems Miss Bingley is not above the general tendency in our now-related families for infatuations with people below their stations."

"Below their—Darcy!" She hit him with a pillow. "Though I suppose it did turn out well in the end."

He was going to respond, but she grabbed his arm very suddenly. "I am in need of a bucket, *please*."

He understood enough to get her a chamber pot and turned away as she was ill. Perhaps they would need the doctor after all. But it did break the serenity in the air of their bedchamber, and more pressing matters began to invade his mind again, even though his wife's health was at the forefront. He called for a maid again who collected the pot. "Elizabeth—"

"It is nothing. Probably that awful inn I stopped at last night. I should have known better, but I was starving." She was sitting up now and looking less pale. "Perhaps we should get to the business of letting poor Mr. Bingley down."

"Or cheering him up," he said.

Bingley, when summoned and given the purpose in a note, made uncommonly good time to the Darcy residence. By then, Elizabeth had persuaded her husband to let her come downstairs into the sitting room where much tea was forced upon her, and she had her satchel brought to her.

"Mrs. Darcy," Bingley said, obviously relieved to see her alive and well. "We were quite worried about you. Should I write Jane?"

"My father went straight to Chatton, so she is informed by now, but her letter must not have reached you if she wrote one. Anyway, there are other things pressing." She opened the sack and presented him with the documents, which he sat and inspected for some time without saying anything.

"These will hold up in court?" he finally said.

"It is not a matter of courts," Darcy said. "Lord Kincaid must merely be exposed, and he will doubtless be scurrying off in some direction. Though it will distress her greatly, you may take comfort that this will not break Miss Bingley's heart."

"How it is to be done, though—"

"In great privacy, for the family's reputation—and especially your sister's." Darcy, as usual, already had a plan. "May I suggest you tell her in private if he does not see fit to confess it himself?"

"And how will we convince him to do this and yet not expose his plot to all of Town?"

"I will do it," Darcy offered. "I have confronted him and bested him once; this should be simple enough, and I am far enough removed from you that it will complicate things less if there is a resulting scandal that must be covered up. I will take all the documents and go to his lodging at once. Now that we have proof, this can no longer stand to wait."

Elizabeth decided to leave out that Darcy had just lingered half a day with his wife like a newlywed. "And what am I to do?"

They both looked at her.

"I'm serious!"

"Elizabeth, you have done more than both of us in less time," Bingley said. "I can ask no more of you, other than to recover your health and perhaps write to Jane that you are here and recovering." He stood up. "I will return to my house and pretend nothing clandestine is occurring. And if Lord Kincaid is there— which he should not be—I will send him home right away."

"And I always thought you incapable of deception," Elizabeth said.

Bingley was still trying to decide whether to take that as a compliment or not when they parted.

Unfortunately, there were no servants to greet Darcy at the door to Lord Kincaid's lodging, and he was forced to stand in the cold until Lord Kincaid himself let him in. "Oh, Darcy, do come in."

Darcy entered. The place was as it had been described— grand, but lacking furniture and other embellishments. "I apologise for the state of my rooms, but I believe that can be excused, all things considered," Kincaid said. "I've simply been too busy to get even the most basic things done, as you can see.

Not properly English at all—I should be more attentive. Would you like me to—," but as he turned around to face Darcy after shutting the door, he was presented with what Darcy was fairly sure was the very legal marriage contact between him and some Scottish woman named Fiona.

"We can dispense with the pretences now, I believe," Darcy said. Not having to force himself into being agreeable with this man was extremely relieving; he felt as if the weight was off his shoulders already, despite the utter severity of the situation. "If your banking records were not enough to condemn you, I believe this would do for any family, no matter their standing or desperation to marry off their sister. And Bingley cares for his sister a great deal."

"You can stop waving that in front of me; I know what it is," Kincaid said, quickly regaining his composure. He was not at ease now and did in fact make no pretences, but he was not a snivelling villain. He stood up straight, readying himself as a fencer would for a match. "After all, that is my signature. No, Mr. Darcy, I will not deny it."

"Even if you agreed to divorce Lady Kincaid tomorrow, which to my knowledge you have refused to do many times despite abandoning her, it would hardly make a good impression on your intended in-laws. Nor would the nonexistent fortune you found in Australia. I do not know your true intentions, but I will surmise that they had something to do with Miss Bingley's personal fortune. In fact, it would be best to assume that you would merely disappear sometime after you had funnelled all of it away, as you did with Lady Kincaid, and not something worse."

"So you are going to assume the best," Kincaid said. "How very nice of you, Darcy. You are indeed the knight in shining armour, forever rescuing the Bingleys from their ridiculous romantic entanglements, as they have not the wits to do so themselves."

"As you are a deserter, a liar, a thief, and would this day be a bigamist if Bingley had granted his consent, I can only expect that you would stoop so low as to insult anyone you cared to," Darcy snapped back. "But I will not stand for it. You do not give Mr. Bingley enough credit. It was only his fine senses that brought me here in the first place and Miss Bingley giving herself away as having no deep affection for you. Perhaps there was nothing in you to inspire great love."

"There is nothing in her to inspire great love," Kincaid said. "You of all people know that. You spurned her for years, so at least on this issue we see eye to eye."

"Just because I did not wish to marry Miss Bingley does not mean we could ever see 'eye to eye' on her," Darcy answered. "You are, once again, totally incorrect in your assumptions. She is a woman of great intelligence and dignity—everything you said to me at the club when you were pretending to be entranced. In fact, I respect her a great deal more than almost all of the other women I had known previous to meeting my wife and Mrs. Bingley."

"Fancy words from a man who can afford to make them," Kincaid seethed. "I'll admit, you've been a clever opponent and would see that there was more to the match than pure, deep love—whatever that is, if it exists beyond medieval romances. But how you managed to get my own marriage contract and before I broke Bingley down—that was most impressive."

"Credit my wife, as that is where credit is due," Darcy said. "Even from afar, she was suspicious."

"Why? Because Caroline is so dislikeable that she could not imagine someone would marry her without direct sight on her fortune?"

Aggressive stance again because his opponent knew his weakness. Darcy again had to defend Miss Bingley, the woman whom he had shrugged off even after she had spent years pursuing him. An admirable attempt, but that he believed in her faults was obvious enough by their history. Fine, he could parry. "Because my wife trusts Mr. Bingley's instincts, which are keener than people think. It had nothing to do with Miss Bingley at all. Had I come to Town and discovered her horribly in love with you, I would not have been so eager to find fault. She is my sister by marriage, and I hope to see her happy." No, he could not do this forever. He needed to strike, be offensive. "And though this will distress her, she will know the truth of it. You will tell her."

Kincaid laughed. "You tell me I am a liar and a crook, and now you expect me to be noble for no reason? Already I am beyond saving in the family's eyes, so the matter, as far as I'm concerned, is concluded. Why should I put myself out and expose myself to that woman again? You know she can be quite the vicious snake when not being fawning and pretentious."

"You will not walk away from this; let me make that clear. Your brother is on his way now, and he will deal with you in whatever matter you Scots do up there; I care not. But I could make it much worse than that if you do not apologise to Caroline and beg for her forgiveness, whether she grants it or not—which we both know she shall not, and you will be at the mercy of that vicious tongue of hers. I only wish it would be proper for me to be there." He held up the satchel. "I have not only your marriage documents but copies of notes from all of the banks whence you have borrowed money. Money I know you have no way of repaying unless your brother comes through for you, and from Elizabeth's description of his attitude toward you, he will not be in a generous mood when he arrives, and you will quickly be in debtor's prison—that is, unless you are allowed to make your escape." His stance expressed his finality; the choice was before Kincaid.

The earl merely shrugged. "I am not intimidated by you, Mr. Darcy. You are not master of London, and I assume you are here to avoid a scandal for your extended family. So I may have to face my brother, but I will not face that woman again. I see no reason to put myself in such a position. And do you really think it will make her feel better? That she will run to her four-eyed paramour?" He laughed. "Did you know he proposed to her? That spineless servant had the audacity to propose to perhaps the vainest woman in West London!"

This, Darcy did not know, but he could not reveal it and made every attempt to hide it. He hoped he was successful. "The choice is before you. Debtor's prison or escaping to wherever you can manage before the real Lord Kincaid gets here. Please choose, as I am a very busy man, and you are very boring."

"You are a bad liar; you are very intrigued by what I have to say. But I will not take up any more of your precious time, Mr. Darcy. My answer is no. I will not grovel to Caroline Bingley or any other Bingley or anyone related to the Bingley family by marriage or otherwise. That includes you. I will only grant you the small favour of leaving town before the scandal hits. Perhaps that will diminish it. I care not either way." He waved Darcy off as one would a servant. "So you'd better get out of this disreputable house and give me my chance before all those creditors and relatives of mine arrive."

"That is your final answer, then?"

"Do I stutter? Is my accent incomprehensible to you?" As their conversation had turned negative, his Scottish accent, which he usually took great pains to disguise for good London society, had increasingly slipped out. "No, Darcy. I will have nothing more to do with any Bingley or you. Now as you are a proper English gentleman, certainly more than this Scottish rogue, you will do me the honour of leaving my house." He gave him a very stiff, mocking bow.

"You are making a serious mistake," Darcy said with all of the severity he could muster and then turned to the door.

"No, it is you who are making the mistake."

Darcy's hand had not reached the doorknob when he heard the gunshot. By then, it was too late.

Chapter 7

THE SHOT HEARD 'ROUND TOWN

As Darcy slumped sideways, leaning against the column as his body sunk to the floor, Kincaid had two matters immediately pressing. The first was a candlestick to his head. It was not enough to knock him unconscious entirely, but the shock and pain of it was distracting enough that it sent him sideways where his body was met with a wooden chair. Caught between two very hard places, he trembled and then fell, smashing face forward onto the marble floor.

"Mrs. Darcy!"

"Mr. Bingley!"

For they were both very surprised to find the other there, each one holding an impromptu weapon, having emerged from opposite rooms.

Elizabeth dropped the candlestick, horrified at her actions. "I just meant to hit him a little!"

"So did I!"

"I've been shot!" Darcy said.

Bingley dropped the chair and joined Elizabeth as they abandoned the unconscious Kincaid and ran to Darcy who was only sitting up because his body had fallen against the column and so was propped up. From the front he looked fine, if a little pale, but a quick inspection revealed that the pillar and the back of his coat were both quickly soaking with blood.

"Darcy, are you all right?"

Darcy gave Bingley a look he would normally bestow on a complete idiot.

"Well, he's conscious at least," Bingley said. "Where does it hurt?"

Darcy didn't respond at first, apparently more than a little stunned at this new prospect of being shot in the back. Finally he gasped and said in a tiny voice, "I'm a little cold, to be honest."

Elizabeth put her hands on his cheeks. "Stay with us, please, darling."

Darcy did not respond. He was clearly struggling to keep his eyes open. "I'll get help," Bingley said.

"Get the constable! And a decent surgeon! Darcy will not be cut up by some student!"

Bingley could only nod as he disappeared out the door, barely stopping to close it behind him. Meanwhile, Elizabeth removed her coat and placed it over Darcy who was shivering and trying to say something. "Shhh. You don't have to say anything." She inspected him again and saw no blood in the front, only blood pouring out his back. As far as she could tell from the tear in the fabric, he'd been shot in the upper chest very close to the shoulder. "The bullet hasn't gone straight through." She didn't know if that was good or bad. All of the blood was making her nauseous, but she swallowed it down. There was no time for that now. "Darcy?" His eyes were closing again, and she dared to shake him, just a little. "Fitzwilliam Darcy, for the record, if you die, I will never forgive you."

His face gave no indication that any of her words were registering, but he was making an attempt to keep himself awake. "Lizzy—"

"Don't tire yourself. Please, just stay with me." She did not even notice the entrance of the constables that Bingley had alerted. She did not hear their questions. "Darcy, please."

He smiled. "I—I love you." And then his eyes rolled back into his head, and there was no more visible struggle. Elizabeth hugged his chest and wept until someone pulled her off to make way for a man who seemed to be some kind of doctor. Bingley was nowhere in sight.

This man felt Darcy's pulse and put his head to his chest. "He's alive. He's just unconscious from the shock."

"I take it this is not his home," said the constable, turning to Elizabeth.

"No," she said, trying to collect herself. Darcy was alive. "No, no. It's that man's—the man who shot my husband." She pointed to Kincaid. The pistol had dropped from his hand on impact from her strike and was lying next to him. "I'm Mrs. Darcy. We have a house in the West End. Can he be moved?"

"It would be best to try to stop the bleeding first," said the apparent physician. He called for a constable to help him get Darcy to a couch as another held Mrs. Darcy and kept her from running to her husband. "'Sit okay if we cut off the garb? Some gents get angry—"

"No, no, do whatever you have to do." She was a little annoyed at the constable holding her back, but she had not the strength to resist him. Instead she watched helplessly as they cut away the sleeve of Darcy's coat and shirt, exposing the wound, which the physician immediately covered with the cloth from his undershirt and pressed down on.

Time seemed to be moving in another realm; Elizabeth thought only moments had passed since she had seen her husband go down, and yet they were bandaging him, and before she knew it, someone had taken away Kincaid in chains, and Mr. Bingley appeared soaked and half covered in mud from the waist down. He was flanked by a curly-haired man with glasses and a large black bag. "This . . . is . . . Dr. Maddox," Bingley said between heaving breaths. Had he actually run the whole way to his townhouse? "Very good . . ."

Dr. Maddox bowed to Mrs. Darcy and the constable and turned immediately to Mr. Darcy and the attending physician. "What are you doing?"

"Trying to stop the bleeding."

"Is there an exit wound?"

"No, sir."

"Then we have to get the bullet out as soon as possible. But that must be done in more sanitary conditions. Here—let me bandage him. Can someone prepare a stretcher? And we'll need several blankets."

The constable holding Elizabeth went to handle these orders; once released, she ran to her husband who was on his stomach and totally unresponsive to her voice. It was Bingley who took her in his arms, and she could feel his heart still pounding, probably from all the running. On any other day, the sight of Mr. Bingley running through slushy, muddy London on a cold November day would be an amusing one, but at the moment, she found no comfort. "He's going to be all right. This is the best doctor in Britain."

"He just . . . he couldn't stay awake. He tried so hard."

"I would actually prefer him to remain unconscious for the trip to your residence," Dr. Maddox said, not facing her, consumed in his work as he tied up the bandages winding them around Darcy's arm. "It will make the trip easier. Someone, please tell me when things are ready."

"Is the bleeding stopped?"

"It won't be until I sew it up, and I can't do that with a bullet in him," Maddox explained in a calm, decisive, but compassionate voice. "I assume he would want this done in his home."

"Yes," Elizabeth said.

"Then can one of you send ahead orders to have water heated to boiling then covered and put outside to cool so it will be ready when we get there?"

"I'll do it," Bingley said, releasing his hold on Elizabeth, and he ran out to find a messenger or to run there himself.

With his patient temporarily stabilised, Dr. Maddox bowed to Elizabeth. "Mrs. Darcy, I assume."

"Yes." She curtseyed to him, but the action was too much for her, and she toppled over. "This is very selfish of me, but I need to be ill."

"I understand." Without question, he helped her to the kitchen where she lost her afternoon tea in a basin. "Look, the stretcher is here. Everything is going to be fine, Mrs. Darcy." He left her when she seemed steady again to attend to his more pressing patient, but sincere as he sounded, she had trouble believing his words.

The short ride to the Darcy townhouse was the most torturous ride of Elizabeth's life. Not only did the usual rocking of the carriage make her queasy, but the fact that the carriage was following a wagon with her husband covered in blankets made it positively unbearable. Only Bingley's presence and calming touch as he held her shaking hands kept her from swooning.

When they stepped out and the servants rushed to them, it finally occurred to her that she would have to deal with Georgiana Darcy, who must have been told by the messenger. "Brother!" the girl cried, and was only kept away from the stretcher by Dr. Maddox who insisted that they'd better get him inside as fast as possible, and it was easier without her in the way. They got him upstairs to an audience of horrified servants and into his bedchamber where everything had been prepared, and the maid was just gathering together extra towels.

The first order of business was apparently who was to go in the room. "Mrs. Darcy, I must insist—," Dr. Maddox said in the doorway.

"No use in that," Bingley said. "If you weren't the doctor and you were still standing in the way, she would strike you with a candlestick right now."

Elizabeth gave Maddox a look of extreme severity, one that made him back out of her way. She did turn back to Georgiana. "Why don't you organise the water we're going to need? Dr. Maddox wants it boiled and then cooled. And we'll need lots of disposable towels."

"Darcy—"

"I know." She hugged her sister. "I know, but I think he would take great comfort in you *not* watching this."

"He's not going to cut his arm off, is he?"

"No . . . No?" She looked at Maddox for confirmation, and he shook his head. "No. Please, help your brother by helping in the kitchen."

Georgiana was not one to put up a fight, and so she disappeared. Maddox emptied the bedchamber of weeping maids and called only for a single servant "with a strong stomach." He allowed Bingley and Mrs. Darcy to stay and asked that the door be closed as he opened his bag and began to unload a strange assortment of instruments onto the bed stand.

Meanwhile, the patient was coming around. Mr. Darcy mumbled incoherently and made some attempt to move, as if he were trying to get off a rough spot on the bed he could not identify. Elizabeth took his hand. "Darcy."

"Can we sit him up?" Maddox said as he washed his own hands. He took a bottle of green liquid and a spoon and pulled up the chair in front of Darcy. "Mr. Darcy, do you think you can swallow?"

Darcy opened his eyes, but his answer was incomprehensible. Maddox filled the spoon. "Open his mouth, please." The servant awkwardly opened Darcy's mouth. "Now, Mr. Darcy, this is not going to taste very good, but trust me when I say it will make this far more bearable." And then he carefully put the spoon in and emptied its contents. "Now, try to swallow." Darcy managed to do as he was told. Everything else, he was fairly oblivious to. "Good, good." Maddox put the jar and spoon aside and took a piece of leather from his bag. "You're going to want to bite down on this."

Again, there was no real answer, but it wasn't expected at this point. They got Darcy on his stomach, exposing the wound, and at Maddox's insistence, Bingley kept Elizabeth turned away, but she would not relinquish her hold on Darcy's hand. From the corner of her eyes she could see Maddox putting his glasses up in his bushy hair and peering close to the wound with his instruments, and it was up to her vivid imagination to invent what was taking place. It did not take much work.

It took a long time, longer than she expected. How long did it take to find a bullet? It was black and metal, and it didn't belong there. Maybe it was buried in bone. Again her stomach turned and threatened, but she swallowed the bile and tightened her grip around Darcy's cold and unresponsive hand. "You're doing well, darling. Did I tell you Geoffrey said his first word? It was his name."

Time and time again Dr. Maddox called for more towels and the warm water. "Aha!" he said finally, holding up his pliers with the small bullet that had brought so much havoc into their lives. He put it on a saucer on the bed stand beside his other items. "Don't dispose of it. Now then, Mr. Darcy, the hole is very small, and the worst is over." He asked the servant for his needles, and Elizabeth sobbed again as Dr. Maddox went to sew up her husband. Only Bingley's firm hand kept her from peeking at the actual procedure. "There. Just one more wash . . . Mr. Darcy, you are a most excellent patient."

It was hard to judge Darcy's reaction to any of this during the operation because he was face down on the bed, his head turned away from Elizabeth, and he made very little sound. It was only when Dr. Maddox gave the order for them to turn him back over was it clear that he was at least partially conscious, but he said nothing when the bit was removed. Dr. Maddox washed his hands for what seemed the tenth time, removed his bloodied smock, and replaced his glasses. "There should be at least four layers of cloth between him and the sheets, and they should be changed at least every six hours," he said to the servant. "No exceptions." Again he reached for the bottle and the spoon, which he washed in yet another dish of clean water. "Now, Mr. Darcy, if you would oblige me and open your mouth . . ."

This time he succeeded in opening his mouth on his own, to the great relief of everyone. He was responsive to commands. He swallowed the green solution with a look of distaste. "I know; it is most unsavoury," Maddox said. "But you're the better with it; trust me. All right, Mr. Darcy needs his rest, and if I would dare to say, Mrs. Darcy, you need some as well—and perhaps a change of clothes."

She had not realised how bloodied her own garments had become, as had Bingley's. "Yes." She wiped the tears from her eyes, kissed her husband on the cheek, and opened the door for the maid to request a change of clothes. "But first, an assessment?"

"Outside, if you would."

He was so polite and yet full of authority, at least in his role of doctor. The three of them stood in the hallway outside the master bedchamber. Dr. Maddox pushed his glasses further up on his nose. "I believe he will be fine. It took a long time because the bullet was very close to several nerves in the neck. If I had extracted it too forcibly, there would have been damage, and he might have lost movement in his arm or his leg. Nerves are tricky things. He has lost a lot of blood, but he is young and healthy, so he should recover in time. And I don't know; he may wish to keep the bullet. Some men prefer it as a keepsake."

"I doubt it, but thank you," Elizabeth said. "What was the medicine you gave him?"

"Not snake oil. It is an opium-based concoction, a recipe I got from a medical book in the Cambridge library. It will greatly decrease . . . well, let us say, his *awareness* of pain. The heart can only take so much, so I feel it is quite necessary." He bowed slightly to Elizabeth. "I would prefer, if the lady would allow it, to remain in the house with my patient until he is more recovered—"

"Of course. You may stay as long as you like, Doctor," she said.

"I will break the news to Mr. Hurst," Bingley said, "and Caroline. It seems I have much news to break."

"Better she hears it from you than town gossip," Maddox said, "though I would suggest a change of clothes before you return home, Mr. Bingley."

"Yes, of course." He put his hand on Maddox's shoulder. "We are forever indebted to you, Doctor."

"Mr. Darcy may not say the same when he first wakes again. He may be cursing me to every layer of hell." He bowed and excused himself.

"Elizabeth," Bingley said with concern. "You do not look well. You should rest, and someone should be with Darcy, anyway."

"How did you know to follow him to Kincaid's apartment?"

"Probably the same way you did. Darcy is so proper that he forgets that other people might not be," he said. "Though if we're counting, I think you did more damage than I did."

"Only because I chose a metal weapon," she said. "I must lend you some of Darcy's clothing, for you cannot go home like that."

"Good, because he is a much better dresser than I," Bingley said. "But don't tell him I said that."

"If I had the strength to laugh, I would," she said as Georgiana appeared on the steps.

"Elizabeth must retire," Bingley preempted her. "I will fill you in on everything, Miss Darcy. The short answer is that he is patched up and recovering."

The sigh of relief from Georgiana was audible. Elizabeth was grateful when he led Georgiana away because she was barely standing on her own and was eager to rush back into the bed-chamber where a maid was waiting. She changed into her night-clothes; Darcy was sound asleep so there was no reason to change behind the dressing screen, but she did it anyway out of habit, at least while the maid was there. Because of all of the towels soaking up blood, she did not get under the covers but stayed above them, covering herself with an extra blanket. Only holding his hand and listening to his steady breathing finally allowed her to drift into sleep. Even in such a state, he was her greatest ally.

LIZZY BENNET AND
FITZERS DARCY

ELIZABETH WAS NOT SURE how much time was passing, as she was lost in her own world beside her husband. In a way, it was reminiscent of their honeymoon, minus all the fun, and Darcy was no conversationalist this time around. Whether he roused at all or not she honestly had no idea because she spent her own time mostly asleep, aside from partaking of a few meals that were served to her on a tray. Dr. Maddox seemed to be in and out, but she paid him no attention until he stopped her from returning to bed. "Mrs. Darcy."

"Doctor," she said, still a little too dizzy to properly curtsey.

"If you would permit me, I would like to inquire as to your health—"

"I am fine," she insisted. "Just overtired."

"Mrs. Darcy," he said, more insistently, "How long have you been ill?"

There was clearly no hiding it from him. "Counting the journey . . . what day is it?"

"Fifth of December."

"So . . . the fifth? Really?"

"Yes."

She did a calculation in her mind. "Then, about two weeks, but . . ." But he didn't interrupt her. He just let the revelation dawn. "Oh, no. I had no idea. I would not have ridden—"

"At this stage, when we cannot even be sure, I would severely doubt that there is any danger," he said, "though I would not repeat the ride if I were you."

"I will know more . . . in a few days, I believe. Until then, not a word of this to anyone."

Dr. Maddox smiled. "I don't think Mr. Darcy is in the condition to process the information if you *did* tell him."

Further conversation was interrupted by Bingley climbing up the stairs. He looked exhausted himself and surprised to find Elizabeth up and about. "Elizabeth. Dr. Maddox."

"Mr. Bingley." The doctor bowed and scurried off like a servant, which, Elizabeth supposed, he technically was, despite whatever entanglements he had with the Bingley family.

"What was that about?" Bingley asked as soon as he was gone.

"I am not a gossip, Mr. Bingley!" she answered. "And besides, it was nothing that concerns you for once, if you can stand not being the centre of attention."

"I am quite accustomed to residing in Darcy's shadow as it is. All of the focus is positively draining," he said. "It is good to see you well."

"It is good to be upright, I admit, but I will feel better when we can say the same about Darcy." But they didn't need to dally on that, for their concerns were wearing on them enough as it was about the man sleeping in the next room. "I've no news of the outside world. You must update me."

"Jane has posted that your father is safely back in Chatton. I decided to write him instead and have him deliver her the news about . . . well, everything, especially Darcy."

Bingley always surprised her with his good sense. "Thank you."

"Anything for Jane. But besides that, our Lord Kincaid is in jail, and I hear his brother has arrived to see to the matter further, but so far, our family has not been implicated. Though, that is not what concerns me."

"And Miss Bingley?"

"I don't know."

She blinked. "What do you mean, you don't know?"

He shrugged in that hapless way of his. "I mean, I went straight home and told her in privacy and with great care, and I have never seen her so emotionless."

"What did she say?"

"Nothing. She dismissed me, but that was all," he said. "I am not at ease with comforting my sister. Perhaps I should have done a better job . . . but I assumed . . . I don't know." He scratched his head, further mussing up his hair in the process. "Maybe she wanted to be alone. And I was so distracted . . . and she has Louisa."

"Who I doubt has ever given her any good advice," Elizabeth said. "Perhaps I will speak with Miss Bingley—when Darcy is recovered."

"Yes." He looked a bit shook up at the discussion of his sister's welfare. "Now that there is nothing pressing . . ."

"You know that is not true."

"What are you referring to—Oh. You mean—"

"Dr. Maddox, yes."

"So Darcy told you. But . . . it is just suspicion."

"And what Kincaid said to Darcy . . . about the proposal."

"We have no way of knowing if that is true."

"I will find out," she said with determination, "when Darcy is awake."

"Yes, our first concern. May I see him?"

She led him into the bedchamber where Darcy was in his usual position, propped up on many pillows. The bleeding had ceased, but there was still a considerable chance of infection, so the sheets were changed regularly. The difference now was that, as Elizabeth approached him, his eyes fluttered open.

"Darcy!" she cried, and rushed closer to him as Bingley hovered over. "Can you hear me?"

He turned his head slightly to the side and said in a hoarse whisper, "I think I am leaning on a knife."

"You were shot. You had surgery." She cupped his cheek. "You're going to be all right. Bingley, get the doctor." She didn't take her eyes off her husband's as she gave orders, watching the obvious pain and confusion in them. "You're going to be all right."

"I love you," he said.

Bingley returned shortly with Dr. Maddox. "Mr. Darcy," the doctor bowed. "I see you have regained your senses. Are you in any discomfort?"

Darcy gave the doctor a look.

"Of course, I'm silly for asking. Please, swallow." He had the spoon and jar already prepared. "There we are. You're going to feel a little light-headed in a bit. You may wish to go to sleep. It's best not to fight it."

Darcy nodded and closed his eyes.

"His colour is returning," Elizabeth said to Maddox. "Do you think so?"

"If he escapes infection, he should be perfectly mended in time. And I have taken every precaution that I know against it. The rest is up to God." He pushed his glasses up on his nose again. "If he is still in pain in half the hour, please call for me, and I will give him another dose, but that is all for now. And he may not be . . . particularly lucid if you try to talk to him."

"Thank you, Doctor, for saving my husband's life."

He blushed at her curtsey, apparently only accustomed to being told what to do and then dismissed. "It's only my job, Mrs. Darcy." And he quickly disappeared.

"A bit shy," she said to Bingley. "How ever did he approach Miss Bingley?"

"I hardly have the details. All I know is he speaks many languages."

Elizabeth took up her place sitting on the bed next to him as Darcy dozed, and Bingley sat in the corner chair, apparently also unwilling to leave Darcy's side. After some time, while the servant brought his visitors some tea, Darcy mumbled something.

"Darcy?" Elizabeth said, taking his hand.

He opened his eyes but did not look directly into hers, apparently unable to focus properly. He looked instead at Bingley. "My God, you are . . . quite red."

Perhaps he was referring to Bingley's hair, which wasn't a proper red but more of an orange. Bingley stifled a chuckle. "Yes, I suppose. How do you feel?"

"Did I ever tell you . . . wait." He paused, and there was a gap in his thinking. "Tell me . . . something."

"All right."

"Eliza Bennet—what do you think of her?"

Bingley had trouble keeping a straight face; Elizabeth gave up entirely and was barely muffling her laughter, which was too much to Darcy's side for him to see. "I think she's a lovely woman and has a very beautiful sister."

"No . . . I mean, yes . . . of course . . . but—she has not . . . the eyes. You know . . . the older one."

"Jane?"

"Yes. Will she dance with me?"

"Jane or Elizabeth?"

"Who?"

"We were talking," Bingley said patiently, "about our wives."

"Oh, yes." And then Darcy said nothing, as if the conversation were finished. In fact, he closed his eyes as if he were going back to sleep, before saying, "Where's the carriage?"

"What carriage?"

"The one that rolled over me."

Elizabeth said, "You were shot, Darcy."

He opened his hazy eyes and looked in her general direction. "Oh." He paused, moving the conversation at his own speed, and added, "How? I'm . . . very good."

"At shooting people in the back?" she said, with mock horror.

"At fencing. I could beat 'im . . . just parry and—" He made a sort of motion with his right hand, but he lacked the coordination to have it resemble anything like an actual parry.

"This was a bullet, dear husband."

"I could—I could parry a bullet." He waved his arm again in that bizarre motion. Finally, Elizabeth put out a hand to stop him.

"Darling, please, don't tire yourself."

He looked at her and made great (and rather slow) attempts to focus his eyes as if he were trying to make sure she was the person he suspected her to be. "I love you, Lizzy Bennet."

"And I love you, Fitzers Darcy."

He nodded and closed his eyes. Both his guests had to leave the room immediately because they could no longer contain their laughter. They shut the door and filled the hallway with it.

"I can't *believe* you got away with that!"

"I'm not sure I got away with it," she said. "Oh, but it was worth it. As horrible as it is to take advantage of a man without his senses, it was worth it."

"Most definitely."

They were not quite recovered from their escapades when Georgiana appeared up the stairwell. "What are you two laughing about?"

"Nothing," they said simultaneously. Bingley wiped the last of the tears from his eyes.

"And I am to believe that?" Georgiana crossed her arms with a Darcy-like look of determination.

"Your brother is . . . indisposed," Elizabeth said, a smile creeping back across her face. "Dr. Maddox gave him something for pain that has made him muddle-headed."

"Oh. Well, let me through, then. Should I not have my fair share?"

"Georgiana—" Bingley put up some protest, but she sideswiped him and went right to her brother's side and took his hand, waking him from his light sleep.

"Brother," she said with a very serious voice.

"Georgiana," he smiled. "Sweet Georgiana."

"I am affianced. I have found the most disreputable bachelor in Town, and I will marry him at Gretna Green on Sunday."

This was a very long sentence for Darcy to comprehend, if he was comprehending anything at all. "All right . . . then."

"So you give your consent?"

"Of course. But first I must . . . castrate him . . . before the ceremony."

Any pretence that laughter was going to be held in by the two onlookers was now entirely abandoned. They all had to leave the room very quickly. As they left, they missed Darcy mumbling, "Kill . . . you all . . ."

The next greatest challenge was getting Darcy sitting up. This was complicated by the fact that, when he was finally lifted into the chair, dressed in underclothing and a robe, he refused Dr. Maddox's medicine, saying it "dulled his senses." He was obviously still in pain, leaning slightly to one side to take the pressure off his left elbow, but he would not hear the doctor's protests, dismissing them with a very weak gesture.

"It is no use," Elizabeth explained. "My husband is the most stubborn man in England."

"And my wife is the most stubborn woman in England," Darcy replied, but his voice was still ragged. "So we are . . . a very well-matched . . . pair."

Elizabeth kissed him on the head, and Dr. Maddox took his leave as Bingley entered, and wife and friend began to update him on the events that had occurred since his trip to Kincaid's apartment, of which he remembered very little. Even without the laudanum affecting his mind, he had trouble coming to terms with being shot in the back.

"Despicable man," was all he said, and had no further comment on Kincaid and seemed to show little interest in how and where he was incarcerated. "What day is it?"

"The tenth of December."

It took him a long time to say anything. It was obvious he was fighting waves of pain. "My God Bingley . . . what are you doing here?"

"What?"

"Jane! Your wife!"

"She is well, and Chatton is not that far of a journey. She has also refused, by letter, to allow me to leave your side until you are recovered."

Darcy grumbled but had no proper counter to this. "Can you send in the doctor? And . . . I require . . . some privacy."

"Of course."

Darcy said nothing as Elizabeth stroked his hair. It was not easy watching her debilitated husband, and she was relieved when Maddox reappeared with the bottle. "No," Darcy said, "I want to ask you something . . . while my mind is clear."

"And then you will take your dose?"

"Agreed." Darcy closed his eyes, and they thought maybe he might be drifting off again, as he had developed a habit of doing, but he was instead apparently refocusing and gathering his energy so he could speak in a clearer, more confident voice when he asked, "Did you or did you not make an offer of marriage to Caroline Bingley?"

Of course, the doctor's terrified stance and mute response gave away all or most of his feelings, but fortunately for him, it was Elizabeth who responded, "Darcy!"

"No, I will settle the matter—*now*. Kincaid told me it was so. And he was not lying, was he?"

Maddox backed away, but he did answer, "No."

"I will assume her response was negative," Darcy continued. "I am a man with some experience . . . in rejected proposals." His head rolled to one side; he couldn't properly hold it up anymore. "So . . . my advice . . . is to fret for a while and then try again."

"Thank you so much for your kindly advice," Maddox said, and furiously shoved not one but two spoonfuls of medicine in Darcy's mouth before leaving in a huff, nearly barging into Bingley on the way.

"What did you say to the poor doctor?" Bingley said, and it was at that point that Elizabeth could no longer hold her laughter and nearly collapsed onto the rim of the armchair. "What? That man saved your life!"

"I think he regrets it now," Darcy responded.

After Darcy had drifted off again, or was at least babbling incoherently, Elizabeth left him in Bingley's charge and went about locating the doctor, who had hidden himself in the kitchen where his various instruments were spread out over a clean towel and he was mixing up his various ointments and medicines. He jumped a little at her entrance and bowed stiffly but realised he could do nothing to get rid of the mistress of the house. "Mrs. Darcy."

"Dr. Maddox, I feel you have not been thanked sufficiently for saving my husband's life."

"Yes, well . . ." he trailed off and went back to his powders.

"I apologise for my husband's very blunt behaviour," she said. "I would attribute it to his current state, but honestly that is the way he always behaves."

Maddox did smile but still said nothing. To take precise measurements, he pushed his glasses up into his hair and brought the measuring spoons up to his face, and she could see the obvious glimmer of intelligence in his eyes—and that he was nearsighted.

"Mrs. Darcy, if you're going to stand there, at least allow me to guess what you are thinking."

"You are welcome to do so."

"You are wondering what Caroline sees in me."

So, there was a problem of his self-esteem. "No, I was thinking precisely the opposite, to be honest."

"Maybe it is my own transparency," he said, "but I do not fully understand why she is held in so little regard by so many of her relatives."

Maybe he was blind both literally *and* figuratively. Elizabeth was dumbfounded, so much so that it took her several moments to develop a proper response. "I do not mean to be ungenerous to Miss Bingley—"

"But you do not care for her."

"It is not—" She could not find a proper way to say it without being cruel. "I cannot recall anything Miss Bingley has ever said to me that was not either outright dismissive or falsely friendly."

"And how should she treat a rival for Mr. Darcy's affec-
tions?" he said, but his voice was so pleasant, so truly pure, that
it was obvious he meant no offence, just idle curiosity. "What is
the socially acceptable demeanour for women in that situation?
Forgive a distant observer, but in my limited experiences with
women, it seems that at least some of them must result to the
most cutthroat of tactics even to stay in the game."

She could not deny it; nor could she deny that the insinua-
tion, however unintentional, made her angry. "And you think
this is a positive quality?"

"It is a *necessary* quality, more of a survival instinct. Caroline
Bingley *must* marry and marry well. To do otherwise would hurt
the entire family's social standing. This seems to be true of most
families of fortune." He looked away from her and down at his
mixing bowls. "My aforementioned endeavour's outcome is then
completely unsurprising."

"But you did it anyway."

"Yes." He would not look at her, but his voice cracked a little when he spoke. "I could not do otherwise. So I made a fool
of myself and apparently now also of Caroline, as it has become
known and she is sure to be a laughingstock. The latter is my
only regret."

Their gazes finally met, and the look on Maddox's face was
immediately recognisable. He spoke of the utter despair of a man
who knew he would never get what he desired and had no hope of
forgetting that. She knew it because she had seen that exact look
on Darcy's face as he stood next to Bingley at Longbourn.

But this time, the answer was not so obvious.

MR. DARCY'S PROPOSAL

WHEN ELIZABETH RETURNED TO the master bedchamber, Bingley spun around and had the expression of a child with his hand in the cookie jar. "Mrs. Darcy."

She crossed her arms. "What were you doing?"

"Nothing," he said. "Nothing at all."

"Were you taking advantage of my husband's condition again?"

"No, absolutely not. I would never, *ever* ask him to will his half of Derbyshire to me, and he would never agree," Bingley said. "Right, Darcy?"

"Happy Christmas," said Darcy, who had been moved back into bed and was propped up on the headboard, his eyes a shade of red. "Lizzy."

Elizabeth shook her head. "Mr. Bingley, as much fun as we're having, I think there are matters we should talk of."

"Yes, yes," he said, wiping the tears from his eyes. "In privacy?"

"I think we're in privacy *now*, unless he is deceiving us."

"Elizabeth, you weren't here when he called me Charlie Bungley."

"Well put," she giggled. "Very well. There is the matter of your sister—"

"Yes." This did succeed to some extent in darkening his mood—or would at least until Darcy spoke again. "Did you speak to the doctor?"

"Yes."

"And did he say anything interesting?"

Now Elizabeth was completely serious. "He is completely in love with her."

While this did not seem great news to Bingley, it had an obvious effect on him, as he pondered for a moment before answering, "I would certainly not object to the match, whatever his own financial status is."

"I do not believe that is the issue."

"No, of course not." He rubbed his chin. "The matter is Caroline's own feelings, which of course have to be reciprocal."

"And you have no idea if they are?"

"I have some idea. I mean, I can't positively think of another person not of our social class that she's given any attention to or even learned the proper name of, much less had multiple, extended conversations with. And that she continues to hide her feelings and is yet completely dismissive of him at the slightest implication—which I imagine she would be if I implied something about her and any other man—is yet another indication. But that does not make the matter perfectly clear."

"These matters are rarely perfectly clear," Elizabeth said, "except of course for you and Jane, as you were practically fawning over each other at first glance. Am I not right, Darcy?"

"Who?" he said. "Bingley and Miss Bennet?"

"Yes, darling. What did you think of them at the ball last night?" she managed to say with a straight face, with Bingley laughing in the background.

"She's . . . too tall for him. He needs a woman . . . very small."

It was some time before they both recovered again enough to be serious. "Someone should talk to Miss Bingley."

"What?" Bingley was horrified. "It is not going to be me. I have already tried."

"But she despises me," Elizabeth said. "And if we get Darcy to do it, he might propose to her or something."

"I doubt very much it would hold up in court."

"That is not the point, and you know it." She turned to her husband. "Would you marry Miss Bingley?"

"What?" He blinked. "No! No . . . he's a nice man, but no. I'm too tall for him."

"If he remembers any of this, he'll kill us both," Bingley said. "Surely you realise this."

"And surely you realise it will have been worth it all the same."

The ride back to his townhouse was sobering enough for Bingley, partially attributed to the cold weather and the letter received from his courier before leaving the Darcys. The letter contained the usual reassurances from Jane of her good health and the importance of his giving his support to Darcy and Caroline, but they had planned (on account of her confinement) to all spend the fast-approaching Christmas in Chatton this year, and he honestly had no idea if it would come to be. Maddox had declared that Darcy would have to walk some length (or any length) on his own before the doctor would give his consent for him to ride in a carriage, and it would not be Christmas without the Darcys. And, of course, there was the scandalous storm brewing in Town, and Bingley was to be the manager of that. But rereading the letter only made him think of Jane, his beloved, suffering because of his own desire to produce an heir, and he could not be there for her without abandoning numerous obligations.

In fact, by the time he reached his front door and was greeted by the servants, his mood was positively dour, almost Darcy-like. As far as he was concerned, he had failed Jane as a husband, Darcy as a friend, and his sister on almost every level. If only Caroline were not being so reserved. He remembered the young Caroline and her tea parties where he was once allowed to sit as the "visiting baby" even though he was four, younger than she or Louisa. They intentionally paid no attention to him and played with their dolls instead, but he was happy to be at the tiny table. And now he was master of a grand table, and it brought him no happiness.

It was late afternoon and Caroline, Louisa, and Mr. Hurst were in the parlour. Mr. Hurst was not unconscious but on his way to being so, but the real surprise was that Louisa was talking to Caroline, not in idle conversation, but as one older woman giving advice to another. As if Louisa Hurst should be one to give marital advice! The idea positively infuriated Bingley. Was there no one who cared for his sister properly?

"Charles," Miss Bingley said, breaking off their hushed conversation and rising to meet him. "I must inquire as to Mr. Darcy's health."

"He is better every day, though it may be a few more days before he is able to travel at all, much less to Chatton."

"Are we to miss Christmas then?"

"I doubt we shall 'miss Christmas,' as it seems to happen every year despite anyone's intentions," he replied. "And I do think we shall be there in time. It is fortunate that it was planned for Chatton and not Pemberley this year."

"Do you not suppose," began Mrs. Hurst, "that we should ride on ahead, and the Darcys should follow with the doctor?"

"You may do as you please," he said, deciding not to specify Caroline at this time. "I am going to stay with Darcy as long as I can with Jane's health."

"Charles," Mrs. Hurst said, now rising, "I feel I must raise some objection to your actions over the past few days."

Bingley, in no mood for this but sensing its necessity, merely crossed his arms and waited for her continuation.

"We have been sitting here, trying to avoid the scandal that surrounds our family, hoping and praying that Kincaid's actions do not reach the ears of our social circles, and you, the master of this house, have spent more time at Darcy's beck and call while he has his own staff of servants and a wife and a sister to attend to him!"

"May I remind you, Louisa," he replied, "that it is the Darcys who are responsible for properly exposing Lord Kincaid or Sir Kincaid or whatever title is appropriate to him. And it is the Darcys who have suffered most from this, in terms of physical weathering. We owe them a great debt. Moreover, I cannot abandon him now."

"So you would abandon your sister in favour of Mr. Darcy?"

Bingley coolly replied, "I believe Caroline is capable of speaking for herself on this matter."

For indeed, Caroline had been silent. She had, to his knowledge, not spoken more than a few words since the whole matter had come out. Nor had she seen Dr. Maddox who was housed at the Darcys, who were not accepting visitors. Bingley towered over her—or more accurately, looked up at her with a very towering expression—and she finally did respond by turning her head and bursting into tears.

"This is it!" Mrs. Hurst shouted. "This is the shame you have brought upon our family."

"Shame? It was not I who introduced her to Lord Kincaid!"

"He is not the issue. You married below your standing and so did Darcy. Did you think this would do nothing to Caroline's prospects? That she would have to smile and beg for a good match?"

Bingley clenched his fists; his voice raised to a level it had never reached in this house before. "I will hear no more of prospects and good matches! Caroline may marry anyone she chooses, and I will support her . . . and him . . . provided that they bring each other happiness."

Mrs. Hurst was horrified. "Our mother—"

"Our lovely mother, whom I love dearly to this day, is no longer the mistress of this house nor is my father the master. That generation has passed, and we are free to do as we see fit. I don't know what nonsense was imparted to you by our mother before her passing, but I will say here and now as the master of this townhouse, the Bingley fortune, and Chatton, that my word is rule, and my rule is that siblings and children may marry according to their own desires. And if it means we are to be the laughingstock of London, I will say that we will just have to spend some time at Chatton until Town finds another family spectacle to obsess over." He turned to Caroline and offered his arm. "Come, Caroline. I believe we have something to discuss."

He took her to the drawing room and shut the door behind him, with instructions that they were not to be disturbed. He knew it was her favourite room in the house, as he often found her there reading or doing some embroidery when the Hursts were out travelling the country . . . how many lonely hours. He embraced her fully, and she did not reject it, weeping for some time into his shoulder while he patiently waited and said nothing. Which suitor was on her mind, which one would bring her to tears and not disgust, he was not fully sure, but he was willing to wager a guess. It was only after she had stopped sobbing and made many excuses—and attempts to escape the room, which his hold on her hand would not allow—did they finally sit on the sofa, brother and sister.

"What I said there was meant in all truthfulness," he said. "Surely you know that by now. It is only that I cannot understand—" He shook his head. "I can understand what you have been through, what you believe is expected of you, but what I do not know is the last piece of the puzzle—how this business with the doctor came about."

"Does it matter?"

"Yes." He did not elaborate as to why. "I dare say it does."

Caroline looked about, fiddling with her hands a bit before speaking. "He was here for some time, you understand, for Mr. Hurst's treatments. And at some point, I don't remember, I was talking to Mr. Hurst, and I said something in French. And Mr. Hurst, being the ignorant oaf that he is, did not understand it, but it was Dr. Maddox, who was at that time I believe mixing the pot, who responded in perfect French. So I countered in Italian and he in German, and I replied the same. Finally he bested me in Latin, of which I have no understanding. I . . . cannot account for it. I must have been starved for conversation that was not with my sister . . ."

He said quietly, "You do not need to account for it."

"And I decided to test his knowledge of the arts, of which he was very knowledgeable. He went to Cambridge when his family was of some fortune and studied literature extensively. Medicine he pursued only later. I have to say . . . except in financial matters, he bests even Darcy in letters, though he said he does not have much time to read and has trouble seeing the print when it is fine. I asked about eyeglasses and . . . I don't know. I saw him every day for an hour while Mr. Hurst bathed—for the conversation. He was always so kind to me, even when I dismissed him. Some of the servants, I know, have this look in their eyes and despise their positions, but he was most obliging. After we began our routine, he seemed almost happy to arrive."

"And this went without notice—I mean, to Louisa and Mr. Hurst?"

"We were rather secretive about it. I suppose because of propriety. He was there to attend Mr. Hurst's gout; our conversations were merely an afterthought. Or, they had to be. There was no way . . ."

When she could not finish, he did, "For it to be otherwise. I understand. But he proposed to you all the same."

"Yes. I cannot say that it did not take me by complete surprise, but there was no question in my answer, even without Kincaid in the picture, as this was a few days before. After that . . . seeing him here became a pain I did not expect." She was crying again, not sobbing, but quiet tears were escaping her eyes. "Charles, do not say something stupid here."

"Fine, I will say nothing I deem stupid. But clearly, we have a difference of opinion on the matter of what qualifies as 'stupid.' I will say, still, that I, Bingley of Chatton, would not look down on such a match and, in fact, would welcome it, if it would bring you happiness. But I do not know if so many years of social condition-ing can be undone so easily. Darcy struggled with it for almost a year."

"As did you."

"No," he said. "I was from the first moment in love with Jane. I was merely persuaded otherwise for a time because I knew not her feelings. But that is in the past, and I am in a very happy marriage, and I wish the same for you, no matter what imagined scandal it brings to us. In fact, I think it would be convenient to have a very good doctor in the family."

"Charles!"

"I mean it, Caroline," he said seriously. "Please, consider my words this time so I do not have to keep repeating them or employ someone else to do so."

She looked away from him, giving him a dismissive sniffle. "Fine. That I will grant you. I will consider it."

His face lit up. She must have caught that. "Very well." He kissed her hand and finally let her go, disappearing upstairs in a rustle of jade silk.

The next step—literally—was to get Mr. Darcy on his feet. While he had enough servants to aid him in this endeavour, Bingley, of course, insisted on being on his right side as they brought him to his feet.

"I am not an invalid!" he insisted, frustrated at all of this protective attention, but despite his protests, he could barely keep to his feet, and only with two supports, and then he managed with one, making it all the way across the room. Dr. Maddox watched on with concentration.

"Well?" said an exhausted Darcy when he was sitting back in his armchair.

"When you can walk with a cane," the doctor said, "I will consider a carriage."

Darcy had not the energy to argue further. He sighed and leaned into his wife, who sat beside him and rubbed his lower back as a servant entered. "Miss Bingley wishes to see you, Mr. Darcy."

"Very well," he said. "Send her in."

Of course, Dr. Maddox immediately fled the room. That did not save him, though, from encountering her in the hallway outside the door. "Miss Bingley."

"Doctor," she said formally, attempting to hide any emotion and thoroughly failing to do so. She entered and nodded to her brother who quickly left. "Mr. Darcy."

"Miss Bingley," he said, and gave a look to Elizabeth, who took it as a sign that she might give them privacy. She kissed him on the head, curtseyed to Miss Bingley, and left the room, shutting the door behind her.

"Mr. Darcy," Miss Bingley began, "words cannot express my appreciation for what you've done."

"Perhaps if I'd known the outcome, I would have been less inclined to do it," he said, attempting to straighten himself. "Of course, I'm saying this now because of my condition, which I'm told will be temporary, because Lord Kincaid had the decency to shoot me in my weak side. In a few weeks, I will of course say that I would have done it all the same."

"For the Bingley family, which is of course your family now."

"For you, Caroline," he said. "You deserve happiness as much as anyone. Even before my suspicions were confirmed, I knew that he could not give it to you."

"That is because you have a great deal of good sense."

"As does your brother, despite conventional wisdom," Darcy said. "*Both* your brothers, in fact."

Caroline fiddled with her fingers. "Mr. Hurst gave no objection to Lord Kincaid."

"But we are no longer talking of Lord Kincaid, I believe. Or at least, I am not."

She smiled uncomfortably. "So there is to be yet another marriage conspiracy in our families?"

"It seems we are incapable of being married without them."

Now she did really smile. "Thank you again, Darcy."

"Anytime, Miss Bingley." He offered his hand, and she kissed it. "Though I would prefer it to be only as often as absolutely necessary."

The very next day, while Darcy was taking his enforced afternoon nap, Dr. Maddox found himself called very insistently to the Bingley townhouse. "Mr. Hurst is making a great complaint," Bingley informed him, trying to keep a straight face while saying it as Elizabeth listened in on the other side of the door. "It's probably nonsense, but you'd best see to it for all of our sakes, and Mr. Darcy is positively sick of all of this attention."

Thus, Dr. Maddox could not invent an excuse to escape. He arrived at the Bingleys' in the late afternoon, dallying for some bit (and unknowingly giving Bingley time to get there). His entrance was, of course, unannounced, but he did pass by Caroline and Mrs. Hurst in the parlour. Mrs. Hurst gave him a look that was positively scornful, but the expression of Miss Bingley made him weak in the knees, and it was some time before he was able to bring himself to climb the stairs.

Mr. Hurst was waiting for him in his room but said nothing as Dr. Maddox made his assessment and prepared his footbath. The wound was not exceptional but was suffering from some minor neglect. Once everything was prepared, Mr. Hurst dismissed him as usual, saying he could walk about the house if he wished, as long as he stayed within shouting distance.

Actually, Dr. Maddox wished very much to stay in the room, but that was not what he was told, so he exited and, of course, immediately encountered Caroline in the hall. "Miss Bingley," he bowed, hoping to avoid her gaze.

"Charles sent me up for—something," she said. "Doctor." But they did not rush off in either direction; they stood there.

Neither, it seemed, could bring himself or herself to leave. "And
. . . and how are you, Daniel?" she said at last.

"Very well," he said, his voice saying otherwise. "Mr. Darcy
is recovering."

"All thanks to your expertise, of course."

He blushed. "I did what any decent doctor would do,
Caroline."

"There are very few decent doctors in England," she said.
"But . . . I must be off . . . on my . . . errand." And she curtseyed
and left for her room.

Maddox took off his glasses and wiped his forehead. There
he dallied for some time before putting them back on and following her down the corridor.

CHRISTMAS AT CHATTON HALL

"COME IN," SAID MISS Bingley in a soft voice, not asking whom it was. The look on her face when he entered was indescribable, so filled with conflicting emotions, but that didn't make her any less beautiful. She said nothing at his entrance or at his shutting the door behind him, which was most improper for two unmarried adults of opposite genders and a great deal of affection.

As his legs were so horribly wobbly, it was very easy to get to his knees. "Caroline—"

"Don't do this," she said, already in tears. "Please."

"I know very well I can offer you next to nothing besides my paltry income, and that it is not very respectable to actually earn an income at all," he said. "I know that our social positions are incomparable and that I cannot provide for the lifestyle to which you are not only accustomed but are deserving and that we shall be forever reliant on your brother. In fact, all things considered, *all* I have to offer you is my total and unconditional love and admiration." He was very surprised, in fact, that he managed to keep his own voice mainly intact as he said it. "If that is not sufficient, then I will trouble you no longer. *Ma se è abbastanza, Caroline Bingley, accettereste la mia mano in unione?*" (But if it is, Caroline Bingley, will you accept my hand in marriage?)

"*Sì*," she replied in the same language. "*Oh Dio, sì!.*" (Oh God, yes.)

There was barely a second before Charles Bingley burst in the room. "You had to do it in a language I don't know! Now I will look like a fool if it wasn't a yes. It was a yes, right?" He looked at both of their faces as Maddox stood up. "I dare say it was. Doctor, I believe you and I are to have a conversation?"

Charles Bingley sat in his chair in eager anticipation. "I could get used to this. Too bad I have no remaining sisters. Though, the bit about Lord Kincaid was most unpleasant, but I have many years to learn more about checking into people's finances before my daughter comes into society. But as usual I am babbling on, and you have something very important to ask me."

Actually, Maddox was grateful for the reprieve, for it gave him time to collect himself. "Mr. Bingley, I would like to request your sister's hand in marriage."

"Granted."

He breathed a sigh of relief. "I feel with all good conscious I must remind you—"

"Of your financial state. Yes, well, Caroline's been riding on the family fortune for years, as have the Hursts, so I see no reason not to add another person to the list, provided you are not a gambler, which I imagine you are not. Though, I feel I must inquire as to what exactly your income is—for propriety's sake."

"I—I have some savings, a few thousand pounds, what I've saved since completing my medical training. And my yearly income at best is another five hundred, but that is entirely dependent on my patient list."

"Your patient list would improve dramatically, I imagine, if your own social standing increased," Bingley speculated. "And there is the matter of you being a very talented doctor. So I cannot say that you are entirely without fortune and bring nothing to the marriage. Not that it is relevant at all to this conversation. If you make Caroline happy, then you are doing all that is required to be my brother-in-law." He stood up and approached the quivering doctor. "I suppose we should shake on it? Is that how it's done? I would usually ask Darcy, but I could hardly bother him at this juncture."

So they shook hands. This was not enough for Bingley who grabbed Maddox and embraced him. "Welcome to the family. I hope you will find it to your liking."

"I think I will," Maddox finally managed to say.

Now formally engaged, there was no problem with the immediate issue of keeping Caroline and Maddox properly apart except at social functions because he was still living with the Darcys. The most pressing matter, now that this one was passed, was, in fact, getting his approval for their return to Chatton. Darcy insisted they go on ahead of him for Jane's sake and then lamented very loudly that he was disgusted that since his injury no one seemed to be listening to a word he said.

Dr. Maddox finally gave his consent for the journey, provided they proceed appropriately slowly and that he oversee the Darcy carriage's progress entirely. At long last, the carriages bearing the Bingleys, the Hursts, the Darcys, and one affianced doctor could start out from Town, heading north toward Chatton and a very expectant wife. "Just in time for Christmas," Mr. Hurst gurgled, and Bingley had to admit that, this year, the holiday had been very far from his mind.

On the first rest stop, Dr. Maddox took the time to try to get Darcy to get up and move about with the rest of them and, finding that he could not, practically forced a dose of laudanum down his throat. Only afterwards did Darcy thank him, which was his way of subtly admitting that he was, in fact, in some considerable pain. When the doctor was sure the laudanum had taken effect, they loaded back into their carriages and continued on the journey. Darcy leaned on Elizabeth's shoulder, drifting in and out.

"He's pretending to be asleep," she said to Maddox, "so he doesn't accidentally say anything ridiculous."

Maddox said nothing, but he did notice Darcy smile after she said it.

The trip proceeded more smoothly then, at least for Darcy and the two other occupants of the carriage. Dr. Maddox buried himself in a book, which amusingly, he had to read with his glasses removed and the text pushed right up to his face. The title was in Latin, and when asked he said it was a very boring medical text and that he would gladly switch to something more amusing to be read aloud if he had anything with him.

On their third day of travel and near the borders of Derbyshire, the carriage abruptly stopped when the one in front of it did. Eventually the carriage door opened with such ferocity that Mr. Bingley practically tore it off its hinges. "Doctor, if you would, it seems we are needed in Chatton most urgently, and they have sent riders for us."

"Is it—?"

"Yes, Elizabeth," he said. "It is a month earlier than expected, but I suppose it isn't an exact science after all. Or perhaps it is—I am not the expert on the subject. But Jane is . . . very expecting. Now."

"Then I must go with you," she insisted.

"I cannot possibly ask that you leave—"

"'M fine," Darcy mumbled. "Lizzy, ride with them."

Maddox coughed, and this apparently was enough of a reminder.

"Bingley, can you give us a moment to confer?" Elizabeth said, as Maddox climbed out. "A very short moment, I assure you."

"Yes, of course."

With the door closed, she turned to her husband, "Darcy, I cannot ride."

"I told you," he said, his voice slurred. "I will be fine."

"No, I mean—I cannot ride." Since he wasn't at his full senses, she whispered the full explanation.

"*Oh.*" It took him even more time to process this news. "Well, then . . ." he broke up in laughter. "I love you."

"As do I."

He put his hand on her belly. "What shall we name it?"

"George."

Darcy only nodded and closed his eyes. Elizabeth held her laughter until they got him out of the carriage and started off with much greater haste for Chatton Hall.

Even the expectant servants of Chatton were not prepared for the onslaught of three overly worried individuals storming in the door, two having ridden on horseback following the other in a coach, barely allowing time for their coats to be removed. The only person immediately in their range was Mr. Bennet, whom Bingley shook by the shoulders. "How is she?"

"I have no idea. Being a man, they won't let me on the same floor as an expectant woman. But she has not delivered, that much I know, and the midwife and my wife are tending to her. But I see you have brought a doctor—"

"Yes," Bingley said as quickly as possible. "Mr. Bennet, this is Dr. Maddox, who is very accomplished and also Miss Bingley's betrothed."

"Very good—*what?*"

"It will be explained, Papa," Elizabeth said, "when there is not something else pressing."

As the three new arrivals ran up the stairs, Mr. Bennet said, "I hope at least he's not Scottish!"

Jane Bingley was in her bedchamber surrounded by her mother, the midwife, the nurse, and several servants. Her face was showing the strain of a woman in the throes of labour, but she was not screaming or otherwise overwhelmed. In fact, she still had a great deal of her senses about her. "Charles!"

"Jane!" he said, practically tossing everyone in his way aside, including his mother-in-law, who would surely object to his intrusion in any other circumstances, as he ran to his wife's side and embraced her as he could, considering her position and girth. "Oh, my lovely Jane, I am so sorry for the delay! I had no idea—"

"It came about so quickly," she said, "but—I am told I am hours away. You are here with plenty of time. Lizzy!"

Elizabeth took up her place on the other side of her sister, a place she would not relinquish for some time as she grasped her hand. "If I could have come any sooner—"

"I know. Please, while I am between pains, how is Darcy?"

"Enduring the other Bingley and Hursts as we speak. Though perhaps Miss Bingley is not so terrible after all." With that, she shot a look at Dr. Maddox who was holding his bag and quietly waiting to be introduced. "But he is recovering well, thanks to the doctor here. Jane, this is Dr. Maddox who is responsible for my husband's good health and is Miss Bingley's fiancé."

"Mrs. Bingley," the doctor bowed.

"Oh. Hello, Doctor—*what?*" Jane said. "I thought—"

"It's a very long story. One I would be happy to tell you," Elizabeth said, "whenever you are ready. But at the moment, would you consent to an inspection?"

"Yes, yes, of course," said the overwhelmed Jane who turned to her husband as Dr. Maddox opened his bag and began removing various instruments. "You will confirm that?"

"I gave my consent. It seems love will not be stymied."

"To *Caroline* Bingley?"

"Yes, dear."

Dr. Maddox had no comment; he was too absorbed in his examination. He took out a tube of glass, pressed it against Jane's stomach, and put his ear on the other end, which they all found very odd but did not question. "Sound," he explained after a minute or so of listening. "It carries better through solids. Well, Mrs. Bingley, my assessment is that you are doing quite well and are some time away from delivery. I know that is not much comfort to you—"

"No," she said as she grimaced, clearly in the midst of another contraction. "But, is it not too early?"

"It is fairly normal for someone under your circumstances. Ah, Mrs. Bingley," he said very formally, "you are aware that you are expecting twins, correct?"

The blank stares of the crowd confirmed his suspicion that was not, in fact, the case.

"Well, then I must be the bearer of the news."

"You are sure?" Jane demanded.

"Quite. There are two heartbeats. And considering your girth . . . yes, I would say twins."

"Oh," she said nonchalantly, and then turned to her husband. "Charles?"

"Yes?"

She then proceeded to strangle him by his cravat. Only the collective forces of Mrs. Bennet, the midwife, and the nurse could get him away from her to save him from asphyxiation.

Only as the hour grew late and the screams grew louder, so much so that they made their way to the front hallway, did Elizabeth Darcy reappear—and only when she was informed that the other carriage had finally arrived. She embraced her husband, who hobbled in, and gave him the news as it was, that Jane was still in labour and Bingley was hiding in his study for his own safety. "How do you feel?"

"Like I very much want to sit down," he said, "on something that doesn't bounce up and down."

She helped him to Bingley's massive study where he took a seat in an armchair, and she whispered the most recent update to Bingley before disappearing back upstairs. Beside Darcy was Mr. Bennet, who had taken up the business of keeping Bingley from drinking himself into a stupor. Mr. Hurst joined them, and the male sanctuary was filled as Dr. Maddox remained mainly with his patient. In the parlour, Kitty Bennet was joined by Mrs. Hurst, Georgiana, and Miss Bingley so finally had some entertainment.

"All things considered, I think I should say you look much recovered and quite well," Mr. Bennet said to Darcy. "But the fact of the matter is I have never seen you worse."

"You didn't see him two weeks ago," Bingley said. "Drink, Darcy?"

To his great surprise, Darcy answered, "I would appreciate it, yes." And he took a shot of whiskey and downed it like it was meant to be medicinal, which it probably was. "What is the news?"

"I am having twins. You?"

"Wife pregnant," he said. "Triplets, surely."

"Oh, this again," Mr. Bennet said with a roll of his eyes.

"To be sure?" Bingley said.

"She is fairly sure. And now we have a doctor in the family to confirm it."

"Convenient," Mr. Hurst said, already taking advantage of the free-flowing alcohol with a large glass of whiskey.

"Yes, yes, we must all endeavour to come down with horrible diseases that only he may cure," Mr. Bennet said.

"I will demur," Darcy said, "having already fulfilled my obligation to make him worthwhile."

"So it is true, then," Mr. Bennet said. "He is affianced to Miss Bingley. It seems I am terrible at predicting marriages. The only one I got right was Jane, and I did not verbally predict it. I let my wife do that."

"No one predicted this." Bingley defended his father-in-law.

"*I* did," said Mr. Hurst.

"Then you will be the best man, perhaps," Bingley said. "For it seems I must give her away, so I am unavailable, and Darcy can barely stand up."

"I will remind you, Bingley, that Lord Kincaid did me the favour of shooting me in the left side, leaving my right arm available to run you through once I am recovered," Darcy said.

"How very nice of him," Mr. Bennet observed.

Jane's labour continued into the night, which was by no means unexpected, and many residents and visitors retired. Darcy refused to do so, but he did fall right asleep in the armchair in Bingley's study, and Elizabeth was satisfied with covering him with a blanket, as she was very busy herself. The Hursts retired, and Kitty was very excited but as a maiden was not permitted to be part of the group surrounding Jane, so she also went to her room with an annoyed huff. Mr. Bennet gave up around the eleventh hour, complaining of his old, stiff body and invaded the female sanctuary upstairs to give his eldest daughter a kiss on the forehead before turning in for bed. Mr. Bingley stayed awake only with the help of his servants, who he demanded rouse him hourly with reports of Jane's disposition, but otherwise he was asleep facedown on his desk.

No one was watching Caroline Bingley, and Elizabeth first saw her again when she was going for more towels. Dr. Maddox was staying wide awake by ingesting what seemed to be gallons of tea, and Elizabeth turned a corner and saw him taking another pot from Caroline. Not wanting to invade their privacy, she stepped back behind the corner but did peer over to see Caroline give him a kiss on the cheek before he went back to Jane's room.

Only Jane's agony was keeping Elizabeth and her mother awake. She screamed; she cursed a number of curses that they could properly identify; and she damned her husband to the ends of the earth. (Fortunately he was not there to hear it.) The midwife remained in the room, but Dr. Maddox gave the orders, especially now with the dangerous complication of two potential newborns. Between contractions, Jane was told the entire tale of the adventures in Town, including both conspiracies to get Miss Bingley out of one marriage and into another. As this was done in front of Dr. Maddox, he blushed and turned away but did not flee with a patient in the room needing his expertise. Jane commented in a rare moment of lucidity that she rather enjoyed the story or would take the time to enjoy it upon retrospection when she was not otherwise engaged.

Eventually there was the inevitable; Jane's contractions would not cease, and even the most uninformed person in the room could tell it was her time.

"Pray for sons, Jane dearest," Mrs. Bennet said, holding her hand.

Jane gasped, "Dr. Maddox, if you are as proficient as they say, then please quicken the process!"

"That, sadly, is beyond my abilities," he said quietly, and merely told her to push.

Charles Bingley's first response to being shook awake was to sit up and shout, "Yes, yes, I consent! By God, yes!" It was then that he came to his senses and, unfortunately, realised that he not only had a pounding headache but a doctor standing over him. "What? What is it?"

"Happy Christmas, Mr. Bingley," Maddox said.

Charles squinted at the grandfather clock and noticed the time. "Yes, I suppose it is Christmas Eve—or day. Is it day?"

"I believe it is. Now." Maddox looked at his watch. "It is precisely four thirty-two in the morning."

"Oh." Charles settled back. Things were coming to him slowly, "Um—"

"You have a son, Mr. Bingley, and another daughter. Congratulations."

Bingley looked up at Maddox, who obviously hadn't slept a wink and was staying up only by force of will at this point. "And Jane?"

"I would hurry if you wish to catch her before she is sound asleep."

"Thank you. Thank you, Doctor." He grabbed Maddox's arm and shook it so violently that he nearly tore it off. "Thank you so very much—um, Daniel."

"My pleasure."

"And, uh, I guess someone should do something about Darcy," Bingley said in passing as he pushed passed Maddox and raced up the stairs. Darcy was still asleep in the armchair.

The Bingley twins, as they would be referred to for some time, had the fortune to be different genders, because otherwise they were almost identical in appearance. Both of them had a small tuft of blond hair like their mother, and both of them were squealing tiredly when Bingley entered the bedchamber, seated himself beside his wife, and took one then two infants into his arms.

"Congratulations," said an exhausted-looking Elizabeth, who then moved out of the way so Bingley could see Jane, who was finally able to lay on her side. Jane's eyes were heavy and bloodshot and her natural motherly glow somewhat lessened for the expected reasons, but she still managed to smile softly at Bingley.

"Shall we name them?" she said, her voice hoarse.

"Now? We can think on the matter, but . . . I would very much prefer the boy to be named Charles."

"I do like the name Charles," she said, and gestured, and Elizabeth passed the boy to Jane, or more accurately, laid him beside her on the bed.

"Perhaps we can finally convince your father to let us name the girl Elizabeth," he said, cradling his second daughter.

"Perhaps," Jane said, and seemed to be drifting into sleep.

He kissed her and had the nurse take the babies and put them in their cradle. He turned to Elizabeth. "Thank you. Happy Christmas."

"Happy Christmas." She was clearly too tired to curtsey. She left without another word, and as she was gone, Charles collapsed on the bed next to his wife and fell asleep.

MR. DABBY OF
PEMBERLEY AND DERBYSHIRE

DR. DANIEL MADDOX LEFT the Bingleys' chambers to find a servant waiting for him. "Your room, Dr. Maddox," he said, gesturing vaguely, and Maddox was too tired to do anything but follow. He was shown not to the servants' quarters but to a proper guest room where he unceremoniously dumped his medical bag on the nearest available surface. The servant in the wig, dressed more finely than he was, did not leave, however, but seemed to be expecting some command. Before the good doctor could think of anything, he was helped out of his clothing and into proper bedclothes. He slid between the fine sheets with only the vague recollection that that was how he used to be treated so many years ago, as the remaining candle was snuffed out for him.

When he awoke it was daylight, but as it had been daylight when he went to sleep, that held no significance to him at all. He reached for his glasses and his watch and found the time to be late in the afternoon.

It dawned on him after a considerable panic that, if he had been needed, someone surely would have roused him earlier. Instead he was alone in a rather large and fine room in complete peace on a perfectly quiet Christmas afternoon. (He had to assume it was the same day.) He found the adjoining chamber ready with a copper tub and warm water set aside and quickly washed himself.

His shuffling around in a daze must have made some noise, for the same servant appeared, bowed to him, and began to offer him a large selection of dress, as Christmas dinner would be happening soon, and he was expected to be there when the bell rang. It only then occurred to him that his usual clothing, which was probably once suitable or could be made to look suitable with the right cravat many years ago, was probably ratty and inadequate for the Bingley dinner table. So for reasons he could not understand fully, he found himself standing on a dressing stand being semilectured by a manservant. "We have a selection of clothing that is available. Mr. Bingley, as I'm sure you are aware, is very much in favour of bright colours, but I believe you are closer to Mr. Darcy in general measurements, though he is—if I can say—a bit dour in his choice of colours. And Mr. Hurst has some collection, but I don't think it can be fitted in time."

"Ah, hmm . . . something of Darcy's would be fine," he mumbled.

"Very good, sir."

He knew how to tie his own cravat, but that option was not given to him, and the level of compliance that was expected of him also prevented him from doing it himself. A little over-whelmed but not of the wits to say it, a more presentable Dr.

Maddox finally emerged into the hallway, which was strangely quiet and empty for the middle of the afternoon. He conjectured that many important members of the household were either still sleeping or were inclined to lay rather low after a long trip and an exhausting birth.

But he was not, it seemed, entirely alone. Around the corner and with amazing speed crawled a small child with dark brown hair. When he hit Maddox's legs, he grabbed the trousers by the knees and attempted to stand up, giggling all the way. While the Chatton floors looked perfectly clean, he thought it best that an infant not be loose on them, and he picked up the boy who squealed with delight. "Da!" Maddox judged him to be nearing his first birthday, by weight and development.

"And who are you?" he said, but the most obvious answer was that he was the Darcys' son. He knew very well that Charles and Jane had a daughter named Georgiana, after Mr. Darcy's sister, and that the Darcys were themselves parents, but he could not properly recall the name of the boy.

"Da!" said the boy. "Yeff!" With his arms now free, he immediately went for the most interesting thing in reach, which were the doctor's glasses.

"No, no, I need those," he said, as the world—except for what was very close, in this case, young Mr. Darcy—became a blur. But they would not be so easily wrestled from the child's hands. Like his father, he had a rather strong grip. "I am being very serious."

There was laughter in the distance, and he looked sideways and saw only the vague outlines of a figure, but the voice was recognisable enough. He smiled. "Caroline."

"Let me help you," she said, approaching him and pulling the item in question from the boy's hands with a strong yank. "Geoffrey, no! Those are not yours!" And she handed them back to him—or at least, he felt her do it—and he replaced them on his face, this time holding the boy out at a considerable distance after doing so.

It was then that the nurse appeared, running down the hallway in their direction. "Master Geoffrey! Oh, thank God!" Her accent was distinguishably local or maybe lowlander. She quickly took the child tightly in her arms and curtseyed to both of them. "I'm so sorry. I swear, I never lets 'im out of my sight and yet 'e gets away!"

"No harm done," Dr. Maddox said with a reassuring smile, and she scampered off, taking the squealing child with her.

"He's a sweet boy," said Caroline, turning back to him. "But he refuses to stay still."

"Much like his father," Maddox observed.

"Are you insulting one of your patients?"

"Hardly insulting," he said nervously, which seemed to make her smile all the more.

"You look quite dashing, Daniel."

"Oh, yes." He squirmed in his cravat. "Thank you. It's, um, borrowed . . . for the feast. When is that, by the way?"

"No one has any idea, as no one's seen my brother all day," she said. "When did my sister deliver?"

"About four in the morning."

"You are a hardy man, Dr. Maddox."

He smiled. "I am when I want to be."

The request of the Darcys, both still in convalescence, to see their son was met with a stream of apologies by Nurse that he had been wandering around and was not fit to be presented to his parents. Elizabeth had to stop her in midsentence to get the word in that she had barely seen him the day before, and he would take his nap with his parents, thank you very much. And thus a hastily scrubbed Geoffrey Darcy was brought to the bedchamber, and Elizabeth took him from the nurse and put him between herself and Darcy on the bed. "And how is my favourite little darling?"

"He's fine," mumbled a half asleep Darcy, and Elizabeth swatted him as her son attempted to climb over her.

"You apparently have been naughty," she said.

"Yeff!" he said, putting his fingers in his mouth. Elizabeth looked over at her husband in horror.

Darcy didn't even open his eyes. "Doesn't count. When he says the 'G' properly I will relent."

"Knowing the Darcy heritage, that may be years from now."

Darcy smiled and pulled his son over to him, picking him up and holding him over so they were face to face. "Say it. 'Father.'"

"Yeff!" Geoffrey squealed. "Da!"

"I believe that is Scottish for 'Father,'" Elizabeth said.

"I will not settle. Recent events have not endeared me to the north." He said to his son, "*Dar-cee.*"

"Dabby!"

"Getting closer." He put his son down so he came to rest on his chest. This time, though, Geoffrey did not squirm his way off but settled into his father's night shirt. "I fear we have been very negligent parents."

"Yes, next time we must prevent a marriage, we will be sure to take him with us."

"I have decided to do all of my marriage preventing at home from now on. Georgiana's suitors will simply have to come to Pemberley."

"And you will be smart enough not to turn your back on them."

"Are you attempting to make me cross?"

"Am I succeeding?"

He turned to her, and they looked into each other's eyes for a moment and then broke into laughter. This did not rouse their son, who was now already asleep on his father's chest. Elizabeth leaned over and kissed him on the head, which did not wake him either. "Perhaps the next one will inherit your dourness. That at least will keep them calmer."

"I've been meaning to speak to you about that," Darcy said. "We need to have triplets. Can you—"

"Darcy!" she said. "If Geoffrey was not sleeping so conveniently, I would thrash you, injury or not! Besides, you know very well I have no control over it, and after last night, I am not particularly inclined to have any more children at all!"

Elizabeth fell into a huff on her side of the bed. Seeing her discomfort but being limited in movement, he reached over and stroked her stomach. "I love you."

"I do hope so."

"Please know that I would ravish you right now if not for— well, several factors." He gestured in the appropriate direction.

"I will be very invasive and annoying, as is my right as your wife, and ask you how you are actually feeling."

"Tired and sore but not in a great deal of pain. I know you are very close to your sister, but may I assume we will escape to Pemberley as soon as the year is up?"

"Why does it seem ages since I was there?"

He thought before answering, "Because when you were last there, almost every member of our very large family was in a decidedly different condition." He blinked. "Was that part of my opiate haze or did Miss Bingley accept the proposal of the doctor who patched me up?"

"Unless something has changed in the past few hours, they are still affianced—and very much in love."

"Well, then," he said, apparently lacking much else to say. "He's a good man, but not exactly what I was expecting. And he must get used to all of this intolerable high society."

"I seem to recall you telling me he was raised in a family of fortune."

"Did I? Oh, yes," Darcy said. "Still, if he is to have a serious income, he must get some kind of high commission. I suppose the best thing to do would be to shoot the king in the back."

"Might even get him knighted."

"Yes." He smiled. "Treason it is then."

"Anything for a brother-in-law."

The traditional Christmas meal was much delayed that year. It took so long to get the meal ready and to properly rouse everyone that Christmas itself was coming to a close when they finally sat down at the table, minus the recovering Jane. No less than eleven people (and one empty seat left respectfully for the new mother) took seats for ham and every delicacy that could be prepared as quickly as possible.

Bingley proudly announced the naming of his two children, or what the naming would be for the baptism—Charles Bingley the Third and Elizabeth Bingley.

"Yes, let's just confuse our own family even further by naming everyone after everyone else still living," Mr. Bennet grumbled good-naturedly. "At least Mr. Darcy has some sense."

"No, Papa, we've already agreed, and if we are to have another son, he shall be named Fitzwilliam," Elizabeth said, and gladly endured the glare from her husband and the stifled laughter from their host.

"You may name him after me if you wish, but please do wait until I'm dead," Mr. Bennet continued, and patted his wife on the shoulder. "Any day now, dear."

"Mr. Bennet! You imply that I would wish it!"

"Well, you spent so many years talking of it, I cannot help but make the assumption." He looked across the table at the horrified doctor. "If you have not surmised it already, this family takes great pleasure at making fun of every other member, no matter how beloved."

"O voi che per la via d'Amor passate," said Maddox.

"Hmm," replied Mr. Bennet, " . . . attendete e guardate?"

"s'elli é dolore alcun, quanto 'l mio, grave," added Miss Bingley.

"Something about a hat. That's all I got," Bingley whispered in Darcy's ear.

"Mr. Bennet!" said his wife. "You know Italian?"

"Of course. How else does one read Dante?"

"Is everyone done showing off that they know more languages than we do?" Darcy said.

"It was not my intention, but it is a pleasing side effect," Mr. Bennet said, and Darcy's mood would have soured further if not for his wife's obvious delight with her father. "Doctor, you may or may not be aware, but I have a daughter studying on the Continent, in a seminary in Paris."

"And what does she prefer to study?"

"Incredibly dull religious texts, in Latin, I'm assuming."

"Oh," said Maddox. "I am more in favour of incredibly grue-some medical texts—in French." He turned to his betrothed. "Would you like me to—?"

"*No,*" Miss Bingley said. "Boccaccio will do fine, thank you."

"I see nothing wrong with the King's English," Darcy said.

"*Nu farey frum thilke palacey honourabley, wharey as thees mar-quis shopee hees marri'ajay,*" recited Maddox.

There was a brief silence before Darcy barked, "And what language was that?"

"English. Chaucer, to be exact."

"Are you sure?" Bingley interjected.

"Quite. It is how he would have pronounced it at readings," said the doctor.

"Are you done emasculating my husband now?" Elizabeth snickered.

"I think he is," Darcy said with his usual extreme formality that came down like a wet blanket.

It was in the days between Christmas and the New Year, 1806, that the place was properly done up for the remaining hol-iday, and a generally festive atmosphere prevailed, punctuated by the combined wailing of young Charles and Eliza Bingley. Georgie and Geoffrey had to be moved from the nursery to

another room to get any sleep at all. Jane spent the better part
of the week in bed, finally emerging under everyone's careful
watch to join the ladies in the drawing room downstairs. "Lizzy,
I feel as though we are both finished with our duties, having
both produced heirs. Though I do love my children, I could not
imagine having another quite yet."

"I could," her sister said, and whispered the news to her, as
it was not being made general knowledge. "Though, it is a particularly daunting prospect."

"Pray it is not twins!"

"I think Darcy will settle for nothing less than triplets," she
said as she bounced her niece on her lap, and Georgie grasped at
the hem of her gown. "Fortunately, he has no say in the matter."

"This may just be utter exhaustion," Jane said, "and I do love
my husband and children most dearly, but I cannot at the
moment comprehend why we were so desperate to get married if
this was to be the end result."

"We should let Miss Bingley have that piece of wisdom
right now."

As they giggled, Jane bade Miss Bingley to join them from
the other side of the room. Caroline Bingley had not undergone
a complete transformation of character since her engagement
and had always toned down her particular air of hauteur since
Jane became the mistress of the Bingley family, but she was often
found distracted and busied herself less with biting remarks. In
fact, they were not to judge, for they had seen little of her since
her arrival, all of them being caught up in their own affairs. She
bowed to the mistress of Chatton and, when offered, took
Georgie into her arms next to Elizabeth on the sofa. Other than

a few scattered mumbles, Georgiana Bingley was less inclined than her cousin to try at speaking, but Nurse assured them that girls were slower to present themselves than boys.

"They are busy gathering wisdom and insults to hurl at them," Elizabeth had said.

Georgie did coo and play at the lace on the edge of Miss Bingley's sleeve, which for once, her holder did not discourage. "I see you have fine taste in clothing," she said. Georgie did not respond.

"Heavens," Jane said, "if she develops an obsession with ribbons, I will have no idea which side of the family to blame. Both my mother and my husband are bemused by pretty colours and shiny things."

"Clearly, there is no hope for her at all," Elizabeth said with a smile.

"You will have to hope for the best with the others," Miss Bingley said, and they both laughed in response. Miss Bingley passed off the child and excused herself.

"Good Lord, did we just have a civil conversation with Caroline Bingley?" Elizabeth immediately asked.

"I think we did. What did he *do* to her?"

"As they are not to be married for three months, I hope he has been a proper gentleman."

"Was it decided?"

"First thaw. The roads will be impassable shortly, and we wish to at least invite the Gardiners and the Fitzwilliams."

"A terribly long time to wait," Jane said. "Or, I suppose not. I had to wait a year for Charles. You at least had yet to realise you were in love with Darcy for all but the last few months."

"And to think, this whole business with Miss Bingley was wrapped up in a few weeks. How fortunate."

"Except for your husband."

"Yes, of course. But he was a good sport through it all. Especially when Mr. Bingley and I were rather bluntly taking advantage of the loss of his senses."

"I imagine you had to," Jane said. "Mr. Darcy does not stand the loss of his senses very often. Best to snatch the opportunity when you can."

Being an overworked Town doctor, Daniel Maddox had forgotten just how much work it was to be idly rich. So much preparation went into the New Year's festivities that even he, only a guest, felt overwhelmed and was looking forward to them being over before they began. He did not envy Bingley's position at all, with two infants, a toddler, and an entire household full of guests to oversee. Of course, as a man of wealth he was not required or even expected to take an active interest in his children at their ages, but Charles Bingley was obviously not that kind of man and was often disappearing into the nursery or carrying his daughter around as he went about his errands.

The doctor's own responsibilities were extremely minimal. Mr. Hurst seemed to be recovering from his condition, and Mr. Darcy had progressed to an inevitable point where he was both sick of doctoring and well enough to have the strength to refuse examination. That left Dr. Maddox time to peruse the considerable library and figure out ways to avoid his soon-to-be relatives. Not that he didn't care for them—in fact, he was quite pleased with them—but he was more accustomed to being the near-invisible doctor servant and not the mysterious man who had somehow won the heart of the proud woman who was *Miss Bingley*. He had no way to explain it so they would understand, nor did he want to explain it or feel compelled to. What she said of him, he had no idea, because now that they were affianced, he saw her only under acceptable social circumstances. This was without question but frustrating nonetheless. They needed to confer, to prepare some sort of strategy, if he was going to endure this seemingly endless assault of family. But he would not approach her about it, not when he wanted to make a good impression on the family, and so conversation was restricted to across the table and chance happenings in the hallway.

It was only when finally he made it to the library before dinner to return the newly finished medical text that he found outdated and not worth the effort that he heard the door close and lock behind him. "Please don't—," but when he turned around, it was of course Caroline. One of the things she liked about him was that he was very clever, however awkward being alone in a room with her suddenly made him. "Hello."

"Tiring, isn't it?"

He looked away but smiled. "Yes, very. But it is the proper way to do things, and I am a proper gentleman now. Or at the very least, I am dressed like one."

"You look very pleasing."

"Thank you," he said, unconsciously straightening his waistcoat. "You look . . . the way you normally look, which is perfect."

It was true that she was ready for the New Year's celebrations with her hair up properly, but that still did not entirely deflate the compliment. He suddenly didn't know what to do with his hands, and it didn't help at all that she took one of them, and he was suddenly terrified that it was too cold and clammy and shaky and she would toss him out.

"You know the terrified look on your face is adorable," she said.

"Oh," was all he could say. "Thank you."

"Considering you were, less than a week ago, staring at a woman's—"

"*Entirely* different. It was a medical procedure. And, um, quite different than—"

"Touching a woman you love?"

"Yes. My experience has mainly been with . . ." He could not look at her, so he stared at her hands. It didn't help. "Forgive me. My years of poverty have led me to forget a particular rule of conduct in this situation."

"I can assure you," said Caroline, "we are breaking it."

"Not *that* rule," he said. "I mean—am I supposed to lie and say I am an innocent?"

"I think—we are not supposed to have this conversation at all."

"Right. Of course." And he was relieved because it was a reprieve—but not for long. Within moments, they were up against the bookshelf, locked in an embrace that was breaking all of the rules, and whatever he claimed earlier to have forgotten came rushing back to him.

When they finally broke off she said, "If you claimed now you'd never touched a woman before, you'd be a very bad liar."

"I am a notoriously bad liar," he said.

"What was her name?"

The question threw him off. He was fairly thrown off any-way. He cocked his head. "Who?"

"I am making the very noble assumption there was only one."

He swallowed and answered, "Lucetta."

"Very Italian."

"She was. I mean, she was Italian—Roman, actually." He could not escape her look. "Oh God, must I tell you everything?"

"You said you are a bad liar, so you might as well."

They did, for propriety's sake, separate lest someone pick the lock, he supposed. "I was studying medicine in the Academy in Paris, and I went to Rome for a lecture of a very noted physician. And being there and having some funds, as my brother had yet to destroy the family fortune, I decided to take a convalescence there of a few weeks. This was . . . um, eight, nine years ago. And some local girl was very, very kind to a young student who liked the local vintage far too much. The end result was that I did not see as much art as I wished to see before I had to return for classes. But I did learn a great deal of the language that is . . . not found in your average textbook. But, you know, it was a very long time ago. And nothing came of it that would . . . be signif-icant. And there, now you have my whole sordid history, which I do hope you will keep in confidence."

"I hardly run to my brother about anything and know better than to open my mouth to Louisa. And there are men in this family with far more sordid pasts than you, Daniel, and I have kept my tongue in front of Elizabeth."

It took him a second to make all of the connections. "How would you even—forget it. Am I forever to be compared to Darcy?"

"Darling, in this family, *everyone* is compared to Darcy."

"I would say, 'poor Darcy,' but as he was foolish enough to pass you over, my sympathy is limited," he said.

It was, apparently, the right thing to say because she kissed him again, and it occurred to him that he knew very little about Caroline Bingley. He knew her personality a bit; he knew she was intelligent and graceful and beautiful, but he didn't know what she was as a woman beyond what she presented to society, which he knew was a façade. He wanted to know what she felt like, what she tasted like—all right, he knew that *now*.

"Caroline," he said between breaths.

"I know," she replied. That was the nice thing. So many things did not need further explanation. They pulled apart again. "Can I confess something to you?"

He gave her a look that made it clear that it was not in question.

"For all of my rather . . . intense courting of various people, I find myself somewhat shocked at the end result."

"Which is?" he said, with a smirk.

"That after thirty years, three months seems like an impossibly long time."

He could not bring himself to contradict her.

Chapter 12

BROTHERLY LOVE

THE FIRST THING TO happen after the new year was the removal of Darcy's stitches, a procedure he described as "not particularly pleasant," but it did not seem to bother him much. The only result was some minor bleeding to be bandaged, and then he was free to go about as he pleased. Immediate plans were made for the Darcys' return to Pemberley. While there would be much travelling between the two estates until the wedding, Mr. Bennet would stay with the Darcys and Mrs. Bennet, and Kitty would aid Jane with her three children.

"Have you seen my son?" Darcy said as he burst into Bingley's study.

Bingley merely held up Geoffrey, who had climbed into his lap and decided to take his nap there. "I couldn't bring myself to disturb him, he appeared and was asleep so quickly."

"That's all right." Darcy took his son and handed him to his exasperated nurse. "Sorry to bother you."

"Hardly. How is the shoulder?"

"I've been told it looks worse than it is. Excuse me, Bingley."
He went to leave, but Bingley stopped him.

"I have a favour to ask of you," he announced.

"Does it involve preventing a marriage?"

"No."

"Does it involve forwarding a marriage?"

"No."

"Am I, at any point, to be shot?"

"I daresay, no."

"I am still hesitant," Darcy said, leaning on the fireplace. "My favours seem to get me in a lot of trouble."

"They also got you a wife."

"So clever you are to point that out," Darcy admitted. "Fine, Bingley. What is it?"

"Dr. Maddox has expressed an interest in seeing Pemberley. If you would put him up until the wedding, I am sure he would be quickly lost in its libraries and be no trouble to you."

"Interesting, then, that he has not expressed this sentiment to *me*."

"Well, there is, ah, the matter of . . ." Bingley coughed. "He cannot stay at Chatton, and I have no wish for him to return to Town." He added, "Caroline would go with him, and the problem would not be solved."

Darcy smirked triumphantly. "So it is a problem?"

"So I have been informed. By various . . . ahem, servants."

"You are such a noble guardian of your sister's chastity. Your parents would undoubtedly be proud."

Bingley's face turned the colour of his hair. "I can always rely on you to state the obvious, Darcy. Just take him to Pemberley!"

"If he wishes to go, he is a welcome guest. However, *I* will not be the one to drag him there."

And so, the train of Darcys, one Bennet, and one doctor set off for the great estate of Pemberley. And it was even done without Bingley getting out his shotgun.

Maddox was impressed at the sight of Pemberley; only his usual shyness hid some of it.

"If you're worried about being lost," Elizabeth assured him, "I still manage it on a regular basis, so there is no reason to be ashamed."

"And I've given up hope entirely," Mr. Bennet said.

Mr. Darcy was greeted most enthusiastically by his staff, even though he had been gone less than two months. A teary Mrs. Reynolds stopped short of actually embracing him. He maintained his dignity.

Bingley was correct in his assessment that the doctor was a most unobtrusive and pleasant guest. He spent many hours with Mr. Bennet in the library, sharing a knowledge of language and literature that gave Mr. and Mrs. Darcy their much desired privacy.

"I knew a Maddox once," Mr. Bennet said. "Stewart Maddox. We were down at Oxford together."

"He was my father," the doctor said. "The Earl of Maddox was my great uncle. My father's personal estate and fortune was inherited by my older brother, Brian, who lost it gambling."

"The ruin of many men," Mr. Bennet observed.

Bingley and his sister were constant dinner guests despite the weather, and Elizabeth was back and forth to see Jane, who was not ready to leave her twins. All in all, there were more comings and goings than usual, and Darcy's only objection to the doctor's presence was that Maddox insisted that Darcy not yet return to fencing and used his authority as a physician to continuously send home Darcy's fencing master.

One night late in January, Bingley delivered a letter that had arrived at Chatton, addressed to the doctor. Alone with Darcy in his study, Maddox tore it open. "It is from my brother." He took off his glasses and read it. "He is asking for money."

"Is this a regular custom of his?" Darcy inquired.

"Hardly. I haven't spoken to him in seven years. After he lost most of our fortune, he spent the remainder to pay for my medical education and ran off to the Continent, presumably to escape creditors. I've not a heard a word of him since."

"How extraordinarily coincidental to recent events. How much is he asking for?"

"Twenty pounds." He closed the letter and replaced his glasses. "I have twenty pounds. I have more than twenty pounds."

"It is still a considerable sum," Darcy said, despite the fact that Maddox doubted it was a considerable sum to the master of Pemberley.

"But not unreasonable. And he is my brother."

"So you are not at all suspicious?"

"Of course I am. But considering what he spent in the old days, it is rather small, and he says it is a fee for rent now that he is newly returned to England. And he *is* my brother."

"So despite his ruining your entire fortune and social standing, you parted on good terms?"

Maddox looked over at Darcy and answered very defensively, "Our father died when I was but twelve. Brian paid for my extensive education and my doctor's license, which gave me a potential living. The latter he probably used for loans on credit he did not have. So while we did have a rather heated discussion about the family fortune, we did not say anything we could not take back, and I wished him well on his escape."

Darcy responded, "You are a more generous man than I. While it's all too convenient on his part for my tastes, it is your money, and you may keep your own counsel on what to do with it."

"And I must write him of the wedding if he hasn't heard. I am unsure of the arrangements, but perhaps there would be somewhere for him to stay in Derbyshire?"

"Of course. He is welcome at Pemberley." Darcy, however, was not particularly welcoming in his tone.

The general instinct to delay the wedding until the thaw was proven to be an excellent idea. Derbyshire endured what the aged Mrs. Reynolds assured them was one of the worst winters she had ever seen, with, at times, even the roads between Pemberley and Chatton impassable. The post stopped entirely for days at a time, and most of the occupants of Pemberley retreated from the long, drafty hallways to the smaller sitting rooms. Darcy dismissed all the servants but those necessary and made sure to have the fires going strongly in all of the fireplaces in active use. Derbyshire was blanketed in white, and to the minor vexation of his parents, Geoffrey Darcy's first word was not a name but the word "snow." He banged on the window, indicating that he wanted to play in it or at least see what it was. Darcy immediately refused, but fortunately Elizabeth had a doctor there to assure him that letting his son handle some snow for a few minutes under shelter of the portico columns would do no harm. What he did touch, Geoffrey mostly quickly consumed, which set off another chain of parental worries and more assurances that snow was, in fact, condensed water and harmless when it was clean. Only Darcy's stern look stopped Dr. Maddox from a long lecture about condensation and how the scientific processes of weather worked.

The wedding preparations were continuing at Chatton, or so Bingley assured them when the Bingleys visited, but on this night, the plans were assumed to be cancelled because it had been snowing for almost a day and not even a courier could get through to inquire as to the attendance at dinner. It was late February, and the weather was sure to break soon, but at the moment, Father Winter was holding his own, and despite all attempts at keeping the fire going, most of Pemberley was freezing. The servants were dismissed to their quarters, and the residents and guests of the house retreated after dinner to a single sitting room. Darcy sat in a chair by the fireplace and tended to it diligently. Mr. Bennet and his daughter were very happy with their books and multiple blankets. For once, Geoffrey was not permitted to run around on the cold floor (for he was now walking, if a bit unsteadily, and had occasion to fall) and stayed securely in his father's arms despite how much he struggled to escape them before falling asleep.

Georgiana, who was well-educated but not a bookworm like her sister-in-law, had found Dr. Maddox very pleasing to have around because she quickly discovered a great interest in middle English texts, of which Pemberley had a small number that were rarely perused, mainly because the spelling of words was almost entirely different and in some cases so was the letter set.

"That cannot be the same word!" she insisted, staring at the very large bound text before both of them on the table. "It is spelled differently."

"The fourteenth century was not a time when England had official spellings," the doctor explained patiently. "This was meant to be read aloud, and as we are often to pronounce words differently in different circumstances, so it is written differently."

Darcy spoke out of nowhere, "The double sorrow of Troilus I tell, who was the son of King Priamus of Troy."

Everyone looked at him, but he seemed unfazed by the attention.

"*Troilus and Criseyde*," Maddox said.

"Yes. I had to memorise the first ten stanzas for my literature exams," Darcy explained. "Though, during the oral section, I was allowed to read the text with our current pronunciation if using the original structure of the words, which I do not properly recall now. Admittedly, it has been some time, and I am not accustomed to hearing it spoken aloud properly." He mused, "I once had to attend a reading of *Sir Gawain and the Green Knight* spoken entirely in the old accent and readily confess that had I not read it ahead, I would not have understood a word."

"How bizarre," Elizabeth said, "that the language should change that much in four hundred years."

"In Chaucer's time, I do believe, the Parliament still used Norman French for administration," her father added. "If we're all going to trade facts, none of us are much for cards."

"I am," Georgiana said, "but brother will never play with me."

"You make me seem like a terrible brother," Darcy said. "You have not asked in years."

"Because I know you detest it! I would not ask that of you. Doctor, do you play?"

"Not well," Maddox said.

"Good," Darcy said. "Best to let your wife win. It gives her the perception that she is in the superior position." The knowing smirk he gave Elizabeth was the only thing that he knew kept her from getting up and smacking him. Dr. Maddox merely blushed, but further comment was interrupted by the bell.

"Good heavens," Mr. Bennet said. "In this weather?"

"And I have dismissed the porters," Darcy said, and handed Geoffrey off to Elizabeth. "It seems I must tend to this myself."

Taking a candlestick and another coat, he left the warm room and walked down the empty halls of Pemberley. It was so cold that even his loyal dogs did not follow him. When he finally reached the massive double doors and unlocked them with his master key, he opened the door to a burst of even colder air and snowflakes. When he recovered, he saw before him a man not in a courier's livery but wearing a shabby coat and no hat at all, his face red from the cold but standing there very pleasantly as if his hair were not snow-covered and soaking wet. "I'm so sorry to disturb you. Is this the Pemberley estate?"

"It is," Darcy said.

"Then I am not lost. I heard there are a great many fine manors in this part of the country. I would very much wish to see the master of Pemberley, if he might be disturbed."

"I am he," Darcy found himself saying. "And you are . . . ?"

"Hello, Mr. Darcy," the man said with a courteous and extended bow. "So pleased to make your acquaintance. I am Brian Maddox."

THE INTRUDER

DARCY APOLOGISED FOR THE lack of staff due to the weather, which seemed to bother Mr. Maddox not in the least, and the master of Pemberley found himself taking his own guest's coat and finding him a towel and a blanket for his hair after he shut the door. "I have sent most of the staff to their quarters," he explained as he led him down the long corridor to the sitting room, "to keep warm. How you made it here, I have no idea."

"This? This is a minor dusting," Mr. Maddox said, attempting to dry his hair, which was a frizzy mess. "You've obviously never wintered in the Carpathian mountains."

"No, I cannot say I have."

"Thank you for letting me in. Obviously, I am here for my brother, who I assume by your lack of further questioning is here."

"You have assumed correctly," Darcy said, his voice carrying its normal levels of reservation, though he was not to be an ungracious host. That would be insupportable. He finally reached the door that led to the warm room and realised he would have to announce his guest himself.

That did not come to be. He barely had properly stepped into the room when Mr. Maddox disposed of his blanket. "Danny!"

"Brian?" Whatever surprise was quickly overcome on the doctor's part, and he put down the book and hugged his brother. Without foreknowledge of their history, one might assume they were the best of friends as well as brothers. "You had to make an entrance, didn't you?"

"Always." He bowed to the crowd, and Darcy introduced them in turn. "Very pleased to meet you all. I apologise for my intrusion, but it was hard to calculate when I would be arriving, and all of the inns are full."

Now that they were standing next to each other, the familial connection was obvious. Brian was shorter but older and did not wear glasses, but they both had the same black hair that curled itself in clumps. The chief difference was that the doctor kept his hair longer in front and trimmed in the back, while his older brother took no effort to hide his face but just kept his locks long everywhere, so it faintly resembled a lion's mane. "I came as soon as I got your letter—and the loan, thank you."

"The post has been inconsistent up here," the doctor said, "at least during the worst of the storms."

"Storms! Ah, to be an Englishman again and consider this a terrible winter. Everyone in Town is all complaint. But I suppose it is relative."

"I assume you have been travelling some," Dr. Maddox said.

"Some! All right, I admit I did not get as far as Russia, but otherwise I've been about. Prussia, Istanbul, Austria . . . by the way, the vampire tale is nonsense—or so I was led to believe while I was there."

"What vampire tale?" Georgiana inquired.

"He is talking of an old legend," Elizabeth explained. "Monsters and all that. Very popular in fiction."

"Gruesome fiction," Darcy said to his sister, "inappropriate and fanciful, at best."

"He's trying to discourage her," Elizabeth said to her father.

"Well, it's certainly not Chaucer," Mr. Bennet said in jest. "Well, Mr. Maddox, your return to England then was most for-tuitous because you are here in time for your brother's wedding."

"So it seems," Brian said, and gave his brother a tap on the arm. "Fate, almost."

"Yes," Darcy said coldly.

"Mr. Maddox," Elizabeth said in her hostess voice, "it is most wonderful to meet you, but I fear I must put my son to bed, and I much desire to hear all of the tales of your travels to the Continent. So perhaps you will save them for tomorrow. I will find someone to set you up with a room, and you may stay in here as long as you wish, but I must retire."

"I completely understand," said Mr. Maddox. "I am sorry for my late appearance, again, Mrs. Darcy." He bowed as most of the rest of them took the hint to retire, leaving the brothers to catch up as the fire burned down.

When Elizabeth finally joined her husband in their bed-chamber, he was not in bed but sitting by the fire in deep con-centration. She let a hand stray in his direction as she passed, and he kissed it. "Well, you can stay up, but I am at least getting under the blankets."

He grunted.

Elizabeth changed into her bedclothes and took her place in the bed that was meant to be exclusively hers but that they always shared, where she crossed her arms and said, "Are you going to make me wait all night?"

"Oh." Suddenly his tone softened considerably. "I'm sorry." And he began to remove the outer layers of his own clothing.

"Perhaps I should have been more specific," she said. "I was talking about Mr. Maddox."

He huffed in disappointment. "You were?"

She bid him come closer and kissed him. "First things first, if Mr. Maddox is to stay here, you must try to be a bit more civil."

"Civil? I was being perfectly civil. I was just being Mr. Darcy," he said. "Everyone knows I am still a gracious host, even if I completely lack any social skills."

Elizabeth laughed as he sat on the bed beside her. "I would not say *any*. But I would say, knowing you very well—and remember, Mr. Maddox does *not*—that you were even more unsociable than you usually are around mixed company. In fact, I would say you were downright suspicious."

"And you are not?" he said, untying his boots and tossing them aside. "The doctor's long-lost brother, who ruined the family fortune and left him in destitution before fleeing creditors and apparently went as far away as Istanbul to do so, suddenly reappears just before his little brother marries into fortune? There is nothing to consider in *that*?"

"I am not saying there isn't," she replied. "But that does not mean you must constantly give him a look like you suspect he's about to run off with the silverware."

"Perhaps that *is* what I'm thinking."

"I am not saying that your fears are completely unfounded," she said, "or even downright sensible. But he is our guest, and we must give him the benefit of the doubt until Dr. Maddox, who knows him better than we ever shall, tells us otherwise."

"You are a very trusting person, Lizzy."

"I am merely a proper hostess. I am by no means trusting of Mr. Maddox. I will be most displeased if you turn your back on him. Though, if you must, perhaps he will hit you on the right, and your scars will be symmetrical."

"I have a scar?"

"I suppose you can't see it. Well, it is very small, and I will be the only one who will ever see it beyond your manservant and Dr. Maddox—or at least I *should* be."

"You will be." He kissed her, and they collectively set their fears and concerns about Brian Maddox aside.

Mr. Maddox proved himself a most pleasant fellow, considerably less shy than his brother, and that, of course, made Darcy all the more suspicious of him. "I trust very few pleasant people," he admitted to his wife.

"You trust very few people," she responded.

Mr. Maddox regaled them all with his tales of the wilds of Eastern Europe, and the only comfort Darcy took in his being a threat to Georgiana's marital status was that he was over fifteen years her senior, which violated no rules of society but certainly would be a bit odd. And as far as Darcy could tell with his very scrupulous eye, his sister was inclined to look at their new guest more as someone out of her age range and therefore merely an interesting enough man. Dr. Maddox seemed pleased enough at his presence, and if he had any serious suspicions, he would not voice them, even when Darcy and Elizabeth both took turns cornering him privately about it.

At long last, the weather cleared, and the roads opened up. "So I am finally to meet the beauty who has captured my brother's heart?" This, of course, made his brother blush. "Well, he's too modest. Someone else will praise her, surely, as you are all family."

There was a very awkward silence. Later in private Darcy lamented, "Why is it I am constantly being called to praise Miss Bingley?"

"You must admit, she has improved since her betrothal," Elizabeth said. "Something about being less haughty and insufferable when in love. I have no idea where I am getting this notion, but it suddenly popped into my head that it might happen to people."

"Dearest Elizabeth, remind me again why I put up with you?"

"It must be my excellent conversational abilities."

The Bingleys arrived in time for dinner. "Jane sends her regards," Bingley said as he entered with his sister. "But Eliza has a sniffle, and she would not leave her."

"I will visit now that the roads are clear," Elizabeth said.

"Well, they're not all that clear. We're barely here, I assure you."

Dinner was a most pleasant affair, as Mr. Maddox got to tell some tales anew and some he had apparently saved. Bingley seemed to be enjoying himself, but whether Dr. Maddox and Caroline were paying any attention was anybody's guess. Elizabeth was only glad that it took the attention away from her husband, who was quieter than usual and had been at every dinner since the older Maddox had arrived. Anyone else who took note of this kept it to himself.

In fact, the first time Darcy spoke at all was in reaction to a servant whispering to him. "Good God!" Darcy said.

"Darcy, what is it?"

He grumbled, "It's snowing again."

They had to scurry to the parlour to see that it was, in fact, beginning to snow.

"Well?"

It took the good doctor a moment to realise the question was directed at him. "What? I'm a doctor, not a scholar of weather. If you want to know how snow is made, I would be happy to tell you. If you want me to tell you *when* it's going to happen, I must disappoint you."

"Mrs. Reynolds," Darcy said to the house manager, "please see to the arrangements for Bingley and Miss Bingley for the night."

It was but a night. Darcy made a quiet joke to Bingley about standing outside Caroline's room with a shotgun, to which Bingley blushed and gave no response. What could happen in one night?

Chapter 14

MOTHERLY INSTINCT

ELIZABETH WOKE UP WITH a start. Her heart was racing, and the very sound of it was audible only due to the complete silence of their bedchamber, aside from Darcy's breathing. She put a hand on her forehead and tried to chide herself out of it, but she could not. Finally, she tugged on her husband, and he half mumbled a questioning response.

"I have had a terrible nightmare."

He flipped over, an act that a month ago would have given him some discomfort. "What was it about?"

"I . . . don't properly remember. Something about Geoffrey." Now that she had said it, her mind was set. "I must see him." She slid off the bed and was putting her clothes back on, which were in a pile on the floor, while her husband sat up in a muddled state of half awake. "Now!"

"I am not one to test a mother's instincts," he said at last, and also found his clothes (they were hanging on one of the bedposts) and was putting on his robe when he heard his wife shake the door.

"It's locked."

He frowned. "I didn't lock it."

"But it is locked. So one could logically conclude that you did lock it."

Now coming to his senses, he put on his slippers and grabbed the set of master keys from the bed stand, shuffling over to a very impatient Elizabeth. "Very well." He put the key in, and it turned, but the door still would not open. "Huh."

"Is it locked from the outside?"

"The bedchamber of the mistress of Pemberley does not lock from the outside," he said. "Very few don't. This is one of them."

"Well, try another key."

"This is the correct key. The door is unlocked." Instead of jiggling the handle, he gave it a push. "I think—I think it's bolted."

"Why would it be bolted? Could there be something blocking it?" She thought about it. Their door was at the end of a long hallway, giving them the appropriate privacy. There was no reason why there would be something in front of the door unless someone had gone out of the way to put it there. "Darcy—"

"I know." His voice now was rising to the level of hers. He gave the door a solid shove, the best he could manage without putting a shoulder into it, which he was not eager to do. "It is bolted." He tugged at the door handle. "I'm sure of it." He ran to the pull cord and rang the bell for the servant. "Someone should come."

"Perhaps if we make a noise," Elizabeth said, unwilling to be idle. "Hello? Is anyone out there? Mr. and Mrs. Darcy are unattended!"

There was no answer. There was only silence. "Damn these thick walls!" he said, and turned to his dogs. "Well, don't just lie there! Bark or something! Make yourselves useful!" In response to their master's pleas, one of them got up, climbed up on his chest with her paws, and licked his chin. "Useless mutt! That's not what I meant when I said *useful!*"

"They cannot understand you, Darcy!" Elizabeth said, in no mood for humour, and neither was he.

Three weeks, Daniel Maddox thought as he lay awake in his bed—*at most. Two, maybe, if this damned snow would stop. My rotten luck.* He looked at his watch again; it was half past midnight, and he doubted he would get any sleep at all. *Maybe I should read up on the circulatory system. That always makes me fall asleep—such a boring system.* He relit the candle and shuffled through the stack of books on his bed stand, but none piqued his interest (or noninterest as it were). *Tristan and Isolde, Troilus and Criseyde—I need something that's not romantic! Or, at least, ends well!* He had his hands on a copy of *The Merchant of Venice,* which he had not read in several years, when the door to his room opened, and his brother burst in. "Hello?"

"Danny," Brian said. He was fully clothed and for once looked serious. "Get up, please."

"What is it? Who's ill?"

"Just—do it, all right?"

A little too startled to comprehend, he threw on his clothing as quickly as possible, which, as a doctor, he was quite competent of doing. "Now what is it?" he said as he stepped out in to the better-lit hallway. And that was when he felt the point of sword on the back of his neck. "Brian?"

Brian looked at him sheepishly, which would normally be endearing but this time failed to be so.

"Drop your things," said a very familiar voice, and Dr. Maddox dropped his black bag and raised his hands. "Turn around."

He did not need to see whom it was to know, but it was nonetheless best to face his enemy. Lord James Kincaid looked considerably worse off than when he had last seen him in passing at the Bingley townhouse. He was unshaven, his clothing a mess, but the most relevant issue was that he was holding a rapier to Maddox's throat, just barely scraping the flesh.

"You're making a mistake," the doctor said, somewhat afraid to swallow. "Pemberley is filled with people. All I have to do is—"

"Not only is Pemberley on a skeleton staff, but that staff, upon hearing a noise from you, will find their chambers locked, and so will everyone else. So we have all the privacy we wish."

Maddox inched away only slightly, and though Kincaid kept his blade up, he did not press him. "Brian, what's going on?"

"Unfortunately," his brother said, "his lordship is the master of ceremonies."

"But you're part of this." He shook his head. "I should have known. How would word reach you in Bulgaria that my situation had changed?"

"Your brother did not spend all of his years on the lam in Europe," Kincaid said. "He spent some time in Australia recently, where he and I came into some financial dealings that did not end well for him."

"Look," Dr. Maddox interrupted, "if you're a creditor and you wish to be paid off, we can arrange something, but not here or now, *please*."

"Your brother paid off his debt to me by giving me the master keys to Pemberley." Kincaid mock bowed to Brian Maddox. "Thank you, Mr. Maddox."

"I can't believe—" But this was not the time for accusations. Or maybe it was; he didn't know. He was not accustomed to having blades pointed at him. "So what can I offer you? Whatever my conniving brother has told you, I am a man of very small fortune and will remain so for some time."

"There are a couple of ways this may proceed," Kincaid said, reaching into his pocket and producing a rolled-up document. "As someone of your intelligence can surmise, my object is Caroline's fortune, which you will have legal access to on your wedding day. Your first option, of course, is to sign papers agreeing on that date to provide me with the funds by check."

"And I suppose my second option is to get run through," Maddox said.

"If you want to be stupidly noble about it, then you may do as you wish, but it will not help at all. For you see, I have, of course, a backup plan. I had much time to think this out properly while I was waiting for your brother to bribe the guard to my cell. Apparently, twenty pounds was sufficient."

Maddox steamed, but he could not be angry with his brother now. There would be time for that later, if he survived. "And?"

"Well, I could run you through or leave you unharmed. I really have no preference. But your refusal to sign brings our dear Caroline into the picture."

Maddox stepped forward with indignation, and Kincaid raised the blade so the doctor had to raise his chin to avoid his throat being cut. "Easy now. I've not done anything to her *yet*. But that option lies open, as you are no match for me, and she is a woman. In fact, with all of the English propriety and social strictures, if I had my way with her tonight, I may well end up married to her tomorrow, thus obtaining my intended goal without even involving you. Unless . . ." And he dragged the blade so it drew blood. " . . . you want to watch."

Maddox's reaction was interrupted by what was obviously the bell ringing in the middle of the night—apparently not part of Kincaid's elaborate plan. He was distracted, and Maddox reached for anything that could be a weapon, despite his lack of abilities, and found only the candlestick mounted on the wall. Before he had time to dislodge it, Kincaid collected himself and struck at the doctor.

Fortunately for Daniel Maddox, he had a certain agility and ducked out of the way. Unfortunately for Brian Maddox, he had not the same agility and was still standing behind him. He gave a small gasp as the rapier went through his chest.

Chapter 15

SCOTLAND THE BRAVE

"THE BELL?" DARCY SAID, perking up his ears.

"I don't like this," Elizabeth said, and in response, her husband grabbed the metal sifter from the fireplace.

"Please, away from the door," he instructed, and when she stepped away, he swung at its top hinges, making a considerable indentation in the fine wooden door but not dislodging the hinges. "Damn it! This will take all night."

To no great surprise, his wife immediately took up a poker and swung it at the bottom set of hinges. He had no time to protest. "If only I had a hammer . . . or an axe. We're coming, son."

Dr. Maddox's first instincts, surprisingly, were to run to his brother who slumped to the ground when Kincaid pulled the blade out. Years of his profession could not undo his inclinations, and he ignored Kincaid almost entirely. Fortunately, the lord did not strike at him again. "What the hell are you—?"

"Shut up, and get me my bag!" He looked over his shoulder. "*Now!*"

"You—"

"Do it, and I will sign your damned contract!"

Kincaid was not prepared for this precise situation and somewhat numbly kicked the bag over to Maddox, keeping his blade up. The doctor tore it open and spilled the contents onto the floor next to his brother who he slapped on the face. "Stay with me." Brian's response was to cough as his brother took scissors and cut his shirt away, revealing a hole in his chest near the collarbone. Blood was running but not gushing, which meant the artery was missed, but as it was also pooling beneath him, he had been pierced straight through. He probed the wound, and his brother gasped. "Oh, be quiet. You brought this on yourself." It was hard to tell if the lung had been hit, but he could do nothing for that, anyway. He went for his needle and thread and immediately began lacing it up.

"Maddox—"

"You can try to kill me, too, if you want," Maddox said, without turning to look at the man who had the rapier pressed against the doctor's back. "But that is your decision, and clearly I cannot stop you either way, so in the meantime, my brother will live to see the day when I can properly slap him in the face for this if I can possibly help it."

"I could go after Caroline."

"Touch her, and I'll kill you," said a voice from behind. It was Charles Bingley in his nightclothes, brandishing a walking stick, which he swung at Kincaid. Despite being an accomplished outdoorsman, he was easily parried by the lord, who, unfortunately, caught the stick and used it to bash Bingley on the head. The master of Chatton dropped to the ground in a heap and did not stir.

"One patient at a time!" was all Maddox said in response as he began to sew up his brother. "Please!"

"All right," Darcy said, looking at the prospect of a door with the area around both its hinges nearly destroyed. "I think I can push it open."

"With your shoulder? Alone? Absolutely not!"

"Lizzy—" But one look from her silenced him. "Fine. On three. One . . . two . . . three!" Together they slammed their combined weight into the door, and it finally came loose, freeing the Darcys from their prison.

"Geoffrey!" Elizabeth cried as they rushed to the nursery, which was just down the hall, only to find the door locked. "Keys!"

Darcy fumbled through his set of keys and found the correct one, which successfully unlocked the door, which had not been bolted.

"Mr. Darcy! Mrs. Darcy!" Nurse, barely awake, curtseyed. "I was woken by that terrible noise, but I couldn't—"

"Open the door, yes," Darcy said as his wife rushed to her son's cradle where he was fast asleep.

"My darling," Elizabeth said as she took her son into her arms. "My baby. Darcy, my baby."

Darcy put his arms on his wife's shoulders and made his own inspection of his son who was now waking from the commotion. "I think he is all right. Whatever is the matter, it is not with Geoffrey." He kissed his son and then his wife, who was still sobbing. "I must find the cause of all this. Please, stay here and keep the door shut to anyone suspicious—especially Mr. Maddox." He turned to Nurse. "Watch over them."

"Darcy—"

"I love you," he responded, and left the nursery. The hallway was silent except for the banging on the door to Georgiana's room. "Georgiana!" he said and quickly unlocked her door, which was of course locked.

"Brother!" she screamed as she emerged, also in her night-gown and robe, and hugged him. "What is going on? I heard all this noise!"

"I have no idea what is the matter, but you should go to the nursery and stay with Elizabeth."

"Is she all right? Is my nephew all right?"

"They are fine, just understandably upset. She woke and found our door barred, and we had to destroy it to get it open." He said very firmly, "Go to her, and stay there unless I call or there is a fire." He kissed her on the forehead. "Go, please."

She did as she was told. Since there were no more banging doors, that left the guest wing, servants' quarters, and that business about the bell. Something was afoul in the halls of Pemberley, and its master would not stand for it. Instead of going to the front door, he took a sword from the wall above the fireplace in a sitting room and followed his instincts to the guest wing.

The scene before him was inexplicable. Dr. Maddox knelt on the floor next to his fallen brother, covered in blood, sewing him up as women seemed to embroider things, if those things involved human flesh. Standing over him, a roguish-looking

Lord Kincaid held a rapier. Behind him, an unconscious Bingley slumped on the floor.

"Mr. Darcy," Kincaid said, "somehow I thought our paths would cross again."

"Despite some people's inclinations for revenge, I, in fact, never cared to see you again," Darcy said, raising his weapon. "I do not associate with filth." He did, it seemed, fence filth, despite his inclination not to. He had two wounded men on the ground, one who needed his concentration, and a lot of people missing, and he knew that even with an uninjured right arm he had not the stamina for a long battle, having expended almost all of his energy just getting the bedchamber door open. He was already breathing heavily, and he hoped Kincaid did not notice this, but if their previous matches were any indication, he was an observant man. "I have no idea as to how you managed this, but I will be a great host and will give you the chance to leave Pemberley now, unharmed, to contend only with the proper authorities and the miserable weather."

"And do you think in your state that you can best me if we were to duel?"

"I believe in my state that I can try," he answered with his usual determination. And that was when they both heard the great battle cry that overruled further conversation. Both fighters were distracted long enough to properly see the man in the great tartan cloth swinging from a chandelier and landing next to Darcy.

"For the Bonny Prince!" cried the man, in full antique Highland costume—great kilt, white shirt, and a blue beret. He was carrying a wooden circular shield and a basket-hilted claymore. "God, I've always wanted to do that!"

"William?" Kincaid finally stuttered.

William took his place beside Darcy, holding up his sword and his shield. "Lord Darcy of Pemberley, I assume?"

"Mr. Darcy, thank you." With two swords now to face Kincaid, Darcy felt a bit more confident, especially because he could barely hold his own sword up. "Might I inquire—"

"Lord William Kincaid," he said.

"My brother," Kincaid said, "making a fool of himself, apparently. Where did you even get that? Aren't great kilts still *illegal?*"

"I knew I'd catch up with you sooner or later," William Kincaid said. "This is for Fiona, brother."

Apparently, Lord Kincaid—the villain of the two—had been holding back at the club in Town, because he was a sufficiently accomplished swordsman to parry not one but two blades and to avoid tripping over Bingley's body in the process. It was only when he was bashed from behind with a broom that he gave pause long enough to strike properly, and he practically fell into both of their blades. As he fell first on his knees, then straightforward to the floor, behind him appeared Caroline Bingley, wielding her impromptu weapon.

"Miss Bingley!"

"Caroline!" Dr. Maddox looked up long enough from his gruesome work to replace his glasses and turn to her. "Are you all right?"

"Is my brother all right?" she asked, and motioned to Bingley. Darcy dropped his weapon and ran to Bingley, turning him over. Charles Bingley groaned as he returned to consciousness, clutching his head.

"Bingley, are you all right?" Darcy said, kneeling beside him.

"I—I think so. Did I miss it?"

Darcy's response was a look. He turned impatiently to Dr. Maddox who turned away from his brother and to Lord Kincaid the elder. "Help me turn him over, please—someone."

William and Darcy helped flip Lord Kincaid over, and Caroline gasped and fell against the wall. "Is he alive?"

"Yes," Maddox said, pulling his shirt open. Kincaid responded by unintentionally coughing up blood in his face. "But both his lungs are pierced. I cannot repair organs. Lord Kincaid, I am sorry to give my prognosis—"

"How long does he have?" Darcy interrupted.

"I don't know. Not long."

"He will not . . . he will not die on Pemberley grounds," Darcy said, losing a bit of composure to exhaustion. "No offence, Lord Kincaid, but your brother is—"

"A rogue, I know," said William Kincaid. "I will take him if someone will show me the way."

"I will," Darcy said, and before anyone could protest, he continued, "I am the only one of us who knows the extent of Pemberley. If he must die in Derbyshire, it will not be on any great estate." He handed the set of master keys to the recovering Bingley. "Go to the servants' quarters and unlock them or unbar them or whatever must be done. And tell Elizabeth all is . . . well. Doctor, does your brother need more tending?"

"Yes, I must repair his back or he will bleed to death."

"Then do so. The servants should be along to aid you."

And with that, Darcy turned to William, who took his dying brother over his own shoulders, and the two of them ran down the main stairs, Bingley following them and turning off to the servants' quarters.

Dr. Maddox turned back to his brother with grim expression. "Brian?" Brian did not respond in words but in a coughing sputter. "Stay with me. I am going to flip you over." But he found it was not an easy task to do. Another pair of arms helped him. "Caroline—"

"What?"

"I can't—you shouldn't see this," he said, as he prepared the scissors to cut away the back of Brian's shirt. "It's . . . unpleasant."

"Not ladylike?"

"Really—I—I must insist—"

She responded by handing him his pliers with an indignant scowl.

"I love you," he said, and went to his work.

"Let me understand," Mr. Bennet said as he sat in the parlour in his bed robe, being served tea by a harried servant. On the couch sat his daughter who would not release her grip on her son, who had fallen back to sleep in her arms. Next to her, Bingley was tended by the servants and sat with an ice pack on his head. Beside him, a nervous Georgiana wrung her hands as they all waited for Darcy and Lord William Kincaid to return. "Not only did I sleep through being locked in my room and the return of the infamous ill-willed suitor, but I also missed a Highland battle in the halls of Pemberley?"

"Yes, Papa. Though it is my own fault for not rushing to unlock your door. I only went to the nursery, and Darcy to Georgiana, and then . . ." Elizabeth said. "Come to think of it, Mr. Bingley, was your door not locked?"

"It was."

"And Miss Bingley's?"

"I did not ask her."

"So . . . you broke down your door?"

"No," he said, repositioning the ice pack. "I picked the lock." He was not prepared, with the innocence of his phrasing, for the stares he was to receive. "What? Is there some reason why a respectable English gentleman should not know how to pick a lock?" The looks were enough of a response, and he sighed and leaned back. "Can I tell the story at a time when my head is not ringing like the inside of a church tower?"

They barely had time to agree to his terms when the master of Pemberley reappeared in the heated parlour, soaking wet and looking as if he would topple right over. This time there was a horde of servants to attend to him before he could even be seated in an armchair with a tub of water put beneath his feet and covered in blankets.

"Lord James Kincaid is no longer with us," he announced with the appropriate gravity. "The constable will be here in the morning or whenever he can make his way here to look into the matter." After all, a member of the nobility, even as an escaped criminal, was dead, and it was hard to determine who exactly had killed him.

"I should send word to Jane," Bingley said. "But I was waiting for—Caroline." The last bit was meant as a greeting, as Miss Bingley entered with a shawl obviously covering a gown that was bloodstained. Bingley succeeded in rising to greet his sister. "How are you?"

"I? I am fine," she said with her usual dignity, marred only by fatigue. Dr. Maddox appeared behind her wearing a different shirt.

"Doctor." Bingley greeted him, and Darcy himself rose before collapsing back into his chair again. "Your brother—"

"I've done all I can. We will have to wait it out, but I think he will be fine."

"Until the constable arrives," Darcy mumbled.

"As master of Pemberley, you may press what charges for theft that you wish, but Caroline and I have agreed not to pursue the matter further. You may take my word on it when I say he is suffering enough as it is for his crimes."

As they would later learn from other sources, Brian had asked, then demanded, then begged for his brother's legendary opium concoction, and Dr. Maddox had very uncharacteristically refused his patient's request every time.

THE CHIEF OF CLAN KINCAID

JANE BINGLEY ARRIVED AT Pemberley with exceptional speed, even when the missive containing the current events did not ask her attendance. With the lateness of the hour, only her sister was there to greet her in the doorway. "Lizzy."

"Jane."

They embraced, and for a moment, no words were spoken.

"Everyone is all right," Elizabeth said, clearly meaning "everyone relevant." "Papa has just retired, and I've put Geoffrey to bed."

"My husband?"

"Oh, it's my fault," Elizabeth said, putting her hands over her mouth. "I shouldn't have let them go."

"Go?"

"The men, into a room to discuss things with Lord Kincaid—the younger brother of James Kincaid. I shouldn't have left them alone."

"Lizzy," Jane asked, "Whatever do you mean?"

Behind closed doors in the parlour, four gentlemen sat around a small table, which was now loaded almost to capacity with wine and whiskey bottles. Mugs and glasses had been nearly forgotten, and there was quite a bit of drinking straight from the bottle, but at the moment, three of the men were cheering the fourth on as Darcy finished the contents of the drinking horn with a long gulp and promptly collapsed back in his chair, the horn hanging by its chain around his neck, a dazed expression on his face.

"Cheers!" Bingley raised his empty glass.

"To the new chief of Clan Kincaid!" said William Kincaid, still in Highland garb but having lost his hat when he tipped over. "Chief . . . wha's his name again?"

"Darcy," offered Maddox, who was having trouble trying to balance an empty bottle on his palm upside down.

"Chief Darcy! Hail to the Chief!"

"Silly man," Darcy said. "Listen to how he says 'to.' 'Heil too tha Chief!'" he said, doing his best to imitate the Scottish burr. "Is there a rule for how long I must contain the wine?"

"Shut up, English! And what kind of English name is Darcy, anyway?"

"'s French," slurred Darcy. "Dah'arceee."

"What? You're not even a proper Englishman? Then what's all this nonsense about?" He turned to Maddox, grabbing him by the arm with an unintentionally harsh twist. "You—you're English, right?"

"By birth," Maddox said, taking a deep breath so he could speak clearly. "But . . . you know . . . the name is not . . . 's Welsh."

"I'm English!" Bingley protested, raising his glass again.

"You?" Darcy said. "Look at you. Look at your hair, man! You're as Irish as . . . as . . . a famous Irishman. I can't be bothered with th' history!"

"He probably has peat bogs growin' in his backyard," William said.

"Hey!" Bingley said, pointing at the Scotsman to his left. "Hey!" he repeated, apparently not completely in his full wits. "Hey, stop it!"

"So none of us are proper English?" Maddox inquired.

"Aye," said William. "To the Bonnie Prince! To the Jacobites!"

"Didn't your prince escape by dressing as a woman?" Darcy said smugly, rocking back on his chair.

"Stop being so smart all the time!" Bingley said. He slammed his hand on the table, which rattled the bottles. "You—you Frenchman! Go back to Napoleon!"

"And fight you? The man who spent the whole battle tonight unconscious on my fine floor?"

"Yes! Wait, no . . . yes! And stop it with Pemberley this, Pemberley that. I'm sick of it!"

Darcy was so drunk, his eyes so unfocused, his speech so uneven in tone, it was hard to tell if he was being serious. "Do not smudge the honour of Pemberley, Bingley."

"O'Bingley," Maddox giggled. "I'm marrying Caroline O'Bingley."

"Okay, you shut up!" Bingley pointed in Maddox's general direction because that was all the hand coordination he had. "This is between me and Darcy! Now you stop talking about Pemberley and how great it is!"

"And why—why should I do that?"

"'Cuz—I know things . . . about you. I could tell that story. You know, the one from college." He turned to William. "He said he'd kill me if I ever told it. But we're like Gaelic brothers or something, so you'll defend me, right?"

"How good is the story?"

"Which one is it?" Darcy said. "Is it one from Cambridge?"

"Yes. I mean, aye, yee, 'tis," Bingley said, doing his best Irish accent and not succeeding very well.

"Fine," Darcy said, crossing his arms and attempting to keep his head up. "Is it the one where I almost duelled my fencing partner in the tavern?"

"No."

"The one where I punched Wickham?"

"Which time?"

"Any one."

"Uh . . . no."

"Um." Darcy was clearly having as much trouble speaking as he was dredging up the memories. "The time I flunked my examinations?"

"You flunked your examinations?" Maddox asked.

"Hung over, bribed the headmaster, took 'em again," Darcy explained. "There, Bingley."

"Not that story."

"Um, all right. How about that girl?"

"Which one?"

"The . . . I don't know, pick one."

"It's not, by the way."

"By God, put us out of the bloody suspense," said William.

THE DARCYS & THE BINGLEYS

"'Kay." Bingley focused his attention on William Kincaid. "So, this one time, it was a moonlit night, and we were studying, um, that play—the one by the Bard."

"*The Jew of Venice*," Maddox said.

"Right. Wait, is that right? Darcy, is that right?"

"*The Merchant of Venice*," Darcy corrected.

"Right. All right. So, we're all studying, and we're talking about Antonio and Bassanio, and Darcy turns to me and he says, he says, 'Bingley, have you ever—'"

Whatever Bingley meant to say was cut off by Darcy socking him in the face. Darcy had to reach over the table to do it, and Bingley went right overboard, his chair hitting the floor. "My eye! You bastard, my eye!"

But he was laughing as he said it, and before long, they were all laughing and pulling Darcy upright, upon which he announced he needed to be sick. "I said I'd kill 'em. He's dead, right?" Darcy said before trying to stand to run out of the room. He was not able to do so and would have gone right over had William Kincaid not caught him.

"Frenchmen. Can't hold down anything stronger than their fancy wines," William said. As he was the most sober of the group, he grabbed a precious vase from the display case and helped Darcy expel the contents of his stomach into it, to which if anyone heard over their giggling, they made no comment. "O'Bingley, you okay?"

"Someone get me up, or *I'm* going to be sick," Bingley announced, and Maddox pulled him and his chair back into a proper position. He removed a hand from his eye, and there was no obvious injury other than some redness around it. "Okay, no more double malt. Single malt *only.*" He attempted to drink from an empty glass and didn't seem to notice this discrepancy. "Seriously, Doctor," he said, gripping his future brother-in-law's shoulder very hard and almost leaning on him entirely, "I'm English—raised just outside London."

"Oh, no worries."

"You should be happy with your choice of wife," William said. "The Gaels, we age well. Right, Bingley?"

"I'm English, damn it! And I'll fight anyone who says otherwise!" Then he thought the matter through. "Anyone I can fight. Uh, Doctor?"

"What?" Maddox had almost gone into a drunken doze.

"I could take you. I could take him, right, Darcy? He's a pacifist!"

Maddox seemed insulted. "Who said I was a pacifist?"

"Do you know how to fight?" Darcy said calmly.

"No."

"Well, then." He looked at William. "Five pounds."

"What? Oh, to see them fight. Who are you betting on?"

"Doesn't matter. I just want to see them go at it. You in?"

William Kincaid took a look at Bingley with his multiple head wounds and Dr. Maddox with his shy demeanour and thick glasses. "I would put five pounds in. Winner gets all ten."

"I will not fight Dr. Maddox!" Bingley announced.

"Maybe if we get some other people in on it . . ." Darcy looked around, but of course no one would offer. "Fifteen pounds!"

"Twenty!" William said. "C'mon, Irish!"

"I'm not Irish!" Bingley said. "Darcy, back me up 'ere."

But Darcy's response was to pass out face-first on the table.

"Frenchmen. Could never stand up to good Scot!"

"I thought he was your chief?" Maddox pointed out.

"Did you say twenty pounds?" Bingley asked, and turned to Jane as she burst in the room. "Can I fight the doctor for twenty pounds, darling?"

"Charles!" she screamed. "You're drunk!"

"No, I'm English!"

"Darcy!" Elizabeth ran to her husband and picked his head up by his hair. That was enough to return him to consciousness. "How much have you drunk?"

"A—oh, Lizzy," he said, his voice nearly incomprehensible. "I lofe you."

Elizabeth released her grip on him, and his head dropped to the table again with a thud. "How much did he have?"

Bingley giggled, and even Maddox could not hold back a smirk. "Have 'im sleep on 'is chest."

"Maybe I should just leave him here," Elizabeth said.

"You're all drunk!" Jane said. "You, Doctor, while your betrothed stands vigil over your dying brother!"

"Scottish tradition," William said in a deep burr. "After'r battle."

"As a cultured woman, I consider myself respectful of other cultures," Elizabeth said, "so I will hold my tongue on this one and put my husband to bed."

"And I the same," said Jane.

"I'm—I can still—" Bingley stuttered. "I can still sit up."

"I will be the judge of that," his wife said very authoritatively. "Come, darling!"

It was not meant to be merely a suggestion, and if there was to be opposition, Charles Bingley was too much in the cups to do it—or, more accurately, in the bottles.

Dr. Maddox refused to be helped up or to bed. He was fortu-nate in that he, aside from the hardy William, was the only one who could stand and walk about, even if he occasionally had to lean on something to get where he was going. But he was a doc-tor demanding to see his patient, and this carried some amount of authority.

Brian Maddox had been put on a mattress under guard in one of the available rooms, where under the doctor's strict instructions, he was to be kept hydrated and clean but nothing else. When Dr. Maddox entered, Brian was awake but could barely lift his head up and had to wait for his brother to join him at his side. He made a quick inspection of the wounds and announced, "If you don't develop an infection, you won't die."

"Lucky me," Brian said in barely a whisper. "Please, could you—"

"No."

Brian turned his head and sighed. "I know, I deserve it."

"Yes."

"I've . . . been a fool. But I never thought . . ." He coughed uncomfortably. "He just said—"

"I don't care what he actually told you," Maddox said. "The man threatened to violate my future wife, and you *let him in*!"

"I didn't—"

"I will be generous and say you are not a fool—just very eas-ily led and a bad gambler."

"I . . . will not deny it," Brian said. "I am sorry."

"Sorry. *Sorry?*" the doctor said, his voice a bit slurred but lacking none of the intensity as he shook his brother, which elicited a cry of significant pain from the wounded man. "If any-thing . . . *anything* had happened to her—"

"She . . . is . . . your fiancée I believe, brother, please—"

"I don't care!" But he did release his brother. "I would have—" He broke off. "I would have *killed you.*"

There was a moment before Brian Maddox, obviously in great pain, could speak again, "You . . . really . . . love her."

"You doubted it?"

"No . . . I just . . . have never seen you angry . . . before," he wheezed. "Or throttle a patient."

Maddox took an uneasy step back and sat on the mattress beside his brother, taking off his glasses so he could wipe his eyes. He was, he had to admit, not in the best of senses, but that did not excuse his behaviour, however much his brother soundly deserved it. If a stitch had come loose, he doubted he had the coordination to repair it properly. He had so many emotions, stronger than the ones he was used to in the years of playing the caring but relatively removed doctor, and an entire bottle of whiskey prevented him from properly processing them all. There he stayed for an undetermined amount of time, his brother either asleep or in so much pain that it prevented conversation, until he was tapped on the shoulder.

"No, no," Maddox said. "I don't need help. I'm quite well." He didn't want any servants bothering him, telling him when to go to bed and when to get up and how to dress and say and do all things proper. He wanted to sit and think, as much as he was capable of doing in his befuddled state.

But the touch was not the touch of a servant's. It was soft and gentle and snaked around the back of his neck. "Caroline."

He put on his glasses again so he could properly see that it was her, and his instincts were proven correct. "You shouldn't—"

"I shouldn't what?"

He realised he did not have a proper answer for her. He was so very tired and still a bit in the cups, and so he only leaned on her shoulder, which was improper but comfortable all the same, and for a while there was silence, except for Brian's laboured breathing.

"I should give him something," he said, "so he can sleep."

"You are very forgiving."

He picked his head up and met her expression. "If you wish, I will not be."

"Nothing happened to me, Daniel."

"Something *could* have."

"But it didn't."

"Are you saying I should forgive him?"

"He is hardly a villain. A bad gambler, an idiot, and a thief, yes, but like you, when he says he had no concept of Kincaid's level of deceptions, I would believe him."

"You are being very kind."

"Well, he *is* to be my brother-in-law."

Maddox smiled and took her hand. "I love you."

"You should retire, dear."

"I should." He stood up with great difficulty, having trouble finding his balance, and went to his equipment on the table, retrieving the green bottle and a spoon. "This does not mean I entirely forgive you for being an imbecile," he said to his brother, who opened his eyes and swallowed what was offered to him. His duties finished, the good doctor drunkenly straightened his coat, looked around, and realised he had not the wits about him to see his way back to his room. Wordlessly, Caroline took his arm, and he did not object. The hallways were empty, as almost everyone else was long asleep or at least at the mercy of their wives berating them for all of the appropriate reasons.

When they entered his room, he dismissed the waiting servant, saying he was quite capable of removing his bloodstained clothing, thank you very much. However, this clothing contained a lot of buttons and most of them he found rather vexing when actually attacked.

"Here," Caroline said, and helped him remove his overcoat.

"I seem to recall . . . this is most inappropriate of a lady," he mumbled.

"Are you objecting?"

He did not have a proper response. All he wanted to be was down to his underclothes and in bed, which happened very quickly. She kissed him on the cheek, and he turned and returned the favour, but not on the cheek.

"If you don't leave," he said, "your brother may burst in with a shotgun."

"I think it has been established that all we have to do is clonk him on the head, and he will be incapacitated."

"Not that a concussion will endear me to him." He pulled her closer to him. It was partially to make his point, partially to do the opposite. "I love you, but—I fear I am not in the most . . . inhibited of moods."

"Neither am I. But I do not have an excuse."

He giggled. "That is true."

They lay together on the mattress, side by side, looking up at the ceiling for some time before Maddox finally said, "If I am to be a gentleman again, I should perhaps act like one."

"Yes."

"And that would require you vacating my bedchambers at once."

"Yes."

Neither of them made a move for some time.

Finally, he turned on his side to face her. "Caroline, my darling, two things could happen. Either it will be something very improper, or I will fall asleep. Neither I would object to, but we should probably make a decision."

"Even in love you are so logical?"

"I *am* a scientist."

She giggled. It was so strange to hear Caroline Bingley giggle when not at someone else's expense—though perhaps it was at his, but not in that way. "Daniel, I love you, but I think I must retire."

"Good," he mumbled, "because I think I am too drunk to do the deed properly."

She snorted into the pillows. "That is what you get for trying to outdrink a Scot."

"And an Irishman."

"Are you implying something about my family?"

He swatted her playfully, but that was all he managed as a response. She kissed him on the forehead, removed his glasses for him, and gathered up her somewhat tousled robes. By the time she reached the door, he was fast asleep.

Chapter 17

THE GREAT BINGLEY HEIST
OF 1785

"MASTER CHARLES, YOU GET back here!"

Mrs. Anne's call went entirely unheeded by the seven-year-old Charles Bingley Junior. In fact, his response was to put as much distance between himself and her as possible in the little time afforded to him. He climbed the old wooden steps of their house with greater ease than he knew she could and practically swung himself onto the second floor by grasping onto the worn railing. While this would give him some time, it did not give him very many places to hide. His own room was too obvious, and he would never invade the sanctity of his parent's bedchamber, even if neither were at home. That left the storeroom (locked) and the rooms of his sisters, and he was still debating his escape plans when he heard the voice of his nurse and governess.

"I see you!" she called indignantly from the bottom of the stairs. "Master Charles, you get down here right now!"

He huffed and darted down the hallway. Having only moments to decide (as the Bingley family house, just outside of

Town, was not very large and not filled with many places to hide), he did what he judged best, which was to burst unannounced into his sister's room.

"Charles!" Caroline Bingley of ten years said with indignation. She was sitting at her dressing table, combing her long hair. "What are you doing?"

He put his finger to his lips. "Shhhh!"

"Charles Bingley Junior! Where did you go?"

In the room, Caroline kept her silence until the noise outside the door died down, at which point she whispered, "You can't just barge into a lady's room!"

"You're not a lady! You're a girl!"

Caroline, only three years his senior, could not correct him easily. "Well, you can't go into a girl's room either!"

"Says who?"

"Says Mama!"

He stuck his tongue out at her, only to be pushed forward by the banging on the door. "Miss Caroline! Is your brother in there?"

"Hide me," he whispered. "I'll make it worthwhile."

"How will you do that?"

"Do it, and I'll tell you."

Caroline bit her lip as she decided, then called out, "No, he isn't."

"Did he come past?"

"No, Mrs. Anne."

"Remember, your lessons are at noon!"

Charles mouthed a thank you and sighed when they heard no more from their governess.

"I *hate* piano," Caroline said.

"Father says you shouldn't say *hate*. You should say *dislike*. It's not *proper*."

"Neither is hiding from Mrs. Anne!"

"You hid me!"

"Because you asked! Why would you do it anyway? She does not make you play the pianoforte until your fingers hurt."

"She wanted me to bathe—*again*."

She crinkled her nose. "You should bathe. You're filthy."

"But I'm not!" And he bared his arms to prove it. "See? No mud, perfectly clean."

"But your hair is a mess." She bid him to come over. "Here." And despite his struggling, her superior strength held him as she scraped the brush across his hair. "Why can't you ever make it look proper?"

"Because I don't spend hours—ow, Carol, that hurts!"

"Because it's a knot. Don't be such a baby about it. Now, you owe me for lying to Mrs. Anne."

Free from her grip, at least temporarily, he reached proudly into his pocket and produced a metal object shaped a bit like a rod with many bumps and strange curves on one side beyond the handle.

"Where did you get that?"

"Father's desk."

She reached out to touch it, and he waved it beyond her reach. "Don't be such a brat."

"Do you want to use it?"

"You don't know how to use it!"

That much was true. They had only seen their father use his lock pick once, when the laundress was stuck in the closet with the old door and he had misplaced the key. "It can't be all that hard," Charles asserted. "Or maybe you're just chicken."

"I'm not chicken!"

"I think you *look* like a chicken."

"Shut up!" She snatched the lock pick from him. "I'm going to use it, just to prove you wrong—not because I want to."

There was no question as to where it would be used. Even with all of the doors that creaked and got stuck or wouldn't shut properly or had their knobs broken sometimes, there was one door that always stayed locked at the end of the hallway. It was Papa's storeroom, and though he gave no grave warnings as to venturing inside, he kept it locked, which led to no end of speculation as to what might be inside. No idea was too gruesome or scandalous, at least when it was very late at night and they were talking. He spent almost no time there, giving them not a chance to peek inside. Papa was most often in Town or occasionally on the Continent and sometimes came home only late at night or not at all, except on Sundays.

As soon as they checked that the hallway was clear, Charles and Caroline scampered down the hallway to the door at the end of it. Charles put the pick in, but it did not unlock it as he thought it would.

"Stupid. You're doing it wrong," Caroline said, and pushed him aside. Her own attempt was no better. The door remained locked. She jiggled the doorknob to no avail.

"That's because you don't have the key."

They spun around to see Louisa towering over them. Being older than both of them at a time when age determined height, this was not very difficult. She was holding in her hand a small, sharp item of the same metal and colour as the pick. "You need the other half."

"Charles!" Caroline said, apparently annoyed that her time was wasted. "So?"

"So? Let me show you," Louisa said, and put her half in, and after some wiggling about, they all heard the door soundly unlock, and the door swung open.

"That's it?" Charles said. "Clothing?"

"Not clothing, Charles. Fabric." For that was what it was. It was shelves and shelves of rolled, piled, and folded fabric and practically nothing else but a chair. "But it is very beautiful." Caroline ran a hand across the embroidered silk in colours she had never seen. The three of them had their way about the room.

"Look at me," Charles said, draping himself in brown fabric. "I'm a monk!"

"I'm the Princess of Wales," said Caroline, wrapped in the prettiest print on the top of the pile.

"And I cannot begin to imagine the trouble you will be in when your father comes home," their governess said with all severity, blocking their escape by standing in the doorway, and they all turned to her. The most terrifying part of it was that they knew it to be true.

Charles thought it was most intolerable that he was last. He was dressed in his best clothes and made to wait in the chair outside his father's study while one after another his sisters were sent to Charles Senior, leaving his son to swing his legs back and forth on the chair that was too big for him. He was almost relieved when he was finally called in.

To his surprise, his father's expression was not entirely malign. Mr. Bingley was seated at his massive desk, which was stacked with endless papers of business. He was not a corpulent man, but he did allow himself the fine French food when he had the chance, so he was not an imposing personage, which, if not for the regular broad smile on his face, could easily have made him an intimidating man. Perhaps he was when he needed to be. All that his son really knew was that his father was very success-ful, so he must have been good at whatever he did.

Charles Bingley Senior said nothing but bade his son to take a seat on the chair, which he practically had to climb into, feel-ing very small indeed and very afraid.

"Charles," his father said. His father usually called him Junior. "I heard about your little exploit today. Do you have something to say about it? The proper Christian thing to do would be to allow a proper chance for a confession." And he crossed his fingers and waited while his son gathered his thoughts.

"I didn't—we were just really—we wanted to know—what was inside."

"But you didn't ask."

"No." He shrunk further into his seat. "We didn't know. Maybe it was awful. Maybe it was . . . not proper."

"And do you really believe your father would do anything scandalous?"

"No," he answered honestly. He had, after all, only respect for his progenitor.

His father was very patient as he began, "Charles, would you like to guess the worth of the cloth in that room? I will aid you by saying some of it is from the Far East."

"I don't know." This was not the time to admit that he was behind in his math lessons. "Um . . . thirty pounds?" He watched his father's face for a reaction. "Forty?" Still nothing. "A hundred."

"I will not torture you. I purchased that collection at some twelve thousand pounds. I plan to sell it at about forty thousand, depending on the current market," his father explained. "I think you are old enough to see now how a fortune is made. Because I intend to have a fortune—not for myself, of course, or my wife— for you and your sisters until they marry well. I work so you will inherit and be a man of society, though that may seem like a daunting prospect, but it is very important that I provide for my children to the best of my abilities." He went on, "I keep it in the house because it is the best of my stock, and my warehouse is regularly robbed. I keep the door locked because even the best of servants cannot always avoid the temptation of Chinese silk. So now you know, and this was your method of discovering it."

"I'm sorry," he said. He would have been crying in shame, but instead he was just overwhelmed at the astronomical numbers flown at him. "I was curious—"

"There is nothing wrong with curiosity, as long as it does not involve the theft of one's father's things. Now, the pick?"

Charles guiltily climbed out of the chair, went around the desk, and presented his father with the lock picks that Louisa had shoved into his tiny hands upon their discovery.

"Thank you. You understand this is an emergency tool, to be used for the old locks when they fail and trap people. It is not a toy."

"It is not, sir."

"Good. And since no damage was done, I suppose I could let you off, provided you do not pull this sort of stunt again."

"Yes, sir," his son said proudly, eager to please his father. It was only later that he and Caroline would decide that "this stunt" referred only to the storeroom, which barely interested them anyway now that the mystery was solved, and many hours were passed picking the locks on their own doors until all three Bingleys could do it with just two of Louisa's hairpins. But this secret they kept to themselves.

1806

Geoffrey was jumping on his head. Of that, Darcy was sure. It was the only way to explain the splitting pain in his skull. Kincaid hadn't gotten him in the head, right? And he wasn't dead, right? The details were a little fuzzy. The pain wasn't.

"Darcy, how do you feel?"

His lovely wife's voice was entirely unwelcome. "Please," he mumbled into the pillow as he found himself facedown on his bed. "The noise."

"Oh, I'm sorry. Was I too loud?" she said, and he covered his ears in defence. "How could you have a headache? I really have no idea, darling."

"Lizzy," he whispered, wildly and numbly grasping for her. "Please—"

"Something about a drinking horn?"

He picked his head up, his vision blurry in the morning light—or afternoon. He had no idea. "What?"

She kissed him, which had its mixture of pleasure and pain. "You are too adorable when befuddled to be tortured further."

"Thank God for that," he said, and put his head back down on the pillow.

It was some time before he was properly roused and put together in a way that he considered presentable and was willing to venture outside his bedchamber, but only after a lot of coffee had been brought up for him.

On the stairway he immediately encountered Bingley who not only had a welt on his head but was otherwise injured. "My God, man, what happened to your eye?"

Bingley looked confused and then stifled a grin. "You socked me, Darcy."

"I did?" he stumbled. Bingley did have a black eye in evidence, and he was not known to be a good liar, so it was probably true. But why in the world would he punch Bingley? "Do you wish to tell me the circumstances under which this occurred? I assume it was more than just being inebriated."

"Are you daft?" This time, his friend felt no compunction to hold back his laughter. "I have no desire to have a matching pair."

"Well, then." Darcy decided it was prudent not to question it. "My apologies."

"Apologies accepted. Oh, and the constable has arrived, so you may wish to gather your memories for the inquest."

"My memories are perfectly clear," he said, adding, "until about the third glass."

"You may wish to leave that out."

"I do not believe it is relevant to the inquest," Darcy said.

"Good point." Bingley added, "And there is the matter of Mr. Maddox."

"How is he?"

"I am not the expert on the subject, but he is alive and has a long recovery ahead of him. Whether he spends it in prison or not is a decision that falls to you."

"Dr. Maddox is not pressing charges?"

"No."

"Nor Miss Bingley, I assume?"

"No, or, not since I asked. She may feel differently now. I've not had the time—"

Darcy put his hand up. He was master of Pemberley. It was time to act like it. "When am I expected to report to the constable?"

"I believe when he is done with Lord Kincaid." He clarified, "Lord William Kincaid."

"Then I must find the good doctor and speak with him if I can first. I assume he is well."

"All things considered, I think he is faring better than either of us."

"Good for him. Sorry again about the eye. Was it really that terrible?"

"I'm not telling you, Darcy."

"That bad," he said, and inquired no further.

Darcy was directed to the library where he found Dr. Maddox trying to distract himself with some text Darcy had not the time to identify. "Dr. Maddox."

"Mr. Darcy," he bowed.

"How is your brother?"

"Recovering." Maddox put his book down. "But very slowly. He has some terrible days ahead of him."

"And you clearly think this enough of a punishment."

"What am I to do? He's my brother."

"He's a fool who has ruined your fortune and your life and had almost gotten us all killed, if I must remind you."

"If you wish to press charges, that is your right, Mr. Darcy."

"You are changing the subject."

"Not very well, apparently."

There was a silence between them, and Darcy stared out the window. When Maddox would not break it and might have even gone back to his reading, Darcy announced, "He cannot stay at Pemberley."

"I understand. But in his condition, I must go with him."

Darcy sighed. Everyone seemed to be making life harder for him than was necessary. "Then I suppose . . . until he is recovered . . . he may stay here. But under guard, of course."

"Of course." Maddox audibly closed his book. "Thank you, Mr. Darcy."

Darcy did not have to look at the expression on Maddox's face to know it was genuine.

On his way out of his meeting with the constable, which was mostly procedure at this point, with an escaped convict breaking into his home and stabbing people, nobleman or not, Darcy was surprised to run into someone he had never met before.

"Mr. Darcy," the man bowed. "It is good to see you again."

The accent was unmistakable. He recognised Lord William Kincaid now back in normal, proper clothing, which included pants. "Lord Kincaid. Thank you."

"I have no wish to further intrude now that my business is concluded. And I must return for the funeral. Thank you, Mr. Darcy, for all of your aid, and I'm sorry to bring James's habits into your family."

"Hardly your fault."

"It is, but I will not press the point. Thank you again," he bowed.

"You're welcome." Darcy took the trouble to properly show out his guest to the waiting carriage.

"*Sealbh math dhuit*," said the Scot from his carriage. "Ask your wife what it means. And hail to the chief!"

Darcy did not reply because he had not the slightest idea what he meant by that.

THE UNLIKELY BRIDE

THE MATTER OF WHO was to be the best man became a severely complicated issue, at least among those who were inclined to chat about it behind Dr. Maddox's back, as apparently he was to have no say in the matter. Darcy was the obvious choice, but it took Bingley to admit over billiards that even he would find Darcy as best man at Caroline's wedding a bit strange. Mr. Hurst could barely stand up through a whole ceremony, and Bingley, of course, had the task of giving his sister away. Brian Maddox, despite being an amiable and very repentant fellow, was nobody's favourite for obvious reasons and was a most inappropriate choice.

"It is a shame that I have not yet developed a horrid disease and therefore do not know him better," he said. "Though perhaps we could consult the *groom* before assigning the position?"

"It's not our fault he cares more for the library than for billiards," Mr. Hurst said.

"Or being in Miss Bingley's sitting room."

"Elizabeth is a bad influence on you," Bingley spat back at Darcy. "I think I liked you better when you just stared out the window during these conversations."

The snow stopped and melted, causing the roads to flood, and it was almost April before the last Bingley sibling was married off to a man of relatively small fortune but an outstanding reputation in his profession. He was offered a sizeable position in Scotland by a certain earl but turned it down saying he preferred his work in London, and his wife liked the social life, and he would forever be at the mercy of his wife's wants and wishes. Lord William Kincaid, who returned to England for the wedding, smiled and shook his hand and said that he understood.

To everyone's chagrin, at least privately, Maddox did (undoubtedly with full awareness of the irony) ask Darcy to stand as his best man. Aside from a few associates from Town and University, he had few guests of his own beyond his brother, who was to depart from England as soon as the amnesty granted to him until the wedding ended was up. Brian Maddox had recovered but walked with a limp, having had a particular nerve severed near his spine, and this was somehow deemed enough of a punishment by his sibling and sister-in-law. Not that anyone beyond the doctor himself felt compelled to be nice to him, but he did attend the ceremony, and whatever understanding had transpired between brothers in the weeks up to the wedding they kept to themselves.

"If my brother is poor in character, it is not my place to judge," Dr. Maddox finally said when cornered, and then would say no more on the matter.

But aside from being the recipient of many cold stares in the church, Brian Maddox bothered no one and smiled awkwardly to the guests who didn't know him as they arrived.

It seemed the last people to actually arrive were the two people the ceremony concerned. Caroline had all of the usual delays of fittings and women doing whatever it is they do when a woman gets married, which Charles Bingley avoided assiduously and, instead, stood in the church with Darcy, despite the fact that this was the last day he would see his sister for some time, as the couple was taking their honeymoon on the Continent. Once again, Bingley found himself in the office of the local pastor with Darcy.

"Your wedding gift?" Darcy said. "If I may inquire."

"A townhouse in West London. Caroline should have her own place."

"Now I feel cheap," Darcy said. "All I got them was a book."

"Well, you are only a—*Darcy!* That's my *sister* we're talking about!"

"I didn't say what kind of book. You have a foul mind, Bingley."

"Don't mock me on my sister's wedding day!"

"I mocked you on yours; I hardly see how this is as bad," was Darcy's reply.

"I'm buying Georgiana a copy on her wedding day!"

"You must be referring to your daughter, because Georgiana Darcy is never getting married. She's taking the veil," he said. "And if it isn't the man of the hour."

Dr. Maddox had finally arrived, looking more nervous than he normally looked—not the Bingley sort of "I can't stay still" nervous, but more of the skittish terrified nervousness, which was not entirely unexpected. "Hello."

"Doctor," Bingley said, slapping him on the shoulder. "Best of luck. If you have any questions on how to entice Caroline, ask Darcy here." And with that, he left to meet his sister.

"Bastard," Darcy said. "Got out of here before I could say anything."

"You don't . . . have any advice?"

Darcy shrugged. "You don't seem to need any. And I assume you are quite acquainted with feminine biology."

"Am I going to have to return this witty brotherly repartee?"

"To last in this family, yes," he said. "A small price to pay, all things considered."

"And I even made it in without a mother-in-law."

"Mrs. Bennet will happily fill the role if you find yourself lacking one," Darcy said. "She may even do it without your formal request."

"I may, then, just have to go deaf as well as blind," the doctor replied.

"See? Not so hard, is it? And if you ever need an insult to hurl at a Bennet, former Bennet, or your illustrious brother, just ask your wife, as she always seems to have one at the ready."

"I have no wish to insult my family."

"I fear you are too good to your family." But Darcy finished it with a more meaningful look.

"Brian will not bother you again, not unless you travel to Bulgaria and gamble with him. And even then, I hear he is a terrible gambler, and you will just take whatever money he has from him."

"And he is entirely untrustworthy and will attempt to take from you whatever income you receive."

Dr. Maddox would not be cowed—not on this subject. "He lacks judgement in all matters of money and assessing people, but he raised me since I was barely more than a boy, Mr. Darcy. Surely you can imagine how this would inspire some lingering affection. He is my brother, and I will love him until the day he is killed by one of his creditors and I am not there to try and save him. That does not mean I did not imply to him that I would not love him more if he were very, very far away from all of us."

"A wise implication." If he had anything else to say, it was interrupted by the music starting up. "Best of luck."

"I think you mean that a little too much, Mr. Darcy."

Darcy did not contradict him as they entered the chapel.

Darcy's claim that his wedding present was merely literary was not entirely accurate. When the Maddoxes returned from Vienna, the doctor was called to sit for an eye examination so the proper lenses could be prepared for him for his own personal microscope, which took another month to complete. Its worth incalculable, he kept it in his laboratory, and Caroline Maddox was being constantly called in and asked if she wanted to see something up close, which she did not, especially because it was usually a bug or a sample of some noxious liquid. She assured him that, while she did love him very much and thoroughly enjoyed being Mrs. Daniel Maddox, it did not mean she had any desire to see the insides of a flea, however fascinating they might be.

They were also back in time for the Season. The Bingleys did not attend because of their infants, and the Darcys did not attend because Mr. Darcy never attended unless he absolutely had to, and now he had not only Caroline's but Dr. Maddox's promise to keep an eye on the very eligible Georgiana Darcy who dined often with them and sent letters to Derbyshire about the happy couple. She also remarked on what the inside of a flea looked like (which she admitted to being a little disgusting and thoroughly blamed her brother for it).

"She was not this way before I married you," Darcy said to his wife, now just barely showing her pregnancy.

"Yes, I suppose I am thoroughly to blame for this, of having two women assaulting your personal honour," Elizabeth replied, handing him back the letter. "And once Geoffrey says proper sentences . . . well, who knows."

"Yeffrey!" Geoffrey said, standing on his father's lap and banging up and down on the writing pad with the ink pot he had somehow gotten hold of.

"So close, and yet so far," Darcy said.

"Just like his father."

"I can pronounce my own name *now*," he said. "I just don't want to."

"So our second son is not to be named Fitzwilliam?"

"I would not subject him to that," he replied. "But the other two, if they are girls, you may name as you like, as I have no objections to any female names."

"I am *not* having triplets."

"I believe you have no say in the matter."

"And I believe the same can be said of you."

"I was thinking very . . . triplet-y . . . thoughts when we . . ." He looked up at his wife, then turned his son properly around to face her. "Son, memorise this look, as it is very important to understanding your mother. It is the look of someone who is very annoyed and wants me to stop talking and start apologising. I should probably do that."

"You probably should," said Elizabeth.

"If only she would come over here, and then I could kiss her without getting up, because you are getting a bit big to be carried about, and then maybe—" But he did not have to say any more because Elizabeth did come over to his side of the desk and let him kiss her on the cheek and then took their son in her arms.

"Oof! You are getting heavy, darling," she said.

"Mama!" Geoffrey said, because saying anything seemed to excite him.

"Mo-ther," his father corrected very patiently.

Geoffrey squealed and pointed. "Fisser!"

Elizabeth laughed so hard she nearly dropped her son. Darcy put his head down face-first on the desk. Geoffrey Darcy looked on, completely unaware that he, by making them parents, had been the final means of truly uniting them.

THE END

ACKNOWLEDGEMENTS

IT WOULD BE UNFAIR of me to not first credit Jane Austen with creating most of these characters two centuries ago, thereby letting them fall into public domain to be used and abused at my whim. I'm proud to say I share two things in common with one of the greatest novelists of all time: a love of these characters and an autoimmune disorder.

This novel could not have happened without Brandy Scott. More accurately, it could have happened, but it would have been full of spelling and consistency errors. If you meet her, shake her hand and don't tell her that some people charge for their editing services.

This novel wouldn't be on the shelves without Deb Werksman—who actually went through the trouble of reading the manuscript and turning it into a book—and her assistant, Susie Benton, for the crucial essentia. Thanks go to my agent, Katie Menick, who undoubtedly put in more time to work on my career than was financially feasible for her.

To everyone at FanFiction.net I owe a great deal: the people who left comments, the people who found mistakes, and the people who just raised my hit count (and therefore my self-esteem) by visiting the page. The same goes for private sites where the story was also posted in a very unfinished form and my historical questions were answered by people more knowledgeable than I. Thank you, Giulia Longhin, for helping me with the Italian translations.

Renata Miller took time out of her busy schedule reading graduate literature papers (which we padded with huge quotes to reach the page expectation) to read, review, and correct my manuscript. Thank you, Professor Miller.

Thank you, Lindsey Abrams, the head of my MFA program at the City College of New York, who was my thesis advisor and let me use this manuscript as my thesis so I could have time to work on it while earning three credits.

Special thanks go to my parents, who encouraged me to pursue a career in the low-paying field of writing, instead of encouraging me to become a doctor or a lawyer.

To Rabbi Yehuda Henkin, who told me I was funny and that I should write a humor magazine: Rabbi, this was the best that I could do. It's not as glossy, but I'm told it makes people laugh. To Rabbi and Rebbetzin Weisberg for the encouragement.

To Dr. Goodman, thanks for all the Klonopin. Now if you could stop mentioning my writing in therapy, that would be nice.

Thanks also go to Mrs. Mary Anne Dietrich, my fourth-grade reading teacher, who was the first nonparental authority figure to officially tell me I should be a writer.

To Felicia Haberfield, thank you for the moral support on a particularly crucial afternoon.

To anyone else I forgot, let me say this: You have no idea how fast this deadline came down on me, and I did not mean to forget you. I really didn't.

To the Holy One, blessed be He, King of the Universe, for that thing He did that time at the place. He knows what I'm talking about.

ABOUT THE AUTHOR

Marsha Altman is an author and historian specializing in Rabbinic literature in late antiquity. She has a bachelor's degree in history from Brown University and an M.F.A. in Creative Writing from the City College of New York. She works in the publishing industry and is writing a series continuing the story of the Darcys and the Bingleys. She lives in New York.